THE SEERSUCKER WHIPSAW

Ross Thomas

"... Riotous affair of public relations and politics in emerging Africa; it's a classic, unforgettable, a joy forever, and if you missed it, hurry and catch up."
—*Los Angeles Times*

THE
SEERSUCKER
WHIPSAW
Ross Thomas

PERENNIAL LIBRARY

Harper & Row, Publishers

New York, Cambridge, Philadelphia, San Francisco

London, Mexico City, São Paulo, Singapore, Sydney

To Harriet

THE SEERSUCKER WHIPSAW. Copyright © 1967 by Ross Thomas. All rights reserved. Printed in the United States of America. No part of this book may be used or reproduced in any manner whatsoever without written permission except in the case of brief quotations embodied in critical articles and reviews. For information address William Morrow & Company, Inc., 105 Madison Avenue, New York, N.Y. 10016. Published simultaneously in Canada by Fitzhenry & Whiteside Limited, Toronto.

First PERENNIAL LIBRARY edition published 1985.

Library of Congress Cataloging in Publication Data

Thomas, Ross, 1926-
The seersucker whipsaw.

Reprint. Originally published: New York : Morrow, 1967. I. Title.
PS3570.H58S4   1985   813'.54   84-47676
ISBN 0-06-080728-8 (pbk.)

85   86   87   88   89   10   9   8   7   6   5   4   3   2   1

Confound their politics,
Frustrate their knavish tricks...
—*Old Song*

whip·saw (hwip′so) v.t. 1. to cut with a whipsaw;
hence, 2. to defeat or get the best of (a person) two
ways at once, as in *faro*, by winning two different
bets in a single play.
—*Webster's New World Dictionary*
of the American Language

THE SEERSUCKER WHIPSAW

— *1* —

My four-city search for Clinton Shartelle ended in Denver where I found him playing shortstop for the Kwikway Truckers in a sandlot park at 29th and Champa. He was playing barefoot and talking it up in the infield.

The scoreboard said it was the top half of the ninth and that the Truckers were leading the Pueblo Ironmen six to five. There was one out with the tying run on first. The bleachers that ran along the third and first base lines were about three-quarters filled with the teams' families, friends, and just people who think a free baseball game is a good way to kill a warm July evening.

I took a seat in the stands next to a fat Mexican who ate tamales out of a newspaper as he gave some advice to the pitcher.

"Burn it in there, baby!" the Mexican yelled through a cupped hand. He had something wrong with his adenoids and whatever it was lent his voice a blasting resonance that crackled in the night air.

"Where do you get the tamales?" I asked.

"Guy's got a cart, right down there by third," the Mexican said. I went over and bought three tamales from an old man with a white pushcart that rolled on bicycle wheels. He used *The Denver Post* to wrap them in, but the individual tamales were bound in real cornshucks. They cost twenty-five cents each.

I went back to the bleachers and sat down by the Mexican again. The pitcher tried another fast ball, but it was low and outside. "How come the guy playing short hasn't got any uniform?" I asked the Mexican.

"Just a minute," he said and gave the pitcher some additional encouragement. "The guy out there was just sitting here watching. Then when Connors got his ankle twisted, he just goes over and talks to the manager and they give him Connors' glove and he starts playing. He ain't bad neither."

"Connors is regular short, huh?"

"He's regular short, but he got his ankle twisted in the second inning when he mistook a hop."

"And the tall guy's been playing since?"

The Mexican chewed the last of his tamale, licked his fingers neatly, and nodded. "That's right," he said after he tidied himself up.

The pitcher took a long windup and tried a slider. It was hit-and-run. The man at the plate got a fat piece of the ball as the runner on first scampered towards second. It was a hard-hit grounder to short that took a nasty bounce, but Shartelle pulled it in on the hop and snapped it to second in one smooth motion as if he had been doing it all spring and summer. The second baseman made a nice throw to first in time for the double play.

"How 'bout that?" the Mexican said.

"He can go to his right," I said.

"Not bad for an old guy like that."

"You mean the shortstop?"

"He must be close to forty."

"And then some," I said and walked down from the bleachers towards the bench of the Kwikway Truckers.

I had never met Clinton Shartelle, but I had seen pictures of him in the elaborate dossier that the agency had compiled and bound in a leather folder that made it look like a presentation to Anaconda Copper. We always went sled-length in that agency. The pictures had been mostly news shots, grainy stuff from AP, UPI's Wide World, Black Star, and the rest of the commercial houses. In nearly all of them Shartelle had been in the background, apparently by accident, standing slightly behind and to the right of the photos' principal figures. In most of the shots he wore a preoccupied look, as if he were trying to remember

2

whether he had turned off the roast. In others, he was next to a variety of beaming but somehow glassy-eyed men—young, old, and middleaged—who smiled vacuous smiles and made some small gesture of victory: a thumb and index finger forming an O or hands clasped together over their heads in the boxer's salute.

The pictures showed Shartelle as a man with a face in the shape of a broken heart. His chin came to a rough point and a wide mouth wandered around above it. His nose was on the right track until it got halfway to where it was supposed to go and then it veered slightly to the left. It was a good nose, a strong nose. His eyes in the pictures were dark and direct and the left eyebrow was in a fixed arc that lent him a questioning look. It was a face that gave off, if it gave off anything, an air of preoccupied amusement that stopped just short of cynicism, but not much short.

He was using a towel on the short-cropped hair that was his trademark, when I approached him. The hair met in a widow's peak, was pure white, and had been so since he was nineteen years old.

"That was a nice play, Mr. Shartelle," I said.

He turned to look at me. "Now you'd be a little young to scout for the Pittsburgh Pirates," he said. "Although that was a kindly thing to say to a man of my years."

"It was a fine catch and a good snap to second. I'm Peter Upshaw."

He put the towel on the bench and we shook hands. "My pleasure, Mr. Upshaw."

"I've been looking for you for five days. You've been moving around."

"You come on slow, Mr. Upshaw. But nice."

I smiled. "It's a holdover from the days when I sold mutual funds in college."

"And now you're selling?"

"I'm not. I work for Padraic Duffy. In London."

"Himself?"

"The same."

Shartelle nodded and looked up as the ballpark's lights

were switched off. "And how is the poor Irish lad from Chicago who aspires to be England's noblest lord?" He didn't seem really interested.

"He was in New York for a month recently. We all hoped that they enjoyed having him there as much as we enjoyed him being there."

"He hasn't changed, I take it?"

"No. He hasn't changed."

Shartelle gave me an appraising look and again nodded his head slightly. "He hasn't changed the initials either?"

"No. They still stand for Duffy, Downer and Theims. Limited."

"Prosperous, I hear."

"Very."

"Padraic Francis Duffy—or Pig as we called him."

"He raises them now, in case you're interested."

"He would," Shartelle said. "He would raise pigs just to prove that a pigsty, as long as it's Irish, can be a work of art. Chester Whites?"

"Poland Chinas."

Shartelle produced a package of Picayunes and offered me one.

"I didn't think they still made these," I said.

"You can get them at the tobacco stores, the kind of places that sell nothing but tobacco. Most drug stores don't carry them."

"They're strong."

"I'm getting just a little chilled," Shartelle said. "Why don't we go to my hotel and I'll take a shower and then you can make your pitch." He looked around the deserted baseball field. "For some reason, I don't think this is quite the place to entertain a proposition from Pig Duffy."

Shartelle had a small suite in the old part of the Brown Palace on Sixteenth and Broadway. He had a view of the mountains, furniture that was a cross between Italian Provincial and Midwestern Modern, about two dozen books, and an ample liquor supply. It looked as if he had settled in for a long stay.

4

"You a married man, Mr. Upshaw?"

"Not any more."

"Well, I don't reckon this kind of living would appeal to a married man."

"It probably depends on how long he's been married." Shartelle grinned. "It might at that. Why don't you fix yourself a drink while I take a shower. There's a bucket of ice in the refrigerator and the refrigerator is in the bottom of that thing that looks like an *escritoire*."

I poured a measure of Virginia Gentleman into a glass, dropped in two ice cubes which slopped a little of the liquor over the side, added some water and walked over to the window to see what I could of the mountains at night. There were some lights high up, but at night Denver looked very much like Birmingham, New Orleans, and Oklahoma City which were the three other towns where I had been searching for Clinton Shartelle.

He came out of the bedroom wearing a white shirt, a yellow, green and black striped tie that rightfully belonged to the Lancashire Fusiliers, dark gray slacks, and black loafers. His thick white hair was brushed and lay close to his head in a damp, tidy pile.

"'Denver,' some early settler once remarked, 'has more sunshine and sons of bitches per square foot than any place else in the United States.' He may have been right. I know Pig Duffy would feel right at home here." He walked over to the fake writing desk and put some ice in a glass. "I see you have your drink, Mr. Upshaw."

"I'm fine."

He sat in an armchair and took a sip of his whiskey. From a distance he would look sixty, until you saw him move. The dossier said he was forty-three. Up close, if you blocked out the hair, he looked thirty-two or thirty-three despite the wide mouth and the meandering nose. I decided that it must be his eyes. There has been a lot of nonsense written about childlike gazes, but Shartelle seemed to look out on the world with the lesson-learning gray eyes of a nine-year-old who has been told that he must save the ten-dollar bill he found under the bench

5

in the park. Although he knows he will never find another one, he also knows that he will never again tell anybody if he does.

"What role do you play in the Duffy charade, Mr. Upshaw?"

"I'm an account executive."

"Which side?"

"Public relations."

"In London?"

"Yes."

"While I was taking a shower, I was thinking about your name. You did a series on Hungary a long time ago." He named the paper I had worked for.

"You're right. It was a long time ago."

"And now you're flacking for Pig Duffy?"

"They're calling us public relations practitioners this year."

"How'd you locate me?"

"I checked with the national committee in Washington. They had a rough itinerary. I kept just missing you. My instructions were to make the proposition in person; no phone calls."

Shartelle rose and moved over to the window that looked out on the Denver night scene. "And what is Pig's proposition?"

"He told me to mention the fee first."

"He would."

"It's thirty thousand."

"Oh?"

"Pounds. Not dollars."

"I'll say 'oh' again and put a little interest into it."

"I don't blame you."

"Campaign?"

"Yes."

Shartelle turned from the window and looked at me. "Where?"

"Africa."

He smiled, and the smile grew into a laugh. A delightful laugh. "I'll be goddamned," he said, choked, and laughed again. "I'll be goddamned to hell! Nobody but that shanty-Irish son of a bitch would have the nerve."

"He does have a plentiful reserve."

"Mr. Upshaw, he's got the balls of a brass ape. I've seen high rollers in my time, but for plain green gall there's none that'll match Padraic Duffy, landed gentry."

"He speaks well of you," I said in game defense of my employer.

Shartelle dragged a chair close to mine, dropped into it, then leaned over and tapped me on the knee. "Why, he should, Mr. Upshaw. By God, he should! You don't know about old Pig Duffy and me and it's too long a story to tell right now, but I will say that he *should* speak well of me."

"He said you'd worked together once or twice."

"Did he tell you about the last time?"

"No."

"I don't imagine he tells many people about that, but after it was over, I told him just like I'm talking to you that if he ever so much as mentioned my name in the same breath with his, I was going to clean his plow good." He tapped me on the knee again. "Now I told him that as one Southern gentlemen to another."

"Duffy's from Chicago," I said.

"Not when he's in New Orleans, he's not. In New Orleans he tells folks he's from Breaux Bridge. Where're you from, Mr. Upshaw?"

"North Dakota, Fargo."

"Why, if old Pig got up to Fargo, he'd tell folks up there he was from Mandan. Or Valley City."

"You know North Dakota?"

"Boy," he said, "there's damned few places in this country I don't know. And if I call you 'boy', it's just my purposeful plain way of speaking that seems to put folks at their ease and makes them think I'm not too bright which I probably ain't."

"Just call me Pete."

"I was fixing to."

"I think I'll have another drink."

"You do that. Now what's this about Africa?"

I tried the Virginia Gentleman again. "Duffy has been asked to handle the strategy, campaign management, and public relations for Chief Sunday Akomolo who wants to be premier of Albertia when it gets independence from the Crown come next Labor Day." I needed a breath after that.

"Who's Chief Akomolo?"

"He's the head of the second largest political party in the country—the National Progressives."

"How many in the race?"

"There're fourteen parties—but only three of them count."

"How did Duffy get asked in?"

"Cocoa. He landed the Cocoa Marketing Board account and did his usual promotion job."

Shartelle nodded. "I heard about it. The cocoa futures bounced around some as a result."

"It was a volatile commodity for a while," I said a bit pontifically. "Well, Chief Akomolo is on the Cocoa Board, met Duffy, and got the idea."

Shartelle rose and walked over to the window again. "O.K., let's bring it all out nice and plain. Just what kind of stakes you playing for?"

"No limit. The country's got twenty million people, add or subtract a million or so. It's got one of the best harbors on the West Coast. It's got oil that hasn't been touched, mineral deposits, a solid agricultural economy, and a built-in civil service system that'll run for a hundred years and a day before it breaks down or someone forgets to minute a file. The British have seen to that."

"Who'll count the votes?"

"The Crown."

"So the boy who gets in this time will be counting the votes the next time."

"Probably."

"Then there's really going to be only one election, the first one, because the next time around the ins will have it wired."

8

"You seem familiar with African politics."

"No, I'm just familiar with all politics. It's been my life-study. And in some circles I'm considered a leading authority, and I say that with all modesty."

"You've got the track record, I hear."

"What's Duffy's end?"

"Not as much as you'd think. The entire package is five-hundred thousand pounds. Your cut would be thirty thousand, as I said."

"And if the Chief wins?"

I looked up at the ceiling. "I don't know really. Let's just say that there's probably a tacit understanding that DDT would get the whole thing—advertising, promotion, consultation, marketing, feasibility studies—everything."

"How much is all that, you reckon?"

I shrugged. "I'd guess twenty million annual billing."

"Dollars?"

"Pounds."

Shartelle chuckled and shook his head slowly from side to side. "Now ain't that something? Old Pig's got himself a fifty-six-million-dollar-a-year nigger candidate and he's calling for help. From me. Now that's really something."

"He said you'd say that."

"What?"

"Nigger candidate."

"It bother you?"

"Nothing much bothers me, Mr. Shartelle."

"Let me tell you one thing, boy."

"What's that?"

"It wouldn't bother Pig."

There was a silence that grew. I lighted a cigarette, an honest Lucky Strike, and smoked it without pleasure as Shartelle looked at me with a slight smile. It was the same smile he would have given a fifteen-year-old. That was all right; I felt like thirteen.

"Look, we can sit here all night and you can make snotty remarks about Duffy, but he's paying my salary, so don't get upset if I don't chime in.

Shartelle grinned. "Now, Pete, you're just pissed off

because of the nigger talk, aren't you?"

"No," I said. "I'm not pissed off."

"Now, boy, I could pull out my cards in the N-Double-A-C-P and CORE and show them to you. Or I could put in your hands some kindly letters I got from some of my colored friends who've been right active in all this Civil Rights hoop-te-do. Or as a Southern gentleman I could tell you that I *know* colored folks because I was brought up with them, which I was, or that I had a fine old colored mammy who I loved better than anyone in this world, which I did. I could parade, right before your eyes, evidence—real evidence—that I am probably the world's biggest nigger lover, and to top it off I could describe in detail to you a high yellow I once courted in Chicago and would have married except she ran off with some smooth-talking firetruck salesman. He was of the Jewish persuasion, I believe. Now when I say nigger it's because I plain can't stand to hear some flannelmouth like me from Opelousas or Natchez trying to say Nee-gro and the word just sticking in his throat like a catfish bone. When I say nigger, it don't mean a goddamned thing because I go by the Shartelle theory of race relations, and the Shartelle theory was pounded and shaped out of a hell of a lot of experience with black and white alike and, boy, I'm gonna give you the benefit of long hours of serious thought and hard study, and I'm surely not one for much introspection. I am possessed, you may have noticed, of an outward-going personality."

"I've noticed."

"Well, now. The Shartelle theory of harmonious race relations is simple and straightforward. My theory is that we either ought to give the niggers their rights—not just lip service, but every blasted right there is from voting to fornicating, that we ought to make them have all these rights and enforce their right to them by law, and I mean tough, FBI-attracting law, until every man jack of them is just as equal as you middle-class, white, Anglo-Saxon Protestants. I said *either* and I mean it. Either we give them the right to marry your daughter, if you got one, and fix

10

it so that they'll not only have the same social and educational rights that you have, but the same economic rights—the same ways and means that you've got to the pursuit of happiness out there in one of those fine suburban developments instead of in a slum. And then they'll be just like you white folks with all your sound moral values, your Christian virtue, and your treasured togetherness. 'Course, they might lose something along the way, something like a culture, but that ain't nothing. Now I say either we do that for them—make 'em just like everybody else—or, by God, we ought to drive 'em down in the ground like tent pegs!" Shartelle slammed his fist down on a table to show me how tent pegs are driven.

"What do you mean 'your' social rights, Shartelle? You're in just as deep."

"Why no I ain't, boy. My great-grandmother was a pretty little octoroon thing from New Orleans. At least that's what my daddy told me. And that makes me about one-sixty-fourth colored, which is more than enough in most Southern states. Now who has the better right to say nigger than us niggers?"

"You're putting me on, Shartelle."

"Now I may be, boy, but you'll never know for sure, will you?" He paused and grinned wickedly. "And you don't mean to tell me it would make any difference?"

— *2* —

We had breakfast the next morning. Shartelle had said he wished to study Duffy's proposition during the night. "I want to give it my most careful consideration, just like a Congressman writing to a constituent who's got a plan to build a bridge across the Grand Canyon."

11

At breakfast he was wearing a dark plaid suit pressed to perfection, a blue oxford shirt with a button-down collar, and a striped blue and black tie that he must have borrowed from another English regiment. We ordered sausage, eggs, toast, coffee, and milk for Shartelle. He had his eggs up; I asked for mine over.

"I made a few calls last night, Pete," Shartelle said as he buttered a piece of toast.

"To whom?"

"Couple of people in New York. Pig was doing some bragging there. That's to be expected. But there's something else you might be interested in—you're going to have some opposition."

"What kind?"

"Another agency."

I made the kind of face that Eisenhower did when they told him MacArthur was fired. "Who?"

"Renesslaer."

"My. Or maybe I should say my, my."

"You echo my reaction," Shartelle said. "The name Renesslaer does hit a responsive chord. Like a kid drawing his fingernail across a blackboard."

I thought a moment. "With offices in London, Stockholm, Copenhagen, Brussels, Paris, Madrid, Frankfurt, Zurich, Rome, a dozen cities in the states, Hongkong, Bombay, Tokyo and Manila. What did I miss?"

"Toronto, Sydney, and Johannesburg."

There are all kinds of advertising and public relations agencies. Some are desperate, one-man operations that exist from the commissions paid by equally desperate radio stations and trade publications. There are the swift-moving, hot-eyed agencies that skyrocket to success and then mellow into the pattern of the business world, much like a plumbing fixture manufacturer. And then there are the agencies like Duffy, Downer, and Theims, Ltd., multimillion dollar concerns running on charm, genius, exuberance, and the business morality of a bankrupt carnival. Finally, there are a dozen or so agencies whose size, financial power, and ruthlessness are equalled only by their stunning grasp of the mediocre. It is to these agencies, and the pilot fish which swarm about them, that the nation owes thanks for the present level of its television, radio, and the large chunk of American sub-culture that has been so profitably exported abroad.

Of these dozen or so agencies, Renesslaer was the third or fourth largest, and while the majority of them were making their fortunes by following Menckenian law and betting their all on the bad taste of the American public, Renesslaer had developed a world conscience.

"They've set up, in that agency, a world public affairs section," Shartelle said gloomily. "And it combines all the worst features of Moral Rearmament, the Peace Corps, and International Rotary. They have a speakers' bureau that will fly a speaker any place in the world on twelve hours notice for the guarantee of an audience of five hundred people. And he'll make the speech in his audience's language. They've got an Oceania desk, a Southwest Africa desk, an Italian desk, and an Icelandic desk. For all I know they've got an Antarctic desk."

"I've heard about it," I said. "They send copies of the speeches around. They're translated and arrive all over the world the same day that the speech is given. You'd be surprised how many of them get printed."

Shartelle poured us some more coffee from the pewter pot. He drank his black. I used sugar.

"I remember they handled that special election in California last year," he said.

"Which side?"

"They had the one who used to play the bad guy in the movies. The one who used to play the good guy lost by half-a-million votes."

"You in on that one?" I asked.

"I could have been, but I sniffed around out there and decided it was too dicey. I can't figure that nut vote. But apparently Renesslaer got enough of them switched over at the last second."

I drew some patterns on the tablecloth with my spoon. Shartelle was silent and remote.

"Who's Renesslaer's client?" I asked.

Shartelle fished in his coat pocket and produced a scrap of paper. I wrote his name down. I wanted to ask you about him. Renesslaer's client is Alhaji Sir Alakada Mejara Fulawa. He's a northern Albertian, I understand. What's the Alhaji mean?

"It means he's been to Mecca."

"You mean to say Renesslaer's got themselves a non-Christian for a candidate? What else you know about him?"

"He was educated in England, speaks with a perfect Oxford accent, if there is such a thing. He's rich—I mean the private-Comet, fleet-of-Rolls-type rich. He's the natural ruler of about seven million Albertians and he lives in a palace just south of the Sahara that's something out of *Arabian Nights*. The British love him because he's kept the troublemakers quiet."

"And Pig Duffy wants me to go to Albertia and run old Chief what's his name...Akomolo—*Sunday* Akomolo at that—against this *A*-rab Alhaji Sir Alakada Mejara Fulawa. Oh, ain't he got a name that just rolls pretty off the tongue!"

"From what I've heard he's had a few cut out."

Shartelle shook his head slowly from side to side, a broad crooked grin on his face, sheer delight in his eyes. "I tell you, Petey, it's Richard Halliburton and Rudolph Valentino and Tar*zan* all rolled into one big package and snuffed up tight with a pretty blue ribbon. Man, it's foreign intrigue and Madison Avenue and Trader Horn and *Africa* and Pig Duffy's caught smack in the middle of it, wallowing around and squealing for help, and here comes old Clint Shartelle, all decked out in his pith helmet and bush jacket just a-rushing to the rescue. My, it's fine!"

"Call me Peter," I said. "Call me Pete, call me Mr. Upshaw, or hey you, but for God's sake don't call me Petey."

"Why, boy, you're getting touchous again about my language."

"Oh, hell, call me anything."

"Now I take it that you are going to be working this

campaign for Chief Akomolo?"

I nodded. "I drew the short straw."

"Just what will your duties be?"

"I'll be the writer. If there's anybody to read it."

"Well, now, that's fine. What kind of writer are you, Pete?"

"A fast one. Not good, just fast. When I'm not writing I can sharpen the pencils and mix the drinks."

"And just what does Pig want me to do?"

I looked at him and grinned. It was the first time I had smiled all morning. "Mr. Duffy said that he would like you—and I quote—'to inject a little American razzmatazz into the campaign.'"

Shartelle leaned back in his chair and smiled up at the ceiling. "Did he now? What do you think I'll be doing?"

"You have the reputation as the best rough-and-tumble campaign manager in the United States. You have six metropolitan mayors, five governors, three U. S. Senators, and nine Congressmen that you can honestly claim credit for. You've defeated the sales tax in four states, and got it passed in one. You got an oil severance tax passed in two states and got the resulting revenue earmarked for schools in one of them. In other words, you're the best that's available and Padraic Duffy told me to tell you he said that. You're to do whatever has to be done to get Chief Akomolo elected."

"I tell you, Pete, I'm just about at the end of what might be called a sentimental journey."

"How's that?"

Shartelle reached for the check, signed it, and rose. "Let's go take a little walk." We left the hotel and headed up Broadway towards Colfax. Shartelle puffed away on one of his Picayunes.

"I happened to drop by that baseball game last night just after I'd bought a house," he said. "I didn't do too bad for an old fellow."

"You're forty-three. When Kennedy was forty-three he was playing touch football with a bad back."

"I admit I'm a bit spry, but I owe it all to the wisdom

of youth and my precocious reading habits."

"You mentioned something about a sentimental journey back there," I said. "About a block back."

"The sentimental journey is associated with my youth. I used to live in this town, you know."

We turned up Colfax towards the golddomed capitol where there is a marker that reads that at this exact spot the city of Denver is 5,280 feet above sea level. A mile high and a mile ahead.

"I lived here in a house with my daddy and a lady friend from 1938 to 1939. Not too far from that ball park which is—you might have noticed—in a somewhat blighted area. It was a plumb miserable neighborhood even then. I was sixteen-seventeen years old. My daddy and I had come out here from Oklahoma City in the fall driving a big, black 1939 LaSalle convertible sedan. We checked in at the Brown Palace and my daddy got himself a lease on a section of land near Walsenburg, found him a rig and crew, and drilled three of the deepest dry holes you ever saw."

Shartelle touched my arm and steered us into a drugstore. We sat in a booth, and ordered some more coffee.

"Well, sir, my daddy went busted again. He had wildcatted in Oklahoma City and brought in ten producers in the eastside field there and he had a potful of money, even if he did have to spend a spell in jail for running hot oil. He swore up and down that there was oil in Colorado. And, of course, he was right. He just drilled in the wrong place."

The waitress brought us coffee. Shartelle stirred his. "We moved out of the Brown Palace and rented that house I bought yesterday. Me and my daddy and his lady friend. Her name was Golda Mae, a nice looking little thing. It was surely hard times, but I just went on with my lessons and let my daddy worry about the finances."

"What lessons?" I asked.

"My Charles Atlas lessons, boy. I went through the whole course of Dynamic Tension. Clipped an ad out of *The Spider* and sent off for it. That's when my Daddy was in

16

the money in Oklahoma City. Hell, it wasn't anything but isometrics, the same thing that everybody is doing now. But I followed the instructions like they were the gospel—and that's why I'm so spry today."

"So what are you going to do with the house you bought?"

Shartelle put a hand out in front of him and made an abrupt shoving motion. "Now don't push me. When I'm telling, I like to tell my way. Not too long after the money ran out, Golda Mae moved on and it was just my daddy and me. I was sorry to see her go, because she was a mighty pleasant person. So one day my daddy calls me in and he says, 'Son, I'm not making enough to support us both so I guess you're going to have to be out on your own for a while. But I tell you what, you can have the LaSalle.'

"That offer of his was generous, even if it was worthless. You see it was winter and we didn't have enough money for alcohol so the block froze on the LaSalle and it busted wide open. But it was the only thing he had to offer and he made the offer and we didn't talk about the fact that the LaSalle wasn't worth a dime. I just thanked him and declined politely, the way he'd taught me." Shartelle paused and stirred his coffee some more. "So yesterday I bought the house in Denver, and I bought three others in New Orleans, Birmingham and Oklahoma City. They are the four my daddy and I lived in longest. I own them now and whenever I want to I can walk in and look around at the rooms and remember, or not remember."

"You're going to live in them?" I asked.

"No, I'm going to be landlord. I'm going to rent them for one dollar a year to poor colored folks. The only condition is that I can come in and look around when I want to. That's not too much to ask, is it?"

"Not for a dollar a year."

"I didn't think so."

We got up. I paid the cashier and we walked back down Colfax to Broadway. It was a bright cool July morning in Denver and I looked around trying to project how it was almost twenty-seven years before when a seventeen-year-old was admonished to drive off in his legacy except that the legacy had a broken block.

"What happened to your father?" I asked.

"I don't know," he said. "We lost touch after a while. I haven't heard from him in twenty-five years."

"Ever try to locate him?"

Shartelle looked at me and smiled. "I can't say that I did. Do you think I should've?"

"I wouldn't know."

We walked on in silence. Then Shartelle asked, "How soon does Pig want me in London?"

"As soon as possible."

He nodded. "Then we'd better leave today."

— **3** —

At 10 a.m. Greenwich Mean Time the next day, or 4 a.m., Eastern Standard Time, or 2 a.m., Mountain Standard Time, I picked up Shartelle at the Dorchester in London. We had flown all night after making a close connection in New York. Shartelle was wearing a sleepy look, a lightweight gray suit, a white shirt, and a black knit tie. His white hair was brushed and his gray eyes flickered just slightly as he took in my bowler and carefully furled umbrella.

"I let Duffy wear the Stetson," I told him. "I try to blend with the background."

We talked a little at breakfast and then walked the several blocks to the office. Jimmy, the porter, wearing all of his World War II campaign ribbons and then some, welcomed me back. I introduced Shartelle. "Always glad to have an American gentleman with us, sir," Jimmy said.

"Has Mr. Duffy arrived yet?" I asked.

"Just come in, sir. Been here not more than a quarter-hour."

Shartelle followed me up the stairs to my office. I introduced him to my secretary who said she was glad to see me back. There were two notes on my desk to return Mr. Duffy's call. Shartelle glanced around the room. "Either this place is on the verge of bankruptcy or it's making too much money," he said.

"Wait'll you see Duffy's layout."

"The only discordant note you got in here, boy, is that machine, Shartelle said, pointing to my typewriter. It was an L.C. Smith, about 35 years old.

"That's the touch of class, Duffy figures. It cost the firm ten pounds just to have the damned thing renovated. When he shows clients through the office, he tells them that I wrote my first byline story on it and that I can't write a word on anything else."

"You ever use it?"

I sat down behind my U-shaped desk and swung out a Smith-Corona electric portable. "I use this. It's faster. As I said, I'm a fast writer."

Shartelle lowered himself into one of the three winged-back black leather chairs that clustered around my desk. Each had beside it a slate-topped cube of solid oiled teak and on those were large, brightly-colored ceramic ashtrays.

"Like that good old man said, you got a carpet on the floor and pictures on the wall. All you need is a little music in the air."

I pushed a button on the desk. Muzak gave forth softly with something from *Camelot*. I pushed the button again and it stopped.

Shartelle grinned and lighted a Picayune. "I just noticed one thing," he said. "You ain't got a door."

"The only doors in the place are the front one, the necessary firedoors, the ones that lead to the cans, and four on the women's stalls. Duffy had all the rest of them removed. He says that anytime anybody wants to see anybody they should feel free to poke their heads in. There

19

are no secrets in Duffy, Downer and Theims. It's a mad-house."

As if on cue, the keeper of the madhouse burst in. "Shartelle, goddamn you, how've you been?" he demanded. It was Duffy, dressed for the country. He wore a green tweed suit with a weave so loose that you could poke a ten-penny nail through it without making a hole. His shirt was as pale green as it could get without being white and his tie was a black and green wool. Although I didn't look, I decided that his shoes must be stout brown brogues.

Shartelle uncoiled himself from a black leather chair, shifted his cigarette to his left hand, and slowly extended his right to Duffy. He took his time. A smile that seemed to be of pure delight creased his face as he cocked his head slightly to one side. I was forgotten. Duffy had Shartelle's undivided attention. It was the Shartelle treatment. There was affection and liking in his gaze, but more important, there was a real and deep personal interest in the man whose hand he shook. Had I been Duffy, I would have bought the bridge and probably taken an option on the ferry.

"Pig Duffy," Shartelle said, and his white grin widened. "I swear it's good to see you looking so fit and fine."

Duffy let the Pig go by, not even flinching slightly. He grasped Shartelle's right hand with both of his and shook it some more. He threw his head back and narrowed his blue eyes. "Nine years, Clint. I was trying to remember just where it was, as I drove in this morning. Chicago, the Stockyards Inn."

"July twenty-two."

"Four in the morning."

"Suite 570."

"By God, you're right!" Duffy let go of Shartelle's hand. "You haven't changed a bit, Clint. Did you have a good flight? My boy here take care of you all right?"

"Mr. Upshaw is the soul of courtesy. And, I might add, a crackerjack salesman. I'm here."

Duffy flicked his blue eyes at me. "How're you, Pete?"

"Just fine."

"Did you give Clint all the details?"

"Just the highlights."

"He mentioned thirty thousand pounds," Shartelle said with his warm smile. "That was the brightest highlight of all. What are you doing messing around in Africa, Pig? Ain't that a little out of your territory?"

Duffy rallied. "When I heard about this, I thought the same thing, Clint. I thought, 'Padraic, you have enough on your plate the way things stand. You haven't time to give it the guidance it really needs.' And then I tried to think of someone who could bring off the campaign." He paused, bit his lower lip reflectively, and glanced downwards. His voice softened, and took on a measure of quiet awe. "I decided that there was only one man—not in England, not in the States, but just one man in the *world*. And that was Clint Shartelle." He raised his eyes, looked at Shartelle directly and said humbly, "So I asked Clint Shartelle to help me out." He paused again and then added a line—almost as a throwaway, but not quite—"And more important, to help out Africa."

Shartelle shook his head slightly from side to side. It was the gesture of frank appreciation that the concertmaster pays the performance of the virtuoso. His voice was as soft as Duffy's, and the honeysuckle seemed to bloom as he said, "Put that way, Padraic, no man could refuse."

Duffy brightened, grabbed Shartelle by the arm, and steered him towards 'he forever-open door. "I've got the whole morning open for you, Clint. We'll have a bit of a natter, and then you'll meet the candidate. He flew in two days ago and is leaving this afternoon, but you'll have a chance to get acquainted at lunch." Duffy turned his head. "Come on, Pete." I took it as a nice afterthought.

We walked down the hall past Duffy's two secretaries to where The Hatrack guarded his doorless entrance. The Hatrack was a statue made of welded scrap metal. It stood seven feet high on an onyx base and was supposed to be representative of the Crucifixion. And at least that was its real name. The main crosspiece looked for all the world like the corrugated bumper from a 1937 DeSoto, the kind once held at a premium by the hot rod crowd in Los Angeles. Slightly tight and Philistinish after a particularly good lunch, I once had hung my bowler on it. Duffy wouldn't speak to me for a week, but since then everyone called it The Hatrack. Shartelle gave it an appreciative glance as we moved into Duffy's office.

It wasn't an office exactly; it was more of a huge living room that smelled of leather from the hexagonal pieces of quarter-inch-thick cowhide that served as wallpaper. There was a view of the square and the Embassy, a fireplace with a fire in it, some highly comfortable chairs and a huge oaken coffee table made, Duffy claimed, from the butt end of an ancient giant wine cask. Here and there, placed strategically on small individual shelves that jutted from the walls, were the products of the major clients: a box of instant tea, a package of tissues, a bottle of ale, a model of a jet airliner, a miniature of a bank, a model automobile, a package of cocoa, and a cigarette package. Each had its own niche and to get it, the billing had to top three million pounds a year. There was no desk, but a telephone was handy to Duffy's chair, which sat in a corner behind the immense wine-cask coffee table.

Duffy took his seat and gestured Shartelle and me to chairs. Shartelle gave the room a long and careful appraisal. Then he nodded his head. "You've done right well by the English folks, I'd say," he told Duffy.

"We're growing, Clint, expanding a little every year."

We were interrupted by Wilson Davis, the art director. He didn't knock. He just walked in and stuck a layout under Duffy's nose.

"Hello, Pete," Davis said to me.

"How are you, Wilson?" I asked.

"If he ever makes up his mind what he wants, I'll be all right."

"Giving you a hard time?"

"This is the fourth rough. The fourth, mind you."

"Now that's more like it, Wilson," Duffy said. "Now

that's something that you could say bears the DDT imprint."

"It isn't bad," Wilson admitted.

"All right, then proceed."

"You're not going to change your mind again?"

"No. That's the basis of the campaign I promised. That's the one I'll deliver."

Wilson picked up the rough from the coffee table and left.

"It's like that all day," I told Shartelle. "The DDT open door policy."

"Saves time, really," Duffy said. "Does away with morale problems. That young man is a talented art director— the best in London and as good as you'll find in New York. He wants to see me so he walks in. He doesn't have to work his way past a half-dozen secretaries or assistants. He doesn't have to wait a half-hour outside a closed door, wondering if I'm talking about him. He just walks in, states his business, and a minute later walks out. His time is worth about five guineas an hour. I estimate that this method saves a half-hour of his waiting time plus another half-hour of what I call fuming time when he gets back to his own shop."

"Sounds reasonable," Shartelle said, "and as long as you brought money up, I think maybe I'd better remind you of my usual terms."

"Third now, third halfway through, and a third the week before it's all done. Right?"

"Plus expenses," Shartelle said.

Duffy picked up the telephone and dialed a single number. "Would you find out whether Mr. Theims has countersigned the check for Mr. Shartelle yet? Fine, bring it in."

One of Duffy's secretaries brought in the check. Duffy read it and handed it to Shartelle. "Ten thousand pounds."

Shartelle glanced at it and slipped it into an inside breast pocket. He drew out his package of Picayunes and lighted one. "Pig, old buddy," he said, "just what do you want

23

me to do to earn this money?"

Duffy stared at Shartelle with his china blue eyes, gripped the arms of his chair, and leaned forward slightly. "This is the biggest one of your career, Clint. The most important one. Whitehall has its eyes on this one and so does State. I've been to Albertia, Clint, and it's fantastic. It's the opportunity to carve out a bastion of democracy in Africa. It's the chance to establish your reputation as one of the world's foremost political strategists. But most important, to me—and I know to you—it's the opportunity to elect a good man to office."

"Your client?" Shartelle said.

"Chief Akomolo."

"I guess you heard about Renesslaer," Shartelle said. "They're craving to elect a good man to office, too. Alhaji Sir Alakada Mejara Fulawa—my, that *is* a pretty mouthful!"

The blue eyes of my leader grew cold. "Renesslaer's got Fulawa? Who told you?"

"Some friends in New York. Not very good friends at that. I'm surprised you hadn't heard."

Duffy turned to me. "Did you know?"

"Shartelle told me."

Duffy picked up the phone. "Bring your book," he snapped.

A secretary came in. I don't know where he got them, but there seemed to be a new one every week. After one day, they seemed to know all about the agency and all about the people in it. Then they would quietly disappear to be replaced by someone equally efficient.

"Cable Trookein, New York: HEARTELL BIG R CONNING SKYCHIEF OPERATION PAWPAWLAND. WHY WE UNKNOWN? SEND FULL REPORT PROSCARFACE SOONEST ENDIT DUFFY." The way he barked, it came out all caps.

"No regards?" the secretary asked.

"Hell, no!" Duffy said.

"Let's see, now," Shartelle said, "Big R would be Renesslaer. Skychief would be old Alhaji Sir. Pawpawland,

I reckon, would be Albertia. Who's Scarface?"

"That's Chief Akomolo," I said. "It's his code name because of his tribal markings."

Shartelle chuckled softly. "You wear the secret code ring, Petey?"

"We need a name for Clint," Duffy said.

"How about Shortcake?" Shartelle suggested with a straight face.

"Damn good. Put it on the list," Duffy told the secretary.

"What're you called, Pete?" Shartelle asked.

"Scaramouche," I said and shrugged.

"How 'bout you, Pig?"

"I'm Hiredhand."

"Is it necessary?"

"Yes and no. It wouldn't fool any intelligence operation, but it keeps the casually curious from lifting information that they might sell or gossip about. It's just a minor precaution really."

"It sure as hell wouldn't fool any of the bright boys from Renesslaer."

Duffy smiled pleasantly. "No it wouldn't, Clint. That's going to be your job."

"Just so we get everything nice and clear, Pig, I hope you've told the candidate about the ground rules. First, I run the campaign—from buttons to banquets. Second, I don't handle money."

"I know and the candidate knows," Duffy said. "The money's taken care of. All you have to do is find ways to spend it."

"I'm usually pretty good at that."

"Now here's a thing I want to ask you: can you handle the opposition?"

"Renesslaer?"

"Just."

Shartelle rose and walked over to the window. He looked out for a while and then moved so he could examine the miniature of the bank. "They're a right capable bunch," he said. "I'd be the last to poor-talk them. But since neither of us is going to be playing at home, I might have a slight edge. You've got a research staff?"

Duffy nodded. "One of the best."

"You can count on Renesslaer having the best, so what you've got is second best. But you can turn it loose, if need be?"

"It's at the Chief's disposal—and at yours."

"Way I understand it, this is going to be a three-way race: Chief Akomolo, old Alhaji Sir Prettyname, and somebody else. Who's the somebody else and how much clout has he got?"

"Dr. Kensington Kologo," Duffy said. "He's from the Eastern section of Albertia. The doctor is real: he earned his M.D. at the University of Pennsylvania in 1934."

"What's he got?"

"About a third of the country's population in his region. He also has the iron range plus some tin which gives him a large following among the trade unionists and the more radical younger crowd."

"Sounds like a good base. Does he worry Chief Akomolo?"

"Not as much as Fulawa does."

"Have you checked out whether he's got an agency handling his campaign? I'd sure hate to get out there and find I was being double-teamed by Renesslaer and Doyle Dane."

"It's not an agency exactly," Duffy said and watched Shartelle's face intently.

"What is it?"

"The CIA."

— 4 —

Shartelle slumped far down in his chair, crossed his legs, and stared intently at the ceiling. He made himself more comfortable by folding his arms behind his head. Duffy watched him. I watched Duffy.

"Well, now, old buddy," Shartelle said slowly, "this kind of brings us full circle. You and me, that is. It doesn't seem too long ago that you and Downer and me were taking and losing that French radio station for the grand-daddy of the same outfit."

"That was war time, Clint."

Shartelle looked at Duffy and frowned. "You know, Pig, it always amazed me how you got started over here so smooth-like. I mean you had a going concern from the time you caught a cab at Victoria Station."

"I made a lot of contacts here during the war. You know that, Clint."

Shartelle looked around the room with the gaze of a probate court appraiser. "Yes, I guess you did. And I imagine you still have some, or you wouldn't know about the CIA moving in."

Duffy looked at me. "Nobody but you two knows about it. Nobody but you two had better find out about it. I got this information from someone who owes me a favor. It was a big favor that I'd planned to collect in another way. A more profitable way, I might add. A damn sight more profitable. Now that favor's paid off in full."

Shartelle straightened himself up in his chair. He looked at me and winked. "What's Chief Akomolo going to say to all this?"

"He can't be told, goddamn it, Clint. You know that."

27

"I just wanted to make sure you did."

"He can't be told," Duffy repeated. "Nobody can. What do you expect us to do, issue a release blasting hell out of the CIA for interfering in the internal politics of one of Africa's new and independent nations? Balls. What do you think we're doing—and Renesslaer for that matter?"

"What we got is three American concerns trying to handicap a three-way horse race," Shartelle said. "Now it seems strange to me that one of these candidates hasn't snuggled up to a British PR agency. There're some mighty sharp ones."

Duffy sighed wearily. He looked at his open door and for the first time seemed to wish he had something to close it with. "Chief Akomolo hates the British. Don't ask me why, it's just a way of life with him. They're colonialists. They're the imperialistic power. Fulawa is sold on the Renesslaer bootstrap philosophy. He's also cynical enough to believe it will keep things the way they are for the rest of his lifetime and then some. As for Dr. Kologo, the CIA sold him a campaign that must be based on one thing and that's money. It's the only way I can figure it."

Shartelle leaned forward in his chair. "Now, Padraic, you correct me if I'm wrong. Let's look at it like this: I believe you told me that Dr. Kologo has his base among the trade unionists and the radical younger crowd."

"Anything under forty-five is young," Duffy said.

"Now what's old Sir Alhaji got?"

"The Muslims and the Emirs. It's a little complicated, but he has a tight rein. He also has the political right— if you can call it right."

"What's it right of?"

"Maybe the Social Democrats in Germany or the Labourites here. But not much."

"And Chief Akomolo?"

"He's got the socialists and his tribe—which is the biggest tribe there is except that some of them are Muslims."

Shartelle nodded. "I follow you. Now just how far left is the laborskate bunch that's backing Dr. Kologo? China-left?"

"Christ, no!"

"Not even Russia?"

"No. The trade unionists and the young crowd are just left of everybody else. There are only thirty-one communists in all of Albertia. Thirty-two if you throw in old Mrs. Pryce-Smith who retired there. But she's English and doesn't count. There is no radical right and no radical left. Not as we know it. Everybody's left of center, but not enough so that you can distinguish them."

"Well, now," Shartelle said, "it begins to make a little sense." He rose and started to pace the room. "And hell, Pete, it's better than ever! We got Africa and Jungle Jim and Tribal Chiefs and Secret Agents all sneaking through the rain forest. We got high-powered flacks and bewildered old India hands watching the last of the Empire crumble. We got all this as wild as it can be and just south of Timbuktu!" He turned in the room abruptly. "And sure the CIA wants in, and you know why? It's because they've been badmouthed all over the place about backing the kook groups, the military, the far right extremists, instead of the good, solid lib-lab representatives of the people.

"So in Dr. Kologo they got themselves a candidate—a good man, as Pig here would call him. He's not to the political right, he's not tied up with the military, he's got the support of the unions, and if he wins, then the CIA can leak it out that they supported this good man. If he loses, what the hell. They gave their support to the best man in sight and he lost. At least they weren't supporting the sinister military-industrial complex—if Albertia's got one yet."

"That's not quite it, Clint," Duffy said. "That's a good chunk of it, but not all. Candidates stand for election down there much as they do in England, by districts. Now if none of the three parties gains a simple majority at the center, then a coalition can form the government. This is a likely possibility. And if it happens, then both Chief Akomolo and Fulawa will go courting Dr. Kologo because they despise each other. And the CIA might have the final say on who the successful suitor shall be."

I half-listened as they went on mapping out the destiny of a large piece of African real estate for the next half-century or so. Maybe this was what I had been missing those years that I had stood around in hotel corridors and the drafty halls of government buildings waiting for someone to open a closed door and lie about what they had been saying inside. You never knew really what they actually said or whether they yawned or picked their noses or just talked about women while the administrative aide pounded out the communiqué.

I wondered how Duffy had found out that the CIA was lumbering its way into the campaign and I wondered if two men, very much like Duffy and Shartelle, hadn't been sitting around in a hotel room or some office in Paris or London or Lagos or Virginia when one, turning to the other, had said something like, "What do you think about taking a flyer on the Albertia do? We can send Johnson—he's been moping around the office." And the other one said, "Not bad, Stanley (or Bill or Jack or Rex or Bryan). Why don't you get it down on paper and I'll walk it through?"

The edge that had crept into the voices of Duffy and Shartelle brought me back. I felt I should have been taking notes.

"It was only an offer of help, Clint," Duffy said. "Downer's there now and he could stay on for a couple of months to give you and Pete a hand."

"I don't think I want Downer because I know Downer and I've worked with Downer. I remember the time you and me and Downer were in Liège and trying to get to Aachen and that stupid son of a bitch—"

"Never mind. I remember. All right, Downer's out. Do you have anybody in mind that you'd like to have aboard?"

A secretary brought in a stack of letters and placed them on the coffee table and handed Duffy a pen. "Sign these," she said. "Now." Duffy signed and kept on talking. "We could fly somebody in from the States if you want, or I got a couple of Canadians we could pass off on the Chief as Americans—U. S. variety."

Shartelle was pacing the room again. He waited until the secretary scooped up the letters from Duffy, removed her pen from his coat pocket, and left. "I knew a man once who kept on talking real private business when his private secretary was in the room and one day he came down to his office and they were moving out the furniture and scraping his name off the door."

"I didn't say anything she'd understand."

Shartelle sighed. "You just keep talking. You'll say one here and two there and some pretty little old gal is going to add up to three and you won't know what hit you. But to get back to my need for help, I reckon old Pete here and I can handle it. He *is* coming with me?"

"Yes," Duffy said firmly, "for the duration. You'll be in charge, of course, Clint."

"Oh, I'll just do the thinking and the talking and the nosing around and Pete can do the writing and the administrating."

"You can employ some secretarial help down there," Duffy said.

"When do you expect us to fly down?" Shartelle asked.

Duffy looked at me. "How about tomorrow? If you give me your passports, I'll arrange for the visas this afternoon. Okay, Pete?"

"Sure," I said. "I'll have been back an entire day by then. I can leave tomorrow."

"Now Pete, this is an experience that you could never acquire anywhere else. You're the best we have, and with a little more seasoning like this, there's no telling how fast you'll move up. Downer agrees, and so does Theims."

"He sure talks a pretty piece, don't he, Pete?" Shartelle said with a wide grin.

Duffy got up and moved over to my chair and clapped a well-tended hand on my shoulder. "He's good, Clint. He's one of the best naturals I've ever seen. He's got that ability to synthesize. He's better than I was at his age— and I was one of the best."

Shartelle nodded, without the grin. "I'll say that for you, Pig. You were one of the best."

"I still keep my hand in, you know."

"Doing what?"

"When they need a few words, I can usually come up with them. Now then," Duffy continued. "Your passports." He collected them from Shartelle and me, called the secretary, and handed them to her with instructions to have them back in the afternoon. "I'm having my own physician drop by at four to give you the necessary shots."

"What kind of shots?" Shartelle asked.

"Smallpox, yellow fever, typhoid, and tetanus. Unless you have had them recently?"

"No, I haven't."

The secretary came in again, walked over to Duffy, and whispered something to him. He nodded.

"He's here," Duffy said.

"Who?" Shartelle asked.

"Chief Akomolo. We're having lunch with him in the executive dining room. Special dishes and all. You'll like groundnuts, Clint. We found an Albertian cook who's able to whip up a remarkable potage with them."

"What're groundnuts, Pete?"

"Peanuts," I said.

"Can't say I plan to get all worked up over goober stew, Pig."

"Try it, Clint. Just try it with an open mind."

"Want me to predict the rest of the menu?" I asked.

"What?"

"Chicken curry."

"And hot," Duffy said. "The way the Leader likes it."

"The what?" Shartelle asked.

"The Leader. That's what we call him. It's—well, more precise than Premier and not quite as intimate as Chief."

"I'm going to call him Chief," Shartelle said firmly. "It's the first time I've ever worked for anybody who was a real chief and I'm not going to pass up the opportunity to address him by his rightful title."

Duffy looked pained. "Be polite, Clint. These people are very sensitive. The English don't know how to treat them. In fact, they've treated them shabbily."

"Now, Pig, you ain't telling me how to treat niggers, are you, old buddy, me who was raised with them?" His voice, normally warm and even mellow, developed a cutting edge that had a chill in it. It was the same voice he had used with me when we first discussed the campaign in Denver.

"God knows, Clint, I'm not telling you anything. I'm just saying that the Albertians are sensitive about their treatment from the whites. Especially the British. You can't make any more out of it than that."

Shartelle walked over and admired a painting that Duffy had hung on the leather-covered wall. It was an abstract done in frozen blues that blazed out coldly from the brown and tobacco colors of the room. "You know, I don't feel that I'm going to justify my attitude towards the colored race to anybody else, Pig. Now if you think that my Polite Southern upbringing and my country manners are going to offend this client of yours, perhaps we had just better call the whole thing off. I'll spend a couple of weeks nosing around London, and then just fly on back and there'll be no hard feelings."

"Goddamn it, Shartelle, don't be so childish. All I said was that these people are sensitive."

"This sure is a nice picture," Shartelle said. He turned and looked at Duffy for a long moment. "You'll never learn, will you, Pig?"

"All right, forget it," Duffy said. His face was pinker than usual and little beads of sweat popped out on his wide forehead just below the thinning black hair that he combed straight back. It wasn't thick enough to cover some balding patches. I noticed all this with a sense of satisfaction. "Let's get down to the dining room," he said. "I don't want to keep him waiting."

We walked out the doorless door, past the junk metal monster, and down the corridor to a firedoor. We went through that and down a flight of stairs. With the number of food accounts that DDT had, Duffy had turned the entire first floor of the agency into a hotel-sized kitchen and individual dining rooms where the senior staff could lunch with clients. Duffy led the way and Shartelle and I followed.

The Chief was waiting for us in the dining room. He was seated in a low-backed chair and rose when we came in. I had seen him before at a distance, but we had never met.

"Padraic," he said warmly, "it is good to see you." His English was precise, but muddied with a noticeable accent.

Standing by him was a tall young African. He neither smiled nor frowned. His brown face was fixed in a placid, almost content expression, but his eyes flicked over Shartelle and me, paused long enough to register and classify us, and then moved back to the Chief. The young man was not only tall, he was broad. He wore a chalk-striped blue suit and black shoes that must have been size thirteen, triple E width. He stayed close to Chief Akomolo's elbow, but slightly to the rear. His black eyes roamed the room, rested on Duffy briefly, then back to Shartelle and me, then back on Chief Akomolo. He was a very observant young man.

The Chief himself wore robes of his country. There was the flowing *ordona*, or outer garment, that slipped over the head and fell in graceful folds to the ankle. Loose trousers of matching fabric peeked out from under the robe whose V-cut neck revealed a round-necked shirt that was embroidered with gold thread. A red pill box velvet hat perched on his head at a somewhat rakish angle.

Akomolo's face creased into a smile as he greeted Duffy. They shook hands and the African's eyes glittered behind his gold-rimmed spectacles. Six deeply cut scars formed parallel trenches down each of his plump brown cheeks. They were the markings of his tribe, cut into his face at the age of six and made to fester so that the scars would run deep for the rest of his life.

Duffy introduced me as the former famous foreign correspondent from the great state of North Dakota. I shook hands with the Chief, but his eyes were on Shartelle. I introduced myself to the big African who hovered at Akomolo's side. He said his name was Dekko. "I am the Leader's personal aide," he said in a deep baritone. I told him I was glad to know him.

"And you must be Mr. Shartelle," Chief Akomolo said. His eyes twinkled or glittered some more behind the gold-rimmed glasses. "Padraic has told me so many things about you." He held out his hand and Shartelle shook it firmly and stared back into the Chief's eyes.

"I consider it a genuine privilege to make your acquaintance, sir," Shartelle said. I could hear Duffy letting his breath out.

The *ordona* of Albertia is made on the principle of a tent. It has a hole to poke the head through and the arms find their way out of the poncho-like garment by gathering its folds and throwing them over the left or right shoulder in a graceful, unconscious movement. I decided, as the Chief shifted his folds to his left shoulder, that it was much the same gesture that Roman senators must have used as they arranged their togas.

"You have a considerable reputation in your country, Mr. Shartelle," Chief Akomolo told him. "My personal aide, Chief Dekko, has done a good measure of research on you. Some of your experiences are to be envied."

Shartelle gave a courtly half-bow. "I am glad that you went to the effort to examine my credentials, sir."

The Chief smiled. "It was not because I do not believe my good friend, Padraic, I assure you. He spoke most highly of you and your capabilities. It is only that in an undertaking of such import, I must know my allies and their capabilities. For you see, Mr. Shartelle, I consider myself not a statesman, but more of a politician. As a statesman, I could afford to make mistakes. As a politician, I cannot."

"A fine distinction, and one which has the ring of experience," Shartelle said. He walked over to Dekko and offered his hand. "I'm Clint Shartelle, Chief," he said and gave the huge young man the Shartelle smile.

Dekko's impassive face did not change. He shook hands with Shartelle and made a small bow. "I am honored."

"Now, then, everybody's met everybody," Duffy said. "Shall we have a drink before lunch?"

Chief Akomolo smiled. "You know my preference, Padraic."

"Lemon squash. Right?" The Chief nodded.

"You, Chief Dekko?"

"Bristol Cream sherry, if you have it."

Padraic gave him a speculative glance. "Bristol Cream, of course." There was no tone in Duffy's voice. It was just that the young man had made a mistake. He suddenly knew it and almost lost his placid expression.

"How about you, Clint? Martini?"

"Bristol Cream sherry," Shartelle said blandly.

Before my better nature took over, I said: "Martini on the rocks. Make it a double."

Duffy pushed a button and the agency waiter came in and took the drink orders. We stood in a group talking about the English weather and about the weather in Albertia. Duffy told us of his success in raising Poland China pigs and Chief Akomolo expressed interest in the possibility of raising heat-resisting Brahma cattle in Albertia.

"We drive our cattle four hundred miles down from the north to the abattoirs of the south. Many of them die along the way. All of them lose weight."

"How many head in a drive usually?" Shartelle asked.

"Five hundred to a thousand."

"And you walk them?"

"Yes, along the roads. It causes a traffic hazard, the cattle get sick, the drovers desert. It is a very haphazard business. We should come up with a new program."

They talked on and I listened. It was much like the talk at the pre-luncheon session of the Lion's Club on Wednesday. The Chief talked about his country's economic problems, particularly the cocoa crop. Duffy talked about the eccentricities of a rival's client. Shartelle commented here and there, but spent most of his time in an unobtrusive study of Chief Akomolo.

After the lemon squash, and the Bristol Creams, and the martini we sat down to lunch at the round table. Duffy sat on the Chief's right; Shartelle on his left. The Chief sighed appreciatively as the bowl of groundnut broth was placed before him.

"Your thoughtfulness is sometimes overwhelming, Padraic."

Duffy smiled. "I thought you might be growing weary of English cooking."

"Not only of their cooking, but of the English themselves," the Chief said. "In my heart, I try not to hate them. I try to live by the teachings of the Savior and my Baptist upbringing. Yet they are a cold people, Padraic, cold and unfeeling and vengeful. For three days now I have tried to get this matter of cocoa exports resolved, and for three days I have been going around and around in bureaucratic circles."

"If I can be of any help—" Duffy began the offer, but was cut off by a wave of the Chief's hand.

"You have done too much already. No, they must learn that I am no small boy. When we deal with the top, we have no difficulty. It is only with the minor functionaries that I run into this wall of veiled contempt and bureaucratic inefficiency. 'Of course, Chief Akomolo,'" he mimicked, "'what you seek does require a certain amount of time.' That's what they fail to understand. That I have no time. That right now time is my most precious commodity."

The waiter came in and removed the soup bowls. He brought in a large covered serving dish of silver, placed it in the center of the table, and removed its lid with a flourish. The chief's eyes sparkled behind the gold rims. "Padraic! Curried chicken." He reached for the serving spoon and dumped a large portion on his plate, and began to eat hungrily, making small animal grunts and smacking his lips in appreciation. Dollops of brown grease and gravy spattered his blue *ordona*. Each of us served ourselves. I spooned a small portion onto my plate. As far as I was concerned it was paella with Tabasco Sauce. I shoved it around on my plate some and kept on drinking my martini, congratulating myself on the foresight that had caused me to order a double. Shartelle took a bite, chewed and swallowed. His mouth opened slightly and he reached for a glass of water. They had put all the peppers in. Duffy ate as hungrily as the Albertians. I decided he had no taste buds. Shartelle, I noticed, joined me in shoving his food back and forth across his plate.

The Chief mopped up the last morsel with a piece of bread, popped it into his mouth, and wiped his fingers on the table cloth. His napkin lay unused by his plate. He stretched and yawned hugely. "That was excellent, Padraic. Who cooked it?"

"A student at London University. From Albertia, of course."

The Chief nodded his head. "Of course. The seasoning was just right. Did you enjoy it, Mr. Shartelle?"

"It has a distinct flavor, sir," Shartelle said and smiled.

Duffy passed around cigars but nobody took one. The waiter brought coffee.

"Tell me, Mr. Shartelle, did you know the late President Kennedy?"

Shartelle nodded. "I knew him."

"How well?"

The white-haired man smiled. "Well enough to call him Jack when he was a junior Congressman, Senator when he was Senator, and Mr. President when he was President."

"Did you work for him in any of his campaigns?"

"Just in the Presidential, but I was more concerned with a Senator and a couple of Congressmen. I worked against him in 1956 at the convention when he went after the Vice-Presidential nomination. I was working with Kefauver."

"He is dead now, too, isn't he?"

"Yes."

"Did President Kennedy hold any animosity towards you for working for Mr. Kefauver?"

"A little, but he got over it. After Kefauver won the nomination, Kennedy came to see me. He said, 'I could have had it with your Western states, Clint. I'll remember to look you up next time around.'"

"And did he?"

"He looked me up six months later, right after the election. We came to an understanding."

"I am a great admirer of his. He represented the best of our times and of what your country has to offer. He was one of the few men from whom one could honestly say that one drew inspiration. His death was a personal sorrow to me."

"It was to a great many," Shartelle said. "He had the magic they were all looking for. Good magic."

"Since you are an admirer of Mr. Kennedy, and since you knew him, perhaps you could explain something that has long been puzzling me?"

"I'll try."

"Why wasn't Johnson arrested?"

Shartelle had his cup almost to his lips. He put it down carefully. "I beg your pardon, Chief?"

"What I'm saying is why wasn't Johnson immediately arrested after the assassination? He was obviously the one who would benefit from Kennedy's death. His arrest, it seems to me, should have been a matter of course."

"By whom?"

"By your FBI and your Mr. Hoover," Chief Akomolo said. "Perhaps in conjunction with your military."

"You're not saying it was a plot on Johnson's part, are you?" Shartelle asked, gazing at Chief Akomolo with what seemed to be delight and admiration.

"Not at all. I'm just saying if I had been in your Mr. Hoover's shoes I would have clapped some chaps in jail—Johnson, your Mr. MacNamara, Rusk, perhaps the entire Cabinet. I would have *suspected* something and I certainly would have acted."

"But the Vice-President becomes President upon the death of the holder of office," Shartelle said.

"Exactly, and who's to say that Johnson didn't hire this Oswald? After all it happened in his home state of Texas. That is enough of a coincidence to arouse the suspicions of even the most naïve mind, Mr. Shartelle."

Shartelle gazed at the African with open admiration, a wide white grin on his face. "Chief," he said, "you and me are going to get along just fine. Yes, sir," he said and nodded his head, still smiling. "Just fine."

— *5* —

Albertia is shaped like a funnel and its spout is Barkandu, the capital city. Along the thirty-three-mile strip that forms its claim to the sea are some of the finest white sand beaches in the world and some of the most treacherous undertows. In the middle of the strip of sand is a natural deep sea harbor that divides the city geographically and economically. To the north, towards the interior, are the city's fifty square miles of squalor where the Albertians live on their ninety-six-dollar-a-year average incomes. To the south are the broad boulevards, the neat green lawns, the Consulates, office buildings, hotels (there were four good ones that year), night clubs, foreign-owned shops, department stores, and the Yacht Club.

The site of the Yacht Club was, in the early nineteenth century, the makeshift dock from which a busy slave trade loaded its cargo. The British put an end to the trade— legal trade, anyway—in 1842. The dock fell into disrepair until 1923 when the Yacht Club was built. There were no yachts then, but the name had a nice ring and the district officers could get a cool beer when they came down out of the bush to Barkandu on their semi-annual visits to civilization. The first Albertian was admitted to membership in 1953. He was a doctor who had studied at the University of Edinburgh.

Paul Downer, the Downer in Duffy, Downer, and Theims, Ltd., met us at the airport in a chauffeur-driven

Humber Super Snipe. He was sweating, even in the air-conditioned comfort of the airport. He wore a white linen suit, already soaked at the armpits, a white shirt, blue knit tie and black shoes. He smoked incessantly.

We shook hands all around. "You know each other, I take it," I said to Shartelle.

"Sure, Paul and I know each other. We were in the war together, right, Paul?"

"It's good to see you, Clint," Downer said.

"You staying long?" Shartelle inquired.

"I'm going back on the evening flight. I got a call from Padraic. He said there's too much doing in London. He has to have some help. I couldn't really afford to take the time to come down here—not really. I just did it to help. Politics is not my dish of tea—you know that, Clint."

"Uh-huh."

"Well, I've booked you in at the Prince Albert. I thought we'd go there, have lunch, I'd give you a briefing, and then we'd go over to the Consulate and have a chat with Kramer."

"Who's Kramer?"

"The Consul General," I said. "Felix Kramer. He's been bouncing around Africa since Dulles was Secretary of State. They sidetracked him here in the early 1950's because he spoke excellent Chinese, Japanese, and a few other Oriental languages."

"Logical. But I'm not sure I want to meet Mr. Kramer, Paul."

Downer smiled wisely. "But he wants to see you. Don't forget, both State and Whitehall are vitally interested in this thing."

"Now, Paul, old buddy, you and me had better get some straight. I don't care if the Secretary of State himself wants to cozy up. I'm down here to run a political campaign, and I don't think Mr. Kramer has too many votes."

Downer blushed. He had a pink face and it turned a deeper red. He did it all the time. Sometimes he would blush if you asked him for a match. "Goddamn it, Clint, I've been smoothing things over for you for the last two

41

weeks. State isn't too happy about Americans taking a hand in the internal affairs of another country—especially an African one."

Shartelle drew out his package of Picayunes, took out the last one, looked at the pack regretfully, crumpled it, and tossed it away. "I'm going to miss those," he said.

"Try the local brands," I said. "One is called Sweet Ariels. I've been told they're almost as bad."

Shartelle turned to Downer. "You did say you're catching the evening plane?"

"That's right."

"Well, I tell you what. You just drop us off at the hotel and I'll call Mr. Kramer and Pete and I'll go on over there and pay our respects. Now I know you probably got a million things to do before you get on that plane so don't worry about taking us to lunch or anything and I'll explain things to Mr. Kramer. I imagine he's a smart old boy and he'll be able to fully appreciate your situation. And you can tell Pig when you get back that I won't say anything that will embarrass the firm, or him, or the United States Government, or the D.A.R."

"Well, maybe I should go with you, Clint. I know Kramer and I know his style."

"I surely do appreciate your offer, Paul, but like I said, you must have a million things to attend to. I think Pete and I can explain things to Mr. Kramer so that he won't be too upset about some fellow Americans manipulating the political climate for fun and profit."

"Maybe I'd better give Padraic a call and—"

"There's no need to give Padraic a call. Because if you give Padraic a call, then I'm going to be on that evening plane back to London with you."

Downer mumbled something that passed for assent, turned a shade pinker, and followed us to pick up our bags at customs. A tall, thin young Negro carried them out to the car and put them into the trunk. Or boot, I suppose, since it was a Humber.

"We go for Prince Albert one time," Downer told the driver. "You'll have to learn pidgin, Clint," he said. "They don't understand anything else." Shartelle nodded.

He gazed out the window of the car onto the street scene as we wound our way through the north side of Barkandu. "I'm not sure whether it's the noise or the color," he said.

"What?" I asked.

"Look at it, Pete. All those women sitting by those boxes selling things to each other. Look at their clothes—blues and greens and oranges and purples. And listen to it— hell, it sounds like daybreak on a guinea farm. It just goes on and on."

"The women are the mammy traders," Downer said. "Petty traders, they also call them. They have considerable political influence."

"That a fact?" Shartelle said.

The noise came from all sides. It was the screech of two women arguing with each other, the blast of an outside speaker that dinned Radio Albertia into the ears of the passerby—shrill, oriental, almost atonal music played at top volume. The traffic was dense—horns blew constantly. Goats roamed and snuffled among the litter of the street which was lined by brown, mudwalled houses and stores of one, two and three stories. People swarmed among the goats and chickens. Beggars—not too many—held out upturned and largely ignored palms. Children, naked and almost cool looking, kicked a ball in an impromptu soccer game. A man ran out in front of our car and our driver blew the horn, slammed on the brakes and cursed him. The man ran on, laughing. Our driver said: "He want to die," and turned around and grinned at Shartelle.

He was a good driver, able to bluff and, more important, able to judge when not to.

"The car's yours, by the way," Downer said. "So's the driver."

"What's your name, driver?" Shartelle asked.

"William, Sah."

"You're a good driver, William."

"Thank you, Sah."

"He gets two shillings a day extra when he's away from home," Downer said.

43

"That's twenty-eight cents, I figure," Shartelle said.

"Plenty," Downer said.

Shartelle nudged me. "William, since you're going to be driving for me and Mr. Upshaw here, we'll pay you four shillings a day when you're away from home. If you have an accident, you go back to two shillings. That okay with you?"

"We have no accident, Sah," William said, grinning.

"You'll spoil 'em," Downer grunted.

"If it only costs fifty-six cents a day, I might do just that."

There was a concrete, four-lane bridge across the tip of the curved V of the harbor and William pulled onto it. The bridge arced up, high enough for even the largest freighters to sail underneath to the wharves that lined the shore. Bicycles and pedestrians used a raised walkway that ran along the left hand side of the bridge. A woman, a baby strapped to her back, trotted along the bridge balancing three beams of lumber, at least ten feet long, on her head. The baby slept contentedly. At least it wasn't crying.

"She can keep up that trot for hours," Downer said. "She brings the lumber in from maybe ten, fifteen miles out. Trots all the way. Starts out at dawn. Her husband cuts the wood and shapes it. She trots it into town. She might get a few bob for it."

Across the bridge we came on to Queensway Boulevard It was a four-lane thoroughfare with a strip of carefully tended grass down the center. On each side of the highway, low, hip-roofed houses sat far back on lawns meticulously landscaped with flowers and shrubs. I could recognize palms and hibiscus and bougainvillea. The rest of them were new to me. On one of the lawns two men, using short cane-like sticks to support themselves as they leaned down almost double, hacked at the grass with machetes.

"Now are those boys out there just snipping out the weeds, or are they cutting the whole goddamned lawn?" Shartelle asked.

"They're cutting the lawn."

"With machetes?"

"Lawnmower costs around nine pounds, ten down here. They'll work all day for four bob."

"There must be an acre of lawn."

Downer shrugged. "Helps the unemployment."

The residential area gave way to the business section. White slabs of glass and concrete poked up ten and twelve and fifteen stories into the African sky. Shartelle spotted a Bank of America sign. "That outfit doesn't miss any tricks, does it?"

"Money's money," Downer said wisely.

With a flourish William pulled into the sweeping curved driveway of the Prince Albert Hotel. It was new and its architectural style would win no awards. It was built of poured concrete slabs painted white. The windows were recessed and tinted blue. It was built on the bay and I supposed that one had something of a view from the farther side.

"You wait here, William," Downer told the driver as the robed bellhops took our bags. A smiling Lebanese checked us in and snapped his finger for some more robed bellhops to carry our luggage. The elevators were automatic, but they had operators anyhow. Part of the unemployment solution, I decided. Shartelle and I were given adjoining double rooms and Downer followed me into mine.

The air-conditioning was on full blast and Downer seemed to shiver a little in his sweat-soaked suit. "You better keep the lid on Shartelle, Pete," Downer said.

I tipped the bellhop who gave me a string of "thank you, sahs," and left without showing me where the bathroom was. Maybe he didn't know. I looked for it myself and saw that it contained the standard equipment, even soap, and came back into the room, opened my suitcase, and said: "Why? He's running the show. I'm just supercargo."

"He doesn't understand these people like you and I do."

"Like you do," I said. "I don't understand anybody."

"He can screw us up with the Consulate."

"Kramer's an American, isn't he?"

"Sure he's an American."

"Shartelle understands Americans. He might not understand Albertians, but he understands Americans. I don't think he'll screw us up."

"You don't know him. He goes off half-cocked sometimes and if he goes off half-cocked down here, we can get screwed good."

"I just met him about four days ago, so—as you say—I don't know him too well. But he doesn't give me the impression of going off half-cocked anywhere."

"I knew him during the war," Downer said. "I knew him in Europe. I could tell you some times he goofed it up plenty."

I didn't say anything. I took my shirts and underwear and socks out of my suitcase and put them in the bureau drawer. I hung four suits in the closet. I laid eight ties in another drawer. I put my toothpaste, brush and razor in the bathroom. I wore my hair short—short enough not to need a brush or comb. I had no pajamas, no styptic pencil, no after-shave lotion, no roll-on deodorant, no mouthwash. If I smelled, to hell with it.

"He goofed plenty," Downer said.

"During the war," I said.

"Right. During the war."

I went back into the bathroom and turned on the shower. I turned it to hot and then took one of the tropical suits—made out of air and coal, I think, and guaranteed not to wrinkle—and put it in the bathroom to steam out its wrinkles. Then I sat down in a chair and looked at Downer who was shivering on the bed.

"Are you cold or do you have malaria?" I asked.

"Goddamned air-conditioning," he said. "I take my Arelan. Did you start taking yours before you got here?"

"No."

"You'll catch malaria. Here, take these." He tossed me a phial of pills.

"Like Atabrine?"

"No, they don't turn you yellow."

I went into the bathroom where it must have been 120 degrees and got a glass of water. I popped a pill in and swallowed. "One a day?"

"Better take two. They don't hurt you any."

"Doesn't affect the manhood, huh?"

"That shouldn't bother you while you're down here, Pete —not unless you want to change your luck."

"That's a thought."

"Well, you better keep close check on Shartelle."

"He's running the show."

"I was against it. I told Duffy I was against it. Clint might be the best in the States, but he's not in the States now." Downer paused and lighted a cigarette. His hands trembled and the cigarette shook in his mouth. Maybe he drinks, I thought. It was a vain hope; he wasn't the type. His ego didn't need it.

"You know what Clint's got to watch out for?" Downer asked.

"What?"

"Cultural shock. That's what."

"You think he'll go native, Paul?"

Downer puffed on his cigarette some more. He didn't inhale and when he smoked he took short, rapid sucking puffs and blew them out quickly with little swooshes. It was a mannerism that had long irritated me.

"Not native. He's not Gauguin. I mean that he's been in the States all his life except for that time in Europe with Duffy and me and then we had to lead him around by the hand."

"That's when all three of you were in the O.S.S.?"

"Right. Hell, he could speak a little French, that's all. But Africa's different. A guy like Shartelle may not be able to adapt. Now you and I have lived abroad, Pete. We can take it as it comes. Heat, dirt, diseases, strange customs—these don't faze us the way they might a guy like Shartelle."

"We're sort of cosmopolites," I said helpfully.

"That's right—you put your finger on it. I've lived in London for twenty years now. I spend a lot of time on the Continent. But I feel as much at home in Paris as I do in New York. London's no different to me than Chicago."

"There's a small language barrier," I said.

"In Paris?"

"No. In Chicago."

Downer laughed. "That's not bad, Pete."

He wasn't all that stupid. He had a great passion for detail, he worked hard, he could—upon occasion—turn out workmanlike copy fast, a knack he had picked up from Hearst where he had spent his working life until Duffy brought him into DDT in 1952. But he was sententious, pedantic, and god, how he could talk. He believed in the infallibility of Duffy, Downer, and Theims, Ltd. He bought all the products, used them faithfully, and touted them to his friends. His clients—the accounts he handled—had no faults. If they had had any faults, they wouldn't be DDT clients.

"I'll break him in easy—not too much shock all at once," I said.

Downer nodded. "That's smart. And listen, Pete, if you get in a bind—any kind of bind—and you need help, I'm as close as the phone."

"I'll remember."

"Now then—the house in Ubondo is open and staffed. Here's a set of keys." He tossed them to me. "The account at Barclay's is in your name. It's got around five hundred quid in it and use it for expenses. Revolving fund sort of thing. When you run low, send in a chit and we'll top it up. You'll pay the staff—here's a list of how much they get. Pay them monthly and let me give you some advice: don't lend them any money. You'll play hell getting it back. Food you can get at the supermarket in Ubondo. You'll have to do the shopping—you can't trust the staff to do it. Charge everything and settle the bill once a month."

"How big is the staff?"

"Five—plus the watch night. Six."

"What the hell do two men need with six servants?"

Downer sighed. "Look, Pete. You need a cook. You need a steward. You need a small boy to help the cook and steward. You need a driver—that's William. You know him already. You need a gardener—you've got an acre-and-a-half of grounds. And you need the watch night."

"The what?"

"The watch night. He scares away the thieves. It's a kind of insurance—or protection racket—I'm not sure. But whenever anybody fires a watch night, there's a burglary within a week."

"O.K. When is Akomolo expected back from London?"

"He's back. He came in late yesterday. But he's busy so you'll have a chance to look Barkandu over, make any contacts you want, and then go on up to Ubondo. You'll be working out of Ubondo since that's where Akomolo will make his headquarters."

"Anything else?"

Downer thought. "You can introduce yourself around. DDT has already made a reputation for itself down here with the British. They know who we are."

"Cocoa," I said.

"I drink it for breakfast every morning," he said.

"So do I, Paul. Also have a cup at night before bed."

There was a knock on the door. I opened it and it was Shartelle and I think I finally fully realized what the word resplendent meant. Shartelle was resplendent. He wore a seersucker suit that fitted so well it could only have been tailored. It was a black and white cord, and it looked crisp and clean and cool. It wasn't the suit so much as the matching vest. I had never seen a seersucker suit with a vest. He wore a white shirt with a black knit tie. On his head perched a hat. It was at a rakish angle. It was black. It was a black slouch hat. I didn't think they existed. Shartelle leaned against the door jamb and puffed a cigarette.

"You're gorgeous," I said.

He strolled in and turned, giving us the chance to get the full effect. "I've got six more just like 'em. One for every day in the week but Sunday. Then I wear my go-to-meeting suit."

"Does it have a vest?"

"Never seen a seersucker suit with a vest, boy? Why it's the coming rage. How do you like the hat? It's forty years old, I swear. Now do I look like a well-to-do New Orleans cotton buyer or don't I?"

"Sharp," I said. "Razor-keen."

"It just so happens that this was what I planned to wear in Denver," Shartelle said. "The vest was for the cool of the evening. But I think this outfit just might make me a little distinctive here in Albertia. What do you think, Paul?"

Downer was already moving for the door. "Distinctive, yes, really distinctive. I've filled Pete in on the arrangements, Clint. I've got a few things to do before I catch the plane. It was nice seeing you." He grabbed Shartelle's hand and shook it.

"Nice seeing you, Paul."

"Pete, could you walk me to the elevator, I've got a couple of things I forgot to tell you."

"Sure," I said.

He grabbed my arm in the hall. "That's what I mean," he whispered. "You have to watch out for Shartelle."

"The suit?"

"Damn right, the suit."

"Well, it's distinctive."

"That's what I mean. That's what I was telling you about. There's bound to be cultural shock." He jabbed the elevator button again. Surprisingly, the car appeared.

"Cultural shock," he repeated, as he got in. "Remember that, Pete."

"Just whose culture will get the shock?" I asked, but the elevator door had already closed and he didn't hear me.

— 6 —

I went back to my room, turned off the shower, and rescued my suit. I hung it in front of an air-conditioning vent to cool. Shartelle was at the window, gazing out at the harbor. Ours were the rooms with the view.

"Some harbor," Shartelle said. "Lots of traffic."

"They import a lot of stuff—unfortunately it adds up to more than they export and the balance of trade picture is on the gloomy side."

He turned from the window and lowered himself into one of the Scandinavian-type chairs that the decorator had decided would do nicely in Africa. "You get rid of Downer all right?"

"He's gone," I said. "He's worried about us—thinks we may be coming down with either malaria, cultural shock, or both."

"He was always a worrier."

"You knew him in the war?"

"I knew him."

"You don't like him?"

Shartelle yawned. "It's not that I don't like him, Pete, it's just that I don't have any use for him. He means well, but I'd rather have somebody call me a son of a bitch than to say I mean well. Let's forget him. When are we supposed to see Kramer, the old China hand?"

"We're to call him. You want me to?"

"I'll do it," Shartelle said. He picked up the phone and asked for the American Consulate. "That's right," he said. "The American Consulate." He listened for a while and then held the phone away from his head and stared at it. Then he put it back to his ear and said: "Try the United

States Consulate then.... I know I asked for the American Consulate.... Now I'd like to talk to somebody at the United States Consulate.... No, I don't want to talk to somebody in the United States, I want to talk to the United States Consulate." He was pacing now, as far as the short cord would allow. He covered the mouth of the phone with his hand and turned to me: "He wants me to talk to his supervisor."

"I've heard that it usually takes fifteen minutes," I said. "I'll let you make all the calls."

There were three or four more minutes of palaver with the operator's supervisor before the call went through. Shartelle identified himself, asked for Kramer, was told he was out dedicating a USIS library in Eastern Albertia, and was switched to somebody else. Shartelle's eyebrows shot up at a question he was asked over the phone. "Why, yes, we'd be happy to see him.... Yes, that would be convenient. In half an hour. Fine." He hung up and walked back over to the window to look at the harbor some more.

"Kramer's gone for the day."

"I heard."

"But we've got another appointment."

"In half an hour," I said as I changed into my coal and air suit.

"With the political affairs officer."

"Who's he?"

"Clarence Coit."

"Who's Clarence Coit?"

"He was very big in South America at one time. Made quite a reputation for himself.

"Doing what?"

"Setting up coups for the CIA."

We went downstairs to the cocktail lounge and found an Australian bartender who claimed that he could mix a fair martini. He could. We finished two of them and wandered out through the lobby that looked like the lobby in almost any new hotel you find between Miami and Beirut. Lots of marble and murals and rugs and sand-filled butt receptacles. The Lebanese clerks still held down the front desk and the robed Albertians still toted the bags.

William had parked the Humber in the circular drive under the shade of a tree. He saw us, started the car, and pulled up in front of the door. Shartelle started to get in the front seat.

"Mastah ride in back," William said firmly.

"Why?"

"Proper, Sah. Proper Mastah ride in back."

Shartelle got in the back with me. "You know where the United States Consulate is?" he asked.

"American Consulate, yes, Sah. Na far."

"Let's go there."

It wasn't far, only a half a mile or so. It looked as if it had been built just after World War II by some architect who was overly influenced by the southern California mission school of design. It rambled over an acre or so of shrubbery, flowers and lawn, protected from the Albertians by a high, wrought-iron fence, and shielded from the elements by a red tiled roof that looked as if it were made out of old London chimney pots split in half. We drove through the open gates to the front entrance. There were no guards; the Marines would come after independence when the Consulate achieved embassy status.

The receptionist was a brunette with too much lipstick, too little to do, and a St. Paul accent. She summoned an Albertian and told him to escort us to Mr. Coit's office. Then she went back to her nails. We followed the Albertian down a hall that sported some reproductions of Frederic Remington's Indians and cowboys and turned left. "In here, gentlemen," the Albertian said, indicating a door. We went through the door into a medium-sized reception office that was staffed by a small blonde with popped green eyes and a none-too-ready smile.

"Mr. Shartelle and Mr. Upshaw?" she asked.

We said yes and she talked over the phone briefly. "Mr. Coit will be with you in a moment," she said. "Do sit down."

We sat down and Shartelle lighted one of his

Sweet Ariels. The secretary kept on typing. The air-conditioner droned away in its effort to keep the room at seventy-two degrees. There was nothing to talk about. We waited with the resigned air of a salesman and his trainee in the outer office of the purchasing agent who hasn't placed an order in seven months and isn't likely to do so today.

After ten minutes the door opened and a man came out. He gave us a quick look, the kind that is given to cripples by people who like to examine the affliction but don't want to get caught at it. He hurried through the door into the hall.

The telephone on the secretary's desk rang. She picked it up and said yes. She hung up and looked at us. "Mr. Coit will see you now," she said. "Just through that door."

We went through that door and into a large office that contained a desk, some filing cabinets with combination locks on them, some chairs, a coffee table, a divan, a man, and a calendar on the wall. The calendar was of the screwed-up British variety with the days of the weeks in the wrong place. Each day that had passed that month was carefully marked out. The even days were marked out in red, the odd days in green. The furniture was all battleship gray and streamlined to cut down the wind resistance.

The man was behind the desk and he came at us like a rush captain at Phi Delta Theta. There was the firm quick handshake, the bustling around to make sure that the chairs were comfortable, the shifting of the ashtrays to more convenient positions. Clarence Coit wanted us to like him; maybe he wanted everybody to like him, and the best way to achieve that, he may have decided, was to like everybody.

We got settled in the chairs and looked at each other pleasantly. Coit was as tall as Shartelle, around six-foot-two, and he had smooth black hair that he combed straight back over a wide forehead. His features were regular, his teeth were white, and he displayed them in a slightly crooked, deprecatory smile every chance he got. His nose was only a nose, but his chin was nice and firm and jutted just a bit. He had dark blue eyes that were set under thick eyebrows that had no curve. The pupils flicked here and there. They were restless eyes that gave Shartelle's suit a frankly appreciative appraisal.

"I'm sorry that Kramer is out, but I'm damned glad you could drop by this afternoon and I hope I haven't interfered with your schedule." He had a smooth baritone.

I let the spokesman of our team do the talking. If Coit was with the CIA, he could match wits with the professional country boy and may the best liar win. I decided to root for Shartelle.

Giving his elegant vest a tug, Shartelle replied that Mr. Coit surely hadn't interfered with our schedule, that it was still in the making, and because of the nature of our business in Albertia, it was right kind of him to spare us a few moments. As Political Affairs Officer, he might give us some tips that could save us needless drudgery and fruitless quests. It was, the way Shartelle laid it on, as nice a glob of sandy mortar as I'd yet seen him pat into place.

Coit sat through it all, his hands folded on the empty desk in front of him, his eyes fixed on Shartelle, his fine head nodding every now and then to signal the speaker that he was coming through nicely. Coit was a professional listener. If he had turned the act on for me, I would have talked all day, beginning with the time when I was three and they had stolen my tricycle. It was blue with a bell on the handle bars and studded metal plates on the rear axle that a small passenger could stand on.

But Shartelle didn't even tell Coit about his daddy or the LaSalle with the busted block. He just stopped talking and began smiling. It was one of those silences when you feel you should clear your throat or shift your chair or mention the weather. But I had no cue so I looked around the office which had an autographed picture of the President beaming grimly down from one wall. I had the feeling that it was General Services Administration issue and was one of thousands dispatched to embassies and consulates all over the world the day after Kennedy was shot. You could tell from the size of the office and the furniture how much Coit made in a year, but you could tell nothing about him. The personal touches—a painting, a piece of statuary, or a jug full of flowers—were all missing.

Finally Coit got up and walked a few feet to a window and peered out through the Venetian blind. I couldn't tell what the view was. "I appreciate your confidence, Mr. Shartelle," he said to the venetian blind. "And I must confess that I don't envy you the task that lies ahead."

"Mr. Coit, if I couldn't place confidence in a representative of a United States Embassy or Consulate, I think I would be living in a rather shabby world," Shartelle said.

Coit nodded a grave nod and resumed his seat at his desk. "I've only been here a few weeks, but my job has required me to make an intensive study of the Albertian political scene. The more I study it, the more convinced I become that of all the developing nations south of the Sahara, this country is almost alone in its readiness and ability to accept the full challenge that self-rule imposes."

He paused and extracted a silver cigarette case from his inside coat pocket. He was wearing a pale blue worsted mohair tropical suit, a white shirt with a tab collar that had a gold pin stuck through it underneath the small knot of his blue and red striped tie.

Coit opened the cigarette case and extended it to Shartelle who shook his head and then to me. I took one on the theory that it was probably an American cigarette and that he would be happy that someone liked him enough to trust his taste in smokes. It was filtered, but I tore the top off and placed it in the ashtray. Coit didn't seem to notice or mind.

After he and I had our cigarettes going, he began to tell us again why we should sign the fraternity's pledge cards. "As a political scientist—" He broke off to smile his deprecatory smile. "At least that's what that Master's from Johns Hopkins says I am, I have more than a passing interest in those who engage in *realpolitik*. So your name, Mr. Shartelle, is a familiar one to me. And I also remember, quite well, in fact, Mr. Upshaw's brilliant series from Europe in the troubled times of 'fifty-six. I think we can talk among ourselves as professionals in the political realm, although I consider myself an observer, a student, if you would, rather than an actionist."

It was a long speech and during it Shartelle had hooked his thumbs into his vest, cocked his head slightly to one side, and studied a corner where the ceiling met the walls. He nodded emphatically whenever Coit came to a period. I found it a disconcerting response.

"You see, gentlemen," Coit went on, "you have the opportunity to bring to the Albertian voters the chance to decide the future of their country. You can present them with a clear-cut, well-delineated picture of the issues involved. If you succeed, you will have performed a tremendous public service."

Shartelle kept his thumbs in his vest. His chair was tilted back now, and his eyes were still on the far high corner of the room. "Your remarks are most kind, Mr. Coit, and I'm glad you've elevated our job of rounding up the necessary votes to such an exalted mission. It makes me proud, but I hope not too proud, because pride's a sin as you well know. So just in case we don't make the issues as clear-cut as you'd like them, I'd like to share the credit—or the blame—with the boys who are going to be handling Chief Akomolo's opposition...Dr. Kologo and Sir Alakada."

Shartelle kept on staring at the corner so perhaps he didn't see the hair cracks in Coit's composure. Or perhaps he did, because he gave it another exploratory tap.

"There are other outside forces involved in this, you know. One of them is the biggest agency in the world—in the political sense anyhow. It's worked the Far East, Europe, the Balkans, the Middle East...." He paused. "South America."

I watched Coit. The composure was flaking a bit. His mouth was slightly open. His hands were worrying a ball-point pen.

"It's quite an agency to go up against," Shartelle said,

still tilted back in his chair, still studying the top of the room. "You're familiar with—" He paused again, this time to light a cigarette. Coit almost squirmed. "You're familiar with...Renesslaer?" When Shartelle spoke the name he brought the chair down on its front legs and the metal caps banged nicely on the gray linoleum floor. Coit jumped. Not much, but it was a jump. It was hard to tell whether it was because of the noise of the Renesslaer name. He stared at Shartelle.

"Renesslaer?"

"Right. That's the agency I was talking about. They're big all over the world, you know, and they're going to handle old Alhaji Sir Alakada etcetera up north."

"I've heard of them," Coit said. His tone was stiff. He didn't seem to care anymore whether we liked him or not. "Are you sure of this?"

"Oh, quite sure," Shartelle said. "I've been told the deal's all signed and sealed. The boys from Renesslaer ought to be drifting through here any day now and then you'll have to give them that nice little talk of yours about their chance to delineate the issues. They like stuff like that."

Coit said nothing. His hands were now pressed palm up against the bottom of his desk drawer. You could see the muscles bulge in his neck. They were as visible as the bitter dislike in his eyes. He knew then that Shartelle knew. Worse, he knew that Shartelle had been playing with him. Cubebing him, Shartelle called it for some reason I could never understand and was too proud to ask about.

Shartelle got up and stuck out his hand. "Mr. Coit, it has been a pure pleasure to have had this little talk with you. I just hope that we'll measure up to your expectations."

"We're certainly going to try," I said nicely and shook his hand.

But he was a pro. Unless you had been watching carefully, you wouldn't have noticed the hair cracks. They were all gone now. He smiled at us, walked over to the door, and held it open. "Gentlemen, I hope we can meet again soon. You have been most informative. I'll watch your progress—and that of the Renesslaer firm—with much interest, I assure you. We started out and Coit said: "By the way—is there—or have you heard of, any agency handling Dr. Kologo in the east?"

Shartelle stopped and looked at Coit's eyes. Their faces were not more than eight inches apart. "Why, no, Mr. Coit, I haven't. Have you?"

"No, I haven't either."

"If you hear of anything like that, would you let us know?" Shartelle asked.

"Of course," Coit said.

Shartelle looked at him some more and nodded his head slightly. "Of course."

We walked out into the hall and found our way to the front of the Consulate. We walked out of the pleasant seventy-two degrees into the ninety-nine degrees that was the Barkandu afternoon. Both of us hastily put on sunglasses. Shartelle smoked another cigarette while we waited for William to bring the car up.

"You ticked him off," I said.

"Some. He's a cool customer."

"He is that."

"We'll warm him up," Shartelle said. "Come Labor Day he'll sizzle."

— 7 —

On the way back to the hotel, the car got caught in a midafternoon traffic snarl and we were forced to inch along Bailey's Boulevard at four miles an hour. There was no breeze and we sweltered in the thick, palpable heat that made me want to gasp. As a concession to it, Shartelle unbuttoned his vest, took off his slouch hat and fanned himself.

"Fans," he said.

"What?"

"Fans. Remember the funeral parlor ones, the kind that contained advertising?"

"Like the one that the Great Commoner used during the Scopes trial?"

"Like that. We're gonna get us some, Pete. You want to make a note of it?"

I took out a notebook and wrote down "fans."

"How many?" I asked.

"A couple of million," he said. "Better make it three."

I wrote down "3,000,000" after fans. "Think they'll cinch it for us, huh?"

"We can't lose," Shartelle said. "Not with three million fans."

"To be crass, don't you think we'd better have a little commercial on them? Maybe a jingle?"

"You're the word man, boy. Just set yourself to composing."

"I'll give it the afternoon."

"Mastah want me drive?" William asked, skillfully missing a goat by an inch.

"When?" I asked.

"Now, Mastah."

"No."

"I go for brother's house," he announced.

"You have a brother here in Barkandu?" Shartelle said.

"Many brothers, Mastah," William said and smiled his big-toothed smile. "They give me chop. Go small-small time."

"Okay. You go for brother small-small time," Shartelle said. You be back at the hotel, six o'clock. Right?"

"Yes, Sah!" William said.

"How's my pidgin coming, William?" Shartelle asked.

"Very good, Sah," he said and giggled. "Very nice."

"What are your plans for the afternoon, Sahib?" I asked.

Shartelle looked out of the car window at the harbor. "Some harbor," he said. "Well, I plan to get ahold of some hickory nuts and stain my face, slip into my burnoose, and flit about the bazaars to pick up the native gossip. Then I got some planning to do," Shartelle went on, "and I do planning best when I'm in the solitude of my own counsel."

"What you want to say politely without hurting my feelings is that you don't hold with the DDT theory of brainstorming during which everybody spews out everything and a pearl appears among the hawkings."

Shartelle looked at me. "You don't honestly do that— you and Pig and all those grown men?" He sounded horrified.

"Honest to God."

"Does it work?"

"Not for me. But then I'm the type who lurks in the wet forest and throws rocks at those cozily sitting around the camp fire."

"You'd like to be asked to join, huh?"

"So I could say no."

"You got problems, boy," he said.

"I'm going swimming."

"That's healthful. Let's meet for dinner about seven."

"In the bar?"

"Good enough."

At the hotel, Shartelle went up to his room and I found out from the Lebanese desk clerk that the hotel ran a shuttle car to a beach. There was a place to change on the beach, but no shower. I went upstairs and got my trunks, a white duck hat with a floppy brim, the biggest hotel towel I could find, and caught the Morris Minor shuttle. I was the only passenger.

At the beach there was a snack stand that sold Pepsi-Cola and Beck's Bier. I bought a Beck's in its tall green quart size, took it into the shack that served as a dressing room, changed and carried the beer and my clothes out to the beach. It was virtually deserted, except for three or four Albertian children who were running up and down in pursuit of a small brown dog with an enormous tail that waved ecstatically. They never caught the dog but nobody seemed to mind. I put my shoes down on the sand, folded my slacks, shirt and underwear and placed them on top of the shoes as carefully as a suicide who wants to leave something neat to commemorate a messy life. I spread the towel out on the beach, pulled at the brim of my white-duck hat, took a swig of beer, lighted a cigarette, and sat down on the towel and looked at the ocean.

Like the rest of the Dakotans, I felt that anything larger than a two-acre pond held the promise of wild adventure. The ocean was a body of unbearable expectation. I sat looking at the South Atlantic lace itself into combers as the Benguela current rolled up into the Gulf of Guinea. I put the cigarette out, squirmed the beer bottle firmly into the sand, and ran out into the sea. I caught a wave and dived through it. I could feel the undertow, strong and cold, pulling me out towards Fortaleza and Cayenne, eight thousand miles away. I decided I didn't want to go so I swam back, scrambling when my feet touched bottom. Then I tried it again and got the hang of the undertow, playing a game with it to see how long I could last without scrambling to get back. I was a less-than-average swimmer, but that made the game more interesting. If it had been raining, I could have stayed in my room at the hotel and played Russian roulette.

The cigarettes, the martinis, and English food had provoked my chronic malnutrition. Weariness forced me to quit my war against the sea. I stumbled back to the tidy pile of clothes, shook the sand out of the towel, and dried myself off.

The blue jeep drove down as far as it could, until the beach sloped too sharply, and then it stopped. The girl who was driving it got out and walked towards the dressing room shack. She knocked on the door and when there was no response, she went in. She was carrying one of those blue airline bags. The jeep had some white lettering on the top of its hood, but it was too far away for me to read.

I lighted another cigarette and picked up the bottle of Beck's from the sand and swallowed some. It was warm but wet. I watched the dressing shack and in a few minutes the girl came out and walked towards me carrying the airline bag and a large, black and red striped beach towel. She wore a white two-piece bathing suit that was almost a bikini. She moved with an awkward grace that signalled a total lack of self-consciousness.

Her hair was blond, almost white, as if she spent much time in the sun, and she wore it carelessly long. It framed a smooth tan face that would never conceal an emotion. The face was smiling as she walked towards me, swinging the blue bag and carrying the towel. The face was alive— the mouth was wide and full and the smile was dazzling white against the dark tan. She had kind, soft dark-brown eyes that you could learn to trust.

She was all girl. Her breasts formed tan half-moons where they peeked out above the top of her bathing suit. Her stomach sank flatly back from her rib cage and then rounded out nicely to her thighs. Her legs were long and she would stand at least five-seven in heels. It was all there, nicely shaped and molded, in almost perfect proportion, and she seemed totally unaware of it.

When she was twenty feet away she made the smile warmer and said: "Hi, there."

"Hi," I said.

"Would you mind watching my things while I go in? The last time I was here a couple of the kids made off with them and I had to drive back in my suit." She spread the black and red towel on the sand and dropped the bag down on it.

"I'm Anne Kidd," she said and extended her hand. I took it.

"Peter Upshaw."

"You American?"

"Yes."

"I couldn't tell by the way you speak, but then I haven't

given you a chance to say anything, have I? But your hat's a dead giveaway. I haven't seen a hat like that since Daytona."

"It's been in the family a long time."

She smiled at me. "I'm just going in for a little while. Please don't go away."

"I'll be here."

She ran towards the water, and she ran well in the sand. She caught a wave and dived through it and then began to swim with a smooth, effortless Australian crawl. She swam as if she had spent a lot of time in the water. I liked to watch her. She swam for fifteen minutes and then she came running back up the beach, just a little pigeon-toed, but not much, her sunbleached hair hanging wet and straight to her shoulders. She remained lovely.

"You remind me of a fish I once knew," I said.

She laughed and picked up the towel, shook it, and began to dry the water from her body. I watched with interest. "When I was three," she said, "they threw me into the pool at home. It was during a party. My parents thought it was fun. I learned to swim for self-protection."

"You weren't frightened."

"I didn't have time to be, I suppose. Daddy jumped in and my mother followed him, fully dressed, and then all of the guests jumped in and they passed me back and forth like a beach ball. It was hilarious, they tell me. I don't remember it."

I offered her a cigarette after she had spread the towel out and was sitting on it, her knees tucked up to her chin. She refused, but said; "Could I have a swallow of your beer? I'm terribly thirsty."

"It's warm—I'll be happy to get you one from the stand."

"I'm used to it warm. All I want is a swallow."

I handed her the green bottle and she drank and handed it back.

"Where do you drink your warm beer?" I asked.

"In Ubondo."

"You live there?"

"I teach there. I'm with the Peace Corps."

"I never met a Peace Corps before," I said. "Do you like it?"

"After a while you don't think about whether you like it or not. You just do it."

"How long have you been here?"

"In Albertia?"

"Yes."

"Fifteen months. I came down to Barkandu to have my teeth checked. The Baptists have a good dental clinic here. How are your teeth?"

"My own."

"Somebody told me once not to think about yourself anymore than you do about your teeth. That started me thinking about my teeth all the time. Do you think about yours often?"

"Every morning; also every night."

"I like my teeth," she said. "They seem to be the most permanent thing about me."

"How many Peace Corps people are in Albertia?"

"About seventy. Some are up north. There are about twenty of us around Ubondo and there are about forty-five over in the east. You haven't been here long, have you? I can tell because you're still so white."

"Just got in."

"From the States?"

"From London."

"For the Consulate or AID or what? I don't think you're a missionary."

"Not an ecclesiastical one. I'm down here to stir up some interest in the campaign."

"Oh. You're one of *those* Americans. There will be two of you, won't there?"

"Yes."

"They're talking about you at the university in Ubondo. The students are."

"They speak well of us, I hope."

"Not very."

"What are they saying?"

"Let's see—there is something about Madison Avenue techniques—"

"That's to be expected."

"American imperialism disguised as political counsel. Then you're also supposed to be connected with the CIA. Are you?"

"No."

"I'm glad. I really am. Isn't that strange?"

"I don't know."

"Why are you down here really?" she asked.

"It's my job. I make a living doing things like this."

"Aren't you embarrassed."

"Aren't you?"

"Why should I be?"

"I mean joining the Peace Corps. Doesn't that embarrass you?"

"I'm one of those who don't mind caring," she said. "I don't mind if people know about it either. So I'm not embarrassed."

"Why did you join?"

"Kennedy."

"You mean the 'ask not what your country can do for you' thing?"

"That was part of it. I was in Washington when he was sworn in. Daddy was invited because he had made a donation or something."

"This the same daddy who tossed you in the pool?"

"The same."

"It was a good speech," I said.

"So that's why I joined. I thought I could help."

"Have you?"

She looked at me, and then out at the ocean. A breeze had come up and it felt cool against my sweat. "I don't know," she said. "I'm involved, anyway. I was never involved before. Perhaps I've only helped myself. Maybe that's where you have to start."

"But you don't feel the same?"

"Not since Kennedy died. I joined more than two years

after he was shot to prove that it was as much me as anything else. But it wasn't really. It's different somehow."

"He was younger," I said. "That made a lot of difference."

"There was something else," she said. "They talk and write a lot about his grace and style. He had all that and he had a beautiful wife and two nice children. They looked like something out of a bad ad. Yet he didn't seem to think about how he looked—I mean he didn't think about himself so much—"

"Like the teeth," I said.

"Yes. He knew he had what everybody else wanted, but he didn't really care anymore about having it. I'm not making sense, am I?"

"Go on."

"They killed him because he didn't care about what they care about; because they couldn't stand him not being like they were. They killed him not because he was good, but because he was better than anything else around and they couldn't stand the contrast."

"Who's they?"

"Oh—Oswald, all the Oswalds. There're millions of them. And they were secretly glad when he died. I know they were. I don't mean that they were Democrats or Republicans or anything. But they weren't comfortable with Kennedy around and now they're comfortable again. They're got the old shoe back, the Texas tacky, and they can snicker and make fun of him and feel superior or just as good, and they couldn't do that with Kennedy."

"It's a theory," I admitted.

She looked at me and the smile that came my way was chilly. "You're not one to go overboard, are you Peter Upshaw?"

"I said it's a theory."

"I don't mean about that. That's what I feel. I don't give a damn whether you agree with what I feel or not, because I can't change the way I feel. I just said that you're not one to go overboard about anything, are you? You're cautious. And if you're cautious enough then you'll never get caught and if you don't get caught, then you'll never feel anything."

"Tell me something, little girl. Do they still sit around the sorority houses after their Friday night dates and talk to each other about sex and God with their half-slips drawn up to cover their breasts?"

"I guess that was due."

I said nothing and looked out at the waves playing follow-the-leader towards the beach.

"You're married, aren't you?" she asked. Her voice was small and low.

"No. Divorced."

"Do you love your wife very much?"

I looked at her. There was no guile in the question; just a curiously gentle curiosity.

"No," I said, "I don't love her very much. I don't love her at all. Why do you ask?"

"Because you seem lonely. I thought you might be lonely for your wife. But you're not, are you?"

"No."

We sat on the towels on the African sand in silence and watched the ocean. Some gulls tried their luck in the water. The three children chased the small brown dog with the oversized tail along the edge of the surf, then turned and let the dog chase them. They screamed and laughed and the dog barked happily.

"Would you like to go in once more?" she asked.

"Are you?"

"Yes."

"Who'll watch the stuff?"

"We can watch it from the water and yell if anyone comes near it. You can chase them if they try to take it."

"All right."

We ran down to the sea and caught the same wave and dived through it. When we came up we were very close together so I kissed her. It was a brief, wet, salty kiss and she laughed and said "Oh, God," and I knew what she meant. So we stood there in the Albertian sea and kissed each other again and held each other for what seemed to be a long time. Then the laughter of the children and the barking of the dog drew closer. We turned and the children were pointing and laughing at us. We smiled and waved back and they laughed some more and started to chase the dog again. I held her hand and we walked back up the beach. I helped her to dry off and we didn't say anything until we were dressed and were in the jeep and driving towards my hotel. Then I asked her to have dinner with me at seven and she smiled and nodded. We didn't say anything else. She looked at me once and winked.

It has happened that way sometimes, I suppose. But not to me.

— *8* —

After I had showered and changed I went next door and knocked. Shartelle called "It's open," and I walked into a room that was the twin of mine. Shartelle sat on the edge of the bed, with most of the hotel-provided stationery scattered about on the counterpane and the floor. "This mess is the beginning of our campaign, Petey," he said.

"Looks impressive. Busy, anyway."

"How was the water?"

"I fished out a date for dinner."

"White girl?" he asked and arranged some sheets of paper in different order.

"Yes."

"Thought you might have latched on to one of the daughters of the opposition who would do a little peeping for us, but my luck doesn't much run that way."

"I'll do better next time."

Shartelle gathered up a few of the papers and put them

on the desk. "This is going to be mighty tricky," he said.

"What?"

"The campaign."

"We have a chance?" I said, and picked up one of the sheets of paper from the floor and put it on the bed. Shartelle put it back on the floor.

"That's about it."

"Can you buy it?"

He shook his head. "We'd have to bid too high. If we win, it'll be because of their mistakes. We just haven't got the votes."

"So?"

"We're going to help plan their mistakes."

"Sounds dicey."

Shartelle got up and walked over to the window and looked out at the harbor. "Some harbor," he said. "You know where I spent part of the afternoon?"

"No."

"At the Census Office. There's a nice little old Englishman up there, about seven years older than Satan, and he's got the voting strength all broken down—region by region, district by district, village by village. He'd have it down to precincts except they haven't got any."

"And?"

"Like I said, we don't have the votes."

"Do you think Akomolo knows that?"

Shartelle looked at me and grinned. "If he had the votes —or thought he did—we wouldn't be down here, now would we?"

"You have a point."

Shartelle walked back from the window and sprawled out full-length on the bed, his arms folded behind his head. "I think, Pete, we're going to have to whipsaw it. And I ain't done that in a long time."

"Two ways at once?"

"That's right."

"You're the acknowledged expert. Just tell me what you need—and when."

Shartelle stared up at the ceiling for a long moment,

then closed his eyes, and frowned. "You run along," he said. "I'm going to have something sent up. I got an idea somewhere, nudging around in the back of my mind, and I want to see if I can get it to peek out at me. You going to use the car?"

"I don't think so."

"Tell William to pick us up at eight in the morning. We got a meeting at noon in Ubondo."

"Akomolo call?"

"One of his aides."

"I'll see you in the morning," I said.

"I think it's the only way."

"What?"

"Whipsaw it."

I shrugged. "Give it a try."

Shartelle sighed and stretched. "I'll study about it," he said. "It's nudging around there somewhere in the back of my mind."

Outside the hotel I whistled William up and told him to be back at eight the next morning and to have the car ready to go to Ubondo. I then walked to the hotel's bar to try another of the Australian's martinis.

I was about one third of the way through the drink when the bench mark came on. I call them bench marks. The feeling is something like *déjà vu* except that there is no sense of prefamiliarity. They are simply events, not important in themselves, that become milestones in time. They are moments that I measure from. One happened when I was six years old in a park on a swing. I can still remember the touch and feel of the gray metal rungs and the look and texture of the wooden seat, green around the edges and worn to a sand color in the center by a thousand small behinds. There was another bench mark fifteen years later when I was walking across the Tulane campus in New Orleans. I can still feel the muggy weather, see the sky, describe the sidewalk exactly, even the stencilled medallion that said the cement was laid by A. Passini & Sons, 1931.

71

Sitting there in the bar of the Prince Albert hotel, another bench mark came on and I knew that ten years from then, or twenty, I would remember that bar, that drink, and the number of rings the glass made on the dark wood. And I would remember Anne Kidd who walked into the middle of it.

She wore a pale yellow dress that hung straight down and ended just above her knees. It was sleeveless. She wore short white gloves, carried a white purse and had on white shoes—pumps. There was a strand of pearls around her neck. She moved gracefully onto the bar stool and the bench mark ended.

"You look a bit odd," she said.

"Admiring your dress."

"Thank you."

"What would you like?"

"A martini will be fine."

I ordered the drink. "Something happened this afternoon," she said. "To me, I mean."

"I know."

"I never felt like that before with anyone. I liked it. I was afraid you wouldn't be here tonight."

I kept staring at her hair where the light caught it and made it shine like new honey. "It usually happens when you're fourteen or fifteen."

She smiled at the Australian as he served the drink and he smiled back. "He approves," I said. "My masculinity is confirmed. After we finish this we'll stroll past the local gas station so the lads can make a proper appraisal."

"Did you ever do that? Parade your girl friends before the boys at the corner garage or drugstore?"

I shook my head. "The corner garage and drugstore were out by the time I reached puberty. By then it was the drive-in and you showed around ten p.m. in the family sedan. Or in your own car, if you were affluent."

"Were you?"

"Affluent?"

"Yes."

"Sure. He made it off wheat."

72

"Was he a farmer?"

"Is. No, he owns an elevator."

"Where?"

"In North Dakota."

"Do you like him?"

"He's okay. He likes North Dakota. That pretty well sums him up, except for his wife. His second one. She's what I think they used to call a stepper."

"You like her?"

"Yes. She's fine."

"Now I know all about you."

"There's a bit more, but not much."

"Where did you go to school?"

"Minnesota."

"English lit—right?"

"Wrong. Letters."

"Letters?"

"As close to a classical education as Minnesota got that year. It was an experiment. A little Latin, and less Greek. It was to produce the well-rounded man. I think they abandoned it in favor of something called communications shortly after I was graduated."

"A wholesome background," she said. "All Midwestern and chock full of wheaty goodness."

"There are a few edges that still need sanding."

She told me about herself—the bare outline of a life in Florida with parents who were moderately wealthy and moderately young and who got along with each other most of the time. There had been no traumas—her life had run smoothly through high school and college and then into the Peace Corps after eighteen months with a social welfare agency in Chicago.

"It's not much of a life, is it?"

I smiled at her. "It still has a few years to go."

The voice that came over my shoulder was smooth and polished and when I turned to see who belonged to it I wasn't disappointed. He was about six-feet-one, tall for an Albertian, and he carried it straight up and down. The gleam of the leather of his Sam Browne belt matched that of his custom calf-length boots. The crowns on his shoulder said that he was a Major and the uniform I took to be that of the Albertian army. His voice, deep, mellow and smooth as warm grease, had said: "Good evening, Miss Kidd."

She turned, looked at him, and smiled. I envied him the smile. "Major Chuku," she said. "It's nice to see you."

"I didn't know you were in Barkandu."

"I came down two days ago—to see the dentist."

"A smile so lovely should receive every care," said the Major—a slick article, I decided.

"Major Chuku, I would like you to meet Peter Upshaw."

"How do you do?" I said, and we shook hands. He had the weight and the breadth of hand, but he didn't press his advantage. It was just a firm, normal shake.

"You are down from London, Mr. Upshaw?"

"Yes."

"On business or pleasure?"

"Business, I'm afraid."

"I hope then that it will be profitable."

"Thank you."

"Major Chuku commands the battalion in Ubondo," Anne said. "You may be seeing something of each other. Mr. Upshaw is down for the campaign."

The Major's eyebrows arched politely and his forehead took on a few interested wrinkles. "Are you one of the Americans whom we're importing to bring us abreast of the latest political tactics, Mr. Upshaw?"

"Yes."

"Do you happen to be associated with my good friend, Padraic Duffy?"

"I work for him," I said.

"Then we must have a drink together," the Major said firmly. "Surely you will be good enough to be my guest?"

"That's very kind," I said.

We left the bar and found a table. The Major sidled around and held Anne's chair for her. At least it looked like a sidle. He had a round smooth face with a sharp straight nose and small ears that almost came to points.

His hair seemed to lie in neat black ringlets around his head. His mouth was big and wide and he wore it in a darting white smile for company, but when he ordered the drinks from the waiter it straightened itself out into a firm enough line. He had that look of command that you usually find only in experienced kindergarten teachers or general officers.

When the drinks came, the Major insisted on paying. I let him. "Now tell me, Mr. Upshaw. How is my good friend, Padraic? The last time I saw him he was trying to convince me that I should invest heavily in cocoa shares. Sometimes I think I should have followed his advice."

"You met him down here?"

"Yes, when he first came down on the Cocoa Board thing. Chief Akomolo was responsible for Padraic's introduction to Albertia. Do you know the Premier well?"

"We've only met socially."

"An interesting man," the Major said. "And an ambitious one. It was at his house that Miss Kidd and I met. He was entertaining the first members of the Peace Corps to arrive in his region."

"Are you following the political campaign closely, Major?" I asked.

He laughed and made it sound as if he had heard a joke. A funny one. "I have enough difficulty in keeping up with the intramural politics of the army. No, I do not follow governmental politics, only the politicians."

"There is a difference?"

"Of course. Let us say Mr. X is this particular politician of this particular party, while Sir Y is a politician who owes allegiance to another party. I'm really not at all interested in what either Mr. X or Sir Y says, does or promises. I'm only interested in what happens to them. To put it yet another way: I am not interested in whether the jockey stands up in the stirrups on the back stretch—but only if the horse he rides comes in first."

"You give the winner a name?"

The Major smiled. It was the disarming smile of a man who seems to have nothing to hide. "Sometimes," he said, "the winner is called 'Liberty Bell.' Sometimes it might run under the name 'Africa Mine.' Most lately, it's been using 'Martial Air.'"

"I'd put two pounds on the last one if the odds were right."

"I don't gamble, Mr. Upshaw. I prefer the security of flat certainty. Perhaps that is why I have been so unsuccessful with the ladies."

"I'm afraid you're also something of a liar, Major," Anne said. "Your name is often mentioned at Ubondo's hen parties. And it's usually accompanied by a friendly warning, and giggles."

"At the earliest opportunity I should like to demonstrate what lies they tell about one. Especially in a place such as Ubondo. I assure you, Miss Kidd, I am completely harmless."

I tried to remember where I had heard the Major talk before. It wasn't the sound of his voice; it was the faintly archaic phrasing, the almost mannered structure. It all sounded like one of those interminable novels about India or Malaya where the bright young native barrister takes tea with the pretty little thing just out from England and shocks hell out of the crowd at the club.

The Major talked as if he had read the same novels. But he had a look about him which made it obvious that he was out after more than just a cup of tea and a chocolate bickey. As far as I was concerned, he had "Let's Screw, Honey" tattooed right across his forehead.

He turned to me again. "Tell me, Mr. Upshaw, do you really believe that this country of mine is ready for representative democracy?"

"I don't know if any country is ready, except Switzerland."

"I'm really curious, you know. You haven't the air of a chap who'd try to flog a candidate—merchandise him much as one would a motor car or a particular brand of cigarettes. And from my knowledge of Duffy, I doubt that he would be so crass. Just what does a political manager actually do? Mind you, I'm merely curious."

"You'll have to ask Mr. Shartelle," I said. "He's the political expert. I'm just the writer—the phrasemaker. The hack."

"You're far too modest, I'm sure. But I would like to ask him. Perhaps you would have dinner with me in Ubondo this week—Friday?"

"Fine. I'll check with Shartelle."

"Good. And you'll be joining us, Miss Kidd, of course." She didn't pause or hesitate. "I'll be delighted."

"Splendid," the Major said and rose. "Till Friday then."

"Friday," I said, half rising.

He made a short bow and left. He walked tall and perfectly straight and the heads in the bar turned to watch his progress as he moved through the room.

"He's not real," I said. "They cut him out of an old copy of *Cosmopolitan* and pasted him into my African scrapbook."

"He's real all right," Anne said. "Maybe one of your first jobs should be to find out just how real."

Our dinner at the Prince Albert was less than a success. The steak was stringy and had been tenderized to mush by being soaked in papaya juice. The fried potatoes were done to a high cholesterol turn and the salad had been drowned by someone who had inverted the Spanish admonition to be a miser with vinegar, a proffigate with oil. I shoved the food around in circles, dumped something brown and nasty-looking from a Heinz bottle on the steak, gave up, and settled for coffee, a cigarette, and a glass of brandy.

Anne ate hungrily, apparently unmindful of the horror that squatted on her plate. She packed away the steak, the potatoes, the salad, and even the villainous brussels sprouts that she had ordered as an afterthought.

"What do you eat in the Peace Corps?" I asked. "They send you CARE packages?"

"We cook for ourselves. Buy meat and tinned stuff at the local supermarket—they have one, you know. It's not exciting. Just plain British food—"

"Nothing's plainer."

"I'm a good cook," she said. "If you're nice, I'll invite you over. You bring the groceries. I can't afford it."

Somehow we drifted into a mild argument about martinis. Anne claimed that the best were made from Beefeater gin and California's Tribuno vermouth. I argued that it was a New York fad, circa 1956, that was still making the rounds and that gin was gin, especially to gin heads. We found common ground in our conviction that Americans ran the Germans a close race as the world's most unloved tourists, with the English not far behind. We also, for some reason, established a mutual dislike for coconut but parted company over anchovies. I was in the affirmative. We decided we were both against wiretapping in any form and that Jimmy Hoffa was vastly underrated as a natural wit. We split over Bogart. I said he added up to nothing more than a couple of unforgettable scenes in *The Maltese Falcon* and *Beat the Devil*. She said what about *The African Queen* and I said that he should have had his teeth capped and taken his thumbs out of his belt in just one scene or two. We gleefully slandered Dean Rusk, Walter Cronkite, Sonny Liston, and the Johnson daughters. Kind words were said by one or the other of us in memory of the dead, the missing and the neglected: Hart Crane, Ezra Taft Benson, Night Train Lane, Kenneth Patchen, Lana Turner's daughter, Cheryl, Johnny Stompanato and Billy Sol Estes.

"You're fading," Anne said. "I can't go back to World War II. I don't remember anything before 1950."

"Nobody's that young."

"I am."

"I know some guys who were always too young. They were born around 1936."

"That makes them thirtyish. Middleaged."

"Right. Middleaged. They can remember World War II—the eat, drink and be merry *Gemütlichkeit*. But they missed being in it because they were too young. They say it was the last good war. They were also too young for Korea, and although that wasn't such a hot war, they're still sorry they missed it. They say. So they mutter into their Scotch about never having the chance to test their courage truly and well under fire.

"Now there happens to be a very fine war going on in Asia — as sticky a mess as one could hope for. But it doesn't have the clear-cut issues for the lads who were always too young. Besides, they're thirty or so now and their careers have called and the mortgage is due. So, they'll never have that one, right, nice little war with the sides all carefully drawn — good on the left, wrong on the right. They think it will haunt them, but it won't."

"Why?"

"They'll become authorities on World War II and know all the battles and the regiments and the corps commanders, but stay politely silent when the potgutted drones start talking about Guadalcanal and Anzio and Eniwetok."

"Were you a soldier?"

"For a while. In Korea. A replacement in the 45th Division."

"Were you hurt?"

"Not badly."

"How long have you been in London?"

"A long time. Ten years now."

"You're not that old."

"I'm doddering. I was born in 'thirty-two. That was the year my old man sold soy beans short and made a pile. I skipped the second grade, landed at Minnesota when I was sixteen, enlisted in 1950 when I was eighteen, and got sent home from Korea when I was nineteen. I was graduated in 'fifty-three and landed a job on the paper at the same time. Got the chronology?" She was using her fingers to count; they were nice fingers. She nodded.

"I was very bright, they said, so they sent me to Europe as their own very first foreign correspondent in 1955 — late 'fifty-five."

"And what happened?"

"Come October, 1956, there were three stories going: the Stevenson-Eisenhower election at home, Suez, and Hungary. I picked Hungary; they picked reaction election

Europewise. We parted company. I went to England, went to work for Duffy, married my wife, and got divorced by her seven years later."

"Why?"

"I wasn't a very good husband."

"Was she a good wife?"

"We were mutually unsuitable for each other."

Anne looked down at the table and fiddled with her coffee spoon, making a series of X's in the cloth. "I told you earlier I've never felt like this. I've never felt the need for anyone like this."

"So you said."

"It makes me a little afraid. You know what we were doing earlier?"

"When?"

"When we were talking about things—what we liked and didn't like. We were courting."

"I guess we were."

She looked up at me. "I'm in love with you, Peter."

"I know."

"Will it be any good?"

"I think so."

"What will we do?"

"I don't know," I said. "We'll try loving each other for a while. That will be something new for me at least. I never tried it before."

"Really?"

"Really."

"I'm going to love you very much."

"Good."

"I want to stay with you tonight."

"All right."

"You want me to, don't you?"

"Yes, but I'm supposed to make the propositions."

"We don't have time. Am I terribly bad?"

"No."

"Could we have some champagne in the room. Champagne and you and a hotel sounds awfully wicked."

"We'll have champagne." I called a waiter over and with

some difficulty arranged for a bottle of champagne and a bottle of Martell to be sent up to my room.

"We'll wait until it gets there," I said. "I don't fancy any interruptions."

"I'll have to leave you early—around five." She bit her lip, and shook her head slowly. "It's happened so fast and that's such an obvious thing to say." She leaned across the table towards me and her eyes were pleading. "I'm not wrong, am I, Peter?"

"No," I said.

"It's right for both of us, really right?"

"Yes, it's right for both of us and I'm not sure how it happened. I don't know why. I'm not going to think about it for a while, I'm just going to revel in it. I like being in love with you. I like feeling romantic about it. I like the idea that we're going upstairs and drink champagne and love each other. I suppose I'm just happy as hell and it's a very strange feeling."

She smiled at me again. "That was nice. I liked that. Now I know it's all right."

"Good."

We rose from the table and I took her hand. We walked to the elevator and rode up to the room. The champagne was there and so was the brandy. The champagne wasn't very good, but it was cold, and we drank it and looked at each other.

After a glass of champagne she smiled at me and said: "Peter, please be patient with me.

The sheets were cool and I was gentle and smiled at her small cries and when it happened it happened to both of us and we sailed off to where the teddybears have their picnic and then we came slowly back and I kissed her and ran my hand lightly over her face, touching her brow and eyes and nose and mouth and chin.

"Was I any good?" she asked.

"You were perfect."

"We were both perfect."

I lighted a cigarette and smoked it for a while, staring up at the ceiling in the hotel in Africa with the girl whom

I newly loved nestling her head on my shoulder.

Suddenly, it wasn't a bad life. I wondered how I'd got so lucky, but my bed partner started to make small noises again, so I put out the cigarette and quit wondering.

— *9* —

It's ninety-nine miles to Barkandu from Ubondo and the road is a twisting, high-crowned ribbon of patched asphalt that steams in the African sun. On clear stretches, where the rain forest has been cut away, mirages gleam wetly in the distance. Along the road's edge rest the hulks of rusting sedans and trucks whose drivers missed their last curve. The wrecks seem to wait patiently for the junkmen of the forest.

The road from Barkandu leads north to the Sahara, and if you follow it far enough, to where the asphalt gives out to red laterite, and the laterite with its washboard ridges turns into sand and dust, you run into Timbuktu. But that's a long way, farther than most care to travel unless it has taken them an extraordinarily long time to grow up.

Mostly the road to Barkandu is traveled by the mammy wagons which are two-ton trucks with the right door tied open, the driver leaning halfway out, the better to see and the better to jump. The drivers push their trucks down to Barkandu and up to Ubondo and beyond, sometimes making six hundred miles a day, hauling humans and chickens and goats, bargaining for the fare with enthusiasm and flair. What they lack in driving skill they make up for in bravado. Armed with ten-quid juju charms that bear money-back guarantees in case they're killed, encouraged by a couple of sticks of Indian hemp, they charge the approaching traffic. They must dominate all who pass their way.

You can amuse yourself by reading the names of the mammy wagons as they flash by, the drivers mostly teeth and eyeballs as they lean half-out of their cabs, their passengers jolting around in the canvas-covered rears.

"It's better than parlor cars, boy," Shartelle said as William steered the Humber towards Ubondo. "So far, I've spotted 'Don't Spit in the Wind,' 'Sea Never Dry,' 'God, Why Not?' and 'Death, Where Is Thy Sting?' You never read any freight train names as interesting as that; weren't even any names on the Katy parlor cars that could come close."

He was slouched down in the back seat, his black hat low over his eyes, a black, crooked cigar substituting now for the long-gone Picayunes and the discarded Sweet Ariels. His seersucker suit was crisp and fresh, the vest buttoned neatly except for the bottom button, a red and black paisley tie knotted carefully into the collar of a fresh white oxford cloth shirt. He had his feet, encased in black loafers, propped up on the walnut table that opened down from the back of the front seat.

We had started out at nine that morning. He had given me a careful look, murmured something about it being a pleasant day, and asked if I would like some coffee. We had drunk coffee in the dining room at a table that had a view of the bay. "Some harbor," Shartelle said after he had ordered his bacon and eggs. He didn't say anything after that. He was polite.

Anne had left at five in the morning. I had watched her dress and there had been no rummaging to find discarded clothing. She had sat before the mirror of the vanity and brushed her hair and looked at me in the mirror. I had looked back and we had smiled. There was no need to say anything; there would be time for that later. We had time, I felt, to squander.

She came over to the bed when she had dressed and sat down on its edge beside me. She put her hand on my head and stroked my hair. "I have to go," she had said.

"I know."

"You'll call?"

"I'll call you this evening."

I had kissed her then and she had risen and walked to the door, opened it and left without looking back. I lay there and smoked a cigarette and felt the unfamiliar emotions churning and bubbling around inside somewhere. It had been a peculiar old-young feeling, something like being a thirty-year-old grandfather, I suppose, and it had been especially peculiar because I hadn't felt anything towards anyone for a long time. So I lay there and got used to it and watched the sun come up over the edge of the window. After that I got up, showered, dressed, and went down into the lobby to meet Shartelle.

"You know where else I went yesterday?" Shartelle asked around his black and crooked cigar as the car sped towards Ubondo.

"No."

"I went to pay my respects to the Consul General."

"I know. I was with you. He wasn't in."

"I mean after that. Even after I went to see the little old Englishman in the Census Office."

"You mean you went back again?"

"There's more than one Consulate in Barkandu," he said.

"Okay. Which one?"

"Why, the Israeli one."

"Clint, I'm not going to sit here and feed you the lines. You went to see the Israeli Consul General. Why?"

"Well, sir," he said, shifting farther down into the mohair of the Humber's back seat, "I figured to myself this way: If I was a stranger in a town in a foreign country and I wanted to know what was going on, now who would I go to? Why, I said, I'd go look up the Israeli Ambassador, or if he wasn't an Ambassador, I'd look up the Consul General."

"And what would you talk about?"

"Why, kinfolk, boy, kinfolk."

"Whose?"

"His and mine. I got kinfolk in Israel and this little old Jew boy at the Consulate had some in Cleveland that I believe I know. Good Democrats. That made me a *Landsmann*, prid near."

"What kinfolk have you got in Israel?"

"Second cousins on my daddy's side. I figure I'm about one-sixteenth Jewish by blood. Of course, I'm not of the persuasion although I do lean towards their oneist's notions."

"Their what?"

"Their oneist's notions. You know, like the Unitarians."

"I thought Shartelle was French."

"It's purely French, but I think it's also a little Jewish-French, at least that's what my daddy said."

"Okay. What did the Israeli Consul General have to allow?"

"Well, he'd heard about Renesslaer already. He said that there was a team of four through Barkandu three days ago heading north by plane."

"Did he mention any names?"

"No. He said they opened a five-figure pounds sterling account in Renesslaer's name at one of the Barclay branches. High five-figures, he said. He also said that two of them were colored—Stateside colored—and the other two were white."

"We can check them out through London."

Shartelle nodded. "I figured Pig might do that."

"What else did he have to say?"

"Well, he swore he'd deny he said it, but his government is afraid that the British are pulling out too quick. He said he thought that there could be trouble, especially if the election wound up in a donnybrook without a clear-cut win for one side or another—or at least for a strong coalition. He also said he thought he'd never see the day when he would admit that the British could leave any colonial possession too quick. But in this case they were."

"Everything considered, it was quite an admission," I said.

"You haven't seen Martin Bormann around, have you?"

"Who?"

"Martin Bormann. You know, old Hitler's deputy Führer who supposedly escaped from the bunker just before the Russians moved into Berlin."

"No," I said, "I haven't seen him around; not lately anyhow."

"If you do, let the Israeli Consul General know, will you? He's been out here about three years and he figures he could get back home to Tel Aviv if he could get his hands on Bormann—or any other Nazi who's still on the loose. He asked us to keep our eyes open."

"I'll do that."

"You know where else I went?"

"No, but I'm sure I'm going to learn."

"Well, after I had tea at the Israeli's I wandered down around the marketplace—where all those plump little old gals are all gussied up in their blue wraparounds?"

"What did you find out?"

"Well, I bought some razor blades here and some more of these cigars there. Bargained a bit, told a few jokes, and just funned them along. They're real nice little old gals. A bit on the plump side, but neighborly."

"Neighborly," I said.

"Uh-huh. So we got to talking about the election. And they got to arguing back and forth, you know, one of them being for Chief Akomolo and another one being for old Alhaji Sir and the other being for the other guy, the one from the east, uh—"

"Dr. Kologo," I said.

"Doctor, lawyer, merchant-chief," Shartelle said. "Maybe I can keep them straight that way."

"So what was the consensus?"

"The consensus, boy, was that they just don't give much of a shit one way or another because they—the little old

86

plump gals—think they're all crooked and just out for the quick buck."

"We should be able to work that to our advantage."

"You know I told you yesterday I figured we'd have to whipsaw it, but I hadn't quite figured it out and I thought it was nudging around in the back of my mind?"

"I recall."

"Well, it came to me last night and after I got the big one, then the rest of it sort of fell into place. I think I've got it, but it's going to cost a packet and its success'll depend upon the venality of some and the patriotism of others. But successful politics usually does. I'll be needing some fancy writing."

"Such as?"

"Used to be an old newspaper boy that worked on one of these combination morning and afternoon papers that were supposed to be rivals, but are really owned by the same outfit?" He made it that kind of a Southern rhetorical question, the inflection rising until it keened out on the last word.

"Uh-huh."

"This old boy would get up in the morning and go down to his typewriter and whang out an editorial knocking hell out of FDR and Harry Hopkins and all that New Deal crowd. That was for the afternoon paper. Then he'd go out and get a couple of belts into him and come back and whang out another one—this time hoorahing it up for Mrs. Roosevelt, Jimmy, John, FDR, Jr. and calling down the wrath of God Almighty on their enemies and detractors. Now he was what I would call a versatile writer."

"I wonder which editorials he believed?"

Shartelle shoved back his hat slightly and looked at me with a puzzled expression. "Why, he believed both of them, boy. Wouldn't you?"

I sighed and leaned back on the mohair. "You're right, Clint, I probably would."

Well, I figure you're going to be doing some writing something like that old newspaper boy used to do."

"I'm your man. Just put the paper in the typewriter and I'm off. Either side."

William slowed the Humber, turned around and looked at us. I winced as a truck called "It Pains You Why?" nipped by us a couple of inches away.

"Mastah want beer?" William said and redirected his attention to the road.

"Beer?" I asked.

"Yas, Sah, we stop for beer always at halfway house."

"Well, I never had anything against *beer* in the morning," Shartelle said. "Let's stop."

"Fine."

It was a combination roadhouse and gasoline station. It was built of whitewashed mud and inside it had deep wooden chairs with wide arms that looked like Midwestern porch furniture. The chairs were gathered around low wooden tables. A bar stood near the door, conveniently placed underneath the only ceiling fan, which spun at a leisurely and useless pace. A sign painted in an attempt at old English script hung outside over the door. It said the name of the place was The Colony. We sat at one of the tables. A man came over and in a flat American accent asked what our pleasure was.

"Three beers," Shartelle said. "Nice and cold."

"Nice and cold," the man said. He walked back to the bar and uncapped three quart bottles of Beck's. He put them on a tin tray, got some cold glasses out of a refrigerator, the kind that had the coils on top, and brought them over.

"Nice and cold, gentlemen," he said and served the beer. "That'll be twelve and six."

I gave him a pound. Shartelle said: "You're an American, aren't you?"

The man looked at him. "I lived there for a while."

"Whereabouts?"

"You name it."

"Pittsburgh?"

"For a while."

"You own this place?" Shartelle asked.

88

The man looked around and smiled faintly. "No," he said. "I don't own it. I'm just helping out a friend." He stood waiting for more questions, a not-too-tall man, about five-eleven, flat-bellied and lithe. When he moved he moved very much like Shartelle. He had a naturally olive complexion which a lot of sun had burned dark. His hair was cut short and it had some gray in it just over the ears.

"My name's Shartelle, and this is Upshaw."

"They call me Mike," the man said.

"You been here long?"

"Not long; I'm just touring."

"And you're helping out a friend," Shartelle said.

"That's right. A friend."

Shartelle poured his beer into the glass carefully. The man called Mike stood waiting with the tray in hand, patient and poised. "We haven't met before, have we, Mike?" Shartelle asked, talking it seemed to his glass of beer. "A long time ago—maybe twenty years back?"

"You meet a lot of people, but I don't think so." He put the pound note in his pocket and placed my change on the table. "Anything else?"

I said no and the man called Mike went back behind his bar, picked up a copy of the *Times* of London and smiled at the personal ad columns.

William drank his beer out of the bottle, belched his enjoyment, and then went out to talk to the men who ran the gas pump. Shartelle and I leaned back in the porch furniture and drank the beer slowly. When we got up to leave, the man called Mike didn't say goodbye or come back again. He didn't even look up as we left.

Shartelle slumped into his favorite position in the back seat. "You know, Petey, I think I know that old boy and I think he knows me."

"He didn't seem to."

"It was in France during the war...when I was with Duffy and Downer. He was a sight younger then."

"You all were."

"That boy could talk French though—he could fair rattle it off just like he was born there."

"You sure he's the same man?"

"I'm sure, but if he's not sure, then he must have a damn good reason. And he didn't seem to think that his reason was any of my business so I think I'll just let it drop."

The car was back on the road. The traffic was light except for the trucks and an occasional passenger car. I looked out at the rain forest and wondered where the animals were.

I asked William. "Where are all the animals, William?"

"Animals, Sah?"

"Monkeys, elephants, lions, baboons."

"No animals, Sah. Just goat."

"I mean wild animals."

"No wild animals, Mastah. They go long time for chop. We eat them!" He exploded into a fit of giggling.

"Never thought I'd be in Africa and not see any animals," Shartelle said. "Hell, you can see more wild life on a Kansas highway than you can around here."

"Maybe they aren't as hungry in Kansas. Speaking of being hungry, are we invited to lunch at Chief Akomolo's, or is this a purely business call?"

"Lunch, I understand," Shartelle said. "He's having some of the key political supporters in. It's a major policy meeting. I figure on doing a lot of listening, but if I'm called on to say something, don't be surprised at what comes out. Just be ready to back me up—with figures, if need be."

"Figures?"

"Make 'em up as you go along. I'll correct you a pound here and a shilling there to make them seem authentic. You and me might even haggle a bit."

"In other words, you want me to backstop you?"

Shartelle pulled his hat down lower over his eyes and slumped even farther down into the seat. "Petey, that's what I like about you. You don't ask no goddamned fool questions and you don't want to be elected to anything. You just keep that attitude and we're going to be real good friends."

"By the way," I said. "I ran into an army major from Ubondo last night. He's invited us to dinner on Friday. I accepted, for both of us."

"That might be right interesting. You just keep on accepting all the invitations you can get. Then we can throw a couple of cocktail parties and get some mixing and mingling going. I'm afraid it's part of the job."

I leaned back in the seat and closed my eyes and thought about Anne. Shartelle fell asleep for a while under his hat and I didn't have to talk much until we rolled up into the gravel driveway that curved through the acre or so of grounds that formed our compound, and met the five other members of the household staff who were to do our bidding.

— *10* —

To get to Ubondo you leave the crowned asphalt strip and turn off onto a four-laned concrete highway called Jellicoe Drive. It winds up a slight rise and at the crest you get a panorama of the second largest all-black city in Africa. It's a million people living in a sea of tin-roofed houses with one skyscraper, white as a pillar of salt, shooting up out of the rusted roofs that cluster about it. It's the Cocoa Marketing Board building and it rises twenty-three stories into the African sky.

Ubondo is built in a valley and through the middle of it runs the Zemborine River west on its way to the sea. Small boats can navigate the Zemborine during the rainy season and some of them still do, chugging up the 154 miles of meandering river, powered by their tubercular outboard engines.

The Zemborine provides no demarcation between the

rich and the poor of Ubondo. The poor are on both sides and the hovels and fine houses stand cheek by jowl on the twisting streets. Thirty years ago Ubondo got its main thoroughfare when a drunken Irish contractor cranked up his bulldozer, took aim, and smashed a weaving line through the town from the top of one hill to the top of the other. He let nothing stand in his way and since the damage was done, they built the main road along the path he plowed through the town that hot August afternoon in 1935. His name was Diggins and the road is called Diggins Road. He stayed in Africa until he died. He had five wives, all at once, and countless children.

I woke Shartelle up for the view and he shook his head in admiration. "Now, boy, that's what I call Africa. Look at all that squalor. Ain't that something?"

"I never thought of squalor in just that way," I said.

"The old caravans ever get this far down south?"

"No. They stopped farther up north—five hundred miles or so."

"I'd admire to see one coming over that hill with the camels chewing their cuds and the bells jingling from their necks and the Arabs riding up on top of them carrying those long-barreled rifles."

"Shartelle, you've got the goddamnedest preconception of a country of anybody I ever knew."

"Hell, Petey, this is Africa. I've been reading about Africa since I was six years old. I read Mungo Park and Stanley and Livingston and Richard Halliburton and Hemingway and old Osa Johnson and her husband. What was his name—Martin? You remember that story they wrote about the giraffes? They called it 'The Creature that God Forgot.' Now that was one hell of a story. If I was a writer, that's the kind of stories I'd write."

We were winding down through the city itself, past a running ditch in which women were washing clothes. The goats and chickens were thick. The people moved quickly with a jaunty, almost strutting air. William hailed several, waved and they waved back. The street was narrow and the shopkeepers displayed their cloth and cigarettes and snuff and nails and hammers and pots and pans. The stores were about six feet wide and the shutters that locked them up at night served as display racks for the goods.

"I never saw so many little general stores right smack up against each other in all my life," Shartelle said.

"They all seem to sell snuff to each other."

We passed a bank and beauty shop and a drycleaners that looked as if it were going into bankruptcy. Next was a Christian Science reading room, deserted; a bar, packed; a restaurant called *The West End*, and a lonely shack with a closed door that read "Royal Society for the Prevention of Cruelty to Animals."

We came to a stop sign and a policewoman in white shirt, blue cap, black skirt, sturdy black boots and immaculate white gloves directed traffic in a performance of solemn grace that would have done credit to a dancer. Her movements were slow and deliberate, but with a measured rhythm that should have been accompanied by a drumbeat.

There was the noise again, the African noise of shouts and screams, and cries that seem to be of pain but end in shrieks of laughter. The mechanical noise of Radio Albertia blared from five-inch speakers that seemed to be attached to every shop. "That's some Muzak," Shartelle grunted. It was insistent noise—or music, depending upon your ear—backed with a hard beat; and when the beat was strong enough, some of the pedestrians danced to it in curious shuffling steps that reminded me of the march back from a New Orleans funeral that I had seen a long time ago.

Ubondo was no sleepy African village. It was thirty square miles of wide-awake, vibrant, magnificent slum with all of a slum's cynical disregard for self-improvement. It was dirty, dog-eared urban sprawl, rotten at the core, and rotten at the edges. It had been that way when New York was new and it wasn't changing because of the way any wind of change was blowing.

Shartelle leaned forward, looking out the side windows, turning around to stare out the back, a new black, twisty cigar clamped in his mouth, his black slouch hat pushed back from his forehead.

"By God, Petey, I'm going to like this place. My, it's nice and nasty!"

William took a left turn and cut down another boulevard. This one was lined with milroad tracks on one side which eventually passed a grubby station, and on the other side was a racetrack.

"That's racetrack, Sah," William said. "On Saturdays they have many horses."

It was a big track, a mile or a mile and a half. I could see wooden stands along one side of it next to a row of small buildings that I took to be the places where you put your money down. At the near end of the racetrack was a raised podium covered with a round tin roof that looked as if a band might play there on warm Sunday nights.

William turned left and began to wind through what seemed to be the classy residential section of Ubondo. The houses were set far back on lawns, some well-tended, some rather ragged. On one plot a two-story house of faintly American colonial lines dominated two acres of grass and shrubbery. At the driveway an old woman sat patiently beside a wooden box, a collection of oddments that she had for sale spread across it.

William waved at her as we sped by. She waved back and grinned a toothless smile. "That Madame Krinku. Her son is Minister of Transport."

"Her son?"

"Yes, Sah. That is his house. Very fine."

"I hope she makes a lot of money," Shartelle said.

"She make very good money, Sah," William said and giggled. "She sell cigarettes and kola nuts. She make two shilling, three shilling each day."

"That's good money," Shartelle agreed.

The road, a narrow two-lane asphalt or macadam strip, curved and twisted through the area of wide lawns, carefully tended flower beds, and houses set well back from casual view. Most of them had their doors and windows wide open in the heat of the day. Bougainvillea grew in profusion. At the rear of the houses there was usually a row of connected concrete cubicles. Shartelle asked William what they were.

"Quarters, Sah."

"For the servants?"

"Yes, Sah."

"Goddamned slave quarters."

William took another curve that bent around a house to our left. He waved at some Albertians standing in the yard and they waved back and shouted and ran towards the front of the house. William giggled. He made the sharp bend in the road and turned up into a graveled driveway that curved like an inverted question mark across the front lawn of the near acre of ground that spread out from the house. Here, for the time being, was the African headquarters for Dolan, Downer and Theims, Ltd.

There were five of them standing on the front-porch steps of the house with the wide eaves. William pulled the car up and stopped in front of them. The quintet clustered around the car, saying "Welcome, welcome Mastah" as Shartelle and I got out. William introduced the staff:

"This Samuel, cook. This Charles, steward." He pointed to a youth of fourteen or fifteen. "This Small Boy."

"Hello, Small Boy," Shartelle said. The kid grinned.

"This Ojo, gardener. He not speak proper English. Samuel speak him for you." Ojo grinned. He was dressed in khaki rags and tatters, a short broad-shouldered man with bowed legs and a crumpled face that was criss-crossed with tribal markings. We smiled at him.

"And this Silex, watch night." At least it sounded like Silex.

"I am please to make your acquaintance, Sahs," he said and bowed slightly.

"He student at daytime in university," William said.

"And studies all night," Shartelle said.

The cook, the steward and Small Boy were getting the bags out of the car. William, his job of driving done, stood to one side and supervised the task. I noticed that Samuel, the cook, had also assumed a strawboss role.

95

Shartelle and I explored the house. It was a bungalow, Ministry of Public Works, tropical design No. 141. But for all that it seemed comfortable. The folding doors from the porch opened onto a living room. The dining room was to the left. The pantry and kitchen adjoined the dining room. That was practical. To the right was a hall leading to a bedroom and bath. Then there was another smaller bedroom followed by another bath and a bedroom that had a separate outside entrance.

"Which one do you want?" I asked Shartelle.

"Either."

"I'll take the one with the private entrance."

He grinned at me, but said nothing. I told Small Boy and Charles, the steward, where to put the bags.

"Mastah want chop?" Samuel asked.

"No," I said. "We're going out to eat with Chief Akomolo. Did Downer leave any gin?"

"Yes, Sah. Gin and tonic, Sah?"

I looked at Shartelle. He nodded. "Gin and tonic," I said.

The living room was furnished with all the personality and charm of a second-rate Arkansas motel. It had a bookcase without books that served as a divider between it and the dining room. There was a couch made of African mahogany and covered with square pillows that served as seats and back. There were four matching chairs, a desk, a chair for it, some hexagonal mahogany tables, and a bookcase built into the wall—also empty. A dun-colored rug covered the floor.

Silex, the watch night, had disappeared, but Ojo, the gardener, was busy mowing the lawn with a machete. "Now that, goddamn it, has just got to go," Shartelle said.

William was standing by the car watching Ojo. Shartelle called him.

"Sah?" he said.

"Have they got a hardware store in Ubondo?"

"Hardware, Sah?"

"A place where they sell—you know—grasscutters?"

96

A happy look of comprehension spread across William's face. "Yes, Sah."

"How much are they?"

"Very dear, Sah. They cost ten, eIeven, twelve pounds."

"Give him some money, Pete."

I already had my wallet out. I gave William three five pound notes.

"Now take this and go down to Ubondo and kindly get us a goddamned lawnmower. Grasscutter, whatever."

"What kind Mastah want?" William said.

"Ask the head gardener. Ask Ojo. I don't know what kind of lawnmower."

Samuel came in from the kitchen, bearing a tray containing a bottle of gin, two bottles of Schweppes tonic, a bucket of ice, tongs, and glasses. He carried the tray first to me and bent low with it while I mixed a drink. Then he brought the tray to Shartelle.

"We're getting a lawnmower for Ojo," I told Samuel.

"Very good, Sah," he said and smiled.

I took a drink of my gin and tonic. "That was a damned decent thing of you to do, Shartelle," I said.

"Wasn't it."

He leaned back in his chair, his long, seersucker-clad legs stretched out in front of him, a twisty, black cigar in one hand, his drink in the other.

Small Boy ran out of the bedrooms carrying a bundle of soiled shirts, socks, and underwear. He giggled as he passed us. Shartelle waved a benign benediction at him with the cigar.

"You ever have six servants before, Petey?"

"No."

"Man could get used to having six servants around, bringing drinks, cooking dinner, driving the car, watching the kids, mowing the lawn, washing the clothes, cleaning the house, serving the tea at 5:30 sharp in the afternoon. I've been knee-deep in bellhops all my adult life, boy, but I never had six good men and true before to do my personal bidding."

"Gives you a sense of luxury."

"Makes me uncomfortable, if you want to know the truth. Now you'd think that with my fine Southern upbringing I'd be used to colored folks bowing and scraping and coming up to the big house on the hill for Christmas Gift."

"Why, no, Clint," I said. "With that hat and that cigar and that jellybean suit I'd more imagine you astride some Palomino riding through the cotton fields and listening to those happy voices raised in joyful song whose rhythms go back more than a hundred years to—"

"Boy, you do talk a bit of nonsense."

"And then, when the day's work was done in the fields, and the dinner had been served in the old white-columned manse by the Negro butler with just a touch of silvery hair above his ears, you'd jump in your XK-E and roar off to Shartelle City for a night of whiskey-drinking and card-gaming with your cronies. Of course, all Shartelle City has is two stores, a whorehouse, and a cotton gin but they named it after your daddy's daddy—"

"Respect is what you lack, boy, respect for quality folks. Now what I was saying is that I could understand how all this service might tempt a man to linger out here in this tropical paradise, expecially if the only thing he had waiting for him back home was a one-bedroom apartment or a house in Belair Heights or Edgemere Park.

"But to tell you the truth, it just makes me damned uncomfortable so I'm going to turn over the responsibilities of running this menage to you and I'm sure that you'll not only be damned good at planning the menus, but also at counseling this fine bunch of people in their personal problems, attending to their ills, and supervising the general administration of what I'm sure is going to be a might happy household."

I took another swallow of my drink. "No you don't, Shartelle, I'll carry your bag, mix the drinks, and sharpen the pencils. I'll laugh at your jokes and say 'that's right, Clint,' like a parrot, but I'm not going to be honcho on this spread."

Shartelle sighed and stretched. "I'm not much of a drinking man before noon, Petey but I must say this gin and tonic did wonders for my disposition, Care to join me in another one?"

"Why not?"

"How do we get it, just yell?"

"I don't see any buzzer."

"What's that little old skinny boy's name—the steward?"

"Samuel."

"That's the cook. The other one."

"Charles."

"Why don't you call and see if he comes running."

"I'd feel like a goddamned fool," I said,

"Reckon I'll try," Shartelle said. "Charles," he said.

"You talking to me or to the steward? I think you've got your volume turned down."

"By God, it does make you feel plumb foolish, doesn't it?"

"Try it again."

"Charles!" This time he let out a good bellow.

Charles, the steward, yelled back "Sah!" In a moment he appeared.

"Another gin and tonic for the good Mastah, Charles," I said.

"Yes, Sah!"

Each of us mixed another drink from the tray that Charles held before us.

"How much we paying these people?" Shartelle asked.

I fished in a pocket for my billfold. "I don't remember. Downer gave me the list before he left. We pay them once a month." I found the list and unfolded it.

"Let's see—it all comes to forty-nine pounds a month. That's about—what—one hundred thirty-seven bucks a month."

"How does it break down?"

"Well, Samuel gets twelve pounds; William gets eleven; Charles, the steward, gets ten; Small Boy gets four; Ojo gets six, and Silex gets six."

"Merciful God," Shartelle said.

"With Small Boy getting four—plus his quarters—that's forty-eight pounds a year which is about twenty higher than the average Albertian annual income—for a family."

"I don't want to hear any more. You just keep all those depressing facts and figures to yourself. We'll slip a few pounds their way now and then before we leave."

"That's the trouble with you bloody Americans," I said, doing a fair Old Boy accent. "Come down here and first thing start spoiling the beggars."

"We'll let Pig spoil a few," he said. "We'll put it down on the expense sheet as hospitality for others. That makes me feel better just thinking about it."

He rose from his chair and walked out onto the porch. He gazed at the lawn, fingered the honeysuckle vines that provided shade for the porch on the west side, shook his head and came back in. "Wonder how African Bermuda would do in Africa?" he said.

"I used to play golf at a club where they had bent-African Bermuda for the greens. It would grow half an inch and then bend over flat."

Shartelle cocked his head at me. "I once knew a man who raised orchids and actually trained them to—"

The telephone rang before Shartelle could finish his lie. I got up, crossed to the desk, and answered it.

"Mr. Shartelle or Mr. Upshaw, please." It was a man's voice with an English accent.

"This is Mr. Upshaw," I said.

"Mr. Upshaw, this is Ian Duncan. I'm A.D.C. to his excellency, Sir Charles Blackwelder. His Excellency would very much like to have you and Mr. Shartelle drop by Government House tomorrow morning. Would that be convenient?"

"I don't know why not."

"Splendid. Say about ten?"

"All right."

"We'll send a car around."

"Thank you."

"Very good. We'll look for you tomorrow morning, then. Goodbye."

I said goodbye and hung up.

"That was the aide-de-camp to His Excellency, Sir Charles Blackwelder, Governor of Western Albertia, Defender of the Crown, Representative of Her Majesty the Queen."

"And?"

"He would like to see us at ten in the morning. I said all right. You heard what I said."

"What do you know about Sir Charles?"

"He's been Regional Governor for about seven years. He'll go, of course, after independence. Maybe sooner. He started his career here in the 1930's. Was a district officer in the north and then went up rather quickly. Nothing spectacular, but he had the reputation of being a good administrator. The Albertians don't have anything against him other than the color of his skin."

"But he keeps his hand in?"

"Apparently so."

The Humber with William at the wheel and Ojo beside him sped up the graveled drive and came to stop in front of the porch. They got out of the car and went back to the trunk where the yellow metal handle of a lawnmower protruded. William was helping Ojo lift it out as we walked out on the porch.

"Very good grasscutter, Sah," William said. "We make good bargain at eleven pound, four shilling, sixpence."

I walked down the steps and took a look at the lawnmower which looked like any other I'd ever seen or pushed. It had been a long time since I had pushed one. Ojo smiled broadly and ran his hand shyly over the handles. The lawnmower's brand name was Big Boy and the label said that it was made in Toledo, Ohio.

"Ojo very happy," William said, taking out a leather purse and carefully counting my change. By this time the rest of the staff, except for the watch night, Silex, were standing around the lawnmower. "Very nice, Sah," Samuel the cook said. Small Boy touched the lawnmower and received a brisk slap from Ojo who fired a question at Samuel in his unknown tongue.

"Ojo want to know if you or Mastah like to push grass-cutter first?"

"Tell him we appreciate the offer," Shartelle said, "but that we feel he should have that honor."

Samuel thought about that for a moment and then said something to Ojo who grinned hugely. He turned the lawnmower over so that the blades and roller were on top and wouldn't turn, and pushed it to a suitable spot of grass. The servants gathered about him; Shartelle and I observed from the steps of the porch as befitted our station. Ojo flopped the lawnmower over carefully, rubbed his hands on his threadbare khaki shorts, and gave it an experimental shove of about a foot. It cut the grass. An "ahhhhh" and an "ohhhhh" of appreciation went up from his audience. He looked at us and Shartelle gave him the benediction with the twisty cigar. He pushed the lawn-mower six feet straight ahead. Then he turned it slowly and cut another swath of grass for six feet more. Then he was off and his audience dispersed. We watched him for a while as he pushed his lawnmower across the lawn—a short, stubby figure with well-muscled legs—bending happily over the machine, his first brush with automation.

"We'd better start for Akomolo's," Shartelle said.

We got in the car and William backed it to the turna-round place. I watched Ojo and his lawnmower. "Maybe we should get him a basket to catch the grass clippings," I said.

Shartelle puffed on his cigar. "That's the trouble with you Americans. You want to spoil the goddamned na-tives."

— 11 —

Akomolo's compound would have been in the heart of Ubondo's downtown section if the city had had a downtown section. A ten-foot mud wall that needed a new coat of whitewash ran for seventy-five feet along the side that faced the street. The wall had an iron-barred gate that automobiles could pass through once they got by the two tough policemen who guarded it. The top of the wall was encrusted with the bottom halves of broken beer bottles.

Akomolo's house poked up above the wall and from it rose a flagpole. There was no Union Jack, but there was a blue and white banner that hung limply in the breezeless air.

"What's the flag, William?" I asked.

"Party flag, Sah. National Progressives."

"Oh."

William turned into the drive that led to the iron gate and stopped for the two policemen. They came over and looked into the car, one on each side. "Mr. Shartelle? Mr. Upshaw?" one of them asked.

"That's right," Shartelle said.

They looked at us some more and then waved us through. The driveway led past the gate and into a courtyard that was paved with cement. People—men, women and children —stood, sat and lay in the courtyard. Some had small boxes and used their tops to display a grubby collection of cigarettes and kola nuts. Others chatted with their neighbors. Mothers nursed their babies. An old man was curled up in the shade of the wall, fast asleep, or dead.

"Friends of Chief Akomolo," William said, jerking his

head towards the courtyard of people. There were about seventy or seventy-five of them. "He give them chop at night."

The main building in the compound was a U-shaped, three-story, stuccoed house with windows set deep into its thick walls. It had neither style nor flavor, but it looked sturdy. The driveway ran down one side of it towards the rear. William drove the Humber down the drive and turned right behind the building into another courtyard that was enclosed by the same high mudwall and flanked by servants' quarters. A collection of automobiles was parked near the rear wall. There were a Fleetwood Cadillac, a Mercedes 300, a Rolls Silver Wraith, a Facel-Vega, two big Oldsmobiles that looked like a matched pair, a Jaguar Mark X, a Jaguar XK-E with the top down and the left front fender crumpled, assorted Chevrolets, Fords, Plymouths, Rovers, and one lonely-looking Volkswagen.

William pulled up beside the Rolls and parked. Shartelle and I got out. A man in a flowing blue *ordona* hurried over to meet us from the courtyard formed by the Chief's building. William tugged at my sleeve. "I no have chop, Mastah."

"Can you find some around here?"

"I get chop from kitchen here. Not cost much."

"Okay. You be back in a couple of hours. We'll be that long at least."

Shartelle was shaking hands with the man in the robes. He said: "Pete, this is Dr. Diokadu. He's secretary of the National Progressive Party."

Dr. Diokadu was a tall, thin man of thirty or so with a quick nervous smile, brilliant dark eyes, and a high, smooth brown forehead. He looked smart—the way some people do.

"I've been looking forward to meeting you, Mr. Shartelle."

"Thank you," he said. "Are we late?"

"No—not at all. The Leader would like to see you before—"

He didn't finish his statement. It was interrupted by a

104

piercing, off-key blast of what seemed to be a badly-played trumpet or cornet. Then a drum began to pound. Dr. Diokadu smiled nervously. "You must excuse me a moment," he said. "The Ile is coming. I must greet him. You might wish to watch his entrance—it's traditional, you know, and most Europeans find it—oh, well—amusing, I suppose."

Shartelle and I smiled politely. The trumpet or cornet brayed again and a man dressed in lionskins and a grotesque mask, bounded around the corner waving a stick with what looked to be some raccoon tails attached to it. The mask was red and black and green with a hideously-formed mouth that was carved into an impolite leer. The mask had no nose, but the eyes were red and seemed to flash. The top of the mask was adorned by what, from a distance, seemed to be the model of a destroyer or a battleship. The masked figure waved his stick at some of the courtyard's hangers-on and they shrank back, not laughing. The man in the lion's suit shouted something. William was standing by me and he pulled back as the man with the coonskin stick drew near. I saw that the model of the ship on his head was a destroyer and that it had a name: "Ft. Worth, Texas."

"Who the hell's that?" I asked William.

"He small ju-ju man," William said.

Dr. Diokadu stood straight and still in the middle of the courtyard as the ju-ju man shouted and pranced around him, waving his furry wand.

"He get rid of evil spirits before Ile come," William explained.

"Ain't this something," Shartelle said, grinning hugely.

The trumpet blasted again and four men in white robes appeared around the corner. Each carried a tray and on each tray was a single kola nut. The men walked straight ahead after turning the corner. They ignored Dr. Diokadu and he ignored them.

"They bring kola nut from Ile to Chief Akomolo," William whispered.

The trumpet blasted again and the drums rolled.

"Talking drums," William said.

"What do they say?" Shartelle asked.

"They say Ile coming."

Another figure turned the corner dressed in bright blue robes. He carried a gold staff, eight feet long, that had an intricately-carved bird on its end. He used the staff to walk with. He was old and he chanted in a high thin voice as he came.

"He say Ile of Obahma now comes—he say that he is great man and that all who see him—"

"That's just a rough translation," a voice said at my elbow. I turned and a smiling dark man with heavily-framed sunglasses was standing near me. "I'm Jimmy Jenaro," he said. "I'm the Treasurer of the Party."

I whispered my name and introduced Shartelle. "I'll give you the play-by-play," Jenaro said. "The one who is jumping around out there is a small-time, combination witch doctor and court jester. Don't ask me where he got the outfit or the Ft. Worth boat. It's part of his magic. The four guys with the kola nuts are part of the Ile's retinue. The kola nuts, of course, are symbols of friendship and loyalty. Now, the senior citizen with the gold staff is the court herald. That's real gold, by the way. The staff is the symbol of the Ile's authority as the traditional ruler or emperor or king or what-have-you of Obahma. The herald sings his praise. If you'll notice when he says a phrase, the drums pick it up—the intonation, the beat, the cadence. That's why they're called the talking drums. I'll give it to you phrase by phrase—

"People of this land bow down...mightier than all does—or doth—come thy way—prostrate thyselves for the son of lightning, brother of the Moon approaches...."

The old man with the staff walked slowly. He would sing out a phrase and pause and the drums would pick it up. The trumpet would blow. And then he would sing another phrase. Jenaro translated:

"Greater than those from the land of Kush...comes now Arondo, son of Arondo, and son of those Arondos who were in the beginning...He cames now...He comes now...prostrate thyselves for mighty is his wrath, his great wisdom unmatched—or unparalleled, I guess—his valor in war feared and remembered and his fecundity the envy of the world."

The old man had stopped walking and stood near the entrance to the building. He beat the staff on the court-yard in time to his sentences as he chanted some more praise. Around the corner came a six or seven-year-old boy bearing the bell of an eight-foot brass horn on his shoulder. Behind him walked the hornplayer. He gave it another toot. The old man kept on chanting. Next came two men carrying long, skin-covered drums that tapered at either end and were hung around their necks by straps of animal skin. They walked slowly, their heads cocked to hear the chant of the Ile's herald. When a phrase of the chant was ended, their hands beat out its rhythm on the drumheads.

The people in the courtyard silently listened to the herald. Dr. Diokadu still stood in the center of the court-yard straight and motionless. The kola bearers were slightly to one side of the herald who continued his dry, reedy paean for the Ile of Obahma.

"Here he comes now," Jenaro whispered to Shartelle and me.

A car poked its nose slowly around the corner of the building. I could hear Shartelle grunt. It was some car. It was a 1939 specially-built LaSalle convertible, painted a gleaming white, with the whitewall tires mounted in the fender wells.

"Looks like somebody fixed that busted block, Clint," I said.

"Damned if it don't."

It was a seven-passenger limousine and in the back seat, by himself, sat a small man with a straw boater. He wore sunglasses and seemed to stare straight ahead. The straw boater had a large ostrich feather stuck into it and it waved a little in the breeze.

As soon as the car and its occupant came into sight,

William dropped flat on the ground, his head pressed tightly against the cement of the courtyard. Dr. Diokadu went down more slowly, but he too knelt and pressed his head against the cement.

"It's part of the game, fellows," Jenaro said beside us and went down on his knees and pressed his head to the ground. The rest of the people in the courtyard were lying flat. Shartelle waved at the Ile with his cigar and raised his hat—like a gambler in a western who meets the schoolmarm. I just stood there.

The car stopped and the driver got out, prostrated himself in a practiced, hasty manner, got up and opened the door. The Ile took off his sunglasses, tucked them away into the folds of his robe, and allowed himself to be helped from the car. Dr. Diokadu rose from his prostrate position and hurried over to greet him. Jenaro also rose, but William and the rest of the occupants of the courtyard remained flat.

"Plays hell with the threads," Jenaro said, dusting off the knees of his fawn-colored Daks. He wore a white shirt with a yellow and black ascot at the throat, a black cashmere jacket so lightweight that it actually looked cool, and black suede loafers. From the breast pocket of his jacket peeked a yellow and black handkerchief to match his ascot. I caught Shartelle and Jenaro eyeing each other's sartorial splendor.

The Ile moved around the courtyard, speaking first to one of the prostrated Albertians, then to another. Some he spoke to did a half-pushup, turning their faces to him as they would to the sun. Onto their foreheads he pressed shillings. They stuck there with sweat. Then the beneficiaries resumed their positions. During the Ile's tour of the courtyard, Dr. Diokadu followed closely behind, hitching up his robes nervously.

The Ile stopped where William was lying and said something. William did a half-pushup, lifted his face to the Ile, and replied. The Ile pasted a shilling on our driver's forehead and looked over at us. He was a short man

108

with a smooth, almost round head. His robes were pure white with gold embroidery. He wore the feathered boater with a slightly raffish air. He smiled and showed us a nice supply of gold teeth. He continued to look at us incuriously, said something to Dr. Diokadu, and nodded at Jenaro who bowed. As the Ile passed Shartelle he looked quickly to the right and left—and winked. Then he moved off towards the building and disappeared through the passageway, Dr. Diokadu and the retinue close behind.

"Sorry I wasn't here when you arrived," Jenaro said. "But I got tied up with the Leader. He wanted us to get together either before the Ile arrived or after he left. It looks as if it will be after. They're going to have to go through the formal greeting routine for a while, so why don't we have a beer?"

"You lead the way, Mr. Jenaro," Shartelle said.

"Just call me Jimmy. Ohio State, class of '55."

Shartelle grinned. "I took notice that you spoke like a native."

"Majored in business administration, lettered in golf—believe it or not."

"I believe it," Shartelle said.

"I'm just laying my credentials out."

"They're impressive," I said.

"The Leader keeps a little beer tucked away among the lemon squash," Jenaro said. "I think we can promote three bottles."

He led us up a flight of stairs, down an outside balcony, and into a room that seemed to be an office. "The Leader's study," he explained, and walked to one side where a small three-foot office-type refrigerator sat next to some filing cabinets. Jenaro produced three bottles of beer, opened them, and motioned us to seats. He sat on the edge of the desk.

"I saw Downer a couple of days ago. He said you were due."

"We got in yesterday morning."

"Nice trip?"

"Fine."

"You're the Treasurer of the Party, right?" Shartelle asked.

"Right. The bag man, the fixer—if you know what I mean."

"I believe I've heard the terms."

Jenaro put his beer on the desk, and walked up and down the room. "There are three of us going towards the center—the federal parliament. The Leader, me—because I've got the safest district in the country—and Diokadu. You just met him. He's our theoretician. Smart."

He stopped in the middle of the room, assumed a putting stance, and aimed one at an imaginary hole. I judged it was a ten-footer.

"You hold a post in the regional government?" Shartelle asked.

"Minister of Information," he said.

"That could be useful," I said.

Jenaro nodded, aimed another imaginary putt, shot, and sighed. "I missed. I should have stayed in the States and turned pro. Maybe Gary Player and I could have teamed up on one of those Saturday afternoon TV golf tournaments. That would knock hell out of them in Cape Town, wouldn't it?"

Shartelle stretched his long legs out and took a sip of beer from the bottle. Jenaro hadn't offered any glasses.

"That's a nice suit," Jenaro said. "Seersucker?"

"I had this cloth run up for me special by a little old unionbusting mill down in Alabama. I can get you a few yards if you like."

Jenaro walked over and fingered Shartelle's lapel. "Could you?"

"I'll make a note of it," I said. "We'll get Duffy to fly it down."

"Just get it to London," Jenaro said. "My tailor's there."

"How do you see the political picture, Jimmy?" Shartelle asked.

Jenaro took careful aim and sank a twenty-footer. I started to tell him he was wiggling his butt too much, but didn't.

"Very rough. We've got the money; all we lack is votes."

Shartelle nodded. "You can't run a poll, can you?"

"I'm as close as they've got to one," Jenaro said. "We can't run a real poll because we don't have the trained interviewers. And if we did have trained interviewers to do an in-depth thing à la Oliver Quayle or Lou Harris, the interviewers would have to speak ninety-odd dialects. We can take a spot survey, check the voters in the market-place, on the road, wherever you find them, but it won't mean much. We've got the tribal thing here in the west and over in the east. Up north, the Muslims are putting the fear of God or Allah into the people."

"How do you figure it then?"

Jenaro walked behind the desk and slumped into the swivel chair. He propped his legs up on the desk and crossed his ankles.

I don't know. Unless we come up with something, I'm afraid the Leader, Diokadu and I are going to be the loyal opposition. But then I'm no great strategist. I can tell you down to a penny how much we've got in the coffers and how much we can tap a guy for. I know them all because I've been playing politics since I was sixteen years old. They shipped me off to the States to get rid of me, in fact. When I came back I made a pile in the import business and I got to know the business crowd—and that's the same bunch in any country.

"So what I do is get in my Jag and go for bush. You know, park it at a government resthouse, change clothes and ride off into the boondocks on a bicycle. I talk with the villagers. Most don't know who I am and I've got a gift for languages so the dialects come easy. I talk to them; they talk to me. I find out what they're bitching about that week, and then come back and try to get it fixed so that the Leader can take the credit. I sometimes think that's what all ministers should be doing instead of riding around in their Mercedes."

"Been the downfall of many a politician I've known," Shartelle said. "Let me ask you this: you know the trade union boys pretty well?"

111

"Uh-huh."

"How they going?"

Jenaro made a small gesture with his hand, turning it palm up and palm down. "Who knows? Depends on who got to them last."

"Who's the top man?"

"The Secretary-General of the Trade Union Congress."

"That corresponds to our AFL-CIO."

"Roughly, except the Secretary-General doesn't have to run for office every two or four years. He's appointed for life."

"Dedicated?"

Jenaro looked up at the ceiling. "To a point. He and I have had a few business deals together. He's not above taking a profit, although it's a dirty word in any speech he makes."

"Has he got the power?"

"The real stuff?"

"That's right."

"He's got it."

"Will he make a deal?" Shartelle asked.

"For money? He doesn't need money."

"He needs something."

Jenaro got up from the desk and walked the length of the room.

"He'd want it in writing."

"How do he and the Chief get along?" Shartelle asked.

"Okay. Not close. Not distant. They're aware of each other."

"Well, I've got an idea. It might help do the job."

"Talk it over with the Leader."

"Well, now, Jimmy, the Chief seems to be a fine up-standing man who just might not want to get all involved in what I've got in mind. What I need is someone who might serve as the Chief's emissary to organized labor—not out in public, mind you—but somebody who might drop the word where it would be most productive."

Jenaro sat on the edge of the desk again. He moved around a lot. "We used to have some guys at Ohio State from the South who talked just like you. They'd talk and talk and the first thing I knew I was down fifty bucks in a poker game. But no offense. Wait till you get a bunch of Albertians together if you want to go all around Robin Hood's barn before you get to the point. First they start out with the parables. Then come the proverbs. After the proverbs come the veiled metaphors. Then—maybe then, if you're lucky—somebody might get to the point."

Shartelle brushed a bit of ash from one well-cut lapel. "It's my Southern upbringing, sir. We put a lot of store by polite conversation."

Jenaro grinned. "Shit. What you want is for me to make a deal with the Trade Union Congress, right?"

"There's something like that in the back of my mind. Also, I might just have another role for you to play in this campaign."

Jenaro rose and walked up and down the room again. "Clint," he said, "we might just get along."

"I'm sure we will. I'm just sure we will."

An Albertian in a white coat poked his head in the door "Time for chop, Sah."

"Now you meet the rest of the crowd, including the Ile. Not only does the Ile have votes, but he has money. That's one reason we butter him up. And, of course, he is the traditional ruler."

"I think he winked at me," Shartelle said.

"I know he did," I said.

"The old boy has been around in his own way. He puts up with the romance and ritual because the people like it—or seem to."

"My, I thought it was fine!" Shartelle said. "Here he comes on with that old witch doctor prancing around in front of him wearing that Ft. Worth, Texas boat on his head and all those people flopping down on their faces. And then comes that old man with the gold staff a-tappin' and a-chantin' his praises. Hell, it was better than Father Divine. And then here comes that eight-foot horn and the drums a-talkin' and then old Himself, sitting up straight and proud with those Hollywood shades and that straw hat with the ostrich plume floating out of it. Here he comes in that 1939 LaSalle limousine just like my daddy used to have. And then he gets out of the car, just as casual and calm as you please, and walks around sweat-pasting shillings on the folks' heads. I wouldn't have missed it for the world."

"Shartelle's got his own notions of what Africa should be," I told Jenaro.

"Tarzan and Timbuktu?"

"Something like that."

Jenaro smiled and turned to Clint. "Just stick with me, Dad. I'll see that you're not disappointed."

— *12* —

We met them all—from the Minister of Home Affairs to the Premier's assistant administrative aide. There were forty of them in the big room with the long table, take away or add a couple, and they moved around in a brilliant display of best-day robes and a babble of shrill conversation, not much of which Shartelle and I could get. We were the only whites in the room.

Chief Akomolo welcomed us warmly. "After this is over, I was hoping that we could get together. Can you stay?" We told him we could. He instructed Jimmy Jenaro to keep us in tow. Jimmy said: "Just stand still. They'll all drift by before we sit down to chop."

Each of the forty-odd men in the room made his way to the end of the room where the Ile sat on a foot-high dais in a chair fashioned from some kind of animal horn. When each got there he prostrated himself before the Ile, murmured a few words, and moved away. The Ile sipped on a bottle of orange squash and smiled blandly at the gathering. He looked a little bored.

They passed then—those who had not yet done so—

to Chief Akomolo, shook hands, made their greetings, and then moved on to the drinks table. A number of stewards squirmed through the crowd bearing bottles of Ballantine's Scotch which they pressed on anyone who would hold out his hand. I noticed that a few of the guests tucked a bottle or so away in the folds of their robes.

"You want a drink?" Jenaro asked.

"Scotch and water, if you can get it without trouble," Shartelle said. I asked for the same. Jenaro stopped a passing waiter and told him to bring us three Scotches with water. He brought back three fifths and three glasses of water. Jenaro sighed, put two bottles down by a baseboard, uncapped one and poured us all a drink.

"For someone who never touches the stuff, the Leader runs up a hell of a monthly booze bill," he said. "But it's what they expect—the squeeze, the dash, the tip, the bribe. They all expect it and feel insulted if they don't get it."

First we met the Minister of Agriculture, and then the Minister of Public Works, and then the Minister of Transport, followed by the Minister of Trade and Commerce, who came just before the Minister of Internal Affairs and Labor, and after the Minister of Health. They all had a rough jest for Jenaro and a kind word of greeting for Shartelle and me. They were polite, a little shy perhaps, or maybe it was just suspicion. They moved on to talk among themselves.

"Some of them run their Ministries, some don't," Jenaro said in a low voice. "All of us—even I—depend on our Permanent Secretaries who are, with just a couple of exceptions, all British. They're damned good, too, but after independence, they'll be on their way out. Some immediately—some in a couple of months—a few longer. It's the Albertization process."

Some of the lesser chiefs and notables came by to be introduced. Shartelle was gracious and charming. I was warmly polite. These were the hangers-on, the toadies, the go-fors who surround any political activity and sometimes, surprisingly enough, prove useful. They'll do anything at anytime for anyone in power. In the States, they would be hanging around the county courthouse.

"What happens when the British leave?" Shartelle asked.

"They're training some good chaps to take their places, and they're training them well. Of course, the British will get their lumpers."

"What's that?" I asked.

"It's a lump sum compensation for having their careers interrupted." Jenaro paused to make a couple of more introductions. "For instance, suppose you were a bright young guy of twenty or twenty-one or twenty-two, just out of service after World War II with a fair education, and you hoped to come to Albertia in the colonial service. You go into a ministry in a rather low position, or for bush as assistant district officer, and you stick with it. You work yourself up by the time you're thirty-five or thirty-six or thirtyseven to Under-Permanent Secretary or Assistant Permanent Secretary—and then you have the rug yanked out from under you. Or perhaps you're forty or forty-five or fifty or older—but not old enough for full retirement. So what do you do, go back to London and sign up at the Labour Exchange?"

"Sounds like a reduction-in-force," I said.

"Something like that. So we made a deal with them. They get out and depending upon their years of service, they get a lump sum payment. If a guy has been here for say, fifteen years, he gets about three-thousand quid. That's the lump. But in addition to that he gets about a thousand quid a year for the rest of his life. No strings attached."

"You wanted them out bad, didn't you?" Shartelle said.

Jenaro nodded. "Bad enough. And, of course, they can take their lumpers now and get the hell out—and a lot of them are. But a lot more of them are staying for as long as they can. Funny, but I could never see the Amis staying under similar circumstances."

"If we ever dreamed we weren't desperately wanted and liked and loved by all, we'd be on the first plane out," I said.

Jenaro introduced us to a straggler, an old man who

frowned at us, scolded Jenaro in the tribal dialect, and then hurried off to see the Ile. "God knows who invited him," Jenaro said. "Probably the Leader."

The tall broad Albertian who had been with Chief Akomolo at Duffy's office luncheon in London came through the door. In London, he had worn a suit. In Albertia, he wore his robes and he moved on sandaled feet across the room with grace and dignity and a peculiar aura of power. He went immediately to the Ile and the little man's round face beamed as the younger man knelt before him in— my romantic notions told me—respect, not awe, as a returning, successful Roland would kneel to Charlemagne.

Shartelle poked me in the ribs. "There's old Bristol Cream. My, he cuts a fine figure in those white flowing robes and that saucy little cap perched up on that good-looking head."

After exchanging a few words with the Ile, the big man made his way to Chief Akomolo. The same look of genuine pleasure appeared on the Chief's face as the pair shook hands. He gestured towards us and the man in the white robes turned and moved our way.

"His last name's Dekko, in case you forgot," Shartelle said.

"Chief Dekko, call him," Jimmy Jenaro said.

"Mr. Shartelle, it is indeed a pleasure to see you again." He put his big hand out and Shartelle took it.

"I've been looking forward to it, Chief Dekko."

"Really?" the big man said. "Why?"

It would have stopped some people momentarily, I guess. Me, for example. Even Duffy. Not Shartelle. "Because I wanted to get to know you better, and we didn't get much of a chance to talk in London."

"That's true. Why don't we sit together at chop?"

"I'd be happy to, sir," Shartelle said.

"And Mr. Upshaw, is it not?" He put out his hand and I took it.

"Chief Dekko," I said.

"Hello, Jimmy," he said to Jenaro. "I am very angry with you."

"Why?"

'You told me you'd teach me to play golf—that was last month. You haven't called, you haven't stopped by."

"You've been in London."

"For a week—it's been a month. You must keep your promises."

"I'll call you tomorrow."

"What time?"

"Nine—make it nine-thirty."

"Do not forget, Jimmy. It is good to see you gentlemen. I have anticipated this meeting. Now I must greet some others, but Mr. Shartelle, you and Mr. Upshaw must sit with me at table."

"That's kind of you," Shartelle said.

"I will be back."

We watched him move among the men in the room, a foot taller than most, a hundred pounds heavier than some. A big, tough, young man with all the natural poise and grace of a half-tamed panther.

Jenaro watched him and shook his head. "Well, that's the boy."

Shartelle watched him and nodded his head. "He's got the smiles. I'd also say he had the inside track."

"He does indeed," Jenaro said. "When the Leader goes to the center, Dekko becomes Premier of the Western Region."

"Young," I said.

"Thirty-one," Jenaro replied. "He's got it all—brains, looks, ability, and the most naive, trusting manner that you could hope for."

"Must go over real nice with the folks," Shartelle said. "He could move amongst them."

"Could and does. Never forgets a name, never forgets a face. That golf thing. He just mentioned once that he'd like to get more exercise and I suggested that he learn golf. I offered to teach him—some time. But he remembered and now you'd think I didn't come through with the Buick dealership."

"I'd say that boy will do all right in politics," Shartelle

murmured. "Unless, of course, the Colts are looking for a new fullback."

"Soccer's his game," Jenaro said. "And cricket."

"Might even turn him into a roll-out halfback if he's got the speed," I said.

"Might," Shartelle agreed.

Chief Akomolo made his way to the head of the long table that had five places at its T. He picked up a knife and rapped sharply on his bottle of squash. The babble died and he looked at the dais where the Ile sat smiling benignly. The Ile looked around the room and then nodded his head. Jenaro caught Shartelle and me by the arm. "This is a political meeting, so the Leader, Dekko and Diokadu and I sit at the head table. You guys sit across from each other in the next seats down."

Chief Dekko was gesturing to Shartelle and pointing to the seat that Jenaro had mentioned. We sat down, Dekko on Chief Akomolo's right, Dr. Diokadu on his left, Jenaro next to Dekko.

After we were seated, one of the white-clad men who had borne the kola nuts for the Ile brought in a table that fitted cleverly across the arms of the throne of horns. Another brought in a plate of what, from where I sat, looked like chicken and goop. The old man with the gold staff thumped his way over from a corner, took a dirty-looking spoon out of his pocket, and dipped into the food. He shoveled the spoonful into his mouth, chewed, swallowed, and thumped the staff three times. It was time to eat.

In my time I have eaten in army mess halls with apes who thought that Emily Post was the name of a hooker, and I've been the prison route, eating at the mess with no-forehead felons on either side. I have dined at smokers with members of the American Legion who catapulted butter from the blades of knives. And I have sat down to break bread with the rest of the bums and winos at the Harbor Lights and Last Hope Havens. Nothing bothered me. I'm not too particular. But the dinner at Chief Akomolo's was a memorable experience.

The stewards brought the food—an entire broiled or roasted chicken for every man. There were forks and knives to eat them with but they were largely ignored. Plates of hot curry were passed down the table, each man scooping off a double handful or so—with his hand. I took a handful and then looked around for the napkins. There weren't any. I used the table cloth like everybody else. I tried the curry and the *fou-fou* and the palm wine and the French wine that was passed from the head table down. Anyone thirsty took a drink from the bottle and the bottles kept coming. When a chicken was done with, the bones were thrown over the shoulder—just like Charles Laughton in *The Private Life of Henry VIII*. I looked around for some Great Danes. There weren't any.

Then came the plates of sardines fresh from the can— apparently still a lingering delicacy flavored by British rule. There were a couple of cans to the diner. I tore off a leg of chicken, gnawed it, and tossed the bone over my shoulder. Nobody noticed. Nobody minded. I tried the curry again and it was no worse than Border chili. I sampled a lump of gray paste and it reminded me of the tamales in Denver, only twice as hot. The bottles of wine had gone around until now everyone had two or three sitting before him—partly full. I snatched one, a nice Moselle that I remembered, and gulped it down to chase the burn. The wine wasn't chilled, but it helped.

I looked at Shartelle as he scooped up three fingers' worth of curry and popped it into his mouth. His face was streaming with grease and he wiped it off with the back of his hand and then wiped his hands on the table cloth, talking all the while. He winked at me. Jimmy Jenaro saw the wink and grinned.

Chief Akomolo sat at the head of the table, talking first to Dr. Diokadu, who ate sparingly and with a knife and fork, and then to Chief Dekko who looked to be the mightiest trencherman of them all. He put down three chickens and, like Father William, polished them off all but the bones and the beak.

The noise at the table was just below one long shout.

Shartelle leaned across to me and said: "Boy, I haven't been to a feed like this since the last time I was at a Cajun barbecue at the Opelousas yam festival."

Jimmy Jenaro leaned across the table and said, "This is just a quiet businessman's fellowship lunch. Wait 'til we have a feast day." I nodded and kept on chewing and poking more in before I'd swallowed that.

"Do you like our Albertian food, Mr. Shartelle?" Chief Dekko shouted above the shouting.

"Mighty tasty, Chief," Shartelle said, tore off a piece of chicken breast, sopped up some sauce made of pure Cayenne and water, and popped the morsel into his mouth. "It's what I call nicely flavored."

"I thought it might be too hot for you," Dekko said. "If it is—"

"No, sir," Shartelle said. "I'd just call it passable warm; spicy you might say," and the tears of pain glistened in the brave man's eyes for only a moment.

At the end of the hall the Ile sat in lonely majesty and ate a tropical chocolate bar and drank another bottle of orange squash. He smiled his golden smile and then yawned a couple of times. When he yawned, the eating stopped; lunch was over. It had lasted a little over an hour. There were a few polite belches which were greeted with appreciative grunts from neighbors. The chief steward hurried to take away the tray containing the candy bar wrapper and the bottle of pop. The Ile arose, nodded, and the procession left the way it had come—the herald singing the Ile's praises, the drummers beating their litany, the long horn squawking its message to the waiting populace.

Everyone sat stone-still at the table as the procession made its way out the door. Nobody looked at the Ile, except Shartelle and me. The Ile looked straight ahead until he got to Chief Akomolo and then said something to him in the dialect, indicating Shartelle and me with a wave of his hand. The Chief nodded but remained mute. The procession passed on, bound for the 1939 LaSalle.

Chief Akomolo leaned towards Shartelle. "The Ile has

121

invited you to attend him at his palace on Wednesday next. I believe it is important that you should go."

"We would be honored, sir," Shartelle said.

"Good. Chief Jenaro will call for you."

Chief Akomolo rose and rapped his squash bottle for attention. The noise subsided, chairs were scraped back, some lighted cigarettes. It was speech time at Rotary after the Thursday lunch, or at the board meeting of the quarterly get-together of vice-presidents, regional directors, and staff of the International Union of Widget Makers. The speeches began. First came Chief Akomolo. He talked gravely, using a minimum of gestures. His eyes sought out the individual faces of his audience and he drove home points to them—sometimes gently pounding a fist into the palm of his hand. He was the chairman of the board, telling of the progress that had been made—but also pointing to the major challenges that lay ahead and must be met, could be met, and would be met. He sat down.

He was followed by Chief Dekko who looked to be the executive vice-president, the comer, the go-a-long-wayer. He looked down at the table and he started talking to it in a deep, low voice. Then he put his hands on his hips and rocked back and forth a few times, looking straight ahead over the heads of his audience to that far distant point, that source of personal strength. He drew from it. It warmed him, and his voice rose and it got almost to a shout—and he had them then and he played with them. He teased them with his voice and his face and with his eyes and the amen corner shouted his praises. And finally the voice rose slowly to the peak again—almost to that shout that never came, and then it dropped, and his head dropped, and he talked to the table once more. A last simple, slowly uttered phrase, and he sat down.

There was quiet, then clapping, then pounding of the table, and cries of approval. The young chief sat there, head bowed, himself overcome by the strength of his belief in what he had said.

Then Dr. Diokadu, the statistician, the bearer of facts,

got up and read from the number report. He consulted a ledger as the chairs scraped and shifted, a few more drinks were drunk, coughs were coughed, and cigarettes lighted. Nobody listened carefully and Dr. Diokadu didn't seem to be interested in the report either. When he sat down there was polite applause which he acknowledged with a sardonic nod.

And finally from the head table, Jimmy Jenaro—the public relations man, the fixer, the hotel-room-getter, the young brash joker who could tell a story well and did— even if it was a bit dirty. He told a few to get started, and they laughed and slapped each other on the back and grinned knowingly into each other's faces. Then Jimmy got serious and talked gravely and quietly for a few minutes and they nodded their heads in equally grave agreement. Then he left them laughing with a couple of quick ones and they gave him twice as much applause as they gave Dr. Diokadu.

Then each of them got up and gave his appraisal of the situation and how the new moves and proposals would affect his territory. There were the mumblers, the precise and crisp, the ramblers, the droners, the would-be comedians, and those who were too shy to say much of anything.

It was quite a talk session. It lasted two hours and Shartelle and I sat through all of it. It couldn't have been nicer if someone had spoken in English.

— *13* —

There were only six of us at the meeting held in Chief Akomolo's office. The guests had departed in polite haste as soon as the last speaker sat down. I presumed that they went home. There were no offices to go back to, no secretaries waiting with stacks of mail to be signed. All government business closed at two every afternoon. Years ago the British had decided that it was too hot to work in the afternoons, so regular hours were eight to two on weekdays; eight to twelve on Saturdays. None of the Albertian ministers objected.

Akomolo sat behind his desk. The rest of us sprawled in low chairs and couches, groggy from the heat, the huge meal, and the speech marathon. The Albertians had shucked their robe-like outer garments and Shartelle, Jenaro and myself were down to shirtsleeves. The shirts were soaked with sweat. It was stifling in the small office. A ceiling fan turned slowly and creaked as it turned. Additional refrigeration was supplied by two oscillating floor fans that blew the air around some. A few strips of flypaper which hung here and there had a fair catch.

Behind his desk, Chief Akomolo arranged some papers, shifting them into neat piles, and then stowing them away in the desk drawers which he kept opening and closing. He talked as he worked:

"We are here, gentlemen, primarily for the benefit of Mr. Shartelle and Mr. Upshaw, to discuss the basic strategy and issues of the campaign. I must say that I stress the word 'basic' because we can merely touch upon what we consider the key issues."

He stopped opening and closing his desk drawers, took off his gold-rimmed eyeglasses, and wiped them clean with a handkerchief. He held them up to the light at arm's length and squinted to see whether they were clean enough. They were. He put them back on.

While he was doing all that he said: "Dr. Diokadu, would you outline the major issues for our two guests?"

Diokadu was seated on a couch next to Chief Dekko who sat perfectly still, his huge bare forearms resting on his knees, his eyes fixed on the floor. Diokadu thought momentarily and said: "Unemployment, that's first. Agricultural prices and development, that's two. Education, three, and four, medical services. The fifth would be industrialization, but that is scarcely an issue. None opposes it."

"Transport," Chief Dekko said, still staring at the floor. "We are a highly mobile country with an infant transport system."

"Transport," Diokadu agreed.

No one spoke. The silence grew as Chief Akomolo gazed down at a spot on his desk between his arms that rested on the borders of the leather-edged blotter. Then he looked up and gazed at the ceiling for a while where the ornamental fan spun uselessly. "And peace," he said. "Peace among our regions and resolvement of our tribal differences. Peace, too, in the world. That must be our recurring theme."

Dekko looked up from his favorite spot on the floor and smiled. "A war in Vietnam does not concern the villager who cannot feed his family because he can find no work."

"We cannot ignore the responsibility that independence entails," Akomolo said firmly. "We cannot turn our back on the world and isolate ourselves selfishly. The door has been opened; the invitation has been extended. We would be derelict if we did not accept it."

"It won't win any votes," Jimmy Jenaro said. "Everybody's for peace."

Before Akomolo could speak, Dekko smiled again and said: "Do we really have so much to contribute to world peace? Are we so wise—or strong? A weak man seldom ends a market brawl."

Akomolo came back with: "A man who ignores his neighbors should not complain of loneliness." I thought that must have lost a little in translation.

The battle of old saws threatened to continue, but Shartelle rose quickly, walked across the room, and leaned against the wall, his arms folded, a slight smile on his face. By standing, he assumed the role of moderator. The faces in the room turned towards him. I wondered how many times in how many rooms he had done the same thing.

"Gentlemen," he said, "I think you have pretty well

125

established the major domestic issues—unemployment, agriculture, education, health and transportation. Seems to me you're differing only in the shade of emphasis that you think should be placed on Albertia's role in the councils of the world." He paused, reached into a vest pocket and took out a black, twisty cigar. He lighted it, puffed a couple of times, and continued: "I think that'll work itself out during the campaign. If it looks like more emphasis on world affairs is needed, we'll just shift gears. At least it seems that you're agreed within the party, so that's the big thing. But in all those principal issues you mentioned, it seemed to me that there was just one thing missing." Shartelle paused and puffed on his cigar some more.

"Taxes," he said. "Now in my experience, taxes can be the trickiest issue of all."

That started it: a fifteen-minute lively debate on taxes which I didn't bother to follow. I wasn't going to take sides on whether the tax on petty traders should be raised or lowered. If they decided to tax the oil companies, I was automatically for it, so that precluded much personal interest. They could soak the rich, too, I decided. The only trouble with that was that the wealthy passed the tax laws and they weren't going to legislate themselves into the poorhouse. So it would be the small farmer, the worker, the petty-trader, the people like Ojo our gardener, who would pay for the trips to the United Nations, the peace missions to Hanoi, and the cocktail parties on Government House lawn after the dawn of independence. Ojo wouldn't like the tax program whatever it was.

After taxes, the discussion continued in general for another half-hour. Dr. Diokadu sketched out the issues in more detail for us, joined by Akomolo and Dekko. Jimmy Jenaro said little. Shartelle and I listened, asking an occasional question now and then. Whenever the discussion threatened to go abroad, Shartelle steered it back with an adroit phrase, a skillful comment. It was nice to watch him work.

Finally, Chief Akomolo said: "I have decided to ask Dr.

Diokadu and Chief Jenaro to work with you closely in any capacity which you may wish, Mr. Shartelle. Our discussion for today, however, must come to an end. I think it has proved most fruitful."

"It has to us, I'd say, sir," Shartelle said. "Now I know it's been a mighty long day already, but I'd sure like to invite these two gentlemen over to our house to continue this for a little while. We've got only six weeks for this campaign and there's lots of planning and plotting to be done yet. I'm sorry to ask you this, Chief Jenaro and Dr. Diokadu, but it needs to be done."

"Of course," Akomolo said. "Are you free?" he asked the pair. They nodded. "Chief Dekko and I would like to join you," Akomolo said, "but we have some quite pressing party business to attend to."

"That's most understandable," Shartelle said.

We were all standing now. The Albertians, with the exception of Jenaro, were slipping their robes over their heads. The rest of us got into our jackets. The close office had grown hotter and it smelled a little like a locker room. Chief Dekko stretched mightily. "Mr. Shartelle, I would like to see you and Mr. Upshaw tomorrow. Will that be possible?"

"We've been asked to Government House at ten o' clock," Shartelle said.

"Then perhaps at 11:30. I will drop by your place."

Since Diokadu and Jenaro had their own cars, they agreed to meet us at our house in a half-hour. We said goodbye to Chief Akomolo and Dekko and walked out into the hot, bright late afternoon. We found our driver, William, asleep behind the wheel, and Shartelle gently shook him.

"Reckon we can go home now, William."

"Yes, Mastah," the driver said. He backed the car out of its slot, and went out the gate past the two cops and turned towards the center of town. If the Western Albertian government closed down at two in the afternoon, the rest of the country didn't. The streets were jammed, and

127

we were stuck five minutes at one crossroads waiting for a herd of rackribbed cattle to be driven across by the clubs of the drovers.

"Those are the sorriest looking critters I ever did see," Shartelle said. "Boy, they ain't even canners or cutters."

"Look at those horns, though," I said. "Must be about the same breadth as the Texas longhorns."

"That's a fact," he agreed. "Wonder if those drovers are going to hoorah it up a little tonight in the local saloon? Five hundred miles they walk'em, old Chief Akomolo told us. They're just plain gristle."

The cattle passed and William sped us home. We got rid of our coats as soon as we got inside. Samuel the cook, and Charles the steward, were on hand to hang them up. "I serve tea now, Mastah," Samuel said.

"You want any tea, Pete?"

"I think it's the form."

"Okay. Tea."

It was cooler inside the wide-eaved house. A breeze blew through the folding doors that led to the front porch. The ceiling fan turned at a brisk clip and I noticed that it could be regulated to go even faster. We sank back in the Ministry of Works chairs and waited for the tea.

"What do you think of Jenaro?" Shartelle asked.

"He seems to know his way around."

"We start making use of it this afternoon."

"How about Diokadu?" I asked.

"He'll do. He's got the facts and figures in his head, or in that pile of papers he's always got tucked under his arm. He's a real professor, ain't he?"

"Uh-huh."

"Well, we'll soon see. When I throw it out, if they don't light on it like a duck on a June bug, we may as well take the next plane back."

"That rough?"

"You see that crowd at lunch."

"Saw and heard."

"Not much help there. Those boys have had their hand in the honeypot so long they think that bees don't sting.

But that Dekko's all right. He's got the look about him. You only see that look a few times in your life."

"What look?"

"The winner's look," Shartelle said.

Samuel brought in the tea tray and set it down on a low, round table.

"Thank you," I said. "Shall I pour and one lump or two?"

"Two," Shartelle said. I dropped in two lumps and handed the cup to him. "You like tea?" he asked.

"I'm used to it."

"Think we could get old Samuel to drop a couple of ice cubes into it? If we've got to have it, boy, I'd sure admire to have it iced up a little."

"I'll see what I can do tomorrow. It'll take careful explanation."

I could hear the Jaguar shift down into second as it slowed for our driveway. Jenaro, big dark shades over his eyes and a checked cotton cap on the back of his head, threw a little gravel as he braked the car to a stop in front of the door. He jumped out and came in.

"How jolly, chaps, I'm just in time for tea," he said.

"You don't have to," I said.

"Good, I'll pass." He slumped into an arm chair, took off his glasses and hat and placed them on the floor. "Diokadu will be here in a minute," he said. "He had to stop by his office to pick up some papers."

We talked idly for a few minutes until Dr. Diokadu arrived, a fat sheaf of papers under one arm. He seemed to be as hurried and preoccupied as usual. He accepted a cup of tea, and when he was seated Shartelle began. There was no deference in his voice now. He was mapping a campaign, much like a general outlining a battle. It was his idea, his plan, and it was also his responsibility.

The first thing. How many speeches have you got Akomolo booked for. You or Doc?"

It may have been the first time that Dr. Diokadu ever had been called Doc, but it didn't seem to bother him. He produced a notebook that was tucked away in his file.

"Three a day, every day between Monday and election eve."

"Could he speak more often?" Shartelle asked. "I mean could he find more audiences?"

"He could if he could get to them," Jenaro said.

"Start booking him at every crossroads and general store, wherever he can find five people or five thousand. How's his health—I mean can he take twelve, even fifteen speeches a day? They won't all be long ones."

"He's in good health," Dr. Diokadu said. "He takes excellent care of himself."

"Okay," Shartelle said. "Now Jimmy. I need two helicopters. Where're the closest ones—and I don't mean London."

Jenaro thought for a moment. Then he snapped his fingers. "The oil company has two."

"You have a connection?"

"Right."

"Get them. Promise them subsurface rights for the entire country. But get them here by Monday. Can you?"

"I'll have them here."

Dr. Diokadu had his notebook out now.

"Doc," Shartelle said. "Have you got backup papers for the main issues? Farm, unemployment, and so forth?"

"I have them right here. I thought we would discuss them this afternoon."

"Believe it or not," Shartelle said, "we just had our last policy discussion about an hour ago. It's your policy and it's your country. Just give them to Pete." Dr. Diokadu handed me a thick sheaf of typed documents. I thumbed through them.

"How long would it take you to give me a *the* speech, Pete?"

I riffled through the documents again. "A *the* speech takes about four hours. Maybe five if the flies bother me."

"We need it tomorrow."

I nodded. "You'll have it."

"How about the rest?"

"Well, there'll be *the* Farm Speech, *the* Unemployment

Speech, *the* Medical Care Speech and so forth. Five or six in all. I can knock out *the* speech tomorrow and maybe a couple of more before I collapse. The rest of them by the next day."

"You're slowing down," he said.

"It's the semi-tropics," Jenaro said. "Saps the vigor of the white man."

"Doc, who's in charge of translating—you or Jimmy?" Shartelle asked.

"I am."

"Okay. As soon as Pete writes one and we look it over, I want it translated and mimeographed into as many dialects and languages as you think necessary."

Dr. Diokadu grinned. "Right. I know just the chaps."

"Now then," Shartelle went on. "When you book these speeches for Akomolo, make sure you find out what dialect or language is most prevalent in the district he's going to speak in. And when he speaks, make sure you've got an interpreter with him. If he can't make himself understood, there ain't no use in him setting that helicopter down."

"You mentioned two helicopters," Jenaro said.

"I need two. One for Akomolo and one for Dekko. No sense in them traveling around together. This is no brother act. And what I said, Doc, about booking speeches for Akomolo, do the same for Dekko. There may be some repetition, but I never heard of it hurting a thing in a political campaign."

"You want translators, bookings, the lot for Dekko, too?"

"Right."

Dr. Diokadu stood up, said "excuse me" and slipped off his embroidered outer robe and flung it into an empty chair. He was getting caught up in Shartelle's planning. Jenaro took off his coat and dropped it on the floor with his hat and glasses. Both were making furious notes now. Shartelle rose and started to pace the room.

"Pete, have you got their cadence?"

"I got it this afternoon," I said. "I'll have to write different speeches. That's no problem. Dekko takes them up the mountain and shows them the valley down below and the lushness that prevails. Akomolo describes what can be done through hard work, determination, and sacrifice. It makes people feel good both ways because they get to the promised land by either route."

Dr. Diokadu looked at me curiously. "How do you know what they said? They were talking in the dialect."

Shartelle paused his pacing in front of Diokadu. "Doc, when you've heard as many speeches as Pete and me you'll know what's being said regardless of the language."

"I got off some nifties," Jenaro said.

"We need a newspaper," Shartelle said. "A weekly every week between now and election. Lots of pictures, big type, and cartoons—political cartoons that don't need captions. It'll have to be English. We haven't got time for the makeover. Jimmy?"

"I know the guy. He'll edit it. He was an exchange student in the States and used to work on the Santa Fe *New Mexican*."

"Get him. And pay him plenty. Doc, you're acquainted in the intellectual circles, I take it."

Diokadu nodded.

"Okay. Set up a committee. 'Albertian Writers and Artists for Akomolo.' When you get it set up—and I expect it to be by the first of next week—we'll tap them for articles—short ones—cartoons, everything we can milk from them. Jimmy: give that guy who's going to edit the paper a call tonight and tell him to start rounding up a staff. Can he find enough reporters?"

"We've got more journalists in Albertia than we have farmers," Dr. Diokadu said.

"Pete. For whatever good it will do, I want a press release every morning and one every afternoon."

"Right. Just give me Akomolo's schedule and an indication of what speech he'll be using. Also I'll keep tabs on the opposition and if they step out of line, he can always rap them back."

"Good. Now, fans."

"I've got a note on that," I said.

"Buttons."

"Big ones," I said.

"Saw a guy lose an election one time because he had little buttons," Shartelle said. "Jimmy, I need five million buttons by the middle of next week. If we get them here, can you get rid of them?"

"Sure."

"Okay. We'll call Duffy tonight."

"Buttons?" Dr. Diokadu asked.

"Metal buttons with a slogan on them," Jenaro explained. "Like 'I Go Ako.'"

"You just wrote it," Shartelle said. "Pete?"

I'll buy it, even if he did steal it from Pogo."

"Same for the fans?"

"Sure."

"Jimmy. Can we make fans here in Albertia with 'I Go Ako' on them? Used to make them out of palmetto some place, I recall. What I was thinking is this: if we could set up cottage industries all over the country with these fan orders, it'd be just like buying votes."

Jenaro wrote furiously. "I know a guy—" he started.

"Get in touch with him. Get it done. Get them distributed."

"Right."

"Drums," Shartelle said softly. "I need me some drums." He was still pacing the room, a twisty black cigar down to a stub between his teeth. The smoke left a trail behind him.

"Talking drums?" Jenaro asked.

"How well do they talk?" Shartelle said. "Can they get a simple message across? Like 'I Go Ako'?"

Dr. Diokadu rose and walked over to the table where the tea tray rested. "Watch," he said. He picked up the tray and set it down on the floor. With his hands he beat a rhythm on the table. "That's 'I Go Ako.' What else?"

Shartelle thought a moment. "Beware or look out for devil in sky. Maybe ju-ju in sky?"

133

"Beware of ju-ju in sky, we'll say," Diokadu decided. "It goes like this." Once more he beat out the rhythm on the table.

"How far do they carry?" Shartelle asked.

Diokadu shrugged. "Not far—maybe a mile."

"Do people understand them?"

"Not everyone, but they ask. They're curious, so they find out."

"Can you buy them?" Shartelle demanded.

"The drums?"

"The drummers."

"Ah!" said Diokadu and got to his feet, a wide smile of delight on his face. "I see. Yes." He looked at Jenaro. "What do you think?"

"It shouldn't be too hard. We get the key drummers set up and give them the money to buy the drummers out in the bush."

"Every night they get a message to drum," Shartelle said. "Sometimes it's cryptic, sometimes it's simply 'I Go Ako,' but I want these goddamned drums beating every night."

"It'll take both Diokadu and me for this," Jenaro said thoughtfully. "But we'll fix it. I don't know how far north we'll be able to go."

"Probably quite far. It's been spreading in recent years."

"Do it," Shartelle said. He walked over and sat down in his chair, his long, seersucker-clad legs sprawled out in front of him. He leaned his head back and yelled: "Samuel!"

There was an answering cry: "Sah!" Samuel came on the trot. "Drinks are in order, I believe, Samuel," Shartelle said.

"Sah," Samuel agreed. He picked up the tea tray, gathered up the cups and left. He was back shortly with a bottle of Scotch, a bottle of gin, quinine water, soda, ice and glasses. He served the guests first and Shartelle last. The pecking order was firmly established.

"Jimmy," Shartelle said, "I want three more phones in this house, desks for that empty room back there, a couple

134

of filing cabinets—one will do—some chairs and a type-writer. You've got mimeograph equipment at party head-quarters, don't you?"

Jenaro had put his drink down to write some more in his notebook. Diokadu looked poised to do the same. Jenaro told Shartelle that the headquarters had all the necessary office equipment.

"Now I know I've given you a lot of work to do," Shartrelle said. "We'll handle whatever we can ourselves, but you know the country, you know the sources, and you know the people. I would like to check with you several times a day. I don't want to set up any regular breakfast appointments, because if you don't have anything to talk about, they get in the way. But you can expect me to call any time of day or night. I expect the same from you."

Diokadu laughed out loud. "I was laughing at myself," he said. "I expected a rather long—and interesting—theoretical discussion about the merits of the various planks in our platform. As a political scientist, I must say that this afternoon has been even more interesting than I imagined possible—and even more illuminating."

"Well, Doc, we've just begun the operation. This is our side. This is what we're going to do. It's not fancy, but it's good, sound political practice. It's exposure of the candidate. Now comes the even more interesting part of our operation."

"What's that?" Jernaro asked.

"We start planning the campaigns for the opposition," Shartelle said dreamily. "We start to whipsaw."

— 14 —

Shartelle did not go into the whipsaw operation that evening, explaining that he wanted "to study about it some more." Diokadu and Jenaro left, the former looking somewhat nervously at his list of things to do today and tomorrow. Jenaro roared off in his XK-E, apparently unconcerned.

"Those boys will do," Shartelle said. "They caught the spirit."

"I'll give you that *the* speech tomorrow."

"Time enough, Petey. We've had a pretty full day."

"It's getting fuller," I said. "We're having some more company."

A medium-sized man dressed in a white shirt, white walking shorts, calf-high white socks and black oxfords had turned into our driveway and was strolling towards the house. He carried a walking stick of twisted black wood that he used to knock a few pebbles out of his path. Shartelle and I went out on the porch to meet him.

He gave us a calm, speculative appraisal from eyes that had squinted into a lot of sun. As he drew near, I saw that the eyes were cool green.

"Evening," he said.

"Evening," Shartelle replied.

"I'm your neighbor," the man said. "Live just around the curve there. Thought I'd pay a social call. Downer said you were due."

"I'm Clint Shartelle and this is Pete Upshaw."

"John Cheatwood."

"Won't you come in and sit a spell, Mr. Cheatwood?"

"Thanks very much."

He dropped into one of the chairs in the living room, and held his black stick across his bare knees. He was about forty-five, I judged, fit-looking, lean, with a good strong face that appeared to have seen much of what the world has to offer.

"Mr. Upshaw and I were just about to have a drink, Mr. Cheatwood. I hope you'll join us."

"Thank you."

Shartelle yelled for the steward and after the drink-mixing ritual we leaned back in our chairs and waited for our neighbor to start the small talk if small talk were in order.

"Your first trip to Africa?" he asked.

"Very first," Shartelle said.

"Downer said you'd be running the political show for Akomolo."

"We're just advisers."

Cheatwood took a swallow of his drink. "It's giving us a bit of a headache," he said.

"How's that?"

"Quite likely be a bit of fuss between now and the election. Elections seem to stir them up and they sometimes get out of hand. But I think we'll manage well enough."

"Who's we?" I asked.

"Beg your pardon," Cheatwood said with an apologetic smile. "I should have mentioned it. The police here in the western region. I'm the Captain in charge."

Shartelle regarded our visitor with new interest. "You going to be in charge of the poll-watching, Captain?"

"Not really. Our job will be to collect the ballot boxes, make sure that they're properly sealed, and transport them to a safe place for counting. We're keeping the place a secret. The various parties will have monitors—or poll-watchers, if you prefer—at the voting spots."

"You expecting trouble?"

Cheatwood nodded his head. "A goodly amount, I'd say. Chaps down here always get excited over elections. They get carried away. And then there're the hooligans.

137

"Hooligans?"

"Quite. Each party has roving bands of paid thugs. They heckle the opposition, break up meetings, try to intimidate voters. Sometimes we have to break a few heads and put some in jail. Chief Akomolo's party, I should add, has its full cadre of hooligans. I suppose it's becoming part of the election apparatus. Tradition, perhaps."

"How do you handle them?" I asked.

Cheatwood warmed to his subject. He was a professional and he liked talking about it. "We have our roving squads, you see, and we're in constant touch with them by radio. These are specially-trained chaps. They have larger wicker shields and rather hefty sticks. They've been trained in mob dispersal and control. I'd say a dozen or so of them can break up just about any riot we can expect. They're extremely fit —none under six feet, by the way, and they enjoy their work."

"Where you expecting the most trouble?" Shartelle asked.

"Here in Ubondo—that's going to be a major trouble spot. Barkandu will be another, but that's out of my jurisdiction. In almost any of the small-to-medium towns you can expect an occasional flare-up. Not to worry, though. We'll keep it in hand."

"How do you see the election, Captain Cheatwood?"

He took another swallow of his drink. "That's what Downer asked me. I'm a policeman, not a bloody politician, but I'd say that you gentlemen have your work cut out for you."

"That's what we've been told."

Cheatwood set his drink down on a table. "I've been here fifteen years now. Came down from Ghana and before that I was in East Africa. Started out in Palestine during the trouble—just a boy then. But I've been through a few of these times when a country is approaching independence. And they all get just a bit violent. A few heads get cracked, some innocent and some not-so-innocent chaps get killed. My job is not to stop all that—which would be impossible—but to keep it to a minimum.

138

If we do that, we think we've done a fair job of work."

"You said you think we have our work cut out for us," I said. "Anything else you might add to that?"

"Well, a policeman hears all sorts of rumors. The hottest one buzzing around now is that Akomolo is spending half the Regional Treasury to buy the election with the help of your CIA. That one's making the rounds at the university. You could call it a typical one."

"But not true," Shartelle said.

Cheatwood waved his stick in a gesture of dismissal. "Of course not. For one thing, if the Premier's crowd wanted to tap the till, they wouldn't go through the Treasury. Too many checks. They'd go through the Regional Development Corporation: set up their own company and then award it a contract to build a school or hospital for twice what it should cost. The intellectual community at the university has a great deal to learn about finance, I'm afraid."

"And you're saying that the National Progressive Party doesn't?"

Cheatwood smiled. "If there are any tricks to fund-raising, I would say that the Albertian politicians mastered them long ago. But that's not my worry. I have another."

"What's that?" Shartelle asked the question as he got up to mix the drinks. He picked up Cheatwood's glass.

"Very light, please." He waited until Shartelle handed him the drink. "My worry is that I don't like surprises. Surprises are splendid, say around Christmas or on one's birthday, but they are a terrible nuisance if one's a copper." He stopped to taste his new drink. "And if one were a politician, I dare say."

"They can be bothersome," Shartelle said.

"Damn it all," Cheatwood said, "I'm afraid I'm not very good at this roundabout palaver."

"Captain Cheatwood, I'd say you were getting around to making a proposition. Now I don't care much for pretty talk, so if you got one, why don't you just say it right out loud?"

Cheatwood placed his drink on the table again and

leaned forward in the chair, his arms resting on his knees, his hands holding the twisted ebony stick. "I'll make it as plain as I possibly can, Mr. Shartelle. I gathered from your colleague, Mr. Downer, when he was here, that your job will be to produce some political innovations. He didn't know what they were, although he pretended to. He does talk a bit, I should add. Now I'm not concerned about your campaign strategy. My only concern is that should you employ some devices—and God knows what they would be—I would appreciate it very much if you would give me a general description of their nature. I assure you that anything you tell me will be held in strict confidence. I would also assure you that I am not setting myself up as a censor. It's merely that if your tactics are going to provoke a riot, I'd like a bit of warning so that I could plan the proper use of my chaps."

"We're not revolutionists, Captain," I said.

He shook his head slowly. "I'm not going to lecture you on the nature of the Albertians, Mr. Upshaw. During the fifteen years I've spent here, I think I've come to know them. And believe it or not, I like them. I just want to keep things as peaceful as possible during the next six weeks. Now then, I said that it is my opinion that neither policemen nor politicians are overly fond of surprises. If you agree to give me a bit of advance notice concerning your plans, then I—in turn—will give you the gen on what we hear. And we hear a good bit, I should add."

"Just one question, Captain. Are you making this same proposition to the other two major candidates?"

"No, Mr. Shartelle, I'm not. I am employed by the government of Western Albertia and my concern is for the affairs of this region. After independence, I doubt that I shall be about long, but I plan to leave with an unblemished record. If that sounds a trifle stuffy, forgive me. It's a policeman's way of thinking."

Shartelle nodded "I tell you what," he said slowly. "We'll brief you on what we're going to do and where. You keep us informed. And we'll both respect each other's confidence. Now which of us should make the T.L. first?"

140

"The what?"

"The Trade Last. It's an American expression that I haven't heard in years. Probably hasn't been used in years. But forget it; I'll go first."

It took about five minutes for Shartelle to give Cheatwood a rundown on the plans for the helicopters, buttons, drums, newspaper, and speaking schedule. He didn't mention the whipsaw operation.

Cheatwood listened well without fidgeting. His face was almost oblong, with a large chin that looked as if it would be painful to shave. His green eyes were fixed on Shartelle and while he listened, he sat as still as any man I'd ever seen.

"Now that we've taken you into the bosom of our family, Captain, maybe you can provide us with a little information that would prove useful."

Cheatwood leaned back in the chair and crossed his leg. He held the ebony stick up before him and stared at it.

"The Army," he said. "I have a few informers in its ranks, but none at the officer level. I did have some at the officer's level, but they were white. The last white officer received his discharge seven weeks ago. It came quite unexpectedly. But keep an eye on it, Mr. Shartelle."

"You talking about a coup, a takeover?"

"Not likely. The Army, especially since it is the first government organization to completely Albertianize itself, has gained a certain amount of political strength. It could toss that strength to the winner—or to someone who looked as if he were going to lose. There would be a high price to pay, of course."

"Interesting," Shartelle said.

"Yes, isn't it? As soon as I hear anything definite, I'll get in touch." Cheatwood rose and Shartelle and I got up, too. "By the way," he said, "you don't know of any CIA involvement in this thing, do you?"

"They don't confide in us," Shartelle said.

"No, I suppose not. But these rumors at the university are damned persistent. I might check out a few sources

141

in the eastern and northern regions; our Old Boy network is still alive—if gasping its last."

Shartelle grinned. "I've never worked a campaign hand-in-glove with the police before," he said. "Should be most interesting."

Cheatwood walked to the door, turned, and leaned on his stick. "You know, something just struck me."

"What?"

"I'm the last white in either the police or the Army."

"Think you'll be around long?"

"Not long, but as I said, the record will be clean."

"Unblemished," Shartelle said.

Cheatwood chuckled softly. "There's something else that's unique about me, you know."

"What?"

"I'm the last white in Albertia who can shoot an Albertian in line of duty." He chuckled again, but there wasn't much humor in it. "My God, what a way to wind up."

— *15* —

I picked up Anne Kidd that night around 8:30 after bribing William five shillings to drive for me. She lived in a so-so apartment near the school where she taught. Two other Peace Corps girls shared the place with her. The furniture was nothing special, but they had decorated the living room with bits and pieces of carved calabashes, native statuary, some Albertian-woven cloth, and a few good pieces of brass work. It looked fine—like a cross between Barkandu and Grand Rapids.

She kissed me lightly on the cheek in front of her room-mates, who were from the West Coast. One was from Los

Angeles, the other from Berkeley. The one from Berkeley had a merry look about her and I put her down in mental reserve for Shartelle should the need arise. The one from Los Angeles came out of the mold that they should have broken before the eighty-four millionth copy was run off. Not plain, but not pretty. Not gay, but not sad. She seemed to be pouting a bit because Anne was going out with a fellow.

I helped Anne into the back seat of the car. "William, this is Miss Kidd," I said.

"Hello, William."

"Madam," William said and gave her a big grin and threw an appreciative look at me. In town one day and already a date. His estimation of me was soaring.

"Where we go, Mastah?" William asked.

I turned to Anne. "Is there a nice, quiet air-conditioned bar in Ubondo?"

"Sure," she said. "One is in the Cocoa Marketing building. They keep it around sixty-five degrees, I think."

"Fine. Cocoa Marketing building."

I held her hand as William drove the car though the ill-lighted streets. The petty traders were still looking for a final sale, and their stands were illuminated with pressure lamps that gave off yellowish-orange flickering lights.

"How're your teeth?" I asked.

"Wonderful," she said. "He just had to clean them. See?" She smiled and showed them all. They were white and very straight.

"Are you thinking about them much?"

"Not as much as I am about you."

"Good clean thoughts?"

"Nope. Some are nice and dirty. I think I had an orgasm this afternoon, just thinking about you."

"You're not sure?"

"Not with that kind; I just started thinking and thinking and the first thing I knew I wanted to be with you and then it happened; or something did. Whatever happened, I liked it. I like thinking about you."

I kissed her then in the back seat of the Humber driving

through the streets of Ubondo. It was a long, deep kiss and we both were a little excited when we came up for air. William kept his eyes straight ahead.

We drove into the parking lot of the Cocoa Marketing building and took a slow elevator up to the third floor. The place was called the Sahara South and it was leased by a Lebanese gambler who—Anne told me—served the second-best dinner in town. I told her I'd take her only to where they served the best dinner and she said that it wasn't air-conditioned. I told her we would sit and sweat and eat well.

It wasn't cool in the Sahara South; it was plain cold. As far as I could see it was just another dimly-lighted cocktail lounge with a restaurant attached and a bar. We sat at the bar.

"You come here often?" I asked her.

"I can't afford it on $82.50 a month. Don't forget I'm living on that plus my supply of motivation, dedication and commitment."

"I'll buy then," I said.

We ordered gin and tonic. Anne shivered slightly in her white cotton dress. It had dark blue or black piping on it here and there and looked what I suppose is still called smart. She knew how to wear clothes.

"You didn't buy that dress on $82.50 a month," I said.

"You like it?"

"Very much."

"That's daddy's contribution to the Peace Corps—keeping me well-dressed. He was against the whole idea in the first place."

"You joining up?"

"No. The Peace Corps."

"Why?"

"Oh, he wasn't against the idea of helping. He just thought Americans should be paid more. He couldn't see sending them all over the world for what he calls 'pissant pay.' He's funny. He said if the people were needed, America ought to hire real pros—teachers, doctors, carpenters, bricklayers—what have you—and hire them at

144

the going scale and send them out to do what he said those kids will only make a stab at. I think I got my structure a little twisted there."

"I follow you," I said.

When the Peace Corps did as well as it did, he wouldn't change his mind. He said if they want to be martyrs, it's probably good for them. But we ought to have the other thing—the pro corps, he calls it—going, too. He kept talking to the AID people in Washington about it, but it never got anywhere."

"What's he do? Maybe you told me, but I've forgotten."

She took a sip of her drink. "That's cold. He does something with shopping centers. Builds them, I think. I asked him once and he said it was too complicated; that sometimes he didn't understand it himself. It's all something to do with selling land and then leasing it back. He just says he deals in land as quickly as he can because they're not making it any more."

We listened to the piped-in music for a while and watched the people. About half were Albertians, some dressed in robes, some in European-styled clothes. The rest were white or tan or pink or olive. There were the businessmen, the British, the car dealers, the insurance salesmen, and the boys just passing through Africa on hopes of turning a quick dollar. A tall young man with a surfer's haircut came into the bar and looked around. He smiled when he saw Anne and came over.

"Hello, Anne," he said.

She introduced him as Jack Woodring, head of the United States Information Service in Ubondo. I offered to buy him a drink and he accepted.

"I heard you were coming up," he said. "They called from the Consulate yesterday—or maybe it was today. Drop by anytime. After 2 P.M., the office is officially off duty and I have a refrigerator. It usually has a pitcher of martinis."

"We'll do that," I said.

"How goes the Peace Corps?"

"Fine," she said. "How's Betty?"

He shook his head. "She came down with something today and I had to go to this thing at Karl's by myself. Those boys are a little far out."

Anne turned to me. "Karl Haunhorst is a German who's gone native and specializes in Albertian art and culture. He gives a soirée once in a while. I went to one about four months ago."

"I'm the walking-talking example of U.S. culture in Ubondo, so I have to go," Woodring said. "That reminds me, I'm supposed to lodge an official complaint with you."

"Lodge away."

"Kramer sent me a rocket asking if you couldn't get the programming changed on the TV station."

"What's that got to do with Pete?"

"He's the official representative of DDT and DDT got the Western Region the second commercial television station in all of Africa. Or is it the third?"

"Second, I think."

"You mean you brought 'My Little Margie' to Albertia?"

"Not me—Duffy. He found a European syndicate that put up half the money to build the station."

"They've only got seventy-five sets in the whole damned country," Anne said.

"They're improving; there used to be only thirty-five."

"I don't get as excited about it as they do down in Barkandu," Woodring said. "Kramer's worried about the violence. I just worry over getting a travelogue about the Grand Canyon shown on what might be called prime time, if you stretched a point. But Kramer said couldn't something be done about the programming. For instance, on Monday there's 'Highway Patrol,' 'The Great Gildersleeve,' 'Richard Diamond,' and 'Meet McGraw.' On Tuesday, there's 'Father Knows Best,' 'The Man Called X,' 'Dragnet,' and 'The Lone Ranger.' On Wednesday, there's—"

"Duffy just bought them a package deal," I interrupted. "All the crap. Maybe next year will be better."

"They've ordered two thousand transistor sets, I hear," Woodring said.

"I wonder who'll repair them when they break down."

"I refuse to let it bother me," he said. "In another year or so they'll develop local programming and then it might serve some useful purpose. Although, damn it, I find myself leaving Wednesday nights free so I can watch 'Gunsmoke.'"

"It's on tonight," Anne said.

"You're right. I've got to go." He turned to me. "I'll tell Kramer I lodged the complaint with the proper authority."

"I'll carry it through to London."

"Be sure to drop by with your partner soon and we'll have a few. They told me his name, but I've forgotten it."

"Shartelle."

"Right." He spread his hands in a free and open gesture. "Drop by any time. If they're throwing rocks at us, just duck."

"We'll do it," I said and we shook hands. He said goodbye to Anne and left.

"He's a nice boy," she said. "They like him here."

"Who?"

"Funny. Both the British and the Albertians. He makes speeches all over the region, shows motion pictures, and when something nasty happens in the U.S., he calls a briefing session for the press."

"That ought to keep him hopping," I said.

"What's Mr. Shartelle like?"

I shook my head. "It has to be seen to be believed. Would you like to?"

She smiled quickly. "Sure. I want to see where you live."

I paid for the drinks and we took the elevator down to the parking lot where I found William asleep. "We'll go home and you can go to bed there," I told him.

"No drive Madam home?" he asked.

"I'll drive her home. A growing boy like you needs his rest."

"Sah!" he said and gave me the wide grin.

William turned into the driveway of the broad-eaved house and parked the car in front of the porch. He handed me the keys, said good night, and moved off towards his quarters.

I helped Anne out of the car. As we walked around it, we could hear Shartelle's voice: He was doing imitations and he had them down pat:

"You goin' out after Miss Kitty, Mr. Dillon?" That was Chester Proudfoot.

"Reckon I am, Chester. Those Greeley boys sometimes turn right mean." That was Marshal Matt Dillon.

"Gosh, Mr. Dillon, I like Miss Kitty and all, but she ain't nothin' but a whore lady."

"That's right, Chester, but she's the only whore lady in town."

I knocked on the folded-back door. "Marshal Dillon?" I said.

Shartelle was stretched out on the couch, a pillow tucked under his head. The television set was flickering in the corner of the room, the sound turned off. He swung his feet to the floor and rose.

"Hello there, Pete—ma'am," he said. "I was too busy doing all the parts and didn't hear you drive up."

"Anne, this is Clint Shartelle. Anne Kidd."

"It's my pleasure, Miss Anne," Shartelle said, making his slight but courtly bow.

He walked over to the television set and turned it off. "I'm certainly glad you folks decided to drop by," he said. "I've just watched 'The Halls of Ivy,' 'My Little Margie,' and I was going right good on 'Gunsmoke.'"

Anne took one of the chairs and I sat on the couch.

"You often do that?" she asked.

"You mean all the parts?"

"Yes."

Shartelle smiled down at her. "For a lonely man of my years, Miss Anne, it's a harmless enough pastime. And I can make the stories come out the way I want."

"He's forty-three," I said.

"Well, I was just fixing to have a drink," Shartelle said. "What you care for, Miss Anne?"

"Gin and tonic," she said.

148

"You need any help?" I asked.

"No. Before I sent old Samuel off to bed, I got him to show me where everything was kept. Just sit there and mind your young lady, boy."

Shartelle came back with three drinks and sat on the couch. His eyes roamed over Anne and he turned to me and said: "Pete, you said you had met an *attractive* young lady down there at the beach at Barkandu. You didn't mention the fact that you had met the prettiest girl I've ever seen in my life."

"My error," I said.

"Miss Anne, Pete tells me you're with the Peace Corps."

"Yes."

And then Shartelle turned it on and started her talking about the Peace Corps and her impressions of Albertia, her likes and dislikes, what she thought could be done to improve it, and what she thought its future would be. He was attentive, interested, and intelligent. Whenever she started to falter or hesitate, he gave her a gentle, verbal nudge and she continued.

Then Anne stopped talking and looked at him for a moment. "Mr. Shartelle, you've pumped me. I thought I was good at getting people to talk about themselves—to open up—but I see I could use a few lessons."

Shartelle laughed and rose, gave his seersucker vest a tug, and smoothed the lapels of his jacket. He picked up our glasses and moved to the dining table where the liquor was. "Miss Anne, you are not only the prettiest young lady I've ever seen, but also one of the most intelligent. And if old Pete here weren't such a good buddy, I just might squire you around myself."

He handed us the fresh drinks. Anne said: "Mr. Shartelle—"

"You just call me Clint, Miss Anne."

"Just what makes you think you and Pete can win this election for Chief Akomolo?"

Shartelle held up a hand. "No—no, you don't, sweet and pretty as you are. You're not going to get me started. Old Pete here's got to get up tomorrow and write us a *the*

149

speech and if you turned those big brown eyes of yours on me, and let that pretty little mouth drop open just a bit, just like you were tasting and savoring every word I said, why I'd be sitting here talking 'til daybreak. Two expert listeners in one house, honey, is plenty. You listen to Pete, here, if you want to put your listening cap on. Now there's a boy who needs some listening."

"Thanks," I said.

"Well, Pete, if you insist, I will start," he said.

"No—no, it's not really necessary. I could do with some listening."

"What's a *the* speech?" Anne asked.

"You tell her, Pete."

"A *the* speech—you can pronounce it 'thee' or 'thuh', it doesn't matter—is simply the major basic speech of a campaign. It sets the mood, the tempo, the tone. The candidate repeats it or parts of it with variations, throughout the campaign. But it is *the* speech. All candidates have one, and after they use it a few times, it becomes part of their personality. It fits them—because it's been tailored for them. They have to have it because if you make five to ten speeches a day, you can't have something new to say each time."

"And you're going to write this?"

"Uh-huh."

"How do you know what to say?"

"That's Pete's specialty, Miss Anne. It's a gift—like being able to play a piano by ear. Pete, I figure, hears the speech as he writes it. But at the same time, he's plotting its course, remembering how the candidate talks, what the major points are, when the peroration begins, and how to end it so that they still want more. Especially how to end it—right, Pete?"

"It's a gift. Like playing a piano by ear. In a whorehouse."

"I think it's wonderful," Anne said.

We talked a little more. Shartelle told Anne some of the latest political gossip from America and said he thought he'd met her daddy once at a national convention. After the drinks were finished, he rose.

"It's been a pure pleasure, Miss Anne, but I think I'll turn in. I've had a long day. I wouldn't leave now, unless I knew I could count upon the pleasure of your presence at breakfast." He bowed his slight, courtly bow and left as we said good night.

"You're officially invited," I said.

She laughed and shook her head slightly. "I've never heard it put so politely."

"Then you'll stay?"

"Do you want me to?"

"God, yes."

"It will be all right, won't it?"

"It will be fine."

I called Silex to lock up and we went out the front door and down the side of the house to the entrance that led to my room. We went to bed and made love for a long, sweet time. When I awoke early in the morning she was still there and I could never recall a day that had held such promise.

— *16* —

After breakfast, I had William drive Anne home. Shartelle started making notes to himself and I began to read the white papers that Dr. Diokadu had brought the previous afternoon. That kept us busy until the Rolls-Royce pulled up in front of the living-room door. The driver, an Albertian, got out and marched smartly up the steps, across the porch, and to the door where he stopped, and came to board-like attention. He was ex-Army.

"Mr. Shartelle, Mr. Upshaw?"

"Yes, sir," Shartelle said.

"Mr. Duncan's compliments, Sah, and would-you-do-him-the-honor-of-accepting-this-transport?" The last part was pure rote.

"Why, we'd be most honored," Shartelle said happily, slipping into his fresh seersucker jacket and giving his vest a slight tug. He got his black hat on his head at a proper angle, clamped a twisty cigar between his teeth, and we went out, down the steps, and into the back seat of His Excellency's Rolls-Royce.

The liveried chauffeur closed the door, went around to the right-hand side where he slipped behind the wheel, and skillfully backed the car to the turnaround spot in the driveway. We rolled grandly down the drive and out into the street, on our way to Government House.

"Now ain't this fine, Petey—couple of country boys sitting up tall and straight in the back end of His Excellency's Rolls-Royce limousine." He shook his head in frank admiration of the fate that had befallen him, gave his cigar a couple of puffs, and tapped a little ash into a convenient tray. "You ever been in a Rolls-Royce before, Pete?"

"I've been in Duffy's Bentley. It's the same car, but it's not really the same."

"What you reckon His Excellency wants to see us about? You recollect his name?"

"Sir Charles Blackwelder. Call him Sir Charles."

"Happy to," Shartelle said. "Be most happy to. I believe he wants to see us about the election and maybe give us a little advice. I believe I'll do him the honor of listening. Man who's been out here as long as he has might just have picked up an idea or two."

The driver steered the big car expertly through the crowded streets of Ubondo, apparently looking neither left nor right, and sounding the mellow horn only at the occasional goat or chicken who failed to recognize the official limousine. The traffic policewoman whom we had spotted the day before saw the Rolls approach and stopped cars from moving in any direction. The driver seemed to take no notice, but Shartelle grinned broadly.

Government House was built on the highest point in

Ubondo, on the peak of one of the hills that ringed the town. The Rolls sped up a winding, metaled road that was bordered by carefully tended flowers and shrubs. The road doubled back on itself several times, and when we were on its outside edge the view of Ubondo was spectacular. Not beautiful. That town would never be beautiful. But it was spectacular.

"Looky there, Pete," Shartelle said. "That sight just makes me shake all over with nastiness...just like I'd chewed up four aspirins."

"It's some view," I replied.

Government House was two stories high, painted white with a red tile roof, and it seemed to have grown from a rather simple, oblong structure into an imposing mansion complete with porte cochere where the driver parked the car. He hopped out quickly and ran around to open the door for us. As we got out, a man of about Shartelle's age started down the steps. He had a smile underneath his brush mustache. He moved down the steps quickly, and held his back stiffly straight. Either he wore a corset, I decided, or he had spent twenty years in the British Army. "I'm Ian Duncan," he told us. "The A.D.C. Let's see, you'd be Mr. Shartelle—" They shook hands. "And Mr. Upshaw." We shook hands. "If you'll just come along, I'll let you sign the book and then I'll announce you to H.E."

We walked through fifteen-foot-high doors into a hall with a ceiling that was even higher. An Albertian clerk dozed over what seemed to be a reception desk. At one side was a stand with a large guestbook. Both Shartelle and I signed and marked the date. Duncan looked on with what seemed to be interest. He nudged the clerk awake and then said: "It's down the hall and to the right." He walked briskly ahead of us, his head back, his chest out, chin in. His heels clicked loudly on the tile floor as we moved past a series of photographs of what I took to be former governors of the region dressed in full regalia. There were some tall-backed chairs along the wall that looked as if no one had sat in them since 1935. Duncan came to a set of twin doors, also fifteen feet high and four feet wide. He grasped the polished brass handles firmly, gave them an expert twist, and shoved both doors open simultaneously. Then he moved smartly to our left and stood parallel with the door. He didn't look at us; he looked straight ahead, and his voice could have been heard across any good-sized parade ground.

"Mr! Clinton! Shartelle! and Mr! Peter! Upshaw! from the United! States! of America!"

Shartelle and I later agreed that there should have been music. Maybe "Dixie" or "America, the Beautiful." There was a good sixty-foot walk to the far end of the long room where the gray-looking man sat quietly at the carved oak desk. Shartelle snapped straight up and I noticed my own muscles responding as we walked that sixty feet, the longest sixty feet in the world. From the side of his mouth, Shartelle whispered: "My, ain't they got style!" As we grew near we could see Sir Charles Blackwelder regarding us with a faintly quizzical expression, as if we were some new and not too reputable neighbors come to call for the first time. He rose to his feet when we were fifteen feet away. There were three comfortable-looking chairs arranged in front of his desk.

The introductions were made by Duncan who sat in the chair farthest to the left. Shartelle sat in the middle and I was placed on the right. Sir Charles lounged in his highbacked executive type chair and smiled at us. It was a slight smile. There were a lot of lines in his face, I noticed, especially around the eyes and the corners of his mouth. It was a good, long wedge-shaped face with gray hair brushed to one side to cover a bald spot. His eyebrows were straight and dark and his eyes were a curious dark blue. He wore a white suit, white shirt, and a green tie fastened in a large knot. There was some kind of signet ring on his left hand.

"Politics, I understand, brings you gentlemen to Albertia," Sir Charles said.

"That's correct, sir," Shartelle said.

"At first I thought it strange that Chief Akomolo should pick an American firm. But then I thought it over, and it wasn't strange at all. Not at all. He hates us, you know. Oh, not individually perhaps—but as a collective whole. The man simply doesn't like the English. How do you get on with him?"

"So far, very well," Shartelle said. I decided that he could be spokesman.

"You're an expert on politics, I believe, Mr. Shartelle?"

"I earn a living at it."

"And you are a public relations expert, Mr. Upshaw?"

"Yes."

"Well, I should say that you both have your work cut out for you during the next six weeks. I can't, for the life of me, predict who's going to win and I really can't see that it will make much difference."

"Only to the winner—and the losers," Shartelle said. "It usually makes a great deal of difference to them."

"To be sure. But I'm not at all convinced that it will make much difference to Albertia as a country after independence. Of course, independence here will be more or less routine. The ceremonies will be kept to a minimum. It will happen three days after the results are in and the winner is acclaimed—or the coalition—or what have you. Then there will be merely a simple formality of handing over the reins of government. I shall be going home before that; I doubt that I shall be back to see it. I'd like to, really."

I found something to say to that, and Shartelle asked: "How long have you been in Albertia, Sir Charles?"

"I came out in 1934. I was posted up north as an assistant district officer. It was different then. I'm not saying it was better, mind you, but it was different. It seems—and perhaps this is just memory playing tricks—but it seems to me that my Albertian friends and I had some rather good times together then. We would laugh more, have jolly parties, occasionally get drunk together, and sometimes I would put a few of them in jail for a day or so. And occasionally they'd play some rather unpleasant tricks on me, but on the whole we got along famously. Out in the bush.

"But tell me, Mr. Shartelle, why do you think your American brand of politics will work here in Albertia?"

"It's not a brand, Sir Charles. It's merely politics."

"And you think it applies to Albertians as well as to Americans—and say the English?"

"It's a theory that'll undergo a severe test six weeks from now," Shartelle said. "Perhaps I could talk about it more learnedly then."

Blackwelder smiled. The aide-de-camp smiled and so did I. Sir Charles leaned far back in his chair, made a steeple of his fingers, and gazed up at his high, high ceiling. "Mr. Shartelle, I have been here for more than thirty years. I speak two of the dialects and I can get by in Hausa. What I'm saying is this: I've lived among these people all my adult life, and yet I don't think I know them. I don't think that I ever know what they're thinking."

"Well, sir," Shartelle said, warming to his favorite subject, people, "I think you underestimate yourself. I'd take you to be a shrewd judge of character, one who can tell pretty much about a man after talking to him for fifteen minutes or so. Do you agree?"

Blackwelder laughed. "I'm most susceptible to flattery, Mr. Shartelle."

"Now I didn't mean that, Sir Charles. I didn't mean that at all. But I'd say that maybe you're too close to the Albertians. Man who spends more than thirty years with anybody is bound to take on some of their notions and characteristics. I'd say that if I were you, and wondered what the Albertians were thinking, then I'd ask myself what I'm thinking, and what I *would* be thinking if I were them. Then I'd just about have it wrapped up."

"I couldn't possibly think the way that they do."

"Well, I don't think you're thinking the way most British think. At least not the ones I've met."

"Neither fish nor fowl, eh?" He smiled. "I'll devote some time to considering it—from both an English and Albertian point of view. Still, Mr. Shartelle, your job is to get votes for Chief Akomolo. How do *you* appeal to the typical Albertian voter—how do you know what he wants, how he'll react, or what influences his tribal feelings and natural rulers may have on him?"

Shartelle thought a moment. "I don't, Sir Charles. All I know is how people react. I think I know what they want because I believe everyone wants essentially the same thing—a sense of being, if you get right down to it. I'm betting a reputation that I've taken considerable pains to build that people, given a choice, will choose what will cause them the least pain. No majority that I've ever known of has voted for personal sacrifice. It may have ended up that way, but they didn't vote for it to begin with. No, they vote for those candidates who they think will cause them the least pain—either economic or social or emotional."

Blackwelder nodded. "Interesting," he murmured. "Pragmatic, to say the least." He rose. The interview was over. "If there is anything I can do to make your stay more comfortable, please let me know." He moved around the desk to shake hands with us. "I can only give you one word of advice, gentlemen. Don't stay in Albertia too long. West Africa, especially Albertia, has a way of getting into a man's blood. It's an unlovely spot, God knows, although during the harmattan it's not bad farther north. Cooler, you know. But there's something about this country that creeps into the very marrow and keeps drawing one back. Ju-ju, perhaps—eh, Ian?" Duncan smiled dutifully. "Well, goodbye."

"Goodbye," we said. Sir Charles Blackwelder walked behind his carved oak desk and sat down. When we reached the door, I glanced back. He didn't seem to have much to do.

Once outside, Duncan offered cigarettes which both Shartelle and I accepted. "Haven't seen the old boy so talkative in weeks," Duncan said. "I'm glad you chaps could drop around —although Upshaw here doesn't do much talking."

"He's just courteous to his elders, Mr. Duncan," Shartelle said.

"Well, I suppose you'll be wanting to get back or I'd

invite you to have a cup of tea."

Shartelle glanced at his watch. "We have an appointment at eleven-thirty. We'll make it another time."

Duncan walked us to the Rolls-Royce where the same liveried driver held the door. We said goodbye and shook hands. The driver closed the door with a solidly-satisfying Rolls-Royce thunk and ran around to the wheel. We started the drive back home. Shartelle gave his usual close attention to the street scene. "I gotta get down here, Pete, and sort of sniff around. Get too far away from it sitting out there in the house. Got to Josh around with them, find out what they're thinking."

"Do it this afternoon. I'm going to be writing."

"Might. Might just."

"Wonder what Dekko wants?"

"Reassurance, probably. Just a little conversation."

"Maybe he'll stay for lunch."

Shartelle grunted. "Ought to give the man more credit than that."

"You're right."

Although we were back at the house by a quarter-past eleven, Chief Dekko was already there, comfortably seated in one of the chairs, a glass of squash in his hand. He had on a fresh set of robes. This time they were orange with white embroidery.

Shartelle watched the Rolls drive away, a little regretfully, I thought. "They do it up nice, don't they, Pete?" he had said on the way back. "You and me walking down that long, long room to where that nice old man sat behind that fancy desk. And that aide-de-camp just bellering out our names like we were junketing senators. You could have heard him over in the next county. I like it. I swear I shouldn't, but I like it."

"All we needed was a little music when we started down the room."

"Maybe 'Dixie' played in march time with a big brass section."

"I'd settle for that."

Dekko rose when we came into the living room and

gave us a warm smile. "I am early and you are on time. That is good. How was Sir Charles?"

"He looked well, Chief," Shartelle said.

"How does he think the election is going—or did he offer an opinion?"

"He asked us more than we asked him, I'd say. He didn't seem to have spotted any trend—one way or other."

Dekko nodded his big, fine head. "I was talking to Chief Jenaro last night after he left you. I understand that you have arranged for two helicopters so that the Leader and I may visit more villages and towns."

"And separately," Shartelle said. "You're running for Premier of the Western Region. Wouldn't do much good if Chief Akomolo went to the center and became Federal Premier unless you had your own spot carved out here in the West."

Dekko nodded. "Then you think I should confine myself exclusively to the West?"

"No. Now I don't mean to flatter you, Chief, nor do I mean any disrespect for Chief Akomolo, but you make a hell of a fine appearance, one that will help the ticket in general. I want you to get as much exposure as you can. That'll mean a dozen, maybe fifteen speeches a day." He smiled at the big Albertian. "I think you're stout enough to stand that for six weeks."

"Now about the speeches—" Dekko began.

"Pete?"

"You'll have a basic speech tomorrow morning," I said. "This will be written especially for you—tailored to your style and method of talking or speaking. If read in its entirety, it should take approximately an hour. But it will be so written that sections of it can be used as five-minute, fifteen-minute, and half-hour speeches. You'll probably be using the five-and fifteen-minute speeches more than anything else."

"That's true," Dekko said.

"After you give it a few times, it will become your speech. You will memorize it, not consciously, but you'll soon find that you won't have to refer to the text. You'll also find phrases that are particularly appealing not only to you, but to your audiences. So you'll begin to edit the speech to suit your audience. I would say that you have a keen audience sense, so you'll be constantly editing. However, the speech is always there if you find yourself in hostile territory and want to go on record."

Shartelle nodded towards me. "He's a pro, Chief."

"It sounds as if you have been giving its preparation a great deal of thought, Mr. Upshaw."

"I have," I lied.

"The campaign starts officially on Monday," Chief Dekko said. "I merely wanted the opportunity to chat with you for a few moments. As you realize, the outcome is of grave importance."

"It has our complete attention," Shartelle said. "I think that both you and Chief Akomolo should devote all of your time to the task of active campaigning. The details— the mechanics of electioneering should be left to us. That's why you've hired us. In Chief Jenaro and Dr. Diokadu, I think we have two invaluable associates."

Chief Dekko gave Shartelle a long, steady look. "You are a most reassuring man, Mr. Shartelle. And a most glib one. I don't trust many men completely. Yet I trust you. And Mr. Upshaw," he added politely.

"I believe we merit that trust, Chief. We're down here to help win you an election. I think we have a good chance."

"Do you really? Why?"

"Because things are developing," Shartelle said. "It's part of the mechanics of the campaign and I'd rather you get out and let the folks get a good look at you than concern yourself with what you pay us to worry about."

Dekko nodded. There was the finality of agreement in his nod. "That makes much sense." He rose. I asked him to stay for lunch. He declined—a bit hastily, I thought.

"We'll be in touch with you in the morning with the speech," I said. "You'll also have ten-to fifteen-minute speeches on each of the key issues. I think I can get those to you by Saturday."

Dekko gave us a half-salute and bounded down the

steps to his car. He moved fast in the noonday sun. Shartelle sighed and leaned back in his chair. "I swear, Pete, I'm turning into a morning drinker, but there's nothing I'd like better than a tall gin and tonic. You want to yell?"

I yelled for Samuel and he gave me an answering "Sah," from the depths of the kitchen. He came out in his khaki uniform; he reserved his whites for serving meals and tea.

After he served us the drinks and we both had long sips, Shartelle said: "I think we'd better get Jimmy Jenaro and Doc Diokadu over here about teatime. I want to start it."

"The whipsaw?"

"Yes."

"We'd better get Duffy on the phone for the buttons, too."

"That's going to take some doing."

"Let him worry about it," I said. "It's cool in London."

"Let me try that phone," Shartelle said. "I think I got me an idea.

He picked up the phone and waited for the male operator to come on. "How you today, sir, this is Mr. Shartelle.... That's good.... Now how's your family?... That's fine.... Yes, my family's fine, too.... Now I'd like to make a long distance call to London, England.... Think you can handle that for me? Why, that sure is good of you.... I bet you do handle a lot of them.... Now I want to call Mr. Padraic Duffy at this number." Shartelle gave the operator the number. "What's your name? All right, Mr. Ojara, now if you'd just get me that number in London and call me back? Fine. Now I want to make a local call before we do that—is that all right? Fine." He gave the operator Jimmy Jenaro's number. He made the appointment for five o'clock that afternoon. Jenaro said he would reach Dr. Diokadu. Shartelle hung up. He turned to me and grinned. "When I get through with the Albertian telephone system, Petey, we're going to have the best service in the country."

"I believe you. But before Duffy gets on the line, I've got an idea."

"Good."

"Buttons are fine—but we need something else. Something useful, but cheap."

Shartelle nodded. "Combs won't quite make it down here because of the length of the hair. What you got in mind?"

"Folding credit card holders—the plastic kind with the candidate's message stamped on in gold."

"Not bad—but why?"

"Samuel was showing me some of his letters of reference this morning. Albertians apparently set great store by them. But he had no place to keep them—except his tin box. Now everybody has something—a driver's license, a tax receipt, letters of reference. Just imagine letting one of those credit card holders—the ten-paneled jobs—drop down to show off your important papers."

"How many, Pete?"

"They can't be as plentiful as the buttons."

"Right. Sort of premiums for the good boys."

"Uh-huh."

"How many?"

"Say a million? They cost about two, three cents each, I remember."

"How much you reckon they weigh?"

"Ounce?"

"Million ounces—" Shartelle stared briefly up at the ceiling. "Okay. I got it."

The telephone rang five minutes later. It was long distance from London. Shartelle held it while the operators talked back and forth. "Thanks a lot, Mr. Ojara," he told the Albertian end.

"That you, Pig?...Yes, I can hear fine....Yes, everything's going just swell....Now, look, Pig, the reason I called is we need some supplies. You got your pencil? Fine. Okay, I need ten yards of seersucker delivered to Jimmy Jenaro's tailor in London. You can get it from a mill I know down in Alabama." He gave Duffy the name of the mill. "No, that ain't all, Pig. I got some more....You got your order pad ready? Okay. I want ninety-four tons of buttons and thirty-one tons of plastic credit card holders all printed up fancy." He held the phone away from his ear. From across the room I could hear the squawk.

"Why, Pig, I guess you'll have to get them in the States . . . and you better get that fancy art director of yours to draw me up some nice-looking buttons. I don't want no teensy ones that you have to squint up to see. I want me some aggressive buttons that just jump out at you. . . . The slogan's 'I Go Ako'. . . . He don't like it, Pete."

"Tell him the Leader thought it up."

"Old Chief Akomolo thought it up himself. Well, now, Pig—*I* like it, Pete likes it, and Chief Akomolo likes it. So I don't give a damn whether you like it or not. I want the party symbol on that button, to—the rake and the hoe thing. . . . Well, if you can't get them in England, I tell you what to do. You get that art director to take the next plane to New York. When he gets to New York you tell him to call one of the brothers up in Rochester and place two million with them. Then place a million with Pittsburgh and another two million with Los Angeles. Flying Tigers will start moving west to east, picking up the Los Angeles stuff first because they usually print faster. Now I want those buttons here by the end of next week—at least partial shipment. And you tell that art director of yours to tell each one of those Jaspers that Clint Shartelle ain't never going to buy another button from them unless they bust their ass. You hear, Pig? Now how about the folding credit card cases? Okay. You'll take care of that. . . . Why, everything's just smooth as grease, Pig. We're visiting around and Pete's writing speeches and everybody is just as happy. . . . You ever check out those boys from Renesslaer who're operating up north? Okay. We should get it today then. One of them has *what* name? Wait'll I tell Pete. No—everything's fine. We'll be in touch if we need something. Goodbye, Pig." He hung up. The phone rang almost immediately.

Shartelle picked it up. "It went through very fine, Mr. Ojara. I certainly appreciate your efforts. . . . I'd say you're about the best long distance operator I've come across. . . . Thank you again."

He sighed and hung up the phone. Then he chuckled. "Duffy's checked out the opposition that's up with old Alhaji Sir. You know, the four boys from Renesslaer."

"And?"

"I don't know. It just makes me feel sort of old."

"What?"

"One of them is named Franchot Tone Calhoun."

— *17* —

After a lunch of fried liver, fried potatoes, Brussels sprouts, and some kind of pudding that Shartelle and I scorned, I gathered up Dr. Diokadu's white papers, picked up the Lettera 22, and isolated myself in the back, far bedroom, the one that had the outside entrance. I read the papers over quickly again. Then I ran the points through my mind, looking for the lead—the news nugget that a reporter would start his story with. When I found it, I pounded out a two-page story—straight AP style. That served as an outline, and it would also serve as a news release the first time the speech was given in its entirety.

I adjusted another mental screw, and recalled Akomolo's speech patterns, his phrasing, his favorite consonants. He said p's well—so I decided to use a lot of p's—populace, progressive, practical, primary, purposeful, and paramount. I discarded paramount. Nobody would know what it meant. Use people instead. When Chief Akomolo spoke, he paused slightly on the p's—giving them a soft, plopping sound that wasn't at all unattractive.

He also liked short sentences. Or at least he spoke in them. So I would write his speech in short sentences. I decided to vary them from nine to twenty words. None would be longer. Because he spoke in a rather pedantic manner, he would have to use active verbs—words that would say more than the sayer.

I adjusted the mental screw some more, tuning in Chief Akomolo, and started to write. I wrote steadily for two hours and then stopped and went back into the kitchen for coffee. On my way back, I noticed a note from Shartelle that read: "Gone to town to pluck a grass root or two. Be back by 4:30 or 5."

I went back to the far room, sipped the coffee, and started banging away at the typewriter again. The speech flowed easily and I heard Akomolo saying it as I wrote. That always helps. I wrote twenty pages in five hours. I spent another half hour editing. That was it. *The* speech was done. I picked it up and carried it into the living room. Shartelle was back, stretched out in a chair, a tall drink in his hand.

"How were the grass roots?" I asked.

"Just tolerable, Pete."

"What are you drinking?"

"Iced tea. I stopped by our one and only supermarket and picked up a package of the instant stuff." He held up his hand in warning. "Don't worry, boy, I was loyal to the firm; I bought the right brand. Then I got me some fresh mint from a mammy trader and I sneaked back into the kitchen while old Samuel was off on his afternoon siesta and mixed us up a jugful. You want a glass?"

"I'll get it," I said. "Where'd you put it?"

"Sit down, boy, and rest yourself. I heard that typewriter clacking away and I wouldn't have disturbed you for the world." Shartelle went back into the kitchen and returned with a glass of tea. "Not bad with the fresh mint in it," he said. "Now when old Samuel comes in with the regular tea, we'll just pretend to drink some."

"That's what I like about you, Shartelle," I said. "You're hard as nails."

I tried the tea. "Not bad. Here, you want to read this?" I handed him the press release and the speech.

"Been looking forward to it," he said.

Shartelle read faster than any man I've ever seen, and

165

I've seen some who can clip off 3,500 words a minute. I had written twenty pages. It would take fifty minutes to deliver the entire thing if it were read at a normal pace. Because he spoke slowly, it would take Chief Akomolo longer. Shartelle read it in three minutes. When he got through, he shook his head in admiration.

"You're some speech writer, Petey. Why, I could hear the old chief up there just a-ploppin' his p's as pretty as you please. And the lead's good, too. It ought to get him some mileage."

"What did you think of the agricultural section?" I asked slyly. Nobody could read that fast.

"The direct subsidy plan is presented in a much clearer fashion than Doc Diokadu has it in his white paper. You got it down so clear and plain that anybody can understand it, if he can understand English. It's a damned good speech, Pete. One of the best *the* speeches I've come across in a long time."

"Thanks. Where'd you learn to read that fast?"

"Why, when I was living with my daddy, he used to follow the market pretty close when he had something to follow it with. And he subscribed to all the papers—I mean all: *The Wall Street Journal, The Journal of Commerce, Barron's, The New York Times, The Chicago Tribune,* and all the farm magazines, 'cause he studied the futures right smart, too. Well, my job was to read them for him and clip out anything that might be of interest. Now I just didn't read fast enough for all that. So there was this ad in *Doc Savage?* How to read faster and better in ten easy lessons?" There were those rising inflections again. I nodded.

"Well, I sent off for that course about the time that I sent for old Charles Atlas's dynamic tension. I got so I could skim the *Times* in ten minutes—that's what I used to practice on —and read every word damned near."

"How's your comprehension?"

"It was bad at first, but it got better and better. Now it's pretty fair, I'd say."

"How do you do it?"

"Why, there's nothing to it. You just start yourself off by reading in a diagonal line down the page left to right and pretty soon you're taking the whole thing in at a glance. It's come in handy sometimes when all you had is a minute to sneak a look at the opposition's campaign plans as they're being taken down in the elevator from headquarters on the fifteenth floor to the mimeograph room on the fourth."

"I imagine."

The XK-E was shifted down into second for the drive and Jenaro roared it up to a stop in front of the doorway with his usual flair and disregard for the gravel. I had seen Ojo that morning run across a piece of gravel with his new lawnmower. He had inspected the blades for fifteen minutes and was down on his hands and knees for an hour looking for more rocks.

Jenaro looked as if he had just come off the eighteenth at Pebble Beach. He wore a windbreaker with arms specially cut to allow for a free swing of the club, a pale green turtle neck sweater of what looked to be soft woven cotton, chino slacks, cordovan golf shoes, and on his head he had a rain hat that matched the fabric of his jacket. A set of clubs nestled in the left-hand seat of the Jaguar whose top was down as usual.

Jenaro bounded up the steps and slipped off his spiked shoes before coming into the house. He looked happy. "I just shot a thirty-two on nine holes, sand greens and all."

"Sounds good," I said.

"Club record's thirty-one. I'll bust it one of these days."

"You look hot, Jimmy," Shartelle said. "Take off your jacket and let me hang it up for you."

"Thanks." Shartelle took the jacket and hung it over the back of one of the dining-room chairs.

"In time for tea again?"

"I hear him fooling around in the kitchen," Shartelle said. "I reckon you are."

"If you could talk him out of a cold beer, I'd be glad to give you a report."

Samuel came in with the tea and Shartelle, with a note

167

of apology, asked him to bring Chief Jenaro a cold bottle of beer. Samuel said "Yes, Sah," but his heart wasn't in it.

After a long draft of beer, Jenaro sighed, belched and wiped off his mouth with the back of his hand. "Diokadu will be along in a moment. He had to pick up some papers, as usual. But I might as well tell you how far I got." He reached into his hip pocket and took out a small notebook.

"First—the fans. I spent an hour with the Minister of Economic Development and his Permanent Secretary. It took me fifteen minutes to sell them on the idea and forty-five minutes to convince the Minister that they all couldn't be manufactured in his village. The plans and specifications have already been drawn up and they've got a team of fieldmen fanning out across the country. We'll have our first sizable order in by late next week. Okay?"

"Good," Shartelle said.

"Two—distribution. I spent last night at party head-quarters and I've lined up the distribution for every-thing—fans and buttons. It's complicated and unless you want me to go into details, I won't. I'll just guarantee you that it will work —and work fast most of the time. We truck them some places; we fly them others. We've got a Dakota—you know, one of the old C-47's—on standby and it'll take a load any place we want—as well as trans-port some of the party faithful if we need a claque. Okay?"

"Good."

"Third item: helicopters. I've got two of them laid on to arrive here Sunday, late afternoon. The goddamned oil company thinks it'll have mineral rights to the whole country when the Leader goes to the center. I promised them everything but money, and they weren't interested in that. Two pilots—one South African and one American. I figure the South African can go with Dekko, who's big enough to make him think twice about any smart cracks."

"Good," Shartelle said. "What kind of helicopters?"

Jenaro consulted his notes again. "The big ones. Two old Sikorsky S-55's. Big jobs. They'll carry eight plus the pilot. Should have two pilots, but we couldn't swing it.

I've got a list of the oil company's refueling stations. They're going to let us use them. But we'll have to pay for the gas. I agreed."

"Damned good," Shartelle said. He was beginning to grin broadly now.

"What did you think I've been doing—screwing off on the golf course?"

"Go on, Jimmy, you're doing great."

"The newspaper. I talked to the guy who used to work on the Santa Fe *New Mexican* and he's hot for it—for a price. We settled on fifty quid a week which is about forty more than he ever made in his life, but not to hear him tell it."

"When you're in a spot, they can smell it," Shartelle said.

"This guy could, but he's also enthusiastic. I gave him *carte blanche* to recruit a staff, make arrangements for the printing, and I'll handle the distribution through headquarters. We'll give it away, right?"

"Right," Shartelle said.

"Okay. As I said, the guy's enthusiastic. I don't know exactly what he's talking about, but I didn't let on since I'm Minister of Information. I wrote it down and I thought I'd check it with Pete, here. He wants to put out an eight-page five-column tabloid, using horizontal makeup, with flush left heads, no column rules, no cut off rules, lots of art and air, and he wants to use heavy condensed Tempo and Tempo medium for the heads, 10 on 11 Times Roman for the body type, with the leads going to 11 on 12, all set on an 11½ pica measure. I think."

Shartelle looked at me. "What do you think, Pete?"

"He knows what he's doing. It'll be mighty pretty. Maybe he can write, too."

"Claims that he can and he's hot to do some exposés about the north and old Alhaji Sir as Clint calls him."

Shartelle rose and began to pace the room. He would go as far as the television set in the corner, turn, and stride over to the bookshelf divider that separated the living room from the dining area.

"Who's going to give him the party line?" he asked Jenaro.

"I will. Anything you furnish me in the way of speeches and news releases goes straight to him, special priority."

"You've got distribution licked?"

"Yes."

"What're you going to call it?"

"*The People's Voice.* It was his idea," Jenaro said.

"Maybe he can't write after all," I said.

"Okay," Shartelle said. "Let's do it."

"Last item—the drums. I only got started on that and then Diokadu took over. He should be here in a second."

It was five minutes before Dr. Diokadu arrived, bustling into the living room with his now-familiar sheaf of papers under his arm. "As usual, I am late," he said. "But I am not as late as usual."

"Tea?" Shartelle asked.

"Please."

I poured.

"We've just been hearing a report from Jimmy here, Doc, and things seem to be moving right along," Shartelle said, lighting himself another twisty, black cigar as he resumed his pacing of the room.

Diokadu drank his tea gratefully and then set the cup and saucer down. He pulled out a legal pad of yellow paper, flipped through a few pages of notes, found the ones he wanted, and then looked up expectantly. "Do you want my report on the drums or the artists first?"

"The artists."

"Right. A committee calling itself the 'Albertian Artists and Writers for Akomolo' was formed last night in Barkandu. On the steering or founding committee are one actor, one poet, two novelists, and two artists. They're all fairly well-known both here and, to a certain extent, in England."

"How much did it cost?"

"One hundred pounds each and each agreed to recruit five new members."

"This week?" Shartelle asked.

"This week."

"Good. Now the drummers."

"It's set. It took most of the day, really. I was on the telephone from nine this morning until just a few minutes ago. I divided the country into fifteen rough areas and then selected a principal drummer in each area. The message will be telephoned to him nightly—or however often we wish to employ him. He in turn will get in touch with the drummers in his particular section. Each of the fifteen principal drummers was willing to settle for two-hundred-and-fifty pounds. Out of this they will take care of the drummers in their section."

"How soon they ready to start?" Shartelle asked.

"Almost immediately. I told them probably Monday or Tuesday."

"Good."

Shartelle stopped his pacing and slumped into an easy chair, his long legs stuck out in front of him, his ankles crossed. "Jimmy," he said, "you know who's spying on you, don't you."

"Oh, sure. From the north it's the present Parliamentary Secretary in the Ministry of Agriculture. He told me he's really working for us, but has to keep up his contacts in the north to be effective. I think they pay him more."

"He's an obnoxious little man," Diokadu said and sniffed.

"How about the east? Who's feeding them information?"

"A boy in my own Ministry," Jenaro said. "I keep an eye on him."

"Uh-huh. Now then, if I were to send off two telegrams to Duffy in London, do you think you could arrange for copies of them to fall into the hands of these fellows— maybe a day or two before Duffy got them?"

Jenaro smiled. "A specialty of the house."

Shartelle turned to me. "Pete, can you get that little old typewriter of yours in here plus the Orphan Annie code ring? We're going to send Hiredhand a secret message."

I brought the typewriter in. "Now then," Shartelle said. "I want you to code us up a message asking Duffy to find

171

us a firm that will do skywriting down here in Albertia between now and election day."

"Skywriting? I don't buy that, Shartelle."

"Now, boy, you don't have to. You just code us up that telegram."

I shrugged and thought a minute as I slipped a sheet of paper into the typewriter. Then I wrote it, took it out of the machine, and handed it to Shartelle. Diokadu and Jenaro looked puzzled. I thought I was beginning to understand. The message read:

HIREDHAND: IMPERATIVE SECURE SERVICE TOPSIDE SCRIBBLERS ALBERTIAWISE. SCARFACE ENTHUSIASTIC. SHORTCAKE CONVINCED LOCAL SCRAMBLE MAKEORBREAK DEPENDS THEIR AVAILABILITY. CONFIRM SOONEST ENDIT SCARAMOUCHE.

Shartelle read it and grinned. "I don't think it would fool Punjab or the Asp," he said. "But it might cause old Sandy to study a bit." He passed it over to Jenaro, who read it and handed it to Dr. Diokadu.

"I'm not quite sure—" Dr. Diokadu began.

Shartelle held up his hand. "Just a minute, Doc, and I'll give you a rundown on the whole thing. I want to get Pete here to bang out another one while he's got the code in his head."

"That wasn't really necessary, Shartelle," I said. "In fact it was goddamned inexcusable."

"Purely unintentional, Petey, but come to think of it, not bad for a pun."

"What pun?" Dr. Diokadu asked.

"Code in his head," I said.

"Oh, yes...yes. Jolly good."

"What do you want from Duffy this time, Clint?" I asked.

"Need me a Goodyear-type blimp."

"Sweet Christ."

I put in another sheet of the paper, thought a few seconds, and hammered out our second secret coded message of the day. Even Sandy would get this one at first glance.

I handed it to Shartelle who read it and passed it on to Jenaro. He read it aloud:

"HIREDHAND: IMPERATIVE WE SECURE BON-NEANNEE CIGAR FOR USE ALBERTIAWISE. SCAR-FACE HOT PROIDEA. SHORTCAKE CONVINCED NECESSARY PROELECTION SWEEP. SUGGEST NEWYORK CHECK AVAILABILITY. MONEY UNOB-JECT ENDIT SCARAMOUCHE.

"Boy," Shartelle said to me, "you are a natural-born conspirator. Those are two of the worst secret messages I've ever had the pleasure of reading." He turned to Jimmy Jenaro. "Now that first one—about the skywriting—I want that to fall into the hands of the Renesslaer boys up north. One of them's named Franchot Tone Calhoun."

"You're kidding," Jenaro said.

"I ain't."

"Okay. That I can do. Then you want Duffy to get this in a day or so?"

"Right. Now the other one I want to fall into the hands of whoever's ramrodding Dr. Kensington Kologo's campaign in the east. Now make sure they don't get them too easily and make sure that they understand that these are top secret and all. You follow."

Jenaro smiled. "You don't have to draw me a map, Clint."

"Didn't figure I would."

Dr. Diokadu shook his head sadly. "Some place, some place far back, about fifteen minutes ago, I became hopelessly lost. I think it all started with the pun."

Shartelle grinned, threw his head back and shouted for Samuel who responded with his usual "Sah!" from the netherworld of his kitchen. "Thought now that teatime's over, we might have a drink. I swear I think that gin and tonic is habit-forming."

Samuel brought the drinks. Jenaro had another beer; Diokadu decided to try orange squash and gin, and Shartelle and I tried the gin and tonic.

"Now then, Doc. It's simple. I want the opposition to learn of our secret weapon—skywriting and the use of a helium-filled blimp. Now if my understanding of the Renesslaer psychology is right, they're going to try to get the skywriting before we do. That's been the secret of their success in advertising and public relations all over the world. In television, they sponsor only the tried and true. When situation comedy was the rage, they sponsored a raft of situation comedies. When the cute, low-key ads took hold, they started producing cute, low-key ads. They're imitators, not innovators. I doubt if they ever had a fresh idea of their own, but they can take somebody else's and do it a hell of a lot better. Now I figure they'll think skywriting is just the ticket and before you know it, they're going to have a team down here that's going to be writing old Alhaji Sir's name all over the sky. Has he got a short nickname by the way—like Ako?"

"He's called Haj," Dr. Diokadu said.

"Now that's just fine," Shartelle said. "They can skywrite that real easy. Now how about their party's symbol?"

"It's a pyramid," Diokadu said.

"That's not bad either. Give me a piece of that typewriter paper, Pete."

I handed him one and Shartelle sketched on it quickly and then handed it to Diokadu who nodded and passed it to Jenaro who handed it to me. It looked like this:

"Me no vote for man in sky, Mastah," I said.

"Well, now, Pete, that's just what I hope the reaction is. But we gotta be certain. Now here's where Jimmy comes in."

"How?" Jenaro asked.

Shartelle leaned back in his chair and looked dreamily up at the ceiling. He had a slight smile on his face. I had come to know that smile. I felt sorry for whomever he was thinking of.

174

"Jimmy, I need me a poison squad."

"A what?"

"Have you got some good old boys down at party head-quarters who'd be something like traveling salesmen back in the States? You know, they're mixers and minglers, go around to all the villages and towns and talk to the folks. Bring the latest gossip."

Jenaro nodded carefully. "I know what you mean."

Shartelle kept looking at the ceiling. "They'd travel in pairs. Wouldn't be identified with the party in any way, shape, or form. They'd just sort of drift into town and when the conversation turned to politics, and I imagine it does, they'd have just a couple of quiet comments. Know what I mean?"

Jenaro nodded again.

"Now say that Renesslaer does get a skywriting team down here. Have you got some boys that could get hold of their schedule in advance?"

"I've got them," Jenaro said.

"Uh-huh. Now suppose we sent the poison squad out —maybe a day ahead of where the skywriting was to take place. And these two good old boys, these traveling sales-men, sort of bring up the skywriting casual-like?" The South was rising again at the end of Shartelle's sentences.

We all nodded this time.

"Now one old boy turns to the other and says: 'You know, Ojo, I do not believe that the vapors from the plane in the sky destroy a man's sex, do you?'"

"And Ojo—or whatever his name is—says: 'I have heard it said in the last village that the strange smoke is a deadly gas and that it has made many widows whose husbands still live.' Or however they talk. I think maybe I'm overly influenced by H. Rider Haggard. Then one of them—I don't care which one—says: 'I cannot believe that the villages over which the name of Haj was written are doomed to have no more sons.' And they keep it up, mov-ing on from town to town, village to village, just ahead of the skywriting plane.

"Now, Jimmy, you got a hundred or so boys that you

175

could send out to do that little job?"

Jenaro shook his head. It was a shake of admiration. "It just might do it, Clint. We can work the sexual taboos. Sure, we got the boys—in fact, the party faithful we've got would find it just about on a par with their capabilities. They won't have to do much more than buy beer and talk, and they're good at that, if nothing else. It just so happens that I ordered a hundred Volkswagens about two months ago. Looks as if they'll come in handy."

Dr. Diokadu held up his glass and said: "Do you think I might have another gin and squash? It's rather refreshing." I called Samuel and he served us another round.

"It is a lie, of course," Dr. Diokadu said. "The smoke from the plane is harmless."

"It's harmless, Doc. It's just a chemical and crude oil that's squirted into a hot exhaust. And that's what the poison squad will say—that they *don't* believe that the smoke will cause impotency and sterility. But you're right; it's a lie. It's a lie in its conception, its intent, and its execution. Do you think we shouldn't?"

Diokadu sighed. "The Leader will not like it; Dekko won't stand for it."

"I wasn't planning on letting them know," Shartelle said. "They're not to know. Their job is to campaign out there among the folks. If the gutter has to be worked, then that's our job."

"You need something else, Clint," I said. "You can't bank on the secret messages alone."

He nodded and rose to pace the room again. "We need two men," he said to Jenaro. "They must be of fairly high rank in the party. They must have unimpeachable integrity. And they must be willing to make a sacrifice."

He waited. Jenaro and Diokadu exchanged glances. "Go on," Jenaro said.

"I want them to defect. To cross over to the opposition. One to Sir Alakada's side; the other to Dr. Kologo's camp. They'll bring information, of course. You'll provide them enough harmless stuff to make it look authentic. But the most important tidbit they will carry is confirmation of our banking everything on the skywriting and the Goodyear-type blimp. They'll have to be a couple of actors, and they shouldn't be closely tied together. Have you got a pair like that?"

"Quit looking at us, Clint," Jenaro said. "Damned if I'll defect."

"Not you two. But a couple of bright, young types. You're going to have to appeal to their patriotism, party loyalty and sense of adventure."

"More likely to their wallets," Diokadu said. "I have two in mind." He mentioned two names. They meant nothing to me. Diokadu looked to Jenaro for confirmation. Jenaro nodded his head slowly. "One's a lawyer," he said. "The other is an administrative type. They're both tied to the party and are on the rise. They talk a good game— give the impression that they're on the inside." He nodded, abruptly this time. "They'll do.

"Who makes the approach?" Shartelle asked.

"Diokadu. He's the party theoretician. They'd think I was trying to con them."

Shartelle looked at Diokadu who didn't look happy. "All right. I'll contact them this evening. Both are in Ubondo."

"The usual reasons for defection—" Shartelle began. Diokadu held up his hand. "We've had enough defectors in the past, Mr. Shartelle. I know the reasons for defection."

Jimmy Jenaro got up and walked across the room. He sighted an imaginary sixteen-foot putt, wiggled his hips too much, but tapped it into the hole. "The poison squad, Clint. What's their line about the blimp—providing there is a blimp?"

"It's simple," Shartelle said. "They don't believe it's really carrying an American A-bomb."

"They call it the boom bomb back in the bush," Jenaro said.

"And the drums will be used to plant the fear of impotency and death," Diokadu said. "Two very strong fears,

177

Mr. Shartelle. But suppose the opposition denies it?"

"Ask the public relations expert," Shartelle said, pointing his cigar at me.

"They can't deny a rumor—or they give credence to it," I said. "They can't stop using the planes for skywriting, or the poison squad will start taking credit for ending it. They're boxed, anyway they go—providing they go. The same holds true for the blimp. If they quit using the blimp, then the angry protests of an aroused citizenry paid off. If they deny it, why should they deny something that doesn't exist? It's like a press release that starts out: 'Johnny X. Jones today denied widely-circulated rumors that he is an embezzler.' "

Diokadu shook his head. "But we're not counting on this to win the election, surely. It's trickery, it's deceit, and it's a package of lies—cunning, to be sure—but still lies."

Shartelle nodded his head. "If the people vote for Chief Akomolo, they'll be voting for his program. If they want to vote against the other two leading parties, they'll have no place to go but into Akomolo's camp. Now, Doc, you know he hasn't got the votes, and I'm not sure he'll have them even if he makes a speech on the hour, every hour between now and election day. But I want to guide our opposition's mistakes; I want to encourage them. I want to keep them busy running around on useless jobs. I want them to exhaust their energies on their own bungling. I want to create dissension in their headquarters and panic in their hearts. And when something like this starts, there's a damned good chance for panic."

"I'll go along with you, Clint," Jenaro said quietly. He turned to Diokadu. He said a phrase or a sentence in the dialect. Diokadu nodded back.

"I just said that the hands of our enemies are not without blood. They've pulled some real shitty deals on us in the past. I've got no compunction about Clint's idea. It's cunning as you said—and tricky. If it works, we're bound to pick up votes—a lot of votes."

"I will agree, but the Leader must not be told the details," Diokadu said. He smiled, a trifle ruefully. "As a political scientist, Mr. Shartelle, I am learning a great deal about the seamier side of politics. It seems to be the side where the votes are won and lost."

Shartelle smiled back. "They're won and lost every place, Doc. I just want to cover all bets. That leads me up to another question. How about the labor union, Jimmy?"

"I talked to the guy. He's willing to dicker, but he won't go for a general strike. He's saving that, he said."

"How far will he go?"

"He'll pull out one—it's well-disciplined. They'll stay out until he tells them to go back."

"Which one?"

"The one that'll cause the biggest stink." Jenaro grinned happily. "The Amalgamated Federation of Albertian Night Soil Collectors."

— 18 —

Diokadu left, the now-familiar sheaf of papers tucked under his left arm, his right hand hitching up the folds of his *ordona*. Jenaro remained seated.

"You busy tonight?" he asked.

Shartelle looked at me. "I'm free," I said.

"We're two short at our poker school. You care to join us? It's at my place."

"I don't know about Pete here, but I reckon *I* could stand a lesson."

"It's not that kind of a school, Clint," I said. "It's just what the British call a regular game."

"That a fact? How much you play for, Jimmy?"

"Pot limit."

"Man could get hurt in a game like that. What time's it start?

"Nine."

"Pete?"

'I'll play."

"You take checks?"

"Sure," Jenaro said.

"Who else is playing?"

"Me. A couple of Permanent Secretaries—British. And Ian Duncan, the ADC to Blackwelder. You met him. He married money, by the way, and plays a little wild."

"No wild games, though?"

"No. Just five-card stud and draw."

"Sounds like a most intelligent and relaxing way to spend an evening. We'll be there at nine."

Jenaro's house was about a mile from us, a two-story affair with a three-car garage that housed his Jaguar, a new Ford station wagon, and a sedate Rover sedan. He met us at the door and introduced us to his wife—a young, pretty Albertian with an almost fair complexion and an impeccable British accent. She wore slacks and a sweater made out of some minor miracle fabric. Jenaro called her "Mamma" and introduced us to five of six children who, he said, were all his.

Servants bustled about getting us drinks and Mrs. Jenaro and Shartelle chatted about nothing in particular. Ian Duncan was the next to arrive, followed closely by a thin, redheaded man called William Hardcastle who was Permanent Secretary for the Ministry of Economic Development. Last to arrive was the Permanent Secretary of the Ministry of Home Affairs, Bryant Carpenter, who looked a little like Anthony Eden. Mrs. Jenaro saw that we all had drinks, then excused herself and herded the children to bed.

"Who wants to play poker?" Jenaro asked.

We followed him into a room that seemed to be furnished for nothing else. There was a seven-sided table covered with green baize that had shallow, wedge-shaped compartments where you could stack your chips. A green-shaded, 300 watt lamp hung from the ceiling. Comfortable-looking chairs with arm rests were waiting for the gamblers. The only other furniture in the room was a sideboard that held ice, liquor, beer, glasses, and soda. There was also an air-conditioner that had brought the temperature down to around seventy. It looked like a place where a lot of money could be won or lost.

Jenaro brought out the chips and tossed six packs of Bicycles on the table. We all took seats. I found myself between Hardcastle and Carpenter. Shartelle was between Jenaro and Duncan.

"For the benefit of our American cousins," Jenaro said, "I'll repeat the rules. It's dealer's choice as long as you play five-card stud or draw. Pot limit with four raises. No wild cards, no joker. You mix your own drinks."

He ripped open a pack of cards, shuffled, and fanned them out on the table. "Draw for deal." While we drew he passed each of us a stack of blue, red and white chips. "Everybody starts with fifty pounds. The whites are a shilling, the reds are ten bob, and the blues are a pound." He drew his card and turned it over. It was the nine of hearts. Ian Duncan won the deal with a queen of diamonds.

"Draw," Duncan said. I watched him shuffle. He did it competently enough, but without flair. He was no mechanic.

"Jacks or better?" Shartelle asked.

"Jacks or better," Duncan agreed.

"Those rules you spelled out were plain as sin, Jimmy," Shartelle said, "but there's one thing else I'd like to ask. I was just wondering if you all look kindly on check and raise? Some folks' feelings get hurt when it's used in a friendly game."

"Check and raise is the norm, Mr. Shartelle," Carpenter said drily. "It was introduced, I should add, by Chief Jenaro who described it as a basic American custom."

"It's just nice to see that some of the more civilized aspects of our culture are being adopted in foreign lands, Mr. Carpenter."

I looked at my cards. I had drawn a pair of nines. Hardcastle opened for ten shillings and I stayed. So did everybody else. I drew three cards. Shartelle drew one; Jenaro, two; Hardcastle, one; Duncan, three, and Carpenter, three. I looked at mine. I had improved to two pairs—nines and fives.

Hardcastle bet a pound. I called. Carpenter folded. Jenaro saw the pound and Shartelle raised five pounds. Duncan folded. Hardcastle looked at Shartelle. "The raise from the one-card draw. I'll only call."

I folded. Jenaro tossed his hand into the discards. Shartelle said: "Jack-high straight" and laid out his cards.

Hardcastle shrugged and displayed two queens. "Openers," he said.

It went much like that for two hours. I won five good pots and managed to stay even. Shartelle was the big winner. He played smart, cold poker. Jenaro was good, but tended towards flashiness. Duncan played hunches and was down fifty pounds. Hardcastle and Carpenter were erratic players, sometimes lucking out. I decided it was only a matter of time before they were caught.

We took a break at eleven and Jenaro's steward served sandwiches. I drank a bottle of beer with mine.

"How do you predict the election, Mr. Shartelle?" Hardcastle asked through a mouthful of roast beef and bread.

"Looks better and better. But since you're in the Ministry of Home Affairs, I'd say you'd be in a much better position to judge than me."

"We just look after the police, the firemen, the post office, and government printing, plus a few other odd jobs. We let chaps like you and Jimmy here look to the politics."

"Are you leaving before or after independence?" Duncan asked Hardcastle.

"I'm here another six months. The Minister has demanded that I stay on for at least that long. He says I'm the only one who understands the blessed postal system.

Of course, he's wrong. I have young Obaji coming along nicely. He should be more than well-suited by then. Very intelligent fellow."

"They run their Ministries much better than they play poker, Clint," Jenaro said.

"How long have we been playing together?" Carpenter asked.

"Five years now—at least I've been in the school that long," Duncan said. "And I've lost a pile, too, I don't mind saying."

"Upshaw," Hardcastle said, "d'you find it rather strange business, hopping into a country like this, sizing up the political situation, and then trying to change it or influence it, overnight, so to speak?"

"It's different," I said. "But it seems to be a growing industry. In England or the States a candidate won't blow his nose in public until he's consulted his public relations counselor."

"Do you actually believe that public relations is a business?"

"Sure. I know it is."

"But is it a profession?"

"Like a doctor or lawyer or certified public accountant?"

"Quite."

"No. I'd say it was a calling—just like the lay ministry. You don't need any special training or education, you just get the call, announce you're a public relations expert, whatever that is, and you're in business."

"That sounds suspiciously as if you'd like to see some sort of licensing regulation," Duncan said.

"Not at all. To be a real success in public relations, you have to be half charlatan and half messiah. The same qualifications make a good teacher or a good Member of Parliament or U.S. Senator. In fact, you can go a long way in just about anything with those qualifications. Look at Shartelle, for example."

"You're not in public relations, are you, Shartelle?" Carpenter asked.

"No, sir, I'm not. I'm just a man who dabbles in politics

183

because it's a pleasant way to make a living without having to carry a briefcase full of papers home every night. And you don't have to catch the 8:22 or 9:17 of a morning. When I was starting out in life I had to make a choice. I could have been either a professional gambler, an oil wildcatter, or a political manager. Same man offered me all three jobs that very same day. I chose the political route and you know what he said to me?"

"What?" said his reliable straight man, Peter Upshaw.

"He said: 'Boy, you probably made the right choice. But don't ever get to feeling that you're better or smarter than your candidate, because they're smart enough and rich enough to hire you, and you ain't smart or rich enough to hire them. And don't ever run for anything yourself because of necessity, you'd wind up with a liar as a candidate.' Now, I followed his advice and I can't say I'm sorry."

Hardcastle produced a cigar and lighted it. "The thing that bothers me is that the Americans are making it impossible for the average chap to run for office, not only in their own country, but it's getting that way at home. Now this election in Albertia is costing a packet. These fans you ordered through our Ministry, Jimmy. Where's the money coming from, although I dare say you won't give me a straight answer."

Jenaro grinned. "Sure I will, Mr. Permanent Secretary. The money's coming from the people."

Hardcastle grunted. "Clever idea though. Using cottage industries to make the fans. Should drum up a bit of support, although we had the devil's own time convincing the Minister that his village shouldn't get the entire order. But if you have any more ideas like that, come see us."

The talk went on for ten or fifteen minutes more and then it was back to the cards. The game settled down to five-card stud more often than draw. I played careful, dull poker, pairing only a couple of times on the first three cards and once going for a heart flush that busted on the fifth card with a three of clubs. Then Hardcastle, on my right, got the deal and announced a game of draw. I looked at the cards he dealt me and found four sixes and a nine of spades. It was my open. I checked and prayed. Carpenter opened for a pound and Jenaro bumped him five pounds. Jenaro had hit. Shartelle stayed; so did Duncan and Hardcastle. Then it was six pounds to me and I raised the bet by ten pounds.

"The sandbag just landed on the back of my neck," Jenaro said. I smiled politely. Carpenter folded. Jenaro raised my ten pounds another ten and Shartelle stayed. Duncan called and Hardcastle, after a moment's hesitation, tossed in his hand. I called and raised twenty. Carpenter folded, Jenaro, Shartelle, and Duncan called.

"Cards?" the dealer asked.

"One," I said.

"None," Jenaro said.

"Well, now," Shartelle said. "I'll take two."

"I'll play these," Duncan said.

I had drawn a queen of hearts. I waited for someone to say something. "First raise bets," the dealer said. "Your bet, Jimmy."

Jenaro looked at me and grinned. "The first pat hand bets twenty-five quid into the sandbag raise." He shoved some chips into the center of the table.

Shartelle shook his head sadly and tossed his hand into the discards. Duncan, also holding a pat hand, shoved twenty-five pounds into the pot. "Call," he said.

"Up to you, Pete," Jenaro said.

"See your twenty-five and raise fifty," I said.

"Call," he said.

"Call," Duncan said.

It was a nice pot. I put my cards down carefully, face up, and tried to keep from looking smug. I didn't call my hand; I was going to let somebody else do that, but nobody ever did. The door to the poker room burst open and the steward darted over to Jenaro and babbled at him in the dialect.

Jenaro got up quickly, said "excuse me," and hurried out of the room. He took his cards with him. We sat and waited for him to come back. He returned in three minutes

185

and beckoned Carpenter, the Permanent Secretary of Home Affairs. "You'd better get on the blower." The man who resembled Anthony Eden moved quickly through the door. He asked no questions.

"What's the trouble?" Duncan asked. "I couldn't follow your steward, he was going too fast."

Jenaro tossed his hand on the table. He had a low spade flush. "The game's over," he said. "The Captain of police has been found murdered in a driveway." He looked at Shartelle and then at me. "The driveway belongs to you two."

Carpenter came back into the poker room. "It's Cheatwood, I'm afraid. I've just talked to a couple of Privates on the force who identified him." He turned to Shartelle. "Your watch night found him. Multiple stab wounds."

The three Englishmen looked at Jenaro. "You call it, Minister," Duncan said softly. There was a tone of encouragement in his voice, and there was also deference. They were the trained civil servants. Jernaro was The Minister. They had brought him along, coached him in the art of administration, and now he was to act. He was a star pupil; they wanted him to act well. Jenaro didn't hesitate.

"Who's next in line to Cheatwood?" he asked Carpenter.

"Lieutenant Oslako."

"Ring up your Minister and tell him to appoint Oslako Acting Captain. And tell Bekardo that I said we need him made Acting Captain tonight, not tomorrow. That means Bekardo will have to go down to the Ministry. If he objects, tell him to call me. You get the necessary paperwork moving, Bryant."

"Right. I'll call Oslako first and tell him to take charge of the investigation."

"Ian," Jenaro said to the aide-de-camp. "This isn't your cup of tea, I know, but would you ring up my Permanent Secretary and tell him to get his butt down to the Ministry and start getting a statement manufactured on Cheatwood's death. It's to be issued in the Premier's name."

186

"Right away," Duncan said. "Anything else?"

"No. Just tell him I'll be there shortly. He'll know what to do." He turned to Hardcastle. "You knew Cheatwood well?" Hardcastle nodded. "Can you take care of the family—Mrs. Cheatwood, the children? Get a doctor if need be—break the news? I'm giving you the toughest job."

"Not at all, Jimmy. I'll take care of it."

"Thanks very much." The three of them left and Jenaro turned to us.

"We'd better get over there. You follow me so I can identify you before you get shot."

We followed the Jaguar and made the mile in a little over a minute. Three police cars were there by the time we arrived and Jenaro took charge. He beckoned a Sergeant, the only noncommissioned officer in sight. The Sergeant moved over smartly, came to attention, and saluted. "Sah!"

"How long have you been here?"

"Five minutes, Sah. No more."

"You're to take full command until Lieutenant Oslako arrives. Follow your normal routine. Keep the curious out. Don't touch anything."

"Sah!" the sergeant barked and saluted again. By now there was a small crowd composed mostly of servants from the various compounds. Silex, our watch night, was telling—with descriptive gestures—how he'd found the body and promptly reported the matter to the police and Chief Jenaro. I had the feeling he would be telling the story for years.

Cheatwood's body lay in the dirt and gravel halfway up our driveway in a pool of light furnished by the headlamps of a police car. The left side of his face rested in the dirt; his green eyes were open and empty. His left hand was in a position that could have helped him to rise if he had been alive. It clutched half of his ebony walking stick. The other half was a few feet away. I thought that he might have smacked somebody with it. The back of his shirt was soaked with blood and the earth and gravel around him were darkened with it. Alive, he seemed to have been a quiet, calm man. Dead, he seemed to be in a violent spasm that was temporarily suspended. Jenaro turned and talked to one of the policemen. Shartelle and I walked over to the body.

"Reckon he had something to tell us?"

I shrugged.

"Take a look," Shartelle said. "By his right hand." The hand had the index finger extended stiffly. The finger had dug two shallow trenches in the dirt and gravel. The first trench was a curve; the second was a straight line.

"Could be a 'C' and an 'I,'" I said.

Shartelle nodded and stepped casually on the scrabblings in the dirt, erasing them under his shoe. "Could be an 'A' is missing."

"Could be," I said. "If it is, I think we'd better know it before anybody else does."

Jenaro walked over to us. "Buddy, could you spare a drink?"

"Sure."

"I could use it," he said. "The Lieutenant won't be here for ten minutes or so and there's no sense in me trying to play Inspector Jenaro."

Inside, Shartelle mixed the drinks and handed one to Jenaro who took a large swallow. "You know," he said, "we've inherited some of the British traditions that will be with us for a long time. Like general disapproval of having a cop killed. Cheatwood had been here a long time. He knew a lot of people."

"Lots of enemies?" I asked.

"A policeman's usual accumulation. He was fair—that was his reputation. Even scrupulous. You'd met him, hadn't you?"

"He called on us the other day," Shartelle said. "Dropped in to let us know we had neigbors."

"They'll bury him tomorrow."

"I don't think we knew him well enough to attend the funeral," I said.

A medium-sized Albertian knocked on the edge of the

folded French doors. He wore the police uniform and the insignia of a Lieutenant.

"Chief Jenaro," he said politely. "I'm sorry I'm late."

Jenaro introduced us to Lieutenant Oslako whose uniform was a stiffly-starched khaki shirt, equally stiff khaki walking shorts, a Sam Browne belt, a visored cap that he kept tucked under his arm, thick white wool socks that almost reached his knees, and high-topped shoes—the kind that are called clodhoppers in some sections of the States. Shartelle's section, I thought.

"You were informed that you are Acting Captain?"

"Yes, sir."

"The killer or killers must be found, Lieutenant."

"Yes, sir. I considered Captain Cheatwood my friend."

"Carry out the investigation with that in mind."

"May I ask a question, sir?"

"Yes."

"May I ask Mr. Shartelle and Mr. Upshaw whether they heard—"

"They were with me," Jenaro said. "Ask their watch night and their servants."

"Yes, sir." The lieutenant saluted, did a smart about-face and went out into the night to find out who had killed his boss.

"I'd hate to think they killed Cheatwood just to mess up the vote counting," Shartelle said.

"No chance," Jenaro said. "If that were true, I'd be the prime suspect. He'd worked out the handling of the ballots months in advance with the people in Barkandu and in the Ministry of Home Affairs here. It'll go just the way he planned it."

Jenaro took a final swallow and rose. "Thanks for the drink. I have to go down to my Ministry."

"What or who killed him, Jimmy, in your opinion?"

Jenaro smiled slightly. "He was white. That helped kill him. Maybe he had a couple of pounds in his pocket. That would help, too. Or maybe for no reason at all other than it was time to kill someone."

189

"Independence fever?" Shartelle asked.

"Something like that. Africa Now, maybe. I doubt that we'll ever know really. But someone wanted him dead; they stabbed him enough."

After Jenaro had gone, and after the police had crawled around the lawn on their hands and knees with flashlights, looking for the murder weapon and knowing damned well they weren't going to find it, and after they had taken away Cheatwood's body and sprinkled sand on the spot where he had bled on the dirt and gravel, Shartelle and I decided to have a night-cap.

"Who do you think killed him?" I asked Shartelle.

"Not you, not me, not Jenaro, and not those three bad poker players, although they're real nice fellows. I figure that leaves about twenty million live suspects."

"He was too smart a cop to be taken by a drunk-roller."

Shartelle nodded. "I was just wondering how much grit you've got to have to lie out there in the dirt with the life oozing out of you while you try to find the strength to claw a name in the ground with your finger. It must have been something mighty important."

"It was to him," I said. "I wonder if it ever will be to anybody else?"

— *19* —

To Shartelle, she was always the Widow Claude. Her name was Madame Claude Duquesne and she stood at Major Chuku's side, welcoming guests as Anne, Shartelle and I arrived for the Friday night party. We had picked up Anne at her apartment earlier where Shartelle had inspected the roommates without displaying much interest, not even in the merry one from Berkeley. We had gone on to the Sahara South for a drink and from there to the Major's home.

It was a garden party. The Major lived, somewhat beyond his means, I assumed, in a large two-story house with fake beams poking through the stucco exterior. His lawns were as neatly kept as ours and his shrubbery, flowers and plants even better. Japanese lanterns, the special kind they now have that keep mosquitoes away, were strung about the garden. It was a black-tie affair and Shartelle wore his madras dinner jacket with a certain flair, I thought. I wore a white one with a shawl collar and Anne said I looked keen. We arrived after about half the guests were there. The Major, in white dress uniform, stood by a table loaded with iced champagne. Madame Duquesne stood at his left.

When Shartelle saw her as we came around the corner of the house, following the path that led to the garden, he stopped still and stared for a full half-minute. "Petey," he said in a reverent voice, "that's the prettiest little old Creole I've ever laid eyes on and that takes in New Orleans and Baton Rouge, too."

"How do you know she's Creole?" I said.

He looked at me and sniffed. "Boy, us Creoles can spot each other a country mile away."

"She makes me feel dowdy," Anne said. "She's wearing a Balenciaga. I thought I was going to show off with Neiman-Marcus."

"You're prettier," I said, but it didn't sound convincing. Madame Duquesne was a brunette and her hair was cut short. It framed a face that was almost perfectly oval and seemed to have been delicately carved out of new ivory. Her mouth may have been a little wide, but a slightly pouting lower lip looked as if it demanded to be bitten. A straight, barely turned-up nose revealed nostrils that seemed to flare in passion. Her eyes, I rhapsodized, were flashing black promises of a thousand nights of exquisite variations. That was her face—if your eyes ever got above her legs—which were the long, slim kind with knees that seemed faultless, perfectly curving calves, ankles that your hand would fit around so that your thumb and fingers would overlap, and that slight, somehow provocative, curve on the lower shin that a lot of dancers have. Her dress clung to thighs and hips that called for a pat, and just managed to cover a part of her breasts. I kept staring at her breasts, waiting for the dress to slip.

"Heel, Prince," Anne said.

"No offense, Miss Anne, but that little old girl just makes a man's mouth water," Shartelle said. He forgot his manners for once and moved quickly over to Major Chuku.

"Major, I'm Clint Shartelle."

The Major smiled at him and extended his hand. "Mr. Shartelle, I'm so glad that you could come. Allow me to present Madame Duquesne who is doing me the honor of serving as hostess for my little party. The Major switched to rapid, fluent French and said to Madame Duquesne: "Permit me to introduce M. Clinton Shartelle. He is the American political expert whom I mentioned earlier this evening."

Madame Duquesne smiled at Shartelle and extended her hand. "I have been looking forward to meeting you, Monsieur." Her English had a faint accent.

Shartelle gracefully bent his snow-white head over her hand and replied in smooth, liquid French: "Madame, the pleasure must be entirely mine. I now know why I came to Africa. Perhaps you will join me in a glass of champagne later?"

She nodded and smiled again. "I will be looking forward to it."

The Major had a bleak look about him when he heard Shartelle rattle off his French. He recovered enough to greet Anne warmly and to give me his firm handshake. He introduced Anne to Madame Duquesne, again in French. He was not only a slick article, I decided, he was also a show-off.

"That is a most striking gown, Madame Duquesne," Anne said as they exchanged handclasps. "Paris, isn't it?" She also spoke French.

Madame's eyes roved over Anne's dress. "Yes—and

thank you, my dear. Major Chuku has told me that you are with the American Peace Corps. I admire you for it and I must say that you look lovely tonight."

There are advantages to having a degree in letters, even from the University of Minnesota. The six months I spent at the University of Quebec as part of my minor in French were finally going to pay off. Once more, the Major made the introduction in French. Madame Duquesne gave my hand a little squeeze. I gave hers a little squeeze back. If I knew Shartelle, it was as close as I would ever get.

"The Major has told me of you, M. Upshaw." She spoke in French this time. "I have been looking forward to meeting you."

"Unfortunately, Madame, the Major has not been advertising *your* existence. I cannot say that I blame him, but I am delighted that you are no longer his secret." It all came out in French, with a Quebec-North Dakota accent perhaps, but still French.

I moved on to Shartelle and Anne who stood by the table where the white-jacketed stewards served champagne and Scotch and brandy. "What were you doing, taking her pulse?" Anne asked.

"Ain't she something, Petey? I'm sure glad you're spoke for, boy, because that leaves the field wide-open for old Clint."

"Where'd you learn to speak French, Shartelle?"

"Why, New Orleans, boy. I didn't speak nothing but French till I was six, seven years old. I noticed you and Miss Anne were talking it pretty good. Where you all pick it up?"

"I started in the eighth grade and took it all through high school and college," Anne said. "Pete picked his up in a Marseille cathouse."

"University of Quebec," I said. "It was a special program."

"Miss Anne, you don't have to be jealous about old Pete here. I'm going to look after that little old Creole just fine. Ain't she got the damnedest eyes you ever did see?"

"He didn't look at her eyes," Anne said.

I finished my champagne and helped myself to another glass. There seemed to be an endless supply. "If you're going to move in, Clint, you're going to have to move the Major out. He seems to have a certain proprietary interest."

Shartelle took Anne's glass and got her a fresh drink and one for himself. "Boy, true love will find a way. It always has."

"You're gone, huh?"

"I am smitten, I will confess. Ain't she something, though?"

Anne looked up at Clint and smiled. "She's nice, Clint. I like her very much even though I've just met her."

"I have an idea we might all be seeing a good deal more of her," he said and drank his champagne down. He gave his black tie a careful tug. "I think I'm going to move around a bit and talk to some folks."

"Going to check her out, huh?"

Shartelle grinned. "Well, sir, I just might mention her name in passing."

We watched him wander through the guests, a tall man with close-cropped white hair who moved with a strange, rough grace. If he saw someone who looked interesting, he would stick out his hand and say: "I'm Clint Shartelle from the United States. I don't believe we've met."

"I think half the people here are going to think he's the real host," Anne said.

"He likes it. He honestly likes it and he doesn't know the meaning of a phrase such as 'his kind of people.' If they breathe, they're Shartelle's kind."

"He likes you, Pete. And it's a special kind of liking."

I smiled at her. "He's all right."

"You almost said something nice."

"It's getting easier."

Jimmy Jenaro suddenly appeared at my elbow and I introduced him to Anne. "Just call me Jimmy," he said. "Ohio State. Class of '55."

"You'll be able to live that down some day," Anne said and Jimmy laughed delightedly.

"How do you like the threads, Pete?"

"Nice," I said. "But they must interfere with your backswing."

Jenaro was wearing the Albertian *ordona* and it looked as if it contained five or six pounds of hand-embroidered gold thread. It was pure white, loosely woven, and hung in gracefully careless folds that must have taken the tailor hours to get just right. On his head, Jenaro wore a blue cap that looked something like a medieval jester's hat. His eyes were covered by his Miami shades.

I gestured with my head at the party. "The Albertian Army must pay its Majors pretty well, Jimmy."

Jenaro shook his head. "He's got so much loot, he can't count it. His grandmother was the uncrowned queen of the mammy traders. She made a fortune from importing cement. For about ten years, she had the only import license for it. His mother took over then and sent him to the Sorbonne. He finally wound up at Sandhurst. The Army's given him something to do and an excuse to throw parties."

"You know him rather well?"

"I know him. We were kids together,"

"You know Madame Duquesne?"

Jenaro grinned. "Not as well as I'd like."

"Shartelle seems to be taken with her," I said.

"If I weren't of the Christian faith, I might try to take another wife," Jenaro said. "As a Chief, I'm entitled to three, you know."

"I didn't."

"Well, I figure with her and Mamma in the same house, I'd have just about all I could take care of. But I don't think Mamma would stand for it."

"Where is Mamma?" Anne asked.

"Home with the kids," Jenaro said. "Where else? Come on, I'll introduce you around."

Most of the guests had arrived. Approximately half of them were English or European. The rest were Albertians. Jenaro's failure to bring his wife proved to be the exception. I met—or met again—some of the political leaders who had been at Chief Akomolo's luncheon. Their wives stood by their sides, dressed in brightly-colored cloth that seemed to be wrapped around them in a series of intricate and symbolic folds. Their head-dressings, usually of matching material, were even more intricately shaped.

Following Jenaro we met what must have passed for the cream of Ubondo society. There was a Supreme Court judge; a trio of lawyers—solicitors, I suppose; two doctors, one white, one black; an automobile dealer; a Light-Colonel in the Albertian Army; an Albertian Airways pilot; four English Permanent Secretaries of various ministries including William Hardcastle; an Italian contractor; four or five Lebanese businessmen including the gambler who owned the Sahara South; Jack Woodring of the USIS and his wife who wanted to know if I'd heard that the Dodgers had won thirteen straight; two representatives from the British Council, the UK counterpart to USIS, one of whom insisted he was half-American; another automobile dealer; four associate professors and instructors from the university; an Army Lieutenant; another young Lieutenant in the Albertian police; two crewcuts from the Peace Corps who didn't seem bothered by their lack of black ties; a representative of the Ford Foundation who wanted to know if I knew that the Dodgers had won thirteen straight; and a lot of other people whose names I didn't get, but whose eyes lighted up when they heard that I was Mr. Shartelle's associate.

We made the circuit, towed by Jenaro, moving to the left, then around, and back to the table where the drinks were being served. Shartelle was standing there, his eyes fixed on Madame Duquesne who was in deep conference with an Albertian whom I took to be the Major's chief steward.

"Soon as she gets the serving straightened out, she's going to join us," Shartelle said. "Hello, Jimmy."

"Clint."

"How'd the telegrams go?"

"They're gone."

"How about our two defectors?"

"Diokadu's got them lined up. He says they each need a statement outlining their reasons for defecting."

Shartelle nodded. "Pete?"

"It would be wise. They can't switch parties quietly. Their value to the opposition would be lost."

"Can you fix them up with some statements?"

"I'll do it tonight when I get home."

"You can pick them up in the morning, Jimmy."

"Good. By the way, both Dekko and the Leader have gone nuts over their speeches. Dekko says Pete must be a mindreader. The Leader said his is a highly-polished, powerful document of truth."

"They're both right good speeches," Shartelle said. "Diokadu getting them translated?"

"Right."

"How about the shorter ones Pete wrote? The ones on the major points?"

"Those, too."

"Good. When do they change parties?"

"Sunday night," Jenaro said. "Or afternoon. In plenty of time to make the Monday papers. We settled on a thousand quid each."

"Treachery is the last refuge of patriots," Shartelle said.

"Did you make that up?" I asked.

"I think so, boy. Sometimes it just comes out."

Jenaro took the last sip of his champagne and put the glass down on a table. "I think I'll make the circuit again. If I pick up anything interesting, I'll let you know. By the way," he added, "there's nothing new on Cheatwood's death."

Shartelle nodded. His eyes followed Jenaro. He shook his head slightly. "He's sure a natural, ain't he, Pete?"

"He thrives on it."

"You were talking pure skulduggery," Anne said. "It makes me homesick."

"It's sure the same all over, ain't it, Miss Anne," Shartelle said. His eyes sought out Madame Duquesne again. "She's a widow woman, I understand. Husband was the

197

sole importer of a high-class French brandy and some good wines over in Dahomey before he dropped dead of a heart attack about two years ago. She inherited the license and moved on over here to Albertia. Now that's just about every man's dream."

"What?"

"A rich widow with a liquor store, boy. And French at that." He shook his head in deep appreciation.

The widow joined us and said that Major Chuku would like us to sit at his table during dinner. We accepted and Shartelle turned it on. This time he was on full make and the onslaught was undeniable. The widow's defenses began to crumble. Shartelle was witty in English and complimentary in French. He had the widow giggling over the naughty stories he told in Cajun French which he interpreted for us in Cajun English. He made up tales of adventure and conquest, and started Madame Duquesne talking about herself. He listened with deep interest and then got her to agree to join us for drinks at the wide-eaved house after the party was over.

It was a buffet affair and I took advantage of it. There was baked ham glazed with sugared brandy, breast of turkey, and tiny meatballs of pork and veal that swam in rich, brown sauce. There were peas, large and tender, that must have been fresh, a salad of endive and three kinds of lettuce with vinegar and oil dressing that was nothing less than superb. There was cauliflower with a magic cheese sauce and French bread still slightly warm from the oven. There was more, but it had to wait for the second plate that I carefully planned in advance.

"Are you starving?" Anne asked.

"I've been starving for ten years," I said. "For love and food both. I don't know which has been scarcer."

"Well, now that you have the love, it looks as if you're trying to make up for the food. In one night."

Shartelle was following Madame Duquesne down the line, piling his plate high with everything, and chortling with delight. "Pete, would you just look what this little old French gal did for the Major. She supervised this entire spread. My, it looks tasty!"

"I notice that you're not exactly on a hunger strike," I told Anne.

"You bet," she said happily. "When I get a chance to get off that Koolaid and peanut butter kick, I take it."

The Major was waiting for us at one of the round tables that were placed about the lawn. They were covered with fresh white linen. Ice buckets holding several bottles of wine were placed at each table and by them stood white-jacketed stewards.

The Major started to announce the seating pattern which would have had Madame Duquesne on his right and Anne on his left. Shartelle pretended not to understand his French and sat on the Major's right with Madame Duquesne next to him. I let Anne sit next to the Major as a consolation prize. A steward poured the wine, which the Major tasted and approved with an airy wave of his hand.

I ate. I ate the ham and the turkey and the little meatballs swimming in the rich, brown sauce. I ate all the peas and the salad and half a loaf of French bread. I finished up with the cauliflower and then asked Anne if I could get her some more of anything.

"I would like some more salad," she said sweetly and I thanked her with my big gray eyes. Back at the feeding trough, I speared some fish that I had overlooked before, some more meatballs, ham, turkey and some salad for Anne. This time I tried the wine with the meal and found it to be surprisingly good. I complimented the Major.

"It is all Madame Duquesne's doing," he said. "A bachelor such as I has no knowledge of arranging such a wonderful party. She was kind enough to rescue me."

Dessert was a light French pastry which we washed down with a demi-tasse of coffee and some brandy which I supposed was the brand that the Widow Claude held the license to import. It was excellent.

Shartelle refused a cigar from the Major and got one of his own black, twisty ones going. The Widow Claude's hand kept accidentally touching Shartelle's arm.

"How goes the politics, Mr. Shartelle?" the Major asked.

Shartelle puffed on his black cigar and blew some smoke up in the air. "About like any place else, I'd say, Major. There are some folks who want to get in, and there are some folks who want to keep them out so that they can get in themselves."

"It was unfortunate what happened to Cheatwood."

"Yes, wasn't it? In our driveway, too."

"There is something that I am exceedingly curious about. By the way, do you mind if I ask these questions?"

"Not at all, sir. I'm right flattered."

"What I'm curious about is this: when you direct a campaign such as this, do you become personally involved? I should say emotionally involved, perhaps. In other words, if you were to lose, would you be as sorely disappointed as the candidate himself?"

"That's a mighty good question, Major. I'd say no, I don't get as emotionally involved as the candidate does. Emotion destroys perspective, and the candidate has employed me, among other reasons, to keep the perspective straight. But if he were to lose, I'd say I'd be quite disappointed, but not crushed. I've only lost one campaign and I know I'm bound to lose another some day, so it's always in the back of my mind."

"And you do it purely for monetary gain? I mean, it is your profession?"

"I make a living at it and I do it because I like it. I like the hours and I like the action. I like the involvement of people with people. It's a damn sight more fun than running an insurance agency, I think."

"Your profession, its need or usefulness, I should say, is based on the existence of a popular democracy?"

"It doesn't have to be popular," Shartelle said, staring at the Major. "It just has to be some kind of democracy where folks can vote for whomever they want to pay their taxes to."

"You must believe deeply then in the value of a democratic form of government?"

Shartelle smiled his wicked smile. "Why, no, sir, I don't necessarily. I've often thought that in the United States we could use a benevolent dictator. Trouble is, there's never anybody around who's benevolent enough except me—and I don't have the votes. Don't you ever get that feeling, Major?"

The Major smiled a graceful retreat. "Sometimes perhaps, Mr. Shartelle, but only in the very small hours of the morning. It's not a thought that would be politic for me to give voice to very often."

"I bet it's not," Shartelle said.

The Major turned his attention to Anne, and Shartelle turned on Shartelle again for the benefit of Madame Duquesne. I relaxed and mentally re-ate the meal while helping myself to more of the brandy.

Madame Duquesne leaned over to touch the Major on the arm. "It has been such a long day. I have developed a terrible headache. M. Shartelle has consented to see me home —would you mind terribly if you said goodbye to the guests?"

She lied well, I thought. The Major didn't even twitch. He was all concern. "That's very kind of you, Mr. Shartelle, I can never thank you enough, Claude, for the wonders you worked here today. It was a splendid party. It will be the talk of Ubondo for days to come." I decided he was still right out of the pages of an old issue of *Cosmopolitan*.

She put her hand to her head. "I was most happy to help. I have given full instructions to the stewards. They know exactly what to do."

Major Chuku was on his feet. He helped Madame Duquesne to rise. I didn't think she needed much help.

"Mr. Shartelle, I am obligated to you for your kind offer to see Madame Duquesne home."

"It is my pleasure, sir."

The Major smiled wryly. "I am sure it is."

Anne gave me the signal and we rose, too. We thanked the Major for the party, complimented him again on the food, told him it was a delightful evening, and started for the car. Shartelle and Madame Duquesne were right behind us. She had her own car, an old, topless TR-3 which

201

Shartelle gallantly offered to drive. He helped her in and she wound some gossamer or spider web around her head to keep her hair from blowing. Shartelle started the car, grinned at us, and said: "See you folks in a few minutes." He gave it too much gas and the back tires threw gravel at the Major's house.

I helped Anne into the Humber and we drove sedately home. By the time we got there the TR-3 was parked in front of the porch, the USIA transmitter in Monrovia was playing some American jazz over the radio, and Shartelle and Madame Duquesne were dancing close together on the front porch. Her headache seemed to have gone.

"Petey," Shartelle said, "after you write those two statements, would you mind leaving a note for old Samuel? I think we're going to be four for breakfast." We were.

— *20* —

The next morning Anne lent Madame Duquesne a wrap-around denim skirt and one of my shirts. The skirt had been providently stored away in the bottom drawer of the bureau two nights before along with a pair of bermuda shorts, some loafers and a blouse.

"If I'm going to be leaving here at eight in the morning, I don't have to look as if the party went on all night," Anne had said when she stored the clothing away.

Shartelle looked inordinately pleased with himself and the Widow Claude was glowing and almost purring when I came into the living room. They were drinking coffee and Anne was having her second cup of tea. Shartelle was also reading the two statements I had written the previous night—my price of admission to the revels that had followed.

He put the statements on the small desk, looked at me, and shook his head slowly from side to side. "You're a writing fool, Petey. In one of them you have the lawyer fellow quitting old Chief Akomolo's outfit because the Chief is a threat to—what did you call it—'the discipline that democracy entails.' And in the other one you got that guy quitting the party because the Chief is 'symbolic of the neo-Fascism that threatens to engulf Africa.'"

"Is it not true, Clint?" the Widow Claude asked.

"What?"

"That the Fascists are on their way back?"

"They may be, honey, but they're not hiding behind old Chief Akomolo's skirts. You don't think you gave the opposition too much ammunition, do you, boy? I almost got clean mad at the Chief myself reading that stuff."

"He'll be called worse than that before it's over."

"You called him everything but a white man."

"Even I wouldn't go that far, Shartelle."

During breakfast, which was served in relays by Samuel, Charles, and Small Boy—who was a little nervous— the telephone rang. It was Shartelle's telephone pal, Mr. Ojara, informing him that a long distance telephone call was in the making and that he, Mr. Ojara, was personally supervising its completion.

"Well, I certainly do appreciate that, Mr. Ojara. Now how's your family? That youngest doing all right now? That's good. Yes, my family's fine. All right. I'll wait to hear from you."

Ten minutes later the call came through. It was from Duffy and he was mad. I could hear him squawking as Shartelle held the instrument a good foot from his ear.

"Now you just calm down, Pig, and tell it to me slow. That's right...we asked you to get us some skywriters....You tried, huh...hold on, Pig....He tried to get us some skywriters, Pete."

"He figured out the code after all."

"Well, when they coming down, Pig? Not coming, huh? That is a shame....Yessir, I would be interested in knowing who got'em sewed up—hold on, Pig, let me tell Pete.

He says that all the skywriters in England are sewed up. Somebody got to them first and he's going to tell me who it is in a minute."

"Tell him I think it's a shame."

"Pete says he thinks it's a shame, Pig. Who got them? They didn't! Hold on, let me tell Pete. He says Renesslaer has got them all sewed up."

"Tell him I said that's a shame."

"Pete said that's a shame, Pig." There was some more squawking. Shartelle sighed and held the telephone an additional six inches from his ear. "Well, I don't know how that telegram could have been delayed, Pig. Jimmy Jenaro handled it himself. It sure is a pity though. Reckon we'll have to depend on the Bonne Année cigar, huh? Well, now, that's bad news. Let me tell Pete. He says that Goodyear gave him a lot of doubletalk about a helium shortage and also claimed that the blimps were all booked up for county fairs or something."

"You know what to tell him," I said.

"Pete says that sure is a shame, Pig. I reckon we'll just have to make do. How you doing on the buttons and the credit card cases?" There was some more squawking. Shartelle smiled. "I know it's a lot of work, Pig, but that's your end of the shooting match." He beckoned to the Widow Claude to bring him his coffee and she hurried over with it. Shartelle gave her a small pat on the butt. "Well, we're just working our fool heads off down here, Pig. Old Pete's writing and I'm politicking. The only trouble is that it gets awful lonely for both of us."

Anne giggled.

"I agree, Pig. The skywriting and the blimps were good ideas. I'm sorry we didn't move fast enough. But you can give Pete credit for those ideas. The boy's just full of them."

"Lying bastard," I said.

"We'll try not to mess anything else up, Pig. It's looking better all the time.... I'll do that... goodbye." Shartelle cradled the phone and grinned his happy grin.

"They bought it on the telegrams, Pete. They must be

running scared. Renesslaer's got every skywriter in England tied up and on the continent, too. Pig tried for the States but the planes won't make the hop across the Atlantic because the pilots don't want to play Lindbergh. As for Goodyear, I figure that's sewed up through official government channels. Wonder how they're going to get that goddamned blimp over here?"

"The CIA will find a way," I said.

"And these two old boys who are splitting from the party will just frost the cake," Shartelle said. "My, this has started out to be a nice day!"

"Clint," the Widow Claude said. "Anne and I have been talking while you were on the telephone. We have decided to come and cook dinner for you tonight."

"I've already talked to Samuel," Anne said. "There's no jurisdictional dispute. He wants to learn how to cook American to please the good mastahs."

"Well, now," Shartelle said. "It's getting just perfect, Pete. Here we are out on the edge of the Sahara, in politics and intrigue ass-deep to a giraffe, and the hot sun is shining down, and us sweating like pigs and swilling down gin and tonics, and bang, here they come, right out of the bush, two of the prettiest young ladies in the world offering to cook for us and all, and one with a liquor store at that."

"It's not Africa, Shartelle," I said weakly. "It's not Africa at all. We're not seeing Africa."

"Why, boy, sure we are. You mean that slick-talking Major last night ain't Africa, and all those folks we met at Chief Akomolo's lunch, and that old witchdoctor and the Ile and his fine straw boater? That ain't Africa? And His Excellency and that two-mile walk we took and that a-shoutin' of our names—oh, that was fine! You tell me old Doc Diokadu ain't Africa and Jimmy Jenaro? And even Cheatwood and those good old boys who are Permanent Secretaries? Why it's better than Mungo Park and that whole passel of books by Robert Ruark. Now I admit there's only been one killing and no animals to speak of, but I feel Africa—I feel it when I'm down in the market talking to those little old handkerchief-head general store-keepers. I feel it, boy, and if I feel it comfortable, then I consider it my good fortune and yours too."

"Okay, Shartelle," I said. "It's your Africa. You've got one that nobody'll ever change."

Shartelle gave a satisfied nod at my capitulation. "Now then, it's perfectly all right for these two fine young ladies to offer to cook for us, but I think, Pete, we'd better give them some money to get the groceries. You got any money?"

"I got money," I said. I took out my wallet and gave Anne four five-pound notes.

"That's forty-two dollars," she said.

Shartelle waved his hand magnanimously. It was my money. "Don't worry about it, Miss Anne. You and the Widow Claude just stock us up nice. And if you can teach old Samuel some new recipes, why I might even part with mine for dirty rice."

"For what?" Anne asked.

"You mean to say you never heard of dirty rice?"

"No, Clint, I have never heard of dirty rice."

"Well, now, we've got a treat coming Sunday. Pete has said he's the expert on fried chicken. So why don't you find us about three or four good plump fryers. Pete'll fry us up a mess of chicken and I'll cook up a potful of dirty rice—just get me two, three pounds of chicken livers and gizzards, honey—and you two young ladies can lollygag around in the shade sipping ice tea, as befits your station in life."

Anne looked at me. "You're right," she said. "It has to be seen to be believed. Can you give me a lift, Claude? I've got to go teach some kids."

"Of course. Shall we meet later to do the shopping?"

"I'll call you."

Shartelle and I each got a fond goodbye kiss. The Widow Claude wound the gossamer around her hair to keep it from blowing. Anne let hers stream out behind. Shartelle watched them leave. "Ain't they a sight, Pete?"

"I'm forced to agree."

The laterite-covered station wagon almost took a fender off of the Widow Claude's TR-3 as she pulled out of the driveway. She yelled something obscene at the driver in French and drove on. The station wagon backed up and a face peered out of the rear window. Shartelle and I watched from the porch. An American voice yelled: "Pete Upshaw around?"

"Here," I yelled back.

The station wagon backed up some more and the driver spun it up the drive. I saw who it was then. The trio.

"Good God," I said, "it's Diddy, Dumps and Tot."

"Who?"

"AP, UPI and Reuters."

"My."

"There goes the morning."

"Maybe they know something."

"The only thing they'll know is that they're thirsty."

The AP man I had known from the days when I was my paper's chief and only European correspondent. He was pushing sixty-five now and had been writing about it all since he was twenty-five. The UPI man was an Australian, a beanpole made of fine wires that were going to fuse one of these days. I had known him when he was in the UPI office in London. The Reuters correspondent was Albertian and roamed the west coast of Africa as far south as Angola, but no farther. He was a big deep-purple man with a huge red and white smile.

"What did you call them?" Shartelle asked.

"Diddy, Dumps and Tot. They were three characters in a book I once read who use to tag around together."

"I read the same book," Shartelle said. "I was eight years old."

"I was six."

The AP man's name was Foster Mothershand. He was called Mother, of course. He was from Omaha but that was a long time ago. The UPI's man was called Charles Crowell and he pronounced it Crow-well. He was from Adelaide really, but he told everyone he was from Sydney. I don't remember how I found out that he was from Adelaide. I think his girl friend in London told me. The Albertian with Reuters was born in Barkandu, educated at the London School of Economics, and had once worked on the *Observer*. That was when I'd known him. His name was Jerome Okpari and he had been married and divorced three times.

On a story like this they would go together in their small pack. It was a matter of economics, actually. They didn't particularly like or dislike each other, but Mothershand was getting too old to do the legwork that he once did and Reuters and UPI still paid navvy's wages to its correspondents who didn't happen to be American. Their London offices also gave the expense accounts a long hard stare. Associated Press, on the other hand, was probably paying Mothershand somewhere around $17,000 to $19,000 a year, plus an expense account that was audited once every five years or so. So Mothershand picked up the tab for the car which all three of them put on their expense sheets, a receipt for each cheerfully furnished by the Lebanese rental car dealer.

"Ain't that old Mother sitting there in the front seat?" Shartelle asked as the station wagon braked to a stop in the gravel driveway in front of the porch.

"It is."

"I thought he was dead. I haven't seen him in fifteen years."

Mothershand got out of the car first. He was a tall man, turning to fat, and his stomach poked out the khaki shirt he wore. He had a cocoa-colored straw hat with a red, white and blue band around it that was settled on the back of his head.

"Pete, I've been told that you serve the driest martini south of the Sahara."

"Your source was unimpeachable, Mother. How are you?" He walked up the steps and we shook hands.

"Shartelle, they said you were here, goddamnit, and I said they lied. It's sure as hell good to see you. Been a long time."

"About fifteen years, Mother."

"In Chicago, wasn't it? You were futzing around with some fool thing or other. They'd brought me back to re-Americanize me or something and they thought Chicago would do it. I got rolled for sixty-seven dollars that night by a Clark Street hustler."

"But she was a pretty little thing, Mother. I do recall her."

"Damned if she wasn't. You boys air-conditioned here?"

"Sorry," I said.

"Well, something cool will do." He walked on into the house.

"Peter Upshaw, DDT's gift to the Dark Continent." This was Crowell of UPI unwinding his six-foot-six frame from the back seat of the station wagon.

"Hello, Charley."

"It's nine o'clock and I'm sweating like a bloody nigger. No offense, Jerry."

"You smell like one, too," Okpari said and gave me his big red and white smile. A lot of teeth and a lot of gum.

We shook hands all around and I introduced Shartelle. Then we went into the living room and they sprawled on the chairs and the sofa. They all wore khaki shirts and pants and suede high-topped shoes which the kids in London were calling fruit boots that year.

I yelled for Samuel and he came out from the depths of his kitchen looking somewhat irritated with all the company we were having so early in the morning.

"We've got coffee, gin, tea, whisky, squash and beer," I said.

"Gin and tonic will do nicely," Crowell said.

"Same here," Mothershand said.

"You bloody heathens," Okpari said. "I'll have squash if it's iced."

Samuel waited for Shartelle and me. I looked at Shartelle who shrugged. "Gin and tonic for us, Samuel," he said.

"Sah," Samuel agreed, but you could tell his heart wasn't in it.

Once the business of serving the drinks was done, I

209

told Samuel to leave the tray on the round coffee table. If anyone wanted another, he could get up and get it. Mothershand stretched and groaned. "We just got in from Fulawa's operation up north, Clint. They got a sharp bunch of young lads running that show. From Renesslaer."

"Is that a fact?" Shartelle said.

"You run into Franchot Tone Calhoun?" I asked.

"Real bright colored boy from Massachusetts."

"They have something delightful cooking," Crowell said. "They were all going around as hush-hush as could be, but you could tell they were planning to run a shitty."

"What do you know?" Shartelle said. "What else they doing?"

"Well, let's see. They got bumper stickers already, slapping them on every mammy wagon and Morris Minor taxi they can find."

"That's a good idea," I said.

"Funny thing, though," Mothershand said. "Two days before—or was it one day? It doesn't matter. Whenever it was when we were there. Anyway, the outfit that's running Dr. Kologo's show in the east was going around with the same shit-eating grins on their faces."

Shartelle yawned and stretched out his legs, crossing them at the ankles. "I knew Renesslaer had some boys up north, but I didn't know Kologo had anything going in the east."

"He's got five or six of them in an office there. They say they're from an outfit called Communications, Inc.— out of Philadelphia. Ever hear of them?"

"Can't say as I have," Shartelle said.

"Pete?"

I shook my head. "Must be new."

"I say, it seems as if the Americans are making off with all the loot in this campaign," Okpari said. "I could use that, I think. How much are they paying you, Mr. Shartelle?"

Shartelle grinned. "Not enough, Mr. Okpari. But whatever it is will have to remain a secret between me and the Internal Revenue Service."

"Ten thousand pounds?" Crowell guessed.

"Christ, Charley. Shartelle wouldn't set up a Boston testimonial banquet for ten thousand pounds."

"You come high, Mr. Shartelle?"

"The candidates who win don't think so," Shartelle said. "Fortunately, I ain't had to talk to but one who lost."

"When was that?" Okpari asked.

"Nineteen-fifty-two."

"Bad year for the party," Mothershand said.

"Terrible bad," Shartelle agreed.

"What the hell are you doing down here, Clint? We go up north and over east and those young apes are pounding away on typewriters, and flogging out news releases, and talking about their four-color posters which I told them wouldn't do 'em no damn good at all. But I get down here and you and Pete are sitting around sipping gin at nine o'clock in the morning. No phones ringing. No excitement. You got it bought already?"

"Shartelle and I are just consultants, Mother," I said. "We think a lot."

"Mother, we're down here trying to help Chief Akomolo hammer out a new democracy on the anvil of political action. How's that, Pete?"

"You *are* a phrasemaker." Nobody made any notes.

"How do you size it up, Clint?" Mothershand asked. "Really, I mean?"

"We're going to sneak by, Foster. I'm laying six to five right now."

"I'll take five hundred."

"Pounds?"

"Dollars."

"Bet."

"Six to five is just a little better than even money, Clint."

"Odds'll get better maybe. You come round see us week before election. Probably be up around nine to five."

"You're confident, huh?"

"Shit, Mother. I ain't no freshwater college coach crying before the season starts because his first string quarterback's come down with a dose of clap. I'm *paid* to be

211

confident. It's my *natural* state of being."

"How about you, Pete?"

"I think I'm over-confident. I predict a sweep for Ako-molo. You can use that if you want. Duffy would like to read it in London."

"What are the chances of getting an interview with Ako-molo?" Crowell asked. "I've got enough on the American thing. You know: Madison Avenue today staked out a claim on a new and profitable territory—the seething politics of West Africa."

"I'm not from Madison Avenue," Shartelle said.

The tall thin Australian smiled thinly. "You will be tomorrow."

"Chances are good, I'd say. I'll call the Minister of Information and see what I can do."

I got Jimmy Jenaro on the phone, after trying the how's-your-family routine with Operator Ojara. He set it up for ten-thirty.

"You guys want to come?" Jenaro asked.

"No. You take care of it."

"Right. Tell them to be at the Leader's house at ten-thirty."

"All right."

I turned to the gentlemen from the press. "Ten-thirty okay?"

Mothershand grinned. "You got it running too smooth, Clint. Either you've got it taped, or you're double-crossing somebody. You've got ready access to Akomolo—a hell of a lot better than Renesslaer does to Fulawa or that Philadelphia outfit has to Kologo."

"Always believed in winning the client's confidence first, Mother. Then we set out to win the election and it makes it so much easier."

Mothershand drained his drink and stood up. "I want to go down and see this young USIS guy before we go to Chief Akomolo's. Thanks for the drink and for the appointment. You guys sure aren't much news."

"Like Pete says, Mother. We're just down here consulting."

We shook hands again all around and they said they'd drop back by on their next sweep. We said they were always welcome. Mothershand paused before he got into the car and looked at Shartelle.

"I could use a big one, Clint. I'm serious."

"If I get one, you'll have it."

The older man nodded and eased himself slowly into the car. It backed out, turned in the turnaround spot, and sped down the driveway towards the road. It left little red puffs of laterite dust in the air.

"The first wave," I said.

Shartelle nodded. "Get Jenaro back on the phone and ask him to get hold of Diokadu and get over here. We got some tough planning to do. We'll also need some stuff."

"Like what?"

"Like some little red, yellow and green markers, or flags. The kind you stick in a map to show where the salesmen are — or at least where they're supposed to be."

"Anything else?"

"A map," he said. "The biggest map of Albertia he can find."

— *21* —

We were following Jimmy Jenaro's XK-E down the high-crowned asphalt road to Obahma for the Wednesday meeting with the Ile. Jenaro had his top down as usual. He was hitting close to eighty on the few straights and at least sixty on the curves. William was keeping him in sight, but that was about all. Shartelle was in his usual car-riding position, stumped back into the cushions of the rear seat, his feet cocked up on the folded-down walnut table that the Super Snipe afforded. His slouch hat was pulled low over his eyes and the black twisty cigar was cold and dead in his mouth.

"You notice Jimmy's folding bicycle?"

"I noticed," I said.

"He says he's going to park the Jaguar at the government rest house, slip into some other clothes, some less fancy ones, and do a little work in his district—from the seat of his bike."

"He's not worried?"

"Nope. He just says it's a safe district, and he wants to keep it that way."

"There're still too many red and yellow flags stuck in that map."

"I think maybe we'll start changing some to green maybe next week, or the week after. It's just started, boy."

Jenaro had produced the map and the pin flags on Saturday. An artist from his Ministry of Information had carefully outlined the parliamentary districts in ink and then, under the sometimes conflicting supervision of Diokadu and Jenaro, had stuck green flags in the districts considered safe for Chief Akomolo; red ones in those considered safe for the opposition, and yellow ones in those considered doubtful or up for grabs.

There was no forest of green on the map. Shartelle had brooded over it most of Saturday, questioning Jenaro and Diokadu about what "the old boys down at the precinct level are doing." I later wrote them a letter, signed by Chief Akomolo, which had implored them to get off their butts and start knocking on doors. Diokadu had it translated into the necessary dialects and it had been mailed out.

On Sunday we had canceled the fried chicken and dirty rice. It had been telephone day at the wide-eaved house. Anne and the Widow Claude had made sandwiches which we ate while Dr. Diokadu and Jenaro were on the phone telling the party faithful not to worry, that the two defectors who had switched parties were small fry, that it didn't mean a thing really, and that we were better off without them. Between them they made at least a hundred calls

214

that day. Shartelle had sent William down to the telephone office with an envelope containing a five-pound note for Operator Ojara who had given the long distance calls his personal supervision.

After Jenaro had hung up on his last phone call, he had turned to Shartelle and said: "They're jumpy. They're jumpy and nervous and the damned thing doesn't really get off the ground until tomorrow. Not officially."

"We could certainly use something tangible—such as the buttons," Diokadu had said.

Shartelle had nodded. "They're on the way."

"They don't seem to be too enthusiastic, either," Jenaro had said gloomily. "A real apathetic bunch of nothings."

"Dekko and Chief Akomolo will stir them up," Shartelle said.

I looked at him as we rode the high-crowned road to Obahma. "I got an idea."

"Good."

"The two defectors, as we keep calling them, made a bit of a splash in all of the papers, even the papers supporting Akomolo. Right?"

"Right."

"We don't need them any more—not as living testimonials to our need for the skywriting and the blimp. Right?"

"Go on."

"They recant."

Shartelle pushed himself up to almost a sitting position and grinned at me. "See the error of their ways. Come back to the fold. The return of the prodigal sons. Why, Petey, that's just fine. When they going to do it?"

I thought for a moment. "Two weeks from now. Let them stay on the other side long enough to earn their money and to pick up any information they can. Then we can milk it for all it's worth. I can write them both hallelujah speeches. Then we'll send them out on the campaign trail."

"Goddamn! The repentant sinners. Why we could set

up a whole series of revival meetings, Pete. We could get folks coming down the sawdust trail, if not to the arms of Jesus, at least unto the fold of Akomolo's party. Boy, you are learning! You've got all the makings of developing a fine, devious mind."

"I studied with the master," I said. "He was a true inspiration."

"Revival meetings," Shartelle murmured and slumped back down into his familiar position. "With real sinners who've seen the glory light. My, that's fine!"

The helicopters had been late arriving that Sunday evening, and Chief Dekko and Chief Akomolo were forced to wait at the airport in the waiting room, which was even hotter than the direct sun. Finally, the machines had arrived, one with a sputtering engine, and they settled down on the airport. After introducing themselves, the pilots had assured us that they could fix the engine quickly, and then had spent three hours doing it. Chief Akomolo had fumed. Dekko had grown quiet. Chief Akomolo had said to Shartelle: "This is not a very auspicious beginning, Mr. Shartelle."

"It's down right rotten, Chief. But I don't think we need just stand around here and fret. If we got some time, we should use it."

"As usual, you are right, Mr. Shartelle," Dekko had said in his deep baritone. So while the pilots had tinkered with the plane for three hours, the plotters had plotted. Dekko had displayed a keen grasp of the basic fundamentals of campaigning. He was scheduled to give a minimum of ten speeches a day and he kept telling me over and over how much he liked his speech. Chief Akomolo kept referring to his oration not as a speech, but as "this document of truth" which I thought was a little effusive, but not too much. It was a good speech.

Finally, one of the pilots had come over. He was the American, a forty-four-year-old skybum who still wore a World War II Army Air Corps visored cap with a thousand-hour crush. His name was Bill Wyatt and his first question had been: "Who rides with Wyatt?" It had been some kind of a joke. Chief Akomolo, his translator, another personal aide, and one of Jenaro's savvy boys had followed the pilot out to the plane after shaking hands with us. We wouldn't see the Chief again for three weeks, but he would call in every night.

Then the South African had come over. He was a tall, thin polite man with a carefully cultivated mustache and black hair that he wore full on the sides and thin on the top because he couldn't help it. Dekko and an entourage similar to Chief Akomolo's had followed the South African, whose name was Veale, over to the other helicopter. Veale hadn't made any jokes; I had preferred him to the American. Before Dekko hoisted himself into the helicopter he had turned and waved to us. We had waved back. Chief Akomolo, gathering up the folds of his robes to mount the helicopter's ladder, had also turned and waved. His gold-rimmed glasses glinted in the late afternoon sunshine. We had waved in reply and Jenaro had looked at his Rolex Oyster wristwatch. "They'll just about make it," he had said.

Dr. Diokadu had seemed nervous. "I must confess I am not very confident about them going off like this by themselves."

"Why, Doc, these are the candidates," Shartelle had said. "Those boys have got to be able to go off by themselves. We can plot and plan for them, we can write their speeches and arrange their transportation and make sure they're going to have a crowd, but we can't get up there and make that speech for them. They just got to do that by themselves."

"They'll be okay," Jenaro had said as he turned to head for his XK-E roadster which we were now following to the Palace of the Ile.

"Think he'll like the buttons?" Shartelle asked.

"Well, they're big enough."

A special contingent of one thousand campaign buttons with the "I GO AKO" slogan on them had arrived that morning from New York air mail first class. I recall that the Pitney-Bowes sticker had read $47.55. We had dumped five hundred of them into an empty biscuit tin, driven down to the Widow Claude's liquor emporium, and got her to wrap it up like a Christmas present. We had also talked her out of a case of brandy for the Ile, at the discount rate.

"I cannot support you on transactions like this, Clint," she had said.

"Why, honey, you know I'm going to take care of you."

"Adventurer."

He had kissed her fondly, patted her intimately, and she had beamed at him. They had both seemed a little far gone to me. I only spent part of the day mooning around. We had bought the brandy on the advice of Jenaro: "When you go calling on the native brass around here, you always bring something—no matter how poor you are. Usually, it's just a kola nut, but with you guys it's got to be something special. The buttons are special and the brandy reflects your high regard for his taste. God knows what he'll give you in return—maybe a couple of thirteen-year-old girls. Or boys. By tradition it's something three or four times more valuable than the gift he receives. So he gives away a lot of beer."

Obahma wasn't much. It was a collection of buildings and huts roofed with corrugated iron turned rust-red by rain. The highway meandered through it, jogging left and right for no apparent reason other than that a few buildings seemed to have been built in the middle of the road at one time. Sideroads, unpaved, led down twisting streets to nowhere. Radio Albertia screamed from the five-inch speakers that hung from the open-front stores. The people, dressed more casually than in Ubondo and Barkandu, loped along about their business. Some sat in the sun and stared. Others curled up in shady spots and slept. Jenaro slowed down for the traffic and some people cheered and waved at him as the XK-E rumbled through the town. He waved back and tossed a package of cigarettes to a collection of streetcorner idlers. They scrambled in the dirt for them.

The Palace of the Ile of Obahma was on the edge of town and it wasn't much, either, although a high-red mud wall ran for almost two city blocks around it. Jenaro told us later that the wall was at least five hundred years old. It had been there when the Portuguese had first arrived. The Jaguar drove up to the wall's wooden gate which was guarded by some Albertians who wore a vague sort of uniform. The gate was open. They smiled and waved at Jenaro as he drove through. A collection of goats, chickens and people wandered around in the large courtyard. The building, which the wall shielded, was built in a maze. It was one-storied, and the outward edge that we could see had a veranda running along it. The veranda was covered by the familiar tin roof, supported by poles carved with intricate figures of men and women standing on each other's heads. Some of the carved poles had been replaced by plain wooden ones; some were missing and had not been replaced at all. Jenaro parked his car and we parked alongside. He called over a youngster who wore nothing but a gray oversized undershirt. He barked something at him in the dialect. The youngster picked up a stick and jumped into the Jaguar, looking around for someone to hit. Jenaro gave him a shilling. He came over to our car as we got out.

"If I'm lucky, the wheels will still be on when I come out. You notice the missing posts?"

"Yes."

"The Ile's bastard sons. It's African art and they flog it to the odd tourist. One of them conned an American oil man out of three hundred pounds for one of the better posts. Now that the roof's about to fall down in some places, the Ile has threatened to cut the hands off the next one who bootlegs a carving."

William went around to the back of the car and got out the brandy and the buttons. He impressed a loiterer into carrying the buttons; he carried the brandy himself. A crowd had gathered and its members stood there waiting for something to happen. It reminded me of a small town where the big event of the day is when the 4:16 freight goes through. It doesn't stop, but there's always the chance that it might.

Jenaro pushed his way through the crowd, ignoring the cries of the urchins to "dash me, Mastah." Bighearted Shartelle, however, got rid of all his change. It only cost me four and six. Jenaro led the way through the maze of open doors and windows and idle faces and hands and bodies. The crowd followed at a more or less respectful distance, still waiting for something to happen. Then the drums began and Jenaro stopped and looked around. He spotted another idler, beckoned him over, asked him a question, and listened carefully as the man answered at length. The drums kept drumming. Jenaro handed the man a shilling and turned to me. "I asked him about the drums. I don't have the advantage of childhood musical training like Diokadu. The drums are saying: 'They come from Ubondo, the Chief of the Word and his two White Friends. They come to pay their respects to the Ile of Obahma, mightiest of the rulers,' and so forth and so on. It's a commercial for the Ile, and a warning to leave our cars alone."

Shartelle was taking it all in with an occasional "My!" and an "Ain't that something, Petey?" Jenaro pressed on, as they say, and we arrived at a door where a tall young man sat behind a small desk. Jenaro greeted him in English: "Hello, Prince."

"Hello, Jimmy."

"Is the old man expecting us?"

"Go on in. He's got a couple of supplicants in there now, but he should be through."

"Prince Arondo—Mr. Shartelle and Mr. Upshaw."

We shook hands with the Prince who was dressed in an open white shirt, a pair of cotton slacks, and sandals. He seemed almost cool. He looked us over and said he was glad to make our acquaintance. We went through the door, William and his button-box wallah following. The man set the button box down on the floor and fled. William put his down and prostrated himself quickly. Jenaro sighed, spread out a handkerchief, and knelt on it, touching his forehead to the floor once. Shartelle removed his hat and I smiled what must have been a silly grin.

The Ile was sitting in a highbacked chair behind what looked like a library table. The chair rested on a dais similar to the one in Chief Akomolo's banquet room. The Ile nodded gravely at us and went on listening to the keening of two men who were flat on the floor in front of the table. The Ile wore the same straw hat that he had worn in Ubondo, but it looked as if it had a new plume floating out of it. Jenaro rose, picked up his handkerchief, and wiped off his forehead. "It's some kind of a dispute over cattle. One of them stole a couple of cows."

The Ile said a short sentence. His voice was quiet; it seemed almost bored. The two men rose quickly, and backed out of the room. They almost bumped into us. Jenaro used his foot to nudge William. Our driver hopped up and darted out of the door. The old man who had pounded the golden staff in Ubondo was sitting in a chair at one end of the library table, his head nodding. Several young boys, dressed in white robes, sat on a bench near a door behind the Ile. They were quiet, but they twisted and squirmed a little, like pages in the U.S. Senate on a slow August day.

The room was larger than I had thought originally. But the walk towards the Ile was not as long as the walk towards Sir Charles Blackwelder. Poufs made of red and white leather were scattered about the floor. A number of non-descript Albertians sat against the walls on either side, watching our entrance, and looking as if they hoped we would stumble and fall so they would have something to talk about.

The Ile motioned us to three chairs that were arranged in front of the table. He didn't offer to shake hands. "Welcome, Chief Jenaro; I hope that you are in good health. I wish the same for Mr. Shartelle and Mr. Upshaw."

"I trust that the Ile of Obahma enjoys the best of health, as do my friends," Jenaro said formally.

The Ile's voice was blurred with a heavy accent. He spoke slowly and his English sounded as if he translated it from the dialect first.

"So," he said. "What have you brought me?"

"Insignificant trifles, Ile of Obahma," Jenaro said. "We are ashamed to offer them, but they are contained in the two boxes by the door." The Ile raised his hand and pointed at the boxes. The pages sprang up, rushed over, and carried them to the table. "Open them," the Ile said.

They opened the box of brandy first, ripping off the fancy wrapping without comment. It was a wooden box and they had to find a hammer to prize up the nails. The brandy was packed in wooden excelsior. It had never looked more impressive. The Ile took out a bottle, put on his glasses to inspect the label, and said: "You are too kind."

The second box was opened. He reached in, picked up a button and examined it. He smiled again. His robes were blue that day and he stuck the button on the front of his robe on the round neck band. The pages said "Ooooh" and "Ahhhh." He gave a button to each of them and they ran to show the others what they had. The Ile said something to the old man with the golden staff. He awoke for a moment, thumped the staff on the floor, and shouted something to the hangers-on who ringed the walls. They came forward one by one, prostrated themselves, and accepted a button. One of them who could apparently read translated "I Go Ako" for the rest. They grinned, pinned the buttons on, and then went back to sit by the walls to wait for something else exciting to happen.

The Ile raised his hand again and a page was at his side. It reminded me of Good King Wenceslaus, the part that goes: "Hither page and stand by me...." He said something to the boy who nodded and darted through the door.

"Well, Mr. Shartelle," he said. "Do you plan to make Albertia your home?"

"I have been thinking of it, Ile," Old Possum lied. "It's mighty attractive country."

"Attractive as America?"

"Some parts of Albertia that I have seen are more attractive than certain parts of America."

"But different?"

"Every place is different, I reckon."

The Ile nodded, apparently satisfied. The page came back with three bottles of beer. The Ile handed him a beer opener that was welded to a three-foot long steel rod. He gestured at the opener. "Strange, is it not? I serve much beer. For a while I tried to keep openers for the bottles, but the people took them away for keepsakes. It became too expensive, so one of my sons suggested the steel rod. We have lost only two in the past year."

The beer was cold and we drank it from the bottles. The Ile watched us, apparently pleased that we were thirsty.

"Mr. Upshaw, I have been told that your home is in England. Is that not strange for an American?"

"One sometimes works where one is paid best," I said.

"And the English pay better than the Americans? I did not know that was true."

"I work for an American."

"And whom does he work for?"

"He is in business for himself."

"In England?"

"Yes."

"He could not earn a livelihood in America?"

"He apparently can earn a better one using his American skills in England."

The Ile nodded and sighed. "I find it all very strange. I have more than sixty-five years and the farthest I have been from this place where I was born is Barkandu. That was four years ago. The Queen was there." He paused. We remained silent.

"Are these Americans doing a good job of work, Chief Jenaro?" He was direct enough.

"An outstanding job, Ile of Obahma."

"I have heard the drums these past few nights. They

keep repeating the phrase that is on the medallion. People are beginning to talk about it. Did the Americans suggest the drums?"

"They did."

"One might weary of the same message."

"It will be changed at frequent intervals."

"And Akomolo, is he well?"

"Very well."

"And Dekko, is he well?" The old man seemed to put a little more interest into his question.

"He, too, enjoys excellent health."

"That is good." He paused and seemed to be reflecting. "You are the cunning one, Jim-Jim. In this election, who will win?"

"Our chances are improving daily, Ile of Obahma."

"There is a chance?"

"There is."

"A good chance—or a fair chance?"

"A good chance."

"Would you agree, Mr. Shartelle?"

"I would indeed, sir."

The round face of the Ile went into repose. His lids almost closed over his eyes. His voice seemed low and distant. "You have heard of no trouble, Jim-Jim?"

"None."

"No potential danger?"

"None that I can name."

"No threat?"

"I have heard of none, Ile of Obahma. News reaches your ears more quickly than it reaches the wisest of us. Have you heard anything that we should know?"

The Ile's eyes were closed now. He leaned back in his chair. "The policeman's death was unfortunate. I do not know that it was connected with the election. Yet, it is not what I have heard, Chief Jenaro." The diminutive was gone. "It is what I sense. There is bound to be violence between now and the day of the election. There has always been some. I say that as long as the people are allowed to vote, there always will be. But this which I sense is something else. I have not been able to determine what. But it is similar to the quietness of the air before a storm." He opened his eyes and looked at each of us, one by one. "Should there be danger, come here. None dare violate this Palace. I will make you welcome."

He stood up. The interview was over. We rose hastily. "In your car, gentlemen, you will find a small token. But it does not equal your gift. Mr. Shartelle, I have heard that you admired my automobile when I arrived at Chief Akomolo's last week. It is yours. It will be delivered to your house this evening."

I had seen Shartelle weather some onslaughts, but he reeled before the Ile's. "I couldn't possibly—"

"Ixnay," Jenaro said.

"It is too great a gift, Ile. I'm not worthy." He had recovered.

"It is old. I have several others. Yet I like it. Tell me, could I purchase another LaSalle from the United States?"

"I don't think they are manufactured any more."

"What a pity." He nodded briefly, turned, and left the room.

Shartelle clapped his black slouch hat on his head, stuck a twisty cigar in his mouth, and shook his head in wonderment. We left, saying goodbye to the Prince who still guarded the door, and made our way to the cars. Jenaro paused. "Well, good buddies, I go for bush one time."

"Jimmy, is that nice old man really going to give me that fine car?"

"It's yours. I think it's got about nine thousand miles on it."

"He'd been insulted if I'd refused?"

"Deeply."

Shartelle nodded. "Look, you got a minute? Pete had an idea while we were driving up." He quickly spelled out the evangelistic role that the two defectors would play once they recanted. Jenaro's eyes glittered. "A real come-to-Jesus traveling camp meeting, huh?"

"Exactly."

"Tent and all?"

"Right."

"Leave it to me. I'll fix it by phone this afternoon. Don't worry, I'll just lay on the tent, the sound trucks, the advance men, and so forth."

"Ministry of Information?"

Jenaro shrugged. "Buddy, if we win it, we won't worry about it. If we don't, we'll be a long way off. I don't fancy our jails. I've inspected them."

"Uh-huh."

"Here." Jenaro handed Shartelle a piece of paper. "That's my phone number for the next few days. It's the government resthouse. They'll take messages and I'll check with them once or twice a day at least."

We watched him give the car-watcher another shilling, check to see that his folding bicycle was still intact, and start off towards his district, a medium-sized brown man in Miami wraparound shades, driving an XK-E for bush.

"Tarzan and Timbuktu," Shartelle murmured. We walked over to our car. Two cases of Gordon's gin were in the back seat. William cheerfully put them in the trunk of the Humber. We climbed in and started off.

"Well, there's one thing, Clint."

"What's that?"

"You don't have to worry about a freeze busting the block on your new LaSalle."

— *22* —

William drove the Humber slowly down the high-crowned asphalt highway that wound through the town of Obahma that lay 70 miles from Ubondo, 169 miles north of Barkandu. Shartelle was slumped down into his familiar backseat position. The rusty slouch hat sat low over his eyes, the twisty cigar gathered a nice ash.

"William, you keep poking along like this and we're never going to get anywhere."

William turned his head around and gave us the big smile, but he seemed nervous.

"Madam ask me to ask you, Mastah."

"Madam who?"

"Madam Anne, Sah."

"What she ask you to ask us?"

"If we go now for my village. It is not far."

"How far is not far?" I asked.

"Forty, maybe fifty miles."

"When's the last time you were home, William?"

"Two years ago, Sah. I have letter from uncle. He say my brother is now ready for school. For good school, Sah. Madam say to me that she will see that he go to school where she is teacher."

I looked at Shartelle and said: "As far as I'm concerned, Madam has spoken."

"You're right. William, we go for village."

"Thank you, Sah!" He spun the wheel of the Humber, made a U-turn, barely missing a mammy wagon that went by the name of "Poverty Is No Crime," and sped down the highway in the opposite direction.

"What's the name of your village?"

"It very small. It is called Koreedu. Very nice name."

"Very nice," I agreed.

The rain forest thinned out, the farther north we drove from Obahma. It gave way to fields of stunted trees and grass. Palm groves which looked cultivated cropped up occasionally. On a curve, a family of baboons suddenly loped across the road. The rearguard stopped and chattered at us in what looked to be real rage.

Shartelle gave me a poke. "Lookee there, Pete! Ain't that something? Look at him just standing there and giving us billy hell. Ain't he a pistol?"

"Baboons, Sah. They very good chop."

Shartelle had his head craned around, staring at the

baboons through the rear window. "You don't eat those things, do you, William?"

"Very good, Sah."

"Goddamn it, Pete, that's the very first live animals I've seen in Africa. Baboons."

"There're supposed to be some elephants left around here some place. And rhinos. At least that's what it says on the map."

"I'd sure admire to see some."

"Maybe we'll be lucky."

We weren't, though. All we saw the rest of the trip were some goats and chickens. That far north, traffic grew scarce, and the Albertian or two we passed gave us a cheery wave and a shout of greeting. We waved back.

William turned left onto a laterite road after we had gone what I estimated to be fifty miles. The washboard ridges in the laterite grew deeper and rougher. The car jounced along, spewing up a cloud of thick red dust behind. Finally, the laterite gave out to a one-car trail with grass growing between the two tracks. William kept on driving, a little faster now, eager to get to his village.

"You sure you know where you're going?" Shartelle asked.

"Very sure, Sah. Not far now."

"It wasn't far sixty miles back," I said.

A few people began to appear. I don't know where they came from. There were no houses or huts around. They waved at us and William honked the horn and waved back. In a small clearing, just off the trail, there was a mud-walled building, open in the front, that displayed a faded red Coca-Cola cooler of an early 1939 vintage. William pulled up to the building and stopped. Inside, I could see shelves stocked with a few tins of sardines, soup, biscuits or cookies, canned meat, powdered soap, bar soap, matches, cigarettes and snuff. It was another general store.

"I buy gift for village," William said.

"Is it the custom?"

"Yes, Sah."

"We'll buy the gifts. You got any money, Pete?"

228

I gave William two pounds and told him to get what he thought proper. He came back with boxes of cookies, some cigarettes, some snuff, some tinned jawbreakers, and a half pint of whisky.

"What's the whisky for?" Shartelle asked.

"For village headman, Sah."

"He likes gin?"

"Very much."

"Take the whisky back and trade it for some more cookies. We'll donate a couple of bottles of the Ile's gin."

From the general store it wasn't far to the village of Koreedu. The word had been passed that William was returning, driving a fine car for the two white men. They all turned out to meet us—all seventy of them, including children and dogs. There were some square houses built of mud with round, thatched roofs. There were some shed-like buildings that looked as if they were used to dry crops, if ever a crop were harvested. The street was pale dust. William parked the car and got out. He was embraced by an old man, then by a series of younger men. He answered questions; asked questions, smiled, laughed and talked. His relatives and friends did the same. Shartelle and I stood by the car and watched. It grew too hot for that so we walked over and stood in the meager shade of some palm trees. William ran over to us and asked us to follow him. He led us into the village's largest building. It was cooler inside, but that ended when the village population decided to come in, too.

There were three chairs on a raised platform and the old man whom William had first embraced directed Shartelle and me to sit on two of them. William ran out to the car and brought back the boxes of gifts and goodies. He didn't forget to bring the two bottles of Gordon's gin. Shartelle and I sat on either side of the old man. Speaking in the dialect, William made a small oration and presented the two bottles of gin to the old man with a flourish. That called for a response which took up another quarter of an hour or so. The old man then produced two unlabeled pint bottles of clear liquid and handed them to us. Shartelle rose to the occasion and made a fine five-minute speech on behalf of the United States, Lyndon Johnson, Chief Akomolo, the party, Padraic Duffy, Anne Kidd, the Widow Claude, himself and me. He also threw in a few words about the grave responsibilities and duties which William shouldered in Ubondo. He sat down to thunderous applause.

The old man insisted that we have a drink of the unlabeled liquid. I asked William what it was.

"Gin, Sah. Native gin."

"Sweet Christ."

"Very good, Sah."

Shartelle uncapped a bottle and took a swallow. I watched to see whether he keeled over. He didn't, so I uncapped my bottle and swallowed some. It wasn't bad. I've drunk worse. But rarely. William then passed out cigarettes to the younger villagers, snuff to the older ones, and candy and cookies to the pickins, as the children were so quaintly called. A woman came forward and began to talk to William earnestly. He shoved her away with a sharp retort. She insisted. He relented. Shartelle and I decided to give the native gin another go.

"Mastah, woman here want you to look at her pickin."

"Why?"

"She say he sick."

"How is he sick?"

"He sick for three, four days now. Cry all time."

"Does she want me to come with her?"

"Pickin just outside. She bring him in."

Shartelle sighed. "All right, I'll look at him."

William spoke harshly to the woman. Maybe he was due to be headman someday and was just practicing for the job. The woman shoved her way through the packed, now airless, meeting hall where the villagers stood and sat, eating their cookies, smoking their cigarettes, and passing around the Gordon's gin. The woman came back carrying a naked year-old baby who was loosely wrapped in a piece of blue cotton cloth. He was a boy and he squawled, his eyes screwed up tight, his stomach distended and hard. She deposited the boy at Shartelle's feet and backed off into the protective custody of the crowd. Shartelle knelt by the baby who racketed off some more screams. He sounded as if he were in bitter pain. Shartelle patted him on the head, probed his stomach, looked into his mouth, and felt the joints in his legs and arms.

"William, get me some boiling water," he said.

"You're shooting the wrong scene, Manny. The kid's already born."

"Nothing wrong with this kid except pellagra, rickets if he don't get some vitamins, and colic. I know a colicky kid when I see one. I can cure him, too."

"What with?"

"Wild yams. Pound 'em up into a mush and feed it to him. Clean him out good."

"That what the boiling water is for?"

"Kid needs a tranquilizer. Can't get wild yam mush in him till he calms down."

"Where you going to get a tranquilizer?"

Shartelle gave me his wicked grin. "Boy, you just look and learn. You're going to see one of the oldest tranquilizers for kids in the history of the world."

William brought in a small primus stove with a pot of water that bubbled on top of it.

"I need sugar, William. A pound maybe. Brown or white, it doesn't matter."

William translated this quickly to the crowd. Three women darted away, squirming through the packed audience who moved in closer for a better view of Dr. Shartelle's matinee performance. The women were back soon with the sugar, which they handed over to William who handed it to Shartelle. The sugar was brown and it was kept in paper spills. Shartelle took a look at the water and told William to pour about half of it out on the dirt floor. William poured and part of the crowd jumped back. He set the pot back on the stove. "Get me a small, clean stick, William," Shartelle said. William demanded a stick and a man who was cleaning his teeth with one that had a sharp point sacrificed it for the operation. It also entitled him to a ringside seat. Shartelle took the stick in one hand and a spill of sugar-filled newspaper in the other. He poured the sugar into the boiling water, stirring slowly.

"William, get me the biggest rooster they got."

"Rooster, Sah?"

"Cock—male chicken—man chicken."

"Sah!" William translated quickly to the crowd. "Ahhhh," the crowd said. Now the white fool makes sense. He will sacrifice a cock. Someone else burrowed through the crowd bearing a scrawny rooster. He held him out to Shartelle. Another man offered his machete. "Just hold him there a minute," Shartelle said.

He finished pouring the sugar into the boiling water and kept stirring it with a spoon until it was a thick syrup. Then he asked for the Gordon's gin and poured a thimbleful into the pot. He stood up. "Turn the rooster around and hold him tight," he told William who told the rooster holder.

Shartelle inspected the rooster's rear carefully, selected the longest, biggest tail feather, and gave it a quick jerk. The rooster squawked. The kid set up a new howl. Shartelle took the tail feather and dipped it into the syrup until it was completely coated. Then he waved it gently in the air to cool. He gave it to the baby who put it in his mouth— at least part of it. He quit squawking and sucked on the syrup. It was sticky. He liked that. He was only whimpering now. The more he sucked on the feather, the stickier he got, and the better he liked it. He gurgled a little, and wiped his face with the syrupy feather. He liked that even better. He dragged it across his stomach and almost smiled when it tickled and left a syrupy trail.

"Never seen it fail," Shartelle said. "The stickier they get, the better they like it. They can suck on it and it's sweet. They can mess with it and it just gets nastier and nastier. Just a taste of alcohol. Nothing a baby likes more, boy. Any baby."

He turned to William and told him to tell the mother how to use the wild yam paste to cure the baby's colic.

William understood and sought the mother out in the crowd. He translated to her, and to the fascinated audience. She went shyly towards the baby, scooped him up, sticky, syrupy feather and all, smiled nicely at Shartelle, murmured something, and darted through the crowd which parted for her.

Shartelle and I had another drink of the native gin and then got out of the building. "Get that brother of yours, William, and let's get going," I told him.

"He here, Sah." William pointed to a small boy in khaki shorts and white undershirt who giggled and darted behind a stout woman who seemed to be his mother. William talked to her and she talked to the boy who took William's hand. "This is Kobo, Sah. He is my brother."

"Hi, there, young fellow," Shartelle said. The kid ducked his head into William's side.

"He's your real brother?" I asked.

"Very close," William answered and I didn't have the heart to ask him what he meant.

The old man who had given us the gin hobbled up with another present—a live hen. He extended her to Shartelle who, with his usual charm, accepted gracefully and kept his speech of acceptance to two minutes. The villagers crowded around the car as William, a big man among them now, got into the front seat with Kobo and the hen. Shartelle passed out a couple of handfuls of "I Go Ako" buttons which he had pigeonholed somewhere and the recipients "ahhhed" them. We shook hands with the headman, and with anyone else who wanted to, and got in the car. William backed it around slowly and then drove off. I thought the woman whose skirts Kobo had hidden behind was crying. She ran after the car for a little way, waving. So did some of the other villagers. Kobo sat still and straight in the front seat, stroking the hen. He had tied her legs together.

We rode in silence for a half-hour or so. Then the hen began to cackle. It cackled some more and then became quiet. Kobo turned around in the seat, a shy smile on his face. His hand came up and he held an egg in it. He offered the egg to Shartelle.

The white-haired man smiled and took the egg. "Thank you, sonny," he said. "Thank you, very much."

— *23* —

It is difficult to remember whether the trouble with the hooligans started three weeks or four weeks after Captain Cheatwood was stabbed to death on the driveway. West Africa dulls any sense of time. Days begin with a cup of tea and each morning is the same as the one that opened the day before. Flowers bloom, fade, and bloom again without apparent regard for seasons. It's always July in West Africa. A hot July. A journal or diary could be filled with ditto marks.

The trouble came when the roving bands of political hooligans—of all parties—decided to expand their operations. Devised as a form of patronage that offered a few shillings a day and the opportunity to be a general nuisance, the hooliganism broadened into highwaymanship. No longer content with heckling the opposition speakers and harassing their audiences, the gangs started throwing blockades across main roads and robbing the passengers of private autos and mammy wagons.

Chief Akomolo was the first Albertian leader to crack down. He ordered Acting-Captain Oslako to stop the banditry. The job kept the Captain busy. His force was limited and the hooligans had fast transport. They would hit an intersection of highways at six o'clock in the morning. Seven hours later, three hundred miles away, and out of the Captain's jurisdiction, they would be busy robbing somebody else. Oslako and his men managed to capture a few hooligans. Even more important, or useful, they managed to kill some in the process. The Old Boy network among the British civil servants got cranked up again and both the northern and eastern regions announced their determination to eliminate the highwaymen. After the police in those regions caught and killed a few, the robberies stopped.

Captain Oslako dropped by to see me one afternoon during either the fourth or fifth week of the campaign. It was just after the last of the road robberies. I was sitting on the porch, drinking a glass of instant iced tea, and sniffing the honeysuckle. Shartelle and Jenaro were out on a grass roots swing and I had stayed behind to okay copy on the weekly party paper that was published either on Thursday or Friday. It depended on the whim of the printer. I also had to file press releases every morning and night and make sure that the buttons, fans and credit cardholders fell into the proper hands. Things had gone smoothly enough. Smooth for Albertia. A plane load of buttons had been forced down in Accra and the Ghanaian military government impounded them on the theory that they were part of a plot by Nkrumah to regain power. The buttons probably are still in Accra, rusting away.

Everybody had buttons by then. Alhaji Sir Alakada Mejara Fulawa's were white with blue lettering and read "HAJ." Dr. Kensington O. Kologo, from the east, had smaller ones that read "KOK" for his initials. Ours were the biggest of all, a good two-and-a-half inches in diameter, with white backgrounds and red letters that formed the "I GO AKO" slogan plus the party symbol of a crossed hoe and rake. Shartelle described them as "damned aggressive buttons." I just thought they were the biggest.

"You look relaxed, Mr. Upshaw," Captain Oslako said after he took a chair next to the honeysuckle and accepted a cold bottle of beer.

"It won't last," I said.

"I suppose not. Those hooligans were causing no end

of bother. I think we've put a stop to it." He had a nice BBC accent.

"Killing a few seemed to help."

"As Captain Cheatwood was fond of saying, 'My men enjoy their work.' "

"He seemed to know his job," I said.

"Did you know him well?"

"No. I met him once. He paid a social call."

"He was an interesting man. He had fantastic sources of information."

"He said he'd been here a long time."

Captain Oslako crossed his lean legs. He was wearing a starched khaki uniform and white wool socks with the clodhopper shoes. The socks looked hot and I wondered if they itched.

"You have no idea why he came to call on you that night—the night he was killed?"

"None. Are you sure that he was calling on us?"

"He was in your driveway."

"Maybe he was forced into it from the road."

"So he could be dispatched in a more secluded spot?"

"Maybe."

"His widow said that he was merely out for a walk," Oslako said. A remnant of my newspaper training made me wince mentally at his use of the word "widow." It recalled a comment by my first city editor about an obituary I had written: "Mr. Upshaw, Mr. Jones has been dead only a few hours. Mrs. Jones will be a widow for perhaps years to come. Let us be charitable and refer to her as his wife, not as his widow."

"Then I suppose he was," I said. "Just out for a walk."

"Some have advanced the theory that his murder inspired the hooligans to turn to highway robbery; that the murder gave license to lawlessness."

"What do you think?"

"To be frank, I don't know. I discount the theory of simple robbery. Captain Cheatwood was too good a policeman to let a common cutpurse get the better of him."

"That's my impression."

236

"It may have been inspired by a personal grudge. Or because he knew something that someone thought he shouldn't."

"And someone killed him to shut him up?"

"Possibly."

"You seem to have an ample supply of theories, Captain."

Oslako sighed. "Many theories, but few facts. I even thought that he may have been killed to prevent him from giving you information which might affect the outcome of the campaign. But you seem unable to substantiate that."

"He had no information, as far as I know."

"Did you talk about the campaign at all?"

"Yes. We talked about the arrangements for the counting of the ballots, the poll-watching, and so forth. Just the mechanics."

Oslako rose. "Thank you for the beer, Mr. Upshaw. I take it Mr. Shartelle is out of the city?"

"Yes. He's making a tour with Chief Jenaro."

We said goodbye and Captain Oslako left. His former superior had trained him well. I wondered if we should have told him about the letter-like trenches that Cheatwood had scrawled in the dirt. I decided to talk to Shartelle about it when he got back.

One of the purposes of the Shartelle-Jenaro tour was to check up on the revival meetings which were then in full progress and which featured the two defectors who were now safely back in the Akomolo fold. I had written each a slightly-embellished speech that revealed in sordid detail how they had been lured into the camps of the opposition with promises of money and orgiastic goings-on. According to my speeches, the one who went north got the most money and the fanciest parties. They had lasted for three days and three nights and I described them in prurient, lip-smacking detail. When a twinge of conscience, slight but still noticeable, caused me to suggest to Shartelle that I might stick just a trifle more closely to the facts, he had grinned his wicked grin and replied:

"We ain't in the truth business, Petey."

The defector who had gone east was a lawyer and turned out to be something of a ham. We decided he should go on last. He gave a quiet, calm presentation, made even more chilling by the factual manner in which he recounted the experiences I had dressed up for him.

When the pair switched back to Akomolo's party, they had stirred up interest among the voters. We started to receive reports that the camp meetings were drawing larger crowds than either Dekko or Akomolo. Shartelle and Jenaro had gone to see for themselves.

Anne was busy with some school functions the evening that Captain Oslako came to call, so I had dinner alone. After dinner I went back out on the porch for coffee and brandy and to sniff the honeysuckle some more. While I sat there the talking drums began their nightly commercial. I could recognize the one they played that night. It was "I Go Ako." The following night the drums were again scheduled to attack the vile vapors in the sky. We had heard that one of the skywriting pilots had been stoned at an airport when he landed for fuel.

I had one more press statement to write that evening. It was in praise of Chief Akomolo's efforts as mediator in the week-long strike of the Federated Association of Albertian Night Soil Collectors. It was a release whose writing I found easy to postpone.

Jenaro had finagled the deal with the general secretary of the Albertian Trade Union Congress. I never asked what the payoff was and he never told me. As a boon, however, the general secretary had thrown in the support of the National Union of Unemployed Workers, an organization of growing membership which was useful to issue statements, swell crowds, provide sympathetic pickets, and make a lot of noise.

The strike had gone on for a week throughout the country and the residents of the larger towns, especially Ubondo, Barkandu and the capital cities of the northern and eastern regions, grew restive and demanded a quick settlement. The stench in the areas of Ubondo which had no sewers made me sympathize with the residents.

The night soil collectors were demanding a shilling a day raise; those who drove the honey wagons were asking for one and six because of their higher professional status. At the proper time, Chief Akomolo stepped forward and offered to mediate the dispute. After a twelve-hour bargaining session (starting at six in the evening and continuing until six in the morning, a dramatic touch which I supplied) the Chief had emerged from behind the traditional closed doors to announce an agreement: The night soil collectors were to get an increase of nine pence a day; the honey wagon drivers would get a shilling. The price of night soil collecting would go up 8.3 per cent. I held out for the odd percentage because it was harder for the customer to figure and it also sounded as if the formula had been reached after careful collective bargaining conducted in the best of faith.

"The Chief came out of that night soil mess smelling like a rose," Shartelle had commented. He was back from his tour the day after Captain Oslako visited me. For the rest of the campaign, Shartelle spent most of his nights at the Widow Claude's. During the days we counseled with Chiefs Dekko and Akomolo by telephone. The helicopters had been painted a bright silver with "AKO" in big blue letters on one and "DEKKO" in red letters on the other.

Both helicopter pilots seemed to be without nerves. If they spotted a group of five persons, they set the machines down so that the candidates could hop out and shake hands. Dekko was making up to twenty-five speeches a day. He started at five in the morning and quit at midnight. Dekko toured the surrounding area by car or even bicycle when it got too dark for Veale, the South African, to fly.

Chief Akomolo, older and tiring more easily, kept to a schedule that called for a minimum of a dozen speeches a day, countless visits to homes, plus dinners, banquets, and palmwine drinking bouts. He concentrated on the northern and eastern regions, leaving the west mostly to Dekko. The reports that came back to Jenaro and Diokadu grew encouraging, even optimistic. Jenaro sliced them in half, but the number of green flags on the wall map continued to grow.

The day before the three major candidates were to appear at a mass rally and speech marathon at the Ubondo race track, we received a call from Jack Woodring of the United States Information Service.

"This is the clean-cut American lad from the USIS."

"We don't need any," I said.

"You're going to have visitors."

"Who?"

"The honorable Felix Kramer, United States Consul General, and the only slightly less honorable Clarence Coit, his Political Affairs Officer. You met him."

"I remember."

"They'll arrive this afternoon, but they won't stay for dinner. That's my chore. Would you and Clint like to come? We're having hash."

"Well," I said.

"Anything I can't stand is a poor excuse. We'll make it another time."

"Thanks, Jack."

He said I was welcome and hung up. I turned to Shartelle. "Felix Kramer is dropping by this afternoon with Coit."

"Up for the rally?"

"I'd assume so."

Shartelle and I had spent the morning alone trying to figure out whether the campaign had peaked. We decided that it hadn't, that it was still gathering momentum, but so were the campaigns of the opposition. We decided we had a fifty-fifty chance and that we were pulling away. We ate lunch alone. Anne was teaching school; Claude was running her liquor business. We had hamburgers made of coarsely-ground beef, broiled rare, on buns that Anne had baked herself. The hamburgers were topped off with thick slices of onion, lettuce and mayonnaise. We drank German beer. There were also French fried potatoes.

"Very good lunch," Shartelle told Samuel.

"Madams teach me, Sah. They very good teacher." He disappeared back into his kitchen which Anne and the Widow Claude had had sterilized. Samuel had grumbled at first, but the meals improved. He quickly learned some basic dishes that he prepared skillfully. He also mixed a better-than-average martini.

"The poor bastard's ruined," I told Shartelle.

"Why?"

"None of the British will hire him after having worked for an American. We spoil them."

"There's going to be more Americans here than British pretty soon. Old Samuel will make out. Did you pay them this month?"

"Yes."

"Well, now, Pete, I sort of went around and gave them each an extra couple of pounds, figuring it's Pig's money and all."

"Sort of, huh? That's nice. I raised them all two pounds."

"I'd say we've settled the servant problem in pretty fair style."

We were having coffee when Kramer's Cadillac rolled up to the front, an American flag streaming from a fender staff. Kramer got out first. He was in his late forties, perhaps even fifty, and he was slightly tubby and didn't seem to give a damn about it one way or another. He had dark brown eyes, his head was smoothly bald and tan on top, and the hair around the sides was cut short and speckled with gray. Coit followed Kramer out of the car.

Shartelle and I were on the porch. "If you folks haven't had lunch, I believe we could give you a couple of hamburgers and a bottle of beer that would make you feel plain homesick. I'm Clint Shartelle, Mr. Kramer, and this is Pete Upshaw. Hi, Mr. Coit."

Kramer, wearing a light blue suit with black shoes, mounted the steps of the porch and shook hands with us. "I despise myself for it, Mr. Shartelle, but we didn't have lunch and I can't resist a hamburger." We shook hands with Coit and he said he'd have a hamburger, too. I yelled

241

for Samuel and gave him the order. He brought more coffee for Shartelle and me while the hamburgers broiled. He brought cold beer for Coit and Kramer.

"I'm sorry I missed you in Barkandu, gentlemen," Kramer said, "but I'm glad you had the chance to talk with Clarence here."

"We had a nice talk," Shartelle said. "You up for the rally, Mr. Kramer?"

"That's part of it. We're on a pre-election swing, really. So I may as well ask you what you think—or what you predict."

"Akomolo by a landslide."

"That your honest or professional opinion?" Coit asked.

"I'd hate to separate the two."

"I've heard that Kologo's been making gains," Coit said.

"Now you must have been talking to those young kids from the States he's got running his campaign over there. They're from that new agency in Philadelphia. You recollect its name, Pete?"

"Communications, Inc. I never heard of it before."

"You ever hear of it, Mr. Coit?"

"Yes, indeed," the man from the CIA said. "I believe it's gained quite a reputation for itself in the short time it's been organized."

"Funny I never heard of it," Shartelle said.

"What effect do you think the skywriting is having, Mr. Shartelle?" Kramer asked.

"Why, I think it's doing real fine for the opposition. It's hurting the hell out of us, of course, and I just wish we'd thought of it first."

"I've heard that it's backfiring."

"Is that a fact?"

"Out in the bush they're saying that it causes sterility and impotency—the smoke from the skywriting."

"I never," Shartelle said and clucked his tongue some.

"Does Kologo have a blimp?" I asked.

Kramer nodded.

"Goodyear blimp?"

He nodded again.

"They had all the ideas, didn't they, Clint?" I said.

"Seems that way."

Samuel brought in the hamburgers on a tray and served two each to Kramer and Coit. They ate hungrily while I fetched them another beer.

"Wonder how Kologo's outfit got that blimp over here?" I asked. I didn't care who answered.

"I understand that they dismantled it, flew it over in sections by plane, and reassembled it," Kramer said. I wondered if he knew what Coit's job really was.

"Must have cost a heap of money," Shartelle said.

Coit took a swallow of his beer and said: "Goodyear plans to use it again on a goodwill tour throughout Africa and Europe. They've been thinking about it for some time."

"I thought the goverment had an embargo on the export of helium."

"It's been lifted," Coit said.

"Generally," I asked, "or just in this specific case?"

Coit didn't squirm, but he didn't look comfortable. "For this particular case, I believe."

"Well, it sure is a good idea," Shartelle said. "That old blimp floating up there with Kologo painted on the sides and a streamer a couple of blocks long with his name on it trailing out behind. I bet it's a fine sight to see. Get a lot of votes, too."

Kramer swallowed a belch. "I don't know, Mr. Shartelle. I'd say your more orthodox methods seem to work better. We've been getting some protests at the Consulate about the blimp. It seems that out in the bush for some reason they believe it's an atomic bomb—or that it carries one. I don't know how these rumors get started, but even the French have made a discreet inquiry about it."

Coit changed the subject. "You are convinced then that it's Akomolo in a sweep? He has been getting around, I'll grant you that. Both he and Dekko."

"Let's just say we're confident. By the way, Mr. Kramer, I suppose you heard about the murder of Captain Cheatwood?"

"Yes. I was sorry to hear about it. I'd met him and he

243

seemed highly competent."

"Got stabbed to death right out on our driveway," Shartelle said, looking at Coit.

"Have they found who did it?" Coit asked.

"Not yet."

"What was it, robbery?"

"That's one theory," I said.

"You mean there're more?"

"A number of them. One is that he had some information that somebody wanted him to keep to himself. When it became apparent that he wouldn't, he was killed. Some even think the hooligans did it."

"Do you have a theory?" Coit asked.

"No, we don't," Shartelle said. "We just met him once briefly and we were playing poker the night he got stabbed."

"You didn't have any trouble or anything?" Kramer asked.

"No. Nothing like that."

"Strange he should be killed on your driveway," Coit said.

"Yes, isn't it?" Shartelle said.

We talked some more about the election and showed them the map with the green, yellow and red flags. Kramer was impressed; Coit looked as if he were trying to photograph it with his eyes.

"Give my regards to Chief Akomolo when you see him," Kramer said. "I'm sorry to impose on your hospitality like this, but I enjoyed it thoroughly." He smiled at Shartelle. "I've been following your campaign closely, Mr. Shartelle. I'd say your reputation is intact, regardless of who wins."

"Thank you, sir."

We shook hands again and they walked out to their Cadillac. We watched them leave.

"They sure liked those hamburgers," Shartelle said.

"Coit didn't rise to the bait about Cheatwood."

"I noticed. Either he's one cool customer or he's purely ignorant about it."

244

"He's too clean-cut to engineer a policeman's assassination."

"They said that about somebody else one time," Shartelle said.

"Who?"

"Pretty Boy Floyd."

— 24 —

Anne, the Widow Claude, Shartelle and I went to the rally the next day in the big white LaSalle, with the top down. We'd bought William a new shirt and a pair of slacks. He drove and we sat in the back, Shartelle and Claude in the rear seat, Anne and I on the jump seats that folded down.

The car was recognized by many of the Albertians and some of them prostrated themselves, thinking that the Ile was going by. Their more sophisticated friends got them up with shouts of laughter and a kick in the ribs. Shartelle gave all who bowed the benediction of his waved cigar.

I was once quite good at guessing crowds, but the one at the race track was a puzzler. I had seen Shartelle count a political gathering of five hundred with a sweep of his eyes and miss only by three. He put the crowd down at 252,000 people. My newspaper experience led me to put it down at 250,000. Nobody was ever sure.

A special pass provided by Chief Akomolo got us onto the race track grounds itself. William parked the car and we decided to stick with it. There was no place to go except into a packed human mass that shifted restlessly now and then. The vendors were out, selling food, cold drinks, and popsicles. Some members of the crowd wore all three campaign buttons proudly. There were government clerks dressed in neat white suits and farmers dessed in shorts and undershirts. There were richly-robed northerners and Europeanized professional men from Barkandu. We sat under the shade of umbrellas that Claude had thought to bring and watched the people settle down into groups, waiting for the show to begin.

It began when the two helicopters appeared over the horizon, flying low and in formation, if two can do it. They passed over the crowd, did a few tricks of hovering and going up and down, which delighted everyone and also blew a place clear for them to land. The machines came down about a hundred yards from our car. We could see Chief Akomolo get out first, hopping briskly to the ground. Chief Dekko got out next and moved through the crowd, standing a full foot taller than anyone else. They made their way to the bandstand.

Alhaji Sir Alakada Mejara Fulawa arrived in equally fine style. His Mercedes 600 had four motorcycle cops in front of it and they all played their sirens. The Mercedes bored through the crowd to deposit Sir Alakada at the foot of the bandstand. He wore white robes.

Dr. Kensington Kologo came in a Cadillac. I could see that he wore glasses because they flashed in the sun. Both Fulawa and Kologo were accompanied by a number of aides. Chief Akomolo had only Dekko.

"These are sure 'nough quality folks, Sam, you can tell by their big car." It was Jimmy Jenaro dressed for the racetrack. A bright plaid cotton sports jacket, a yellow shirt open at the neck, and fawn-colored slacks made up the uniform of the day. It was topped by a cocoa straw hat and the wraparound shades. He climbed into the front seat with William.

"What's new?" he asked.

"Not much, Jimmy. We're just waiting for the speaking to begin."

"They changed the schedule," he said. "They're bringing in both the skywriters and the blimp."

"When did you find out?"

"Last night. Late. But not too late to get the word out

to the poison squad. They're all here, circulating through the crowd."

"Now that's just fine."

"I've got another idea," Jenaro said.

"What?"

"Wait and see. If it doesn't work, we'll forget I mentioned it."

"When does the speaking begin?" Claude asked.

Jimmy looked at his big watch. "Soon. Each of them gets an hour."

"Let's serve the lunch, Anne," she said. "Jimmy, you will stay?"

"Of course," he said.

The lunch was one of small, cool sandwiches, very cold champagne, and stuffed eggs.

"I don't know how she does it," Anne said. "I got up early, drove over to her house in the jeep to help, and she had it all done, and she looked as if she had just stepped out of her bath. And then she apologizes because the coffee would take another two minutes and we had to delay breakfast."

"You are silly, Anne," Claude said. "It is nothing, and you were of tremendous help."

We sat in the back of Shartelle's big LaSalle and ate the sandwiches and stuffed eggs and drank the cold champagne. William turned down the champagne, but helped himself to a half-dozen of the eggs.

Chief Akomolo was introduced by the Ibah of Ubondo, who would make all of the introductions. The crowd clapped and shouted for eight minutes and forty-five seconds. It was a warm reception; he was in friendly territory. Loudspeakers were scattered around the race course and the crowd could hear him distinctly, even if most of them couldn't see too well. He gave *the* speech. He had changed it some, but it remained mostly the way I had written it. He had learned to phrase it well and the parts I listened to didn't sound as if he were reading. He spoke for fifty-one minutes. The applause was good and lasted for eleven-and-a-half minutes.

247

After a musical interlude, Fulawa spoke. He had a bass voice and his Oxford accent was pleasant. He talked for sixty-three minutes about the good days to be after independence. They applauded him for seven minutes and fifteen seconds. Dr. Kologo was smart and spoke for only twenty-nine minutes. He had a rapid-fire delivery and, all things considered, he made a good speech in the face of a restless crowd.

While they were applauding him the airplane appeared in the sky and started to trace in white smoke on blue sky the first upright bar in the H of HAJ. The crowd roared and "ohhhed" and "ahhhed." A man standing by our car turned to Jimmy Jenaro. He was a well-dressed Albertian who wore a white suit, white shirt and tie. Steel-rimmed spectacles covered his eyes.

"Sir," he said to Jenaro, "do you believe it's true that the vapors from the airplane destroy one's manhood?" He unconsciously touched the fly of his trousers.

"You're working the wrong territory, Jack," Jenaro said.

"I beg your pardon," the man said. "I am from Barkandu and I came specially today to hear the candidates. But this rumor disturbs me."

Jenaro looked at him carefully. "You're not from Ubondo?"

"No. I am from Barkandu. Have you heard this rumor?"

"Yes," Jenaro said formally. "I have heard it, too, and it distresses me."

"It should not be permitted," the man said.

"You are right, my friend. It should not. The candidate, of course, is responsible."

"Perhaps he does not know."

"Then the voters should tell him at the polls."

The man thought about that. "Thank you," he said. "You talk much sense."

"Not the poison squad?" Shartelle asked.

"Free lance," Jenaro said happily. "He's really worried."

The skywriting plane was a North American AT-6. It was making the mile-long horizontal bar across the big H

248

when the two helicopters took off. Chief Akomolo and Dekko were still on the stage. Arguments about the danger of the smoke seemed to be flaring. There was a scuffle about twenty feet from us. We watched that for a while and then watched the helicopters. They flew straight up.

"He's writing at only nine thousand feet and they're going for the smoke," Jenaro said.

Shartelle grinned. "They're going to fan away the evil vapor, Jimmy?"

"They are indeed."

The American skybum got there first and he ran his rotors through the smoke. The crowd roared its approval. The AT-6 saw what was happening and started to write another H in another part of the sky. The South African took care of that, and hovered in the area so that the sky-writer couldn't complete it. The crowd screamed with delight. William was out of the car and jumping up and down and pointing.

The skywriter got mad and dived at the American sky-bum, trying to move him out of position. He had picked on the wrong boy. The American just sat in the sky, his rotors eating at the smoke.

"Why, Pete, it's just like *Hell's Angels*," Shartelle said. "All we need is a closeup of old Jean Harlow with the plane going down and around and around and some chocolate syrup running out of the corner of her mouth for blood."

From the left, the blimp approached. The South African left the American to harass the skywriter and went after the blimp. Again, the crowd roared with happiness. A tall young Negro frantically pushed his way through the crowd toward our car. He was wearing an American suit, and he was mad. When he got to the car, he demanded: "Are you Clint Shartelle?"

"Why, yes sir, I am."

"Call 'em off, Shartelle." The man had a Massachusetts accent.

"Call what off, sir?"

"Your goddamned helicopters."

"What's your name, boy?"

"Don't call me boy, you white bastard! I'm Calhoun from Renesslaer. Call 'em off!" He was furious.

Shartelle chuckled. "Now would that be Franchot Tone Calhoun? I'm pleased to make your acquaintance. Madame Duquesne, on my right. Miss Kidd. My associate, Mr. Upshaw. And Chief Jenaro, Minister of Information for the Western Region, and, I might add, the gentleman to whom your request should be directed." Shartelle settled back in the leather seat, stuck his twisty, black cigar in his mouth, and grinned wickedly.

Jenaro caught Calhoun by the arm and spun him around. There was no big white smile below his wraparound shades. "Now, boy, what can I do for you?" Jenaro's accent came out pure Ohio. Cleveland, Ohio.

The young American Negro twisted away from Jenaro's hand. "Call off those 'copters. We've got a right to the sky."

"Can't call 'em off. No radio contact."

Franchot Tone Calhoun stood quivering for a moment, his hands clenching and unclenching by his sides. Then he turned and ran off through the crowd.

By that time the South African was turning the blimp around and herding it off towards the horizon. Every time the blimp's pilot would attempt to maneuver, the South African would bring his rotors within inches of the outer skin. The crowd made one continuing roar.

"What if he ripped the outer covering, Pete?" Anne asked.

"I don't know, but I think nothing. They must have it sectionalized by now. But I don't blame the blimp driver. That South African is crazy enough to do it."

The skywriter gave up, wiggled his wings in resignation, and flew off. The blimp pooped along the sky towards the horizon. It showed no evidence of turning back towards the race course.

The two helicopters flew low over the race track and the crowd screamed, "Ako! Ako!" Then the pilots did a few up, down and sideways tricks in unison before settling back to the ground. The crowd mobbed them.

Jenaro grinned some more. "The word will go forth from this place, Pete, of how Ako's machines drove the evil ones from the skies."

"I trust you're giving those two boys a bonus," Shartelle said.

"Bonus, hell. They charged me 250 pounds each in advance before they'd even get off the ground. I've got to go round up my poison squad and send them out." He waved a goodbye and melted into the crowd.

Shartelle shook his head in admiration. "There goes one smart nigger," he said. It seemed to be the highest compliment he could pay.

— *25* —

The green flags which were stuck in the map of Albertia that hung on the wall of the wide-eaved house continued to sprout, replacing the yellow ones that indicated doubtful districts. By the Thursday before the Monday election there were enough of them to indicate that Chief Akomolo would be asked to form the government.

Shartelle liked to stand in the room and squint at the map, puffing on his cigar, a contented smile on his face. Occasionally one of Jenaro's three telephone men would hang up, grin at Shartelle or me, and change another flag from yellow to green. On rare occasions, a red flag would be changed to yellow, signifying that one of the districts formerly wired by Fulawa or Kologo had gone doubtful for them.

"I'd say we've done all the mischief we can, Pete," Shartelle said that Thursday afternoon as we slumped in the chairs in the living room, drinking iced tea and eating some delicate sandwiches that Claude had taught Samuel to make. Samuel called them "small chop."

"Now when you get to this point in a campaign, you hold your celebration. You don't wait until you've won, because there's too many folks around slapping you on the back and wondering whether you could find a job for their twenty-four-year-old nephew who just got out of the state penitentiary. And you don't celebrate if you lose, of course, so the only thing to do is pitch your party when you've done all you can and it looks like you just might sneak in."

"You got an idea?"

"Well, I've been talking it over with the Widow Claude and she knows a kind of retreat over in the next country where it's French and all. Some old boy she knows runs a kind of resort there on a lagoon—they got lagoons in Africa?"

"Beats me."

"Well, the widow says it's on a nice beach and they got nice little cottages and the food, according to her, is *magnifique*, so I figure it ought to be right eatable. Now if Miss Anne could talk the Peace Corps out of her services for a weekend, why I thought we'd all go over to this resort and sort of relax. I might even get drunk, if I feel good enough, and I'm feeling fine right now. How's that sound?"

"Great."

Shartelle took a swallow of his tea. "Sometimes you can sense them, Pete. Sometimes you just know when you've won a close one, and that's the feeling I've got now. And I *do* like it! You got that feeling?"

"I think so. My antennae aren't as keen as yours. But I'll be damned if I can think of anything else I can do."

Shartelle put his tea down and stretched. "You've done well, Pete. Better 'n anybody I've ever worked with. Maybe we can take on another one some of these days."

"Maybe," I said.

Anne and I arrived at the resort over in the next country, as Shartelle put it, around noon the next day. It was called

Le Holiday Inn, but I didn't think anyone in the States was going to sue. It was owned and operated by a round little Frenchman called Jean Arceneaux and he seemed to enjoy the wine from his cellar as well as the food on his table. He was half smashed when we checked in, but Claude had previously assured us that he would be.

Le Holiday Inn was located on a small bay that backed around in an S-curve. The tide kept the white sand beach cleaned off and the water was as fresh as the sea. There were six small, one-room cabins, each with its own tiled bathroom—containing a bidet, which M. Arceneaux pointed to with pride. The cabins were shaded by coconut palms and the beach started almost at their doorways. A thatched pavilion with walls that went halfway up served as a dining room. When it rained, bamboo-slatted blinds were rolled down. M. Arceneaux lived in a small house to which the resort's kitchen was attached. We were the only customers.

Shartelle and Claude were to have left two or three hours after we did. Shartelle had wanted to make a final swing through Ubondo's so-called downtown section. "I just want to nose around a bit, Pete. Me and the Widow Claude will take the LaSalle."

At Le Holiday Inn, M. Arceneaux wanted somebody to drink with before lunch so I obliged. Anne kept pace. M. Arceneaux was not only a noteworthy drinker, he was also a talker. We discussed De Gaulle and M. Arceneaux gave an excellent impersonation. We talked about his liver for a while, and he assured us that the trouble lay in the bad water in the area. He was now confining himself to wine. I remarked that the wine seemed to be running low. A waiter produced another bottle immediately. We drank that and talked about French wine for a while which we agreed was the best in the world. Anne said that she thought California wines were improving, but M. Arceneaux disputed her contention and delivered a fifteen-minute monologue on the history, technique and future of the French wine industry. It was a fascinating, graphic description and Anne agreed that the California wine growers might as well close up shop. We decided to try another bottle of the rare vintage which M. Arceneaux had been saving for just such a special occasion. We drank it solemnly and agreed that it justified his faith. Then we ate. We began with snails and ended with salad. The entree was what M. Arceneaux described as "boeuf Holiday Inn." It was one of the best steaks I've ever had. We voted to help ourselves to another bottle of the rare wine, which went especially well with the beef. After lunch, M. Arceneaux presented us with a bottle of brandy and two glasses. He announced that he planned to retire for his usual nap, and moved off towards his house, weaving only slightly.

Anne and I decided to sit under a palm tree and look at the bay while we drank the brandy. I carried the bottle; she carried the glasses. There was, I decided, nobody else in the world but Anne and me. I took off my shirt and she took off her blouse. I poured us a glass of brandy each and we sipped it as she lay in my arms while we looked at the bay. I moved my hands to her breasts and she shrugged out of her brassiere. Her hands started to explore me and she giggled. "Doesn't that get in your way?"

"Well, it would be difficult to walk around with it like that all day. Fortunately, there's a cure."

"Are there many cures?"

"Quite a few."

"Are there any we haven't tried?"

"A couple of dozen, I understand."

"Can we try them this afternoon, right now?"

"A couple of dozen?"

"As many as we can. I want to try everything with you."

"We can make a start."

"Can we do it the French way?"

"The French call it the German way. Or the Spanish way."

"Can we do it?"

"If you want."

She giggled again. It was a nice giggle. "Let's do it the French way and the German way and the Spanish way and the American way and the English way. What's the Russian way?"

"I don't know."

"Did they invent it?"

"No. But we'll invent the Russian way. We'll think up something."

Anne turned towards me and I kissed her and tasted the wine, the brandy, and the sweetness that was her tongue as it moved around my mouth. Her hands were exploring me now in earnest. She unzipped me and said "Oh, let's go cure it." I helped her up quickly, picked her up in my arms, and carried her into our cabin. We cured it all right, and if there were other national brands, they would have to wait for another day.

Later, I sat under the palm trees with a glass of brandy and watched Anne while she swam in the bay. I decided that I was going to spend the rest of my life at Le Holiday Inn, loving Anne, swimming in the bay, drinking M. Arceneaux's excellent liquor, and eating his unsurpassable food. It was paradise regained.

She came running up the beach, just a little pigeontoed, but not too much, her long blond hair darkened by water but still lovely. She wore a real bikini and I studied her body and the way she moved it as she dried herself with a towel.

"Will it always be like this, Pete? Will we ever quit loving each other so much?"

"No. We'll never quit. We'll live on a beach someplace. I'll drink fine brandy and watch you swim. We'll paint shells and sell them to the tourists. We'll sell Shartelle some."

Anne knelt down and took a sip of my brandy. She looked at me over the rim of the glass. "I feel so good. I feel as if everything were turning out the way it was always supposed to, but never did. Can we make love again tonight?"

"Uh-huh."

"I was thinking about it while I was swimming and I got all excited again. Are you really the world's greatest lover?"

"There is none to compare."

"I think you are. I think you are the greatest everything."

"I have no peer. But then you are not at all bad—in bed or out. In fact, you are probably the most delightful person in the world and I love you."

Anne stretched out on the grass and watched as I took another sip of the brandy. "Will we ever fight?"

"Never."

"And we'll always love each other?"

"Always."

She sat up quickly and hugged her knees to her. If a smile can be radiant, hers was. "I'm so happy, Peter."

"We'll be happy. We've got everything going for us. Everything in the world."

The horn honked twice. It was the mellow tone of the LaSalle. Anne and I got up. I seemed to have a little trouble making it. It was Shartelle, a hundred feet away, bringing the car to a stop with a display of flashy driving. Claude was next to him. Shartelle got up in the car and sat on the back of the front seat. He waved a bottle at me. I waved back my glass, sloshing a little of the brandy. Anne picked up our bottle and poured me some more.

"How're you, Pete, Miss Anne?" Shartelle shouted and took a swig from his bottle. He didn't wait for an answer. "I'm fine, just fine, thank you kindly." Claude got out of the car, shook her head in mock disgust, and started towards us. She had an interesting walk. Shartelle stood up in the seat of the car, tossed the bottle away, and then jumped flatfooted over the convertible's door to the ground. It was a mighty leap.

"My, but I'm spry for a man of my years!" he shouted.

"He's also had almost a full bottle of brandy," Claude called.

He was wearing one of the seersucker suits-with-vest. It looked as if he had just put it on. His shirt gleamed

256

whitely and he sported a bright, solid red tie. The black slouch hat was cocked over one eye. He paused, took out a black cigar, put it in his mouth, and lighted it. He looked at the bay, up at the sky, stretched hugely, and let out a whoop. He jumped up and clicked his heels together. Then he started it—a cakewalk down the one-hundred-foot path to us. I could hear him humming as he came, a tall, graceful man in a black slouch hat, cakewalking his way down the African path. It was a humorous, mocking dance, with trick little pauses, circlings, shuffles and mocking bows. I had seen that funeral procession coming back from a graveyard in New Orleans, and some of them danced the way Shartelle danced. It was part New Orleans, part Africa, and all Shartelle. He kept singing, almost to himself, as he strutted and spun. It was, I suppose, his victory dance.

I finished my brandy, handed the glass to Anne, walked over to a garbage pail and picked up the lid. I started to pound the lid with a stick. It made a fine banging sound.

Then I began to chant: "People of this land bow down...." I banged the lid again, this time in cadence to the words, "The mightiest one of all doth come...." Some more banging. "He walks with greatness in his stride...." Shartelle acknowledged my litany with a wave of his cigar and a spin around. "This master of the sacred vote...this son of lightning, sought by kings...." Shartelle's steps got fancier. He kept on humming, and I kept on chanting: "By Shartelle, the earthmen know him...." I chanted, and banged the lid again. "Know his name from Og to Kush...." Shartelle pranced and I pounded. "Now he comes, this son of thunder...bow yourself before his presence ...shield your eyes lest his brilliance blind you ...quickly now, he comes this way...mightiest of the ballot warriors...the Seersucker Whipsaw comes thy way."

Shartelle took his cigar from his mouth and nodded gravely to his imaginary audience, first to his left and then to his right. "I Am the One!" he shouted happily and gave the benediction with a wave of his cigar. "I Am the One!" He took a final leap into the air, stumbled just a bit, and wrapped his arm around the trunk of a convenient palm tree. He threw his head back, let out another whoop, and looked up at the coconuts. "I'm going to sing you a fine old American folk song," he told them:

> Hey! Trotsky! Make a revolution!
> Hey! Trotsky!Make a fine revolt!
> Chicken à la King in every potsky,
> Everything will be all hotsky, totsky!
> Hey! Trotsky! make a revolution!
> Hey! Trotsky! make a fine revolt!

He looked at us and grinned happily. He took off his hat and held it out, crown down, moving it as if seeking contributions. "Remember the Scottsboro boys, folks. Remember Tom Mooney." Anne and Claude applauded.

"Shartelle," I said, "you're drunk." Anne handed me the brandy bottle and a glass. I poured a drink and handed it to him. He accepted it with his courtly bow.

"I am not drunk, Pete, but I intend to get that way."

"He sang all the way from Ubondo," Claude said. "He taught me words to some very naughty songs."

Shartelle looked around. "How's this place, Miss Anne? My, but you are a fetching sight in that skimpy little bathing suit."

"Why, thank you, Mistah Clint," Anne said and curtsied, which I thought she did very well considering that she was almost naked. "This is a wonderful place. Pete and I are going to stay here for the rest of our lives."

"How is M. Arceneaux?" Claude asked. "A little tiddled?"

"Just a little," Anne said. "But it doesn't seem to interfere with his cooking."

Shartelle went back to the LaSalle and fetched the bags. "Boy," he said, "there's a case of some very fine brandy in the rear seat if you feel like getting it."

I brought the brandy and deposited it in my cabin. Shartelle and Claude disappeared into theirs, emerging a few minutes later in bathing suits. Shartelle slapped Claude on her rear. "Ain't she a fine figure of a woman, Pete!"

She was indeed. Dressed fully, Claude exuded sex. In a bikini, what the imagination had promised was completely delivered. She kissed Shartelle quickly on the cheek and ran towards the water. It was a delight to watch her run. Anne followed and they swam while Shartelle and I sat under the shade of a coconut tree and drank some more of the brandy.

"I reckon I'm going to marry that little old gal, Petey."

"You asked her?"

"Sort of. Man of my age gets mighty cautious."

"You're old, all right."

"Reckon I'm just purely in love."

"An old shit like you. She say yes?"

"Kind of."

"Lot of woman for an old man."

"Now, I ain't that old, boy."

I took another sip of brandy and watched the two girls swim.

"How about you and Miss Anne?"

"I'm just purely in love," I said.

"Gonna marry her?"

"Might."

"Might?"

"Will."

"None of my business, but Miss Anne sure seems like the right one."

Shartelle was wearing trunks, but he retained his hat. He tipped it over his eyes, took a final sip of his brandy, and leaned back against the tree trunk. "Never been more content, Pete. Just sitting here watching two pretty, half-naked women cavorting in the water, drinking fine brandy, and knowing that you've just helped win another one. I do feel good."

"No trouble?"

"When I left, it looked better'n ever."

We drank, ate, swam, told stories and made love the rest of that day, all of Saturday, and part of Sunday. Then we sobered M. Arceneaux up enough to make out our bill.

We had a final glass of brandy with him and headed back for Ubondo. I followed the big white LaSalle. Anne sat close to me with her head on my shoulder.

"It was so wonderful, Pete," she said sleepily.

"It was perfect."

"And we can really live in the house by the sea?"

"For the rest of our lives," I said.

— *26* —

The guards at the gate of Chief Akomolo's high-walled compound recognized the white LaSalle and waved us through on Monday night as Shartelle, Anne and I called to pay our respects to the man who looked to be the next Premier of the Federation of Albertia. Jenaro had been in touch with us throughout the day, as had Dr. Diokadu. The bellwether districts had come in early, and they pointed towards a bare majority for Akomolo's party on the federal level, a sweep for Chief Dekko on the regional level.

We had given William and the rest of the staff the day off to vote and to round up all friends who could drop a ballot into boxes marked with the party's crossed rake and hoe, a convenient symbol for those who couldn't read. The other parties had symbols equally convenient. After our protocol visit with Chief Akomolo, we planned to have dinner at Claude's and then we were all due at Jimmy Jenaro's to wait for the final results.

Akomolo's courtyard was filled with cars, people, and noise. Most of the crowd were market women dressed up in their best blue finery. They stood or squatted in the packed courtyard, giggled, gossiped, and sent up shrill cries of approval whenever a prominent Albertian entered the compound to pay his respects to Akomolo. They even cheered for us. Shartelle gave them the benediction of his cigar. The notables, as well as a raft of hangers-on, were gathered in a large downstairs room, gulping the Chief's liquor and telling each other that they had known all along that he was destined to win. Whenever they could get Akomolo's ear, they told him the same thing. The almost-Premier-elect was standing on the left side of the room as we entered. He was surrounded by a knot of well-wishers who all talked at once. He seemed to be half-listening, politely nodding his head from time to time. He looked tired and the tribal markings on his face appeared more deeply etched than ever.

The Chief smiled when he caught sight of Shartelle. It seemed to be his first smile of the evening and it was one of relief and delight. He moved towards us, both hands extended in greeting. "I'm so very pleased that you could come," he said. "The reports are most encouraging."

"It looks good, Chief," Shartelle said. "Real good. I see you've got the usual bunch of courthouse grifters."

Akomolo lowered his voice. "Jackals."

"I bet they all knew from the beginning that you couldn't possibly lose."

Akomojo nodded. "To a man. But the market women in the courtyard are the best indication. They somehow sense the winner and flock to his house It is traditional. I am not at all sorry that they are here."

By then the party had well-lubricated its collective vocal cords with Akomolo's endless supply of liquor and was beginning to babble at a new and higher pitch. "Let's go up to my study," the Chief said. "We can't possibly chat here."

He turned to one of his aides to tell him that he would be available upstairs. We followed him up the one flight and arranged ourselves on the low couches. Chief Akomolo sat behind the desk, his hands already busy shuffling the papers that covered it. The ceiling fan still turned uselessly. I started to sweat.

"I wanted to take this occasion to thank you, Mr. Shartelle and Mr. Upshaw, for what you have done. I am not so naïve that I do not realize that you employed some—strategems, shall we say—that I might not have approved of had my approval been sought."

Shartelle grinned his wicked grin. "Well, now, Chief, me and Pete just didn't want to bother you with all the little details of the campaign. You had enough on your mind the way it was."

Akomolo made a wry face. "I thought I knew something about the way politics works, Mr. Shartelle. But this campaign has broadened my education immensely. Some day I plan to do a paper on it—perhaps for your *Foreign Affairs* quarterly. Do you think they would be interested?"

"You'll have to ask Pete about that, Chief."

"They would jump at the chance to publish it," I said.

"Well, I suppose it will have to wait a few months, but I think if it were well-done it might stand as a classic portrayal of the use of semi-sophisticated American political techniques in a newly-independent African nation. Perhaps Dr. Diokadu could help me with the research."

"The only thing missing was television and radio," Shartelle said.

The Chief smiled broadly. "Next time, friend Shartelle, I think I will have a bit more to say about the proper use of those two media."

He quit smiling when they came in. There were seven of them, a Corporal in the Albertian Army and six Privates. They filled the small room. The Privates carried rifles—old Enfields. The Corporal held a sidearm—a .45 caliber Colt automatic. He aimed it at Akomolo.

"You are under arrest," the Corporal said. His voice held little conviction. He was a gaunt man with hollow cheeks and a forehead that sloped sharply backward and he seemed old for a corporal. His steel-rimmed glasses threatened to mist over in the heat.

"What is the meaning of this?" Akomolo said. He continued to shuffle the papers on his desk.

"You are under arrest; the military has taken over the government."

"You are a fool."

"You are under arrest!" This time the Corporal screamed it.

Akomolo picked up a pile of papers, opened the top righthand drawer of his desk, and put them in carefully as if he wanted to remember exactly where they would be next Thursday morning.

They shot Chief Sunday Akomolo six times while he was going for his gun.

Akomolo had the revolver halfway out of the drawer when the bullets rammed him back into his chair and the chair, with him in it, was slammed against the wall and stopped there only because it couldn't go any farther. The Corporal had fired his automatic three times. Three of the Privates had fired once. The other three held their Enfields on us.

Akomolo's eyes were open and there was wonder in them, but he was already dead. The body slumped forward, rested briefly on the desk where it bled over some of the papers that it never got the chance to shuffle and tuck away, and then it fell to the floor. Anne gasped a little. It was the only sound the white folks made.

The Corporal jerked a thumb at one of the Privates who had fired a shot. The Private took a machete from his belt, went behind the desk, and leaned his rifle against the wall. He knelt down behind the desk and the machete flashed up and down several times. I didn't count how many. It made a wet, smacking sound. He got up with a big grin on his face. His eyes were shining brightly, too brightly. He held Chief Akomolo's head up and turned it this way and that so we could see it plainly. The Chief's gold-rimmed glasses were still in place. Outside, we could hear the market women shouting and screaming because of the shots.

The Corporal gestured. "Outside," he said. "All of you."

We stood at the ledge of the balcony that ran around three sides of the courtyard. The market women shrieked at each other, pushed and shoved. A few fights broke out. The Corporal took Akomolo's head from the Private and held it up high, moving it from side to side. Some blood dripped on his uniform. One drop smeared an eye-glass. He didn't seem to notice.

"The tyrant is dead!" he screamed. The women didn't hear him. They were too busy screaming themselves. So he yelled it again. Two of the Privates flanked him and grinned down at the crowd. Their grins looked a little mad. I put my arm around Anne and felt her shudder.

Some of the hangers-on from the cocktail party gathered on the fringe of the crowd of women. These were the insatiably curious. The circumspect had fled at the sound of the shots. I could hear engines being started and tires squeal as Chief Akomolo's supporters remembered previous appointments.

The crowd grew quieter. "The tyrant is dead!" The Corporal bellowed again and moved the head around some more. This time they heard him and they went with the winner. They cheered. The Corporal lobbed the head down into the crowd. One woman caught it, lost it, and caught it again. It started to move from hand to hand, the gold-rimmed glasses askew on the face. Somewhere they fell off. Then the head disappeared and the women kicked it around some like a soccer ball. The Corporal rested his hands on the ledge and beamed down at the game.

The market women had a good time kicking the head around for five or six minutes, but they tired of that and surged towards the balcony where the Corporal struck his pose. They wanted something else to happen. The Corporal said a few words to the Privates who flanked him. They grinned, moved quickly to Anne, grabbed her by the arms, and jerked her over to the Corporal. I lunged after them, but two of the soldiers fastened onto my arms and pinned me against the wall. One of them put the muzzle of his rifle under my chin. I struggled some more and got rapped across the ear with its barrel. Shartelle smacked one of the other soldiers with a roundhouse left that sent the man sprawling, his rifle clattering to the floor. Shartelle was almost to Anne when the other soldiers caught him, threw him to the floor, and pounded their rifle butts into his back.

Anne fought all the way. She bit and she kicked and she cursed. The market women watched in silence as the two soldiers attempted to lift her up over the ledge. "Akomolo's white witch!" the Corporal yelled and pointed at her. Anne screamed. The women shouted and laughed and held up their arms for her. Their faces formed a dark sea of hate and rage and lust.

The jeep, its horn blaring, roared into the courtyard followed by a Land Rover. The tough-looking Sergeant-Major who drove the jeep fired three shots in the air with a revolver. Sitting next to the sergeant was Major Chuku. The Privates let Anne go and she stumbled towards me. The pair of soldiers who held me let go and moved away. Shartelle groaned, got to his knees, and pulled himself up until he could half-sprawl on the ledge that ran around the balcony.

Major Chuku was in field uniform and carried a swagger stick. Soldiers in full field equipment jumped out of the Land Rover and formed a wedge behind the Major, their rifles at the ready. The Major used his swagger stick to beat his way through the crowd of women. The Sergeant used his feet and fists. They cleared a path and ran up the steps to where the Corporal and his soldiers huddled. The weapons that had killed Akomolo were abandoned on the floor. I held Anne as she shook uncontrollably. I leaned against the wall because I had to, and watched Chuku and his Sergeant-Major run up the stairs. It seemed to take them a long time. Shartelle was still half-lying on the ledge, one of his hands pressed against his back where the rifle butts had struck.

Major Chuku barely glanced at the Corporal and his soldiers.

"Is Miss Kidd all right, Mr. Upshaw?"

"We're all fine, we're all just great."

"Has Mr. Shartelle been injured?"

"I don't think he has any kidneys left."

"Where is Akomolo?"

"In his study."

The Major darted into the small office and came out just as quickly. He shook his head and pounded the swagger stick theatrically into his left palm. It must have meant that he was upset.

"I will offer a formal apology later, Mr. Upshaw. Now I must ask a question. Did they do this?" He made a vague swing of the stick at the six Privates and the Corporal who had been put into a stiff brace by the Sergeant-Major.

"They did it."

The Major turned to the Sergeant. "Take them over to that wall—there." He pointed with his stick. "And shoot them. Make the women watch."

"Sah!" the Sergeant-Major barked and gave Chuku a snappy salute. The thin Corporal fell to his knees when he heard the news and then sprawled on the floor, screaming. The Sergeant kicked him up and shoved him down the stairs. The Corporal fell once more and got kicked up again by the Sergeant. Downstairs in the courtyard the Sergeant gave a brief command to the wedge of soldiers. Six of them detached themselves from the formation and herded the Corporal and his men over to the high wall that surrounded the compound. The women watched.

The Corporal and the Privates didn't line up against the wall. They just huddled in a bunch. The Corporal was weeping. The Sergeant-Major gave a brief command to his men. They shot the Corporal and the six Privates in a bunch like that while the women watched. Some of the Sergeant's troops had to fire more than once. The Sergeant then walked over and used his revolver to put a bullet into the head of each man, but they seemed already dead to me.

The women cheered. They still went with the winner.

Shartelle, half-lying on the ledge, said: "Shit."

The Major turned to me. "It was not to be this way," he said.

Anne continued to shake. She made small whimpering noises and I held her tightly and stroked her hair. I kept saying, "It's all right, it's all right." I could have said it a hundred times.

Shartelle managed to stand up. His face was twisted and white and he pressed his hands against his back.

"It was not to be this way," Major Chuku said again.

"What way?" Shartelle said. His voice was a croak.

"There were to be no deaths—no shooting."

"Shit," Shartelle said again. He started towards the Major, staggered, and almost fell. I watched him over Anne's head. The Major moved back quickly. "No deaths, huh?" Shartelle said. "No rough stuff, no violence. How about Captain Cheatwood?"

Major Chuku blinked rapidly. "What about Cheatwood?"

"You killed him," Shartelle said. "Or had him killed. In our driveway."

"You're mad."

Shartelle fumbled in his pockets and found a twisty black cigar. He put it in his mouth and lighted it. He seemed almost calm now as he inhaled some smoke and blew it in Chuku's face. The Major waved it away.

"No. I ain't mad. You killed Cheatwood because he found out about your coup."

"This was an unfortunate accident, Mr. Shartelle. I regret that you were involved. But it is not your affair."

"Akomolo was my candidate," Shartelle said. "And you got him killed. How about the rest of them—Old Alhaji Sir and Dr. Kologo? They get killed in unfortunate accidents, too?"

"They have been arrested for their own protection."

"But you couldn't arrest Cheatwood, could you? You had to have him stabbed to death. You, Major, because Cheatwood tried to tell us. He tried to write your name in the gravel and dirt of our driveway but he only got as far as the 'C' and the first bar of the 'H' before he ran out of time. Another two minutes and he would have spelled it out."

"It could have been his own name," Chuku said blandly. "It could even have been your CIA, Mr. Shartelle."

"Could have been, but wasn't, because you couldn't let the poor bastards make their own pitiful mistakes, could you? Not even for a little while. You couldn't even let them screw up their own country for a month or so." Shartelle's voice was still like a bullfrog's, but he went on:

"So you take the losers into what you call protective custody and you kill the winner. Only the winner's dead, huh? My winner."

"It was an accident. Those men had been ordered to stand guard at the entrance of the compound. They were to prevent Chief Akomolo from leaving. They took matters into their own hands."

"They killed my candidate, Major—mine. And they were under your command so that makes you responsible."

"I think you will agree that they have been sufficiently punished."

"How about the ones who killed Cheatwood? Have they been sufficiently punished? Don't give me that crap, Major. It's all over the country, one slick coup. Cheatwood found out and had to be killed. Who backed you? The CIA—MI6?"

"You give us far too little credit, Mr. Shartelle. Even Africans can sometimes manage their own affairs without the help of outsiders. It might be a lesson for you to learn."

"So you went and got yourself a real home-grown coup— just you and the rest of the Army. What're you using for an excuse to keep the British out?"

"A formal statement has been prepared. You can hear it on the radio, or read it in tomorrow's newspaper."

"Something about corruption and the need for austerity and stability in the trying times that will accompany independence?"

The Major permitted himself a faint smile. "Something like that."

The women were leaving the courtyard, prodded along by the soldiers who were under Chuku's command. They left quietly—their gabbling over. The courtyard was silent. Shartelle turned to me. "Miss Anne all right?"

"I want to get her out of here."

He nodded and turned back to the Major. "I'm going to tell you something, sonny. You just made yourself a mistake. You've just pulled off about the most unpopular coup in history and if you ain't got a popular coup going, then you're in trouble. If you'd waited a couple of months, you'd been all right. But the folks have just cast their votes and they'll want to see who won and how they do after they get elected. So, boy, I think you're in trouble with the folks, and if you're in trouble with the folks, then you're going to be in trouble with the money crowd. They can starve you out. And when the folks get hungry enough there's going to be some other Major or Light-Colonel come knocking at your door about midnight and if you're lucky, they may even mark your grave."

"You paint a most dismal picture, Mr. Shartelle. I didn't realize that you were capable of such theatrical hate." He smiled again slightly. "Perhaps it will diminish after you leave Albertia. And you will be leaving, you know, you and Mr. Upshaw, within twenty-four hours. You can take your hate with you."

"Major, you killed my client. My winner." Shartelle tapped himself on the chest. "Mine. You don't know what hate is 'til you've been hated by me."

The Major permitted himself another smile. It was probably his last for the day. "Perhaps you will find a match for your hate, here in Africa."

Shartelle shook his head slowly and stared at the Major. "There's no match for mine, Major. There's none at all."

— 27 —

We were back at the wide-eaved house by seven o'clock.
Shartelle had driven and we saw squads of soldiers pa-
trolling Ubondo. They had stopped us once, politely
enough, and cautioned us to get off the streets. The house
was locked when we got there; no servants were about.

None of us said much on the way home. Shartelle had
gone immediately to the phone, and was talking with
Claude. Anne sat on the couch, a glass of brandy in her
hand, staring at the floor. I stood in the doorway, looking
out into the night and drinking brandy. I was trying to
decide how I felt and I wasn't having much luck. My ear
ached.

Shartelle finished his conversation with Claude and
dialed another number. I didn't listen. There was nobody
in Albertia I wanted to call. I walked into the dining room
and poured another brandy. Then I went back into the
living room and stood by Anne.

"Are you all right?" I asked.

She looked up and smiled. "I'm all right. It's wearing
off. The brandy helps."

"When Shartelle gets through on the phone, I'll get us
reservations."

"To where?"

"To wherever the first plane goes. North, south, west—
it doesn't matter."

"I don't understand."

"It's simple," I said. "We're leaving."

"I can't leave. I know you have to, but I can't. I have
to teach school tomorrow. I just can't leave like that. I
can't leave until I'm through."

I knelt down beside her. "What kind of crap is that? It's over, Anne. It's all over. Done. The good guys are all shot; the bad guys have got the ranch. It's ended."

"No," she said, "it's not like that. School will open tomorrow. It always does. It has to open—especially tomorrow. You see that, don't you?" She put one hand out and gently ran it up and down the side of my face where the soldier had struck me with the rifle barrel. "Does it hurt bad?"

I shook my head.

"The children will be there tomorrow. They'll expect me there and they'll want me there because they'll be confused and a little frightened. I'm something constant in their lives. They didn't lose an election—only the candidates did. I don't know. Maybe the country lost something, too, but you can't penalize the children for that."

"You can resign," I said. "You're not indentured. You can quit and we can get married in Rome or Paris or London or wherever the plane lands."

"I want to, Pete. You don't know how much I want to. But I can't leave. And apparently I can't explain it or make you understand."

"I don't know. Maybe I don't understand words like commitment and dedication and motivation. To me they're just jargon. I know I'm not going to be welcome around here. I don't think the new government's going to like it if I hang around for six or seven months just so I can carry your books home from school."

She looked at me and I could see the tears in her eyes. "I know. I know you can't stay, but I know I have to. I just have to."

Shartelle hung up the phone and walked over to us. He picked up a glass of brandy I'd poured for him and took a large swallow. "That was Jenaro," he said. "He's on the run and heading for the Ile's Palace—driving one of those Volkswagens he bought. He had to make sure that Mamma and the kids would be all right. Dekko and Doc Diokadu are already on their way to the Ile's. I guess you and me can head up there about midnight in the Humber."

271

"You and who?"

"You and me, boy. To the Ile's."

"You're not serious, Shartelle?"

He cocked his head to one side and studied me. "I reckon I am, Pete. Jenaro said they've got an emergency plan. It's part political, part guerrilla. They need some help—somebody to do their thinking, I 'spect."

"What are you going to do, Shartelle? Team up with some jackleg politicians who've gone for bush? Run a guerrilla operation? Christ, you're not Fidel Castro. You're not even Ché Guevara."

"You're not going then?"

"To the Ile's Palace?"

"Uh-huh."

"No. I'm not going. I've got twenty-four hours to get out of the country. If I'm still here after that I might wind up out there on the driveway trying to write the name of whoever it was who stabbed me. No, I'm not going, but then I'm not a guerrilla expert. They don't need me. I don't think they really need you. I just think you got whip-sawed and it's tough to take."

Shartelle walked over to one of the easy chairs and sank into it carefully. He stretched out his long, seersuckered legs. He leaned his head back and stared up at the ceiling.

"Now I ain't going to take offense because I know you're upset, Pete. And it may be just the way you said it. Maybe I was whipsawed and maybe I'm riled about it and acting the fool. But I got some of me tied up down here and if I was to leave like the Major said, it would be like walking off and leaving a good arm or leg or eye behind. I can't do that. They took something away from me, that slick-talking Major and his crowd. And what they took is all I've got. Now I don't know if you understand, boy, but I aim to try and get it back. I can't leave without trying and maybe the trying will be enough. But I know I have to do that."

"What did you lose down here, Clint? A shred of a hot reputation? You didn't lose the campaign, they stole it from you at the point of a gun. It was a holdup, a heist.

The only goddamned thing you've lost down here is your mind."

"He won't let himself understand, Clint," Anne said. "If he let himself, he'd stay and he doesn't want to owe that much to anybody."

"You staying?"

"Yes," she said. "I have to. You know that."

"I know."

I knew what they were talking about but I also knew it was too late. About thirty-four years too late. I knew it was too late for me to join anybody's counterrevolution. Instead I got up and walked back into my room, got my suitcase out of the closet, and started throwing clothes into it. I found a blue denim wraparound skirt and a white blouse in the bottom drawer. I put them in the suitcase. Then I took them out and put them back in the drawer. I didn't seem to need any souvenirs. When I was through packing I carried the suitcase into the living room. Anne was on the telephone. She said "Thank you" and hung up.

"There's a flight at eleven tonight. That was the Consulate. They've already been informed that you're *persona non grata* and you've got space on the first flight. If you've decided to go."

"I don't think I'd like the Albertian jails."

Shartelle was still stretched out in the easy chair, his eyes fixed on the ceiling. "Wish you'd reconsider, Petey. Might be a lot of fun."

"I had enough fun tonight."

Shartelle sat up slowly, took a notebook and a pen from his pocket, and started to write. He handed the note to me. "William's back, just stuck his head in the door while you were packing. He'll drive you down to Barkandu in the LaSalle. I'll take the Humber and make sure that Anne gets home safe and sound."

"Thanks. What's the note for?"

"Remember that little old bar halfway between here and Barkandu—The Colony? The place where the American called Mike was?"

I nodded.

"Give him that note on the way down. Go ahead and read it."

The note said: "Mike: if you're running what I think you're running, I'll need some. Madame Claude Duquesne in Ubondo is my contact. Shartelle."

I folded the note and put it in my pocket. "You can get her killed this way," I said.

Shartelle puffed on his cigar and looked at me thoughtfully. "I reckon that's my business, boy, and hers."

William drove the LaSalle to the front of the porch. The top was up. He came in, looked at me, started to say something, changed his mind, picked up my bag and carried it to the car.

"I'd better get packed myself," Shartelle said. He gave me a half-salute as he moved towards the bedroom door. "If you change your mind, Pete, let me know. You're about the world's third-best flack. We could use you."

I nodded. "So long, Shartelle."

He paused at the bedroom door, puffed on his cigar, and gave me his wicked grin for the last time. "So long, boy."

Anne was still sitting on the couch, holding the glass of brandy. I sat beside her. "It doesn't end here, you know."

She looked at me and in the eyes that I knew so well there was hurt and pain. "It'll never end for me, darling. I'm just sick, is all. I'm sick because you're going and because I have to stay. I'm sick because I can't be with you."

"It's not for long."

"I'll write every day."

"I'll be moving around."

"You're going back to London."

"For a while."

"I love you, Pete."

"The house on the beach. Remember that."

I kissed her then and held her. "I love you," I said. And then I thought about the line that went: "...loved I not

274

honor more." I was fresh out. When I felt her sobs, rather than heard them, I kissed her again gently on the forehead, rose and walked through the door, down the steps, and got into the car. I sat in the front seat with William. He made no objection.

"Let's go," I told him.

"Barkandu, Sah?"

"The airport."

I looked back, then. Anne sat on the couch in the living room of the wide-eaved house. She was framed by the open French doors. She sat very still, holding the half-empty brandy glass in her hand. She didn't look up as we left. She seemed to be crying.

William drove fast and the old car took the curves well. We were stopped only once by soldiers and made it to The Colony in forty-five minutes. I got out and went inside. The man called Mike was leaning against the bar, listening to Radio Albertia explain the necessity for the coup, and watching his ceiling fan go around and around. There were no customers.

"What'll it be?"

"Scotch. A double."

He nodded, moved behind the bar, and poured the drink. He slid it across the mahogany to me.

"Some trouble, I hear."

"Lots of trouble." I handed him the note. "It's from Shartelle."

He read it and tore it up. He nodded his thanks.

"You staying?" he asked.

"No. Are you?"

"For a while," he said. "Perhaps business will pick up."

"Guns?"

He just looked at me. "Have a drink on the house." He poured us both doubles. I drank, thanked him, and started to leave. I stopped at the door and turned. "Did you know Shartelle before?"

He nodded again. "We met. A long time ago in France. He thought I was French until he stepped on my hand

and I called him a son of a bitch."

"He said he knew you."

"He has a good memory."

I got back in the car and William drove to the airport in fifty minutes. It was jammed, but a representative of the Consulate got my ticket confirmed. I had twenty minutes to wait. "I'll buy you a drink," I told William.

I had another whisky; he had a beer. "Where's your brother?"

"He in school, Sah. Very good school that Madam Anne make for him."

"Will he go tomorrow?"

William looked puzzled. "Yes, Sah. He go every day."

I nodded. "What do you want more than anything else, William?"

He smiled shyly. "I want taxi, Sah."

"One of those Morris Minor things?"

"Yes, Sah."

"How much do you need?"

"Much money, Sah. Three hundred pounds."

I took out my wallet. I had 132 Albertian pounds left. I gave them to William. "Make a down payment," I told him. "It's from Shartelle and me."

They called my plane before he could thank me. I shook hands with him and he followed as far as Passport Control would let him. I got on the plane and it took off. It was just another plane ride. It flew out over the ocean, turned, and flew back over the Barkandu harbor towards the Sahara and Rome. I looked down only once.

"Some harbor," I said aloud. The man next to me pretended not to hear.

— *28* —

Two months later I was sitting in my brand new office, in a brand new newspaper building, in one of those brand new towns that they build on the east coast of Florida out of nothing but water and swamp. The sign on my door was new, too, and it said Managing Editor. I was sitting there, with my feet on my new desk, reading my daily letter from Anne Kidd who wrote: "They've begged me to stay on for another six months as principal of the school. I won't be a P.C. volunteer, just a private schoolmarm. In six months I can train someone to take my place and then leave. I don't think I can explain why I agreed. I just hope you'll understand. Do you?

"I saw Claude yesterday and she gave me a note from Shartelle to send to you. I'm going to copy it verbatim:

"'Small but growing counterrevolution in West Africa seeks competent, well-rounded public relations director to assume full responsibilities. Chance for rapid advancement. Our employees know of this ad.'"

I read the rest of the letter, folded it and replaced it in my pocket. It was the fourth time I had read it. Another time and I would have it memorized.

George Sexton, the wire editor, came into my glass-walled cubicle and handed me a long yellow sheet of AP copy and a Wirephoto. I looked at the Wirephoto first.

"Don't you know those guys?" Sexton asked.

I knew them. There were four in the picture: Dekko in the middle, looking appropriately grim and resolved. Jenaro to his left, a wide smile below his wraparound shades. Dr. Diokadu was on Dekko's right with the usual sheaf of papers under his arm. Shartelle was in the picture by accident, to the left and the rear of Jenaro. He looked as he always looked in pictures: as if he were trying to remember whether he had turned off the roast.

"I know them," I told Sexton and picked up the story. It was by Foster Mothershand and the dateline was Barkandu. It was a mailer and the editorial precede said it was the first interview with Chief Dekko since the coup. It was a well-written story and ran at least two thousand words. Shartelle apparently had made good on his promise to the old AP man.

I read it quickly. Dekko, operating from deep in the bush, was causing the new military government a lot of grief, and it seemed likely that he would cause a lot more. Mothershand mentioned Shartelle in passing and then devoted about five hundred words or so to a think-piece type summary on the future of Albertia. It wasn't particularly cheerful.

"Cut it to eight hundred words and run it on nine," I said. "Give Mothershand his byline."

"How about the picture?" Sexton asked.

"Crop the guy on the left—the white man with the black hat."

"Isn't that your buddy?"

"He doesn't like publicity."

"Sort of miss the excitement, don't you, Pete?"

I looked at him. He was only twenty-three years old. "No," I said. "I don't miss it."

He went back to his desk and I reached into the bottom drawer of mine and took out my lunch—a pint of Ancient Age. I swiveled in my chair and looked out of the big plate glass window that formed one wall of my office. It faced the street. Across the street was a one-story motel and beyond the motel was the ocean. I opened the Ancient Age and took a drink. Two small children, a tow-headed boy and a girl, walked by, flattened their noses against the plate glass, and studied the Managing Editor at work. I toasted them with the pint, took another drink, and put it back in the bottom drawer. The boy stuck out his tongue at me.

I turned to the typewriter, put a sheet of copy paper in, thought a moment, and typed:

ANNE KIDD
c/o USIS
UBONDO, ALBERTIA
WEST AFRICA

REURMESSAGE TELL SHORTCAKE DOWNTAKE HELP-WANTED SIGN. WORLD'S THIRD BEST FLACK ARRIVING SOONEST ENDIT SCARA-MOUCHE

I yelled for the copy boy, gave him ten dollars, and told him to trot over to Western Union and send the cable. "If they can't do it, call it in to RCA."

I looked out at the ocean once more, then picked up the phone and dialed a number. I did it before I changed my mind. When the voice came on it was the girl's and I knew it would take longer. The man was quicker.

"I would like to make a reservation on the first flight you have leaving for New York tomorrow morning," I said. That was easy. She could confirm it. "I would also like to make a reservation on the next flight from New York to Barkandu." That was harder. "Barkandu is in Albertia," I said. "Albertia is in Africa."

There was a long wait while she called New York on another line. Then she came back on the phone and said, yes, she could confirm that for tomorrow at 4:15 P.M. Eastern Standard Time out of Kennedy. She had one more question, and she had to ask it twice, because I had to think about it for a while. When she repeated it the third time, I said: "No, I don't think so. Just make it one-way."

I hung up the phone and sat there for a moment, staring at nothing. Then I got up, told Sexton I was going out for lunch, crossed the street, walked around the motel and down to the beach. It was late October and the season hadn't started. The beach was deserted. I sat on the sand and looked at the ocean. Three small children chased a large dog down near the edge of the waves. The dog barked merrily and wagged its tail. Then the children turned and let the dog chase them for a while. They kept it up for a long time and nobody ever caught anybody. I sat there, watching them, trying not to think. But the thoughts came anyway.

After a time I rose and brushed myself off. The children and the dog were still running up and down. I bent down and picked up a pebble and threw it at them. Or maybe I threw it at Africa.

I didn't hit anything.

THE PERENNIAL LIBRARY MYSTERY SERIES

Ted Allbeury

THE OTHER SIDE OF SILENCE　　　　　P 669, $2.84
"In the best le Carré tradition . . . an ingenious and readable book."
　　　　　　　　　　　　　—New York Times Book Review

PALOMINO BLONDE　　　　　　　　　P 670, $2.84
"Fast-moving, splendidly technocratic intercontinental espionage tale
. . . you'll love it."　　　　　　　　*—The Times* (London)

SNOWBALL　　　　　　　　　　　　　P 671, $2.84
"A novel of byzantine intrigue. . . ."*—New York Times Book Review*

Delano Ames

CORPSE DIPLOMATIQUE　　　　　　　P 637, $2.84
"Sprightly and intelligent."
　　　　　　　　　—New York Herald Tribune Book Review

FOR OLD CRIME'S SAKE　　　　　　　P 629, $2.84

MURDER, MAESTRO, PLEASE　　　　　P 630, $2.84
"If there is a more engaging couple in modern fiction than Jane and
Dagobert Brown, we have not met them."　　　　*—Scotsman*

SHE SHALL HAVE MURDER　　　　　　P 638, $2.84
"Combines the merit of both the English and American schools in the
new mystery. It's as breezy as the best of the American ones, and has
the sophistication and wit of any top-notch Britisher."
　　　　　　　　　—New York Herald Tribune Book Review

E. C. Bentley

TRENT'S LAST CASE　　　　　　　　　P 440, $2.50
"One of the three best detective stories ever written."
　　　　　　　　　　　　　　　—Agatha Christie

TRENT'S OWN CASE　　　　　　　　　P 516, $2.25
"I won't waste time saying that the plot is sound and the detection
satisfying. Trent has not altered a scrap and reappears with all his old
humor and charm."　　　　　　　　　—Dorothy L. Sayers

Andrew Bergman

THE BIG KISS-OFF OF 1944   P 673, $2.84
"It is without doubt the nearest thing to genuine Chandler I've ever come across. . . . Tough, witty—very witty—and a beautiful eye for period detail. . . ."   —Jack Higgins

HOLLYWOOD AND LEVINE   P 674, $2.84
"Fast-paced private-eye fiction."   —San Francisco Chronicle

Gavin Black

A DRAGON FOR CHRISTMAS   P 473, $1.95
"Potent excitement!"   —New York Herald Tribune

THE EYES AROUND ME   P 485, $1.95
"I stayed up until all hours last night reading *The Eyes Around Me,* which is something I do not do very often, but I was so intrigued by the ingeniousness of Mr. Black's plotting and the witty way in which he spins his mystery. I can only say that I enjoyed the book enormously."
       —F. van Wyck Mason

YOU WANT TO DIE, JOHNNY?   P 472, $1.95
"Gavin Black doesn't just develop a pressure plot in suspense, he adds uninfected wit, character, charm, and sharp knowledge of the Far East to make rereading as keen as the first race-through."   —Book Week

Nicholas Blake

THE CORPSE IN THE SNOWMAN   P 427, $1.95
"If there is a distinction between the novel and the detective story (which we do not admit), then this book deserves a high place in both categories."   —New York Times

END OF CHAPTER   P 397, $1.95
". . . admirably solid . . . an adroit formal detective puzzle backed up by firm characterization and a knowing picture of London publishing."   —New York Times

HEAD OF A TRAVELER   P 398, $2.25
"Another grade A detective story of the right old jigsaw persuasion."   —New York Herald Tribune Book Review

MINUTE FOR MURDER   P 419, $1.95
"An outstanding mystery novel. Mr. Blake's writing is a delight in itself."   —New York Times

THE MORNING AFTER DEATH   P 520, $1.95
"One of Blake's best."   —Rex Warner

Nicholas Blake (cont'd)

A PENKNIFE IN MY HEART P 521, $2.25
"Style brilliant . . . and suspenseful." —*San Francisco Chronicle*

THE PRIVATE WOUND P 531, $2.25
"[Blake's] best novel in a dozen years . . . . An intensely penetrating study of sexual passion. . . . A powerful story of murder and its aftermath."
—Anthony Boucher, *New York Times*

A QUESTION OF PROOF P 494, $1.95
"The characters in this story are unusually well drawn, and the suspense is well sustained." —*New York Times*

THE SAD VARIETY P 495, $2.25
"It is a stunner. I read it instead of eating, instead of sleeping."
—Dorothy Salisbury Davis

THERE'S TROUBLE BREWING P 569, $3.37
"Nigel Strangeways is a puzzling mixture of simplicity and penetration, but all the more real for that."
—*The Times* (London) *Literary Supplement*

THOU SHELL OF DEATH P 428, $1.95
"It has all the virtues of culture, intelligence and sensibility that the most exacting connoisseur could ask of detective fiction."
—*The Times* (London) *Literary Supplement*

THE WIDOW'S CRUISE P 399, $2.25
"A stirring suspense. . . . The thrilling tale leaves nothing to be desired."
—*Springfield Republican*

Oliver Bleeck

THE BRASS GO-BETWEEN P 645, $2.84
"Fiction with a flair, well above the norm for thrillers."
—*Associated Press*

THE PROCANE CHRONICLE P 647, $2.84
"Without peer in American suspense." —*Los Angeles Times*

PROTOCOL FOR A KIDNAPPING P 646, $2.84
"The zigzags of plot are electric; the characters sharp; but it is the wit and irony and touches of plain fun which make the whole a standout."
—*Los Angeles Times*

John & Emery Bonett

A BANNER FOR PEGASUS   P 554, $2.40
"A gem! Beautifully plotted and set. . . . Not only is the murder adroit
and deserved, and the detection competent, but the love story is charming."   —Jacques Barzun and Wendell Hertig Taylor

DEAD LION   P 563, $2.40
"A clever plot, authentic background and interesting characters highly
recommended this one."   —New Republic

THE SOUND OF MURDER   P 642, $2.84
The suspects are many, the clues few, but the gentle Inspector ferrets out
the truth and pursues the case to its bitter and shocking end.

Christianna Brand

GREEN FOR DANGER   P 551, $2.50
"You have to reach for the greatest of Great Names (Christie, Carr,
Queen . . .) to find Brand's rivals in the devious subtleties of the trade."
                                                —Anthony Boucher

TOUR DE FORCE   P 572, $2.40
"Complete with traps for the over-ingenious, a double-reverse surprise
ending and a key clue planted so fairly and obviously that you completely
overlook it. If that's your idea of perfect entertainment, then seize at once
upon *Tour de Force.*"   —Anthony Boucher, *New York Times*

James Byrom

OR BE HE DEAD   P 585, $2.84
"A very original tale . . . Well written and steadily entertaining."
—Jacques Barzun and Wendell Hertig Taylor, *A Catalogue of Crime*

Henry Calvin

IT'S DIFFERENT ABROAD   P 640, $2.84
"What is remarkable and delightful, Mr. Calvin imparts a flavor of satire
to what he renovates and compels us to take straight."
                                                —Jacques Barzun

Marjorie Carleton

VANISHED   P 559, $2.40
"Exceptional . . . a minor triumph."
—Jacques Barzun and Wendell Hertig Taylor, *A Catalogue of Crime*

George Harmon Coxe

MURDER WITH PICTURES P 527, $2.25

"[Coxe] has hit the bull's-eye with his first shot."

—*New York Times*

Edmund Crispin

BURIED FOR PLEASURE P 506, $2.50

"Absolute and unalloyed delight."

—Anthony Boucher, *New York Times*

Lionel Davidson

THE MENORAH MEN P 592, $2.84

"Of his fellow thriller writers, only John Le Carré shows the same instinct for the viscera." —*Chicago Tribune*

NIGHT OF WENCESLAS P 595, $2.84

"A most ingenious thriller, so enriched with style, wit, and a sense of serious comedy that it all but transcends its kind."

—*The New Yorker*

THE ROSE OF TIBET P 593, $2.84

"I hadn't realized how much I missed the genuine Adventure story . . . until I read *The Rose of Tibet*." —Graham Greene

D. M. Devine

MY BROTHER'S KILLER P 558, $2.40

"A most enjoyable crime story which I enjoyed reading down to the last moment." —Agatha Christie

Kenneth Fearing

THE BIG CLOCK P 500, $1.95

"It will be some time before chill-hungry clients meet again so rare a compound of irony, satire, and icy-fingered narrative. *The Big Clock* is . . . a psychothriller you won't put down." —*Weekly Book Review*

Andrew Garve

THE ASHES OF LODA P 430, $1.50

"Garve . . . embellishes a fine fast adventure story with a more credible picture of the U.S.S.R. than is offered in most thrillers."

—*New York Times Book Review*

THE CUCKOO LINE AFFAIR P 451, $1.95

". . . an agreeable and ingenious piece of work." —*The New Yorker*

A HERO FOR LEANDA P 429, $1.50

"One can trust Mr. Garve to put a fresh twist to any situation, and the ending is really a lovely surprise." —*Manchester Guardian*

MURDER THROUGH THE LOOKING GLASS P 449, $1.95

". . . refreshingly out-of-the-way and enjoyable . . . highly recommended to all comers." —*Saturday Review*

NO TEARS FOR HILDA P 441, $1.95

"It starts fine and finishes finer. I got behind on breathing watching Max get not only his man but his woman, too." —Rex Stout

THE RIDDLE OF SAMSON P 450, $1.95

"The story is an excellent one, the people are quite likable, and the writing is superior." —*Springfield Republican*

Michael Gilbert

BLOOD AND JUDGMENT P 446, $1.95

"Gilbert readers need scarcely be told that the characters all come alive at first sight, and that his surpassing talent for narration enhances any plot. . . . Don't miss." —*San Francisco Chronicle*

THE BODY OF A GIRL P 459, $1.95

"Does what a good mystery should do: open up into all kinds of ramifications, with untold menace behind the action. At the end, there is a bang-up climax, and it is a pleasure to see how skilfully Gilbert wraps everything up." —*New York Times Book Review*

FEAR TO TREAD P 458, $1.95

"Merits serious consideration as a work of art." —*New York Times*

Joe Gores

HAMMETT P 631, $2.84

"Joe Gores at his very best. Terse, powerful writing—with the master, Dashiell Hammett, as the protagonist in a novel I think he would have been proud to call his own." —Robert Ludlum

C. W. Grafton

BEYOND A REASONABLE DOUBT P 519, $1.95

"A very ingenious tale of murder . . . a brilliant and gripping narrative." —Jacques Barzun and Wendell Hertig Taylor

UNTIMELY DEATH   P 514, $2.25
"The English detective story at its quiet best, meticulously underplayed, rich in perceivings of the droll human animal and ready at the last with a neat surprise which has been there all the while had we but wits to see it." —*New York Herald Tribune Book Review*

THE WIND BLOWS DEATH   P 589, $2.84
"A plot compounded of musical knowledge, a Dickens allusion, and a subtle point in law is related with delightfully unobtrusive wit, warmth, and style." —*New York Times*

WITH A BARE BODKIN   P 523, $2.25
"One of the best detective stories published for a long time."
                                                  —*The Spectator*

Robert Harling

THE ENORMOUS SHADOW   P 545, $2.50
"In some ways the best spy story of the modern period. . . . The writing is terse and vivid . . . the ending full of action . . . altogether first-rate."
—Jacques Barzun and Wendell Hertig Taylor, *A Catalogue of Crime*

Matthew Head

THE CABINDA AFFAIR   P 541, $2.25
"An absorbing whodunit and a distinguished novel of atmosphere."
                                 —Anthony Boucher, *New York Times*

THE CONGO VENUS   P 597, $2.84
"Terrific. The dialogue is just plain wonderful."   —*Boston Globe*

MURDER AT THE FLEA CLUB   P 542, $2.50
"The true delight is in Head's style, its limpid ease combined with humor and an awesome precision of phrase."   —*San Francisco Chronicle*

M. V. Heberden

ENGAGED TO MURDER   P 533, $2.25
"Smooth plotting."   —*New York Times*

James Hilton

WAS IT MURDER?   P 501, $1.95
"The story is well planned and well written."   —*New York Times*

S. B. Hough

DEAR DAUGHTER DEAD P 661, $2.84
"A highly intelligent and sophisticated story of police detection . . . not to be missed on any account." —Francis Iles, *The Guardian*

SWEET SISTER SEDUCED P 662, $2.84
In the course of a nightlong conversation between the Inspector and the suspect, the complex emotions of a very strange marriage are revealed.

P. M. Hubbard

HIGH TIDE P 571, $2.40
"A smooth elaboration of mounting horror and danger."
—*Library Journal*

Elspeth Huxley

THE AFRICAN POISON MURDERS P 540, $2.25
"Obscure venom, manical mutilations, deadly bush fire, thrilling climax compose major opus.... Top-flight."
—*Saturday Review of Literature*

MURDER ON SAFARI P 587, $2.84
"Right now we'd call Mrs. Huxley a dangerous rival to Agatha Christie." —*Books*

Francis Iles

BEFORE THE FACT P 517, $2.50
"Not many 'serious' novelists have produced character studies to compare with Iles's internally terrifying portrait of the murderer in *Before the Fact,* his masterpiece and a work truly deserving the appellation of unique and beyond price." —Howard Haycraft

MALICE AFORETHOUGHT P 532, $1.95
"It is a long time since I have read anything so good as *Malice Aforethought,* with its cynical humour, acute criminology, plausible detail and rapid movement. It makes you hug yourself with pleasure."
—H. C. Harwood, *Saturday Review*

Michael Innes

APPLEBY ON ARARAT P 648, $2.84
"Superbly plotted and humorously written." —*The New Yorker*

APPLEBY'S END P 649, $2.84
"Most amusing." —*Boston Globe*

THE CASE OF THE JOURNEYING BOY   P 632, $3.12
"I could see no faults in it. There is no one to compare with him."
    —*Illustrated London News*

DEATH ON A QUIET DAY   P 677, $2.84
"Delightfully witty."   —*Chicago Sunday Tribune*

DEATH BY WATER   P 574, $2.40
"The amount of ironic social criticism and deft characterization of scenes
and people would serve another author for six books."
    —Jacques Barzun and Wendell Hertig Taylor

HARE SITTING UP   P 590, $2.84
"There is hardly anyone (in mysteries or mainstream) more exquisitely
literate, allusive and Jamesian—and hardly anyone with a firmer sense
of melodramatic plot or a more vigorous gift of storytelling."
    —Anthony Boucher, *New York Times*

THE LONG FAREWELL   P 575, $2.40
"A model of the deft, classic detective story, told in the most wittily
diverting prose."   —*New York Times*

THE MAN FROM THE SEA   P 591, $2.84
"The pace is brisk, the adventures exciting and excitingly told, and above
all he keeps to the very end the interesting ambiguity of the man from
the sea."   —*New Statesman*

ONE MAN SHOW   P 672, $2.84
"Exciting, amusingly written . . . very good enjoyment it is."
    —*The Spectator*

THE SECRET VANGUARD   P 584, $2.84
"Innes . . . has mastered the art of swift, exciting and well-organized
narrative."   —*New York Times*

THE WEIGHT OF THE EVIDENCE   P 633, $2.84
"First-class puzzle, deftly solved. University background interesting and
amusing."   —*Saturday Review of Literature*

Mary Kelly

THE SPOILT KILL   P 565, $2.40
"Mary Kelly is a new Dorothy Sayers. . . . [An] exciting new novel."
    —*Evening News*

Lange Lewis

THE BIRTHDAY MURDER   P 518, $1.95
"Almost perfect in its playlike purity and delightful prose."
                        —Jacques Barzun and Wendell Hertig Taylor

Allan MacKinnon

HOUSE OF DARKNESS   P 582, $2.84
"His best . . . a perfect compendium."
—Jacques Barzun and Wendell Hertig Taylor, *A Catalogue of Crime*

Frank Parrish

FIRE IN THE BARLEY   P 651, $2.84
"A remarkable and brilliant first novel. . . . entrancing."
                                           —*The Spectator*

SNARE IN THE DARK   P 650, $2.84
The wily English poacher Dan Mallett is framed for murder and has to
confront unknown enemies to clear himself.

STING OF THE HONEYBEE   P 652, $2.84
"Terrorism and murder visit a sleepy English village in this witty, offbeat
thriller."   —*Chicago Sun-Times*

Austin Ripley

MINUTE MYSTERIES   P 387, $2.50
More than one hundred of the world's shortest detective stories. Only
one possible solution to each case!

Thomas Sterling

THE EVIL OF THE DAY   P 529, $2.50
"Prose as witty and subtle as it is sharp and clear. . .characters unconven-
tionally conceived and richly bodied forth . . . . In short, a novel to be
treasured."   —Anthony Boucher, *New York Times*

Julian Symons

THE BELTING INHERITANCE   P 468, $1.95
"A superb whodunit in the best tradition of the detective story."
                        —August Derleth, *Madison Capital Times*

BOGUE'S FORTUNE   P 481, $1.95
"There's a touch of the old sardonic humour, and more than a touch of
style."   —*The Spectator*

Henry Kitchell Webster

WHO IS THE NEXT?   P 539, $2.25
"A double murder, private-plane piloting, a neat impersonation, and a
delicate courtship are adroitly combined by a writer who knows how to
use the language."   —Jacques Barzun and Wendell Hertig Taylor

John Welcome

GO FOR BROKE   P 663, $2.84
A rich financier chases Richard Graham half 'round Europe in a desperate attempt to prevent the truth getting out.

RUN FOR COVER   P 664, $2.84
"I can think of few writers in the international intrigue game with such
a gift for fast and vivid storytelling."
                                    —*New York Times Book Review*

STOP AT NOTHING   P 665, $2.84
"Mr. Welcome is lively, vivid and highly readable."
                                    —*New York Times Book Review*

Anna Mary Wells

MURDERER'S CHOICE   P 534, $2.50
"Good writing, ample action, and excellent character work."
                                    —*Saturday Review of Literature*

A TALENT FOR MURDER   P 535, $2.25
"The discovery of the villain is a decided shock."   —*Books*

Charles Williams

DEAD CALM   P 655, $2.84
"A brilliant tour de force of inventive plotting, fine manipulation of a
small cast and breathtaking sequences of spectacular navigation."
                                    —*New York Times Book Review*

THE SAILCLOTH SHROUD   P 654, $2.84
"A fine novel of excitement, spirited, fresh and satisfying."
                                    —*New York Times*

THE WRONG VENUS   P 656, $2.84
Swindler Lawrence Colby and the lovely Martine create a story of romance, larceny, and very blunt homicide.

If you enjoyed this book you'll want to know about
THE PERENNIAL LIBRARY MYSTERY SERIES

Buy them at your local bookstore or use this coupon for ordering:

Qty	P number	Price
	postage and handling charge	$1.00
_____ book(s) @ $0.25		
	TOTAL	

Prices contained in this coupon are Harper & Row invoice prices only.
They are subject to change without notice, and in no way reflect the prices at
which these books may be sold by other suppliers.

**HARPER & ROW, Mail Order Dept. #PMS, 10 East 53rd St., New
York, N.Y. 10022.**
Please send me the books I have checked above. I am enclosing $_____
which includes a postage and handling charge of $1.00 for the first book and
25¢ for each additional book. Send check or money order. No cash or
C.O.D.s please

Name_____

Address_____

City_____ State_____ Zip_____
Please allow 4 weeks for delivery. USA only. This offer expires 1/31/86
Please add applicable sales tax.